SNOW
COUNTRY
LANE

SNOW COUNTRY LANE

A Novel

SARAH VAIL

ARCHWAY
PUBLISHING

Archway Publishing books may be ordered through booksellers or by contacting:

Archway Publishing
1663 Liberty Drive
Bloomington, IN 47403
www.archwaypublishing.com
1 (888) 242-5904

ISBN: 978-1-4808-8636-0 (sc)
ISBN: 978-1-4808-8637-7 (hc)
ISBN: 978-1-4808-8638-4 (e)

Library of Congress Control Number: 2020902919

Print information available on the last page.

Archway Publishing rev. date: 02/28/2020

ONE

The little girl was the one they'd ordered. Her light brown hair bounced around her sweet face in spiral curls. Her taupe skin and big brown eyes, framed by thick black lashes, revealed her biracial heritage. Five years old and as perfect as a collector's doll in her pink dress, lacy pale-pink tights, and white patent leather shoes. He matched her to the picture they'd sent to his phone.

He didn't know what they did with the children once they had them. He couldn't allow himself to venture down that path. He'd made a bargain with the crooked prosecutor that day three years ago, and he was out of jail and free if he lived up to his end. Besides, he was paid big money and easy money, so he did it. Sometimes the bounty would be up to $100,000 per child, especially for a special order like today's. His girlfriend enjoyed all the gifts, dinners out, and perks his employment brought them. He decided to think of that instead.

The darling little girl rode her fuschia bicycle up the

sidewalk. Sparkly silver tassels fluttered out from the handlebar grips as she pedaled in his direction. Transfixed for a moment, he watched through the van's open window. She approached him slowly, wobbling a little, under the brilliant green canopy of maple trees. The summer breeze picked up the scent of roses from a garden on its way from the west to the east.

He glanced up to see her foster mother meandering toward the house, chatting happily on her cell phone. *Distracted just enough, as if playing her role perfectly,* he thought. Turning the ignition fob, he started the van's engine and let it idle. Slowly, he stepped out of the driver's side and made his way quickly, quietly, to the back of the van and opened the double doors. Earlier that morning, he'd sprayed the hinges with WD-40 so they wouldn't make a sound.

The child rode past him, not even acknowledging his presence. She focused intently on keeping her balance. It made him chuckle, and briefly, the image of his daughter at that age flashed through his mind. Quickly, he pushed it away. Carefully circling at the intersection, she steered her way back toward her mom. The woman had turned her back and was now yelling at the person on the other end of her call. He could hear the sharpness in her voice even at this distance.

The foster mother was still engaged in her heated discussion. Only now, a boxwood hedge obstructed a clear view of the sidewalk. When the little girl was directly across from him, he snatched her off her bicycle, smoothing the measure of chloroform-soaked cotton over her nose and mouth with rainbow-colored duct tape. Her eyes wide with fear, she tried to scream. But the drug only took seconds to start its magic and rendered her unconscious. He had his method down pat. Though she slumped like a dead weight against his chest, to him, she was light as a feather. The riderless pink bike, still upright, faltered for a foot or so before finally toppling onto its side in the grass of a neighbor's manicured lawn. He carefully tossed the little girl onto the clean mattress and pillows in the back of the van and pressed the doors shut. His partner waiting inside would take care of the rest. He couldn't deliver damaged goods. He glanced around cautiously, making certain that no one had seen, careful not to call any attention to himself. Mom still had her back to him.

Days earlier, he'd walked the neighborhood searching for security cameras. He'd parked as far away as he could from the two he'd noticed.

Swiftly, he jumped into the driver's seat. Pulling away from the curb in one seamless maneuver, he made a U-turn and drove in the opposite direction. From time to time, he glimpsed into his rearview mirror to see if the mother had discovered her daughter was gone. When finally she did, he'd put too much distance between them for her to notice the van or see his license plate.

TWO

Tim McAndrews pressed a length of clear packing tape along the top of the last of the cardboard boxes, sealing it closed. The vestiges of his old life were tucked away in the cartons, stacked one on the other, and waiting for the movers to shove them into a dark corner of the attic at the ranch house on the east side of the Cascade Mountains. His single life—college and his first few years with the King County district attorney's office—would be stored there with them. He wasn't going to miss his stuff or the single life. He readily traded Saturdays hanging with his best friends, Scott Renton and Kathy Hope, for waking with Dani in his arms. *Daniela St. Clair.* How had he ever won her? The thought of her brought a rush, warm like a hug, to his whole body. Earlier this morning, he'd felt like the luckiest guy alive as he sat across from her at breakfast. Soft brown curls spilled around her face, over her shoulders, and down her back. Big blue eyes radiated warmth and love, and those lips. Her lips were so kissable it had been hard to tear himself away. Dani was a complete package. Her femininity, tenderness, and beauty combined seamlessly with her intelligent business acumen. God, he loved that woman. And a month ago, she'd married him.

Tim slid back on the polished oak floor, surveying the condo for the last time. Finally, he had days off, and more than he wanted, to consolidate and merge their households. After considering all the pros and cons, together, they decided to make her penthouse on top of her office building in downtown Seattle their main home. It was walking distance to work, the gym, and all the wonderful perks the city had to offer. From the twenty-sixth floor, there were spectacular views of the Puget Sound, the ferryboats, the glittering glass towers, and the distant snowcapped Cascade Mountains, depending on where you were in the massive space.

Tim expected the new buyers for his condo would enjoy all the craftsman woodwork and trim he and his brothers had painstakingly added to the place when he'd bought it just out of law school five years ago. He made the door and window casings, baseboard, and crown moldings in his family's cabinet shop, keeping his father's years of training and his skills honed. With the way things were going at the district attorney's office, he never knew whether or not he'd be forced to use those skills—and sooner than he imagined. He'd been so proud of how that little bit of trim had transformed his unit into art. But today, without furniture, the place looked dark and almost sad.

Tim rolled his shoulders, easing the tension in his back. He'd made a mess of things. He'd made tragic mistakes, life-and-death mistakes, and they sat, murky and black, like an oil slick on the surface of the ocean. He'd shot and killed a man. It was a shadow dulling everything good—his marriage to Dani and his prosecutorial victories.

He slowly stood and scrubbed a hand through his short,

sandy-blond hair. Decisions needed to be made. He was a married man with responsibilities now. Two more weeks, only two, and he'd have to choose. Should he return to work at the district attorney's office; take the offer from Elias Cain with the FBI; join the private law practice of a trusted friend and mentor, Brad Hollingsrow; or just tuck his tail between his legs and go home and work in the family woodworking and cabinetry business with his brothers? After all the money he'd spent on his law degree, and his mother's hopes and dreams for him, that would be a devastating defeat.

Tim walked through the empty rooms, making certain he had packed everything, finally standing and staring through the slatted blinds at the green common area below. He'd done a lot of thinking during his forced leave of absence. After the shooting, the police refused to charge him. It was clearly self-defense. The district attorney, Paul Goddard, convincingly presented his case before the board of commissioners. Goddard reminded them of Tim's stellar conviction record. But the press stirred up controversy and made the board reluctant to keep him on as an assistant prosecutor. In the end, they had—but not without repercussions. They forced Goddard to withdraw Tim's upcoming promotion to assistant chief deputy. Goddard was sure he'd quit, even commented that he would've. Maybe that's what the commissioners hoped for, the easy way out. Goddard begged him to stay. Tim sighed and wandered back to the living room, his mind circling through the past weeks.

Tim remembered that night more often than he wanted to. If he could erase it, he would. He and Dani had only been married for a week when his victim, a stalker and serial killer with his sights set on Dani, broke into their home, intent on murder. Still, the second-guessers thought they knew better how he should've handled it. He shook his head, still in disbelief.

It used to be a man's home was sacrosanct. He was entitled

to self-defense. But not these days. According to Miss Gracie Rose, the chairman of the county commissioners, he had a duty to flee instead. That was rich. They were in Dani's penthouse. They were awakened in the middle of the night. Warden was already at the bedroom door, and a foot of snow prevented their escape through the slider to the deck outside on the opposite side of the room. Flee? Barefoot and in flimsy pajamas? When the man charged them, an eight-inch knife raised and ready, Tim had no choice but to shoot. The man was so crazed it had taken four rounds to stop him.

So, in addition to losing his promotion, he was given four weeks of unpaid leave and was supposed to attend "voluntary" rehabilitation sessions. He had yet to visit one. He wasn't all that sure *he* was the one who needed therapy.

The sound of heavy footfalls coming up the steps outside the open front door returned his attention to the here and now. Movers had arrived, and it was time to go. Tim turned and slipped his arms into the sleeves of the bright blue down jacket Dani had bought him. She'd said the color matched his eyes. He didn't know about that, but he knew she loved him, and to please her, he'd wear any color she wanted him to.

"This is last of it." He was surprised when he turned to see Kathy Hope instead of the movers. Her navy blue overcoat covered her green surgical scrubs. The pants legs were crumpled over the top of a pair of Ugg snow boots, half–tucked in, half–hanging out, giving the impression of a disheveled scientist. That was Kathy. He chuckled to himself. The medical examiner, one of his closest friends, had come here straight from her offices at the hospital. Her blue eyes sparked with almost a dare. She brushed her hair, the color of ripened wheat, away from her face along with her overcoat's hood.

"Hi." She offered him a hesitant but almost guilty smile. She was carrying a work folder. The district attorney's office oversaw both the police department and the medical examiner's office. Goddard was considered hands-on and had a policy that any suspected homicide was to be immediately brought to his attention. He distributed each case right then and there. The ADA assigned was expected to work closely with the police and to keep up with their investigation. Was Kathy bringing him a homicide case? Tim was still on leave. Why was Kathy here with her game face on?

"What's up? I thought you were the movers." Tim gave Kathy a quick hug. "Come in. It's a mess, but ..." Tim gestured for her to enter. "You aren't bowing out of our ski trip, are you?" They were scheduled to depart this afternoon. Kathy didn't ski. That she'd agreed to go at all had surprised him. He guessed Kathy was going only to please her husband-to-be, Scott Renton, another best friend and a Seattle PD detective. Or she'd come to scold him for not going to the counseling the district attorney's office had paid for. With Kathy, a lame excuse for ditching wasn't going to fly, so he kept his mouth shut. In his mind, he did the math. Two weeks a no-show; that was four sessions. The county commissioners might judge that harshly. Voluntary wasn't really voluntary. Kathy was here to remind him he needed to appease them. Her expression was stony like it was when she was going to mother him about something he'd done wrong. He steeled himself for the lecture.

"Tim, it's not a social visit," Kathy said.

"So, I forgot to go to counseling. There's nothing to say. Warden broke into my home. I shot him." He readied himself for Kathy's rebuke.

"What? I don't care if you go to counseling or not. I need your help. And yes, I'm still going on our ski trip." She dragged a heavy box to where he stood and sat down on it, clutching the file folder to her chest. She glanced his way and ducked his suspicious frown by opening the file and shuffling through the papers inside, increasing his wariness.

"Goddard said this case was yours the minute you get back from vacation. I didn't want to wait." She started right off, pushing away his objection with a raised open palm. "Two nights ago, these two boys were dumped outside the emergency room doors of Seattle's Children's. A nurse found them as she went off shift. They both were moments from death. They were practically exsanguinated. The staff did everything they could. Immediately after they died, Dr. Rosen notified me, and I called Scott and Goddard." Kathy lifted her shoulders, and a grimace twisted her face. Tim felt bile rise to his throat. He wasn't sure he was ready to hear about the gruesome things people did to one another this morning. He'd closed that compartment down for the duration of his suspension, and he'd much rather think about skiing. She handed him one of the photos from the folder. He reluctantly took hold of the print. "One look, I freaked. Tim, it's awful."

Tim looked at the picture. He groaned. Instantly, he felt his jaw tighten and clenched his teeth together. The two little boys were twins, not more than six years old. Their blond hair was matted with dried blood, they were nude, severely beaten, and red ligature marks circled their necks, wrists, and ankles. To top off the horror, cigarette burns, still angry and red, dotted their torsos. "Damn!" Tim squeezed his eyes shut and felt disgust surging up from the pit of his stomach. "How could anyone …?" Seeing abused children brought up a mix of emotions: anger, distress, helplessness, more anger—mixing and chilling into a cold rage. Prosecuting the a-hole who did this and seeing justice done was going to be a pleasure. He would go for the maximum. And suddenly, he understood his choice of career paths had just narrowed. Kathy's objective, no doubt.

"Does Scott have any suspects? Are the parents involved?"

Tim asked. He didn't remember how it started, but his best friends always informed him about the cases they were working on, even when he wasn't their assigned ADA. Tim pulled a box over and sat on it, facing Kathy. He remembered when they were kids, up in the tree house his father had built for them, playing at solving mysteries, the three always hashed out all the clues. He also suspected his friends thought it gave them a jump start with the district attorney, and maybe it did. It was no secret Tim was the DA's favorite assistant. But he'd earned it. He'd put the hours in on every case he was given. It was the family work ethic his father had drilled into him as a child. You did your job, and you did it like you were working for God. Back then, he hated it. Now, he was grateful. Hard work brought self-esteem, but most importantly, it brought freedom and self-sufficiency.

"Scott is joining us in a minute. Captain Martin assigned him as the lead detective. Tim, we don't even know who these kids are, who they belong to, who their parents are." She sighed. Her voice cracked with sadness and desperation, and there were tears, held back but still pooling in her eyes. Kathy loved children. This was agony for her. Instantly, he empathized. It was agony for him too.

"What about surveillance video? The hospital has to have that. Did you call Farland? He's in charge of major crimes while I'm on leave." He returned the photos and leaned toward her, resting his elbows on his knees.

"Scott's reviewing the video now. And yes, I called Farland. But he passed me off to Mo." Her lips tightened, and her eyes flashed. Mo was Mohammad Rashad, an ADA in his early forties. He and Kathy had developed a mutual hatred for each other. He dismissed her opinions and wouldn't allow her to testify in court on any of his cases. She was the lead medical examiner and had earned it. Instead, Mo forced her to send her subordinate, Jeff Winsley, to go over her autopsy notes. Why Goddard allowed this was a mystery. A graduate of Columbia Law, Mo never let anyone forget it, as if that alone excused his incompetence. He seemed to harbor overwhelming insecurity around the other ADAs. He'd been hired long before Tim, but Tim had been promoted before him. Tim had heard the other ADAs complain Mo was useless and had been a part of a diversity push by King County. "Mo never returns my calls, Tim. I need you to stay with the DA's office. I can't work with him. Besides that, I'm not sure he thinks the murder of infidel children is wrong."

"Kathy!" Tim sat upright, feeling his scowl creasing his brow.

"Screw you, Tim. I'm not politically correct. I call it as I see it," she defended, standing suddenly. Yep. That was Kathy. He had his reservations about Mo too. But without solid evidence, he was presumed innocent. Tim believed in due process. Rumor and gossip around the office were that Mo associated with a very radical mosque. But rumor and gossip were just that. And usually bull.

"He's nasty to everyone," Tim admitted, slowly rising to his feet. It was true. Mo was an unpleasant guy.

"Well, it doesn't make for a good work environment that he won't help me," she insisted. Tim shielded himself by folding his arms across his chest. He wasn't sure he was going to go back to his old job. He loved court. There was a certain satisfaction when he convinced a jury of a bad guy's guilt and removed the offender from society. Tim believed the Constitution's promise of equal justice before the law. It didn't always happen. But he held on to the ideal; a government of law, not of men, was blind to race, sex, religion, creed, and financial status.

"Goddard had you in charge of the Senchal abuse case two years ago, not Mo. Without your win on that case, he wouldn't be DA at all. You know it, he knows it, and I know it." Kathy plopped back down on the packing crate.

Tim also knew that if he stayed at the DA's office, he might never progress in his career. He'd shot a man. Self-defense or not, promotions were unlikely with that hanging over him. They'd denied him one already. He was only twenty-eight; he had a lot of career time left to be stuck going nowhere.

Tim chuckled and returned to sitting on the box across from her. "Appeal to my vanity and get what you want? All right, tell me what you're thinking, and I'll see if I can arrange a meeting with Goddard. But, damn it, Kath, I haven't decided what I want to do. And you need to try to get along."

She gave him a sassy pout, then said, "Goddard is going to think you are coming back. He'll be all excited." She shrugged an *oh well*. "He'll manage his disappointment if you don't."

"He's not managing his disappointment now." Tim laughed.

Kathy grinned. "I didn't think so." Then she turned serious. "You can't let whoever did this get away with it."

"Shouldn't you be nagging Scott, not me? You don't even have the victims' names or a suspect. They were dumped, so you don't even know where the crime was committed, let alone anything I can use to get warrants."

"Details! Details!" she said and then took hold of his hands and stared into his eyes. The intensity shook him. "That's not the worst of it. Tim, they were sodomized, raped." He gasped, and Kathy's tears were back, welling in her eyes. She tried to be tough, to force them not to fall by jerking her chin up. It didn't work. Tim knew she'd come to him out of frustration, out of that desperate, overwhelming feeling that she needed to do something, anything. The twins were children. He understood. He was already feeling it too.

"Initial lab reports came back. There were traces of Nonoxyl

9. That's a spermicidal emollient, if you don't know." Her voice cracked, and she swallowed hard.

Tim let the evidence settle in his mind. Kathy could connect the forensics, and quickly, the crime would come into focus. He wasn't ready. Damn! He wanted to daydream about skiing with Dani instead.

"Some of the internal wounds and tears had started to heal. I think the boys were tortured for days." She dropped his hands and shuddered. She reached for another picture.

"No." Tim lifted his palm; he didn't want to see it. He could handle a lot of hideous things—had to in his job—but sexually abused and murdered children set his anger on fire. He especially didn't want to see it right before vacation.

Kathy smirked. "McAndrews, you are a six-foot-two wimp!"

He snickered at her. He enjoyed her barbs. "Did he leave DNA?"

"I didn't find semen. But we have a ton of swabs at the lab. If he left DNA, I'll find it. Won't be easy. There was some chemical residue. Maybe soap? The creep may have washed the boys before dumping them. Obviously, he used a condom to cover his tracks."

"Nonoxyl 9 and no semen? He used the deluxe variety of Trojans with extra protection added," Tim mused.

She paused for a moment before speaking, straightened up, and stared at him with surprise. "How do you know about that?"

"What? Did you think I wouldn't know about birth control? Come on, Kath. Remember my rep in college? It wasn't Saint McAndrews."

"I guess I've never really thought about you having sex—let alone practicing safe sex."

He shook his head. "Kath, I'm married." They both

laughed for a second. At least he'd lightened things up for a moment.

She looked down at the ground and cleared her throat. "So, the perp tried to cover his identity," Kathy said, seriousness returning to her voice.

"Cover-ups don't always work. Let's hope the unsub screwed up," Tim stated. He felt his eyes narrowing with contempt. He already hated this perp. "I don't know what use I can be. I'm on reprimand. I'm a bad guy, an out-of-control, gun-slinging cowboy of a prosecutor, according to Gracie Rose anyway. And I'm going on vacation. So are you for that matter." He tried on his most calloused voice. Kathy's stifled laugh proved she didn't believe it. She knew him too well. He was hooked. He wouldn't be able to let a bad guy get away with this.

"Ms. Rose is an idiot. If she were in the position you and Dani were in, she'd be wishing for a good guy with a gun."

They both turned and stood as they heard heavy bounding up the stairs.

"Did you see?" Scott Renton asked, dashing breathlessly into the room, his tweed overcoat flapping behind him like Superman's cape in the wind. Still, his neatly trimmed dark brown hair was in place, and his mustache framed his quick smile of greeting. Before the overcoat slipped back in place, Tim could see the badge Scott had hooked onto his belt and the outline of his shoulder holster. Scott slid his arm over Kathy's shoulder and kissed her on the cheek. "Can you believe it?" He returned his attention to Tim and handed him a computer printout that reflected the first responding officer's notes. "We don't have any identification, no idea who these boys are or where they are from. Surveillance cameras caught some guy in a black hoodie with his face covered by a balaclava. Just dumped them like they were trash. Silver car, Beamer, late model, maybe 2017; both plates were intentionally obscured."

SNOW COUNTRY LANE / 15

"Did you get anything at all?" Tim asked, hopeful. He couldn't go to Goddard with what little they had. They weren't ready for warrants; he had to have more. A suspect would be a great start.

Kathy jumped in. "There was residue from duct tape adhesive on the boys' wrists, ankles, and across their faces. I found a sliver of tape that looked like it might be multicolored or maybe rainbow colored on one of the wrists of one of the boys' sweatshirts. Do they make colored duct tape?" Kathy asked, looking over at Tim.

He bit at his bottom lip. He didn't know, but that would be something Scott would chase down. "If you found traces of glue, he didn't wash them very thoroughly."

"I hope he didn't," Scott said, taking a pen from the inside pocket of his overcoat. "Look, here. The wall next to where he dumped the boys was built with six-inch cinder blocks. From that, we have determined the guy is five foot eleven." He demonstrated on the computer picture. "That's it. How many five-foot-eleven guys driving silver Beamers do you suppose are in Seattle? I guess I'm about to find out," he complained sarcastically. "Seattle's Children's is looking through their database to see if the boys were born in their maternity wing. I've got my team checking all other hospitals in the area. Kathy guessed the boys were around six. I'm having them look for the last seven years. We are looking at all the nearby child sex offenders. We want to see if there are any that used the same signature."

"Any report on the twins in missing persons?" Tim asked.

"I checked. Not in Washington. I instructed my team to look nationwide." Scott rubbed his hand back and forth over his dark eyebrows. He was as upset as Kathy. Tim got it. Together they were reeling Tim into this case and into staying with the DA. He was like a big tuna on a commercial fishing boat line. He could fight, but he wasn't going to get away. "CSI is going through the hospital video frame by frame to see if we can recover anything else."

"What are you expecting from me?" Tim let an expression of skepticism sweep over his face. "You aren't ready for warrants. What can I do on leave of absence?"

Scott's stare bored into Tim. Then with irritation, he said, "You have to stay with the DA's office. You can't break up our team. Go to Goddard. He doesn't much care for me, and we're going to need extra money on this case, likely the FBI, and the budget is short after all the Resistance and Antifa—*marches*."

"Riots, you mean, don't you?" Kathy interjected. "Stop looking at me like that, Tim. You minored in history. And I just told you I'm not politically correct."

"Yeah, I get it."

"Antifa. What a joke. Violent for the sake of violence," Scott said.

"Communists against fascism. As government systems go, they are the same damned thing, just a different vicious killer in charge. In World War II, when the Allies won, and the Communists, a.k.a. Antifa, took over East Germany, the Stasi replaced the Gestapo. Same tyrants, new uniforms," Tim said.

"Will you talk to Goddard?" Kathy asked again. "Please?"

Tim stared at Kathy for a moment. They weren't ready. But the victims were children, cut down before they had a chance to live. They deserved justice, and his friends deserved his help.

"All right. At least we will have him up to speed on the case." Tim angled his iPhone from his jacket pocket. He turned his back to Kathy and Scott when the office picked up. "Hey, Susan, can you put me through to Goddard?"

THREE

Dani McAndrews folded the last ski sweater and placed it into Tim's suitcase yawning open on the red and gold damask bedspread. Outside the penthouse window, gray clouds skimmed across the steel-colored water of the sound toward Seattle. Escaping the rain for a winter wonderland of snow at Christmastime was just what they needed. For the last two weeks, Tim had been in a sad state. He had done the right thing protecting her from Gary Warden. The man had planned to court her, marry her, and murder her for her money. Luckily, Dani had met and fallen for Tim before Warden could put his plan in place. She shuddered when she thought about it.

Why was the district attorney putting Tim through all these hearings and reviews when all he did was guard his home against a serial killer? It was almost as if all the local politicians had lost their minds over gun control and had forgotten about self-defense. There was heated talk of gun confiscation at the city council meetings. They seemed to forget Warden's victims and their families.

Dani had even phoned the district attorney, Paul Goddard, and tried to call in a favor, reminding him of all the money her wineries and beef ranches had contributed to his campaign. It was a stupid stunt. Goddard was already on Tim's side and was as frustrated as she was. The county commissioners were utterly wrong and off base.

Long ago, Dani's father taught her how to use the St. Clair name and money to manipulate situations with politicians to get what was best for the family and businesses. Tim was her family now. She used the family name to get what she could. Goddard assured her Tim was his best and his hardest-working ADA. If Tim knew she'd meddled, no telling how he'd feel. But he'd done nothing wrong, and all she wanted was for him to recapture his joy.

That's when she decided on skiing and snowmobiling, and planninng this trip became a priority. A new pair of K2 skis and a bright blue Polaris, Rocky Mountain King snowmobile waited for Tim at her family's estate at Schweitzer Mountain in Idaho. Oh, he'd be so surprised! Fun would bring him out of the blues he tried to hide from her. In six hours, they'd be on their way. She couldn't wait to escape the dreary gray outside her bedroom window.

"Dani McAndrews," she whispered to herself. She wondered if she'd ever get used to her new name. McAndrews sure had a wonderful ring to it. So in love with Tim, she hadn't given a second thought to taking his name. Her attorney, Brad Hollingsrow, had suggested she keep St. Clair. Instantly associated in business circles with Delight Valley Wineries and Pine Canyon Natural Beef, her maiden name gave her social status and power. Other women friends said taking Tim's name made her his chattel. She'd laughed. Belonging to Tim and he to her was incredible; she could care less what they said. In the end, she decided her family and friends would have to get used to her new identity as Tim's wife: Dani McAndrews.

She started packing his things again. She'd replaced all of his worn-out ski gear with the newest, latest, warmest she could find. Doing this was risky. She knew she'd earn one of his confused and anxious stares when he opened his suitcase and unpacked at the Schweitzer cabin. But she couldn't allow her new husband to have anything but the best of the best. That was the part of being a St. Clair she wouldn't give up. She closed her eyes and could imagine the masculine angles of his face and body. And those eyes—deep blue, strong, and expressive. She turned and fell backward onto the bed, took his pillow and crushed it to her, and his scent teased into the air. She envisioned tossing his trim blond hair and staring into his eyes, her lips so close, longing breathlessly to touch his. Tim's love made her experience a depth of feeling she hadn't known possible. And she spent her time away from him enjoying memories of him.

Tim wasn't used to money. He wasn't poor, but his father taught him to work hard, earn his own way, never burden others, and be responsible at a young age. He'd never strayed from that. When she showered him with gifts, he said it made him uncomfortable. But she could afford whatever she wanted whenever she wanted it. What was the use of having wealth if she couldn't waste some of it?

Dani realized this pampering was precisely the thing that cost both her sisters their once-productive husbands. Now they were entitled boys—spoiled, greedy, and lazy. Once upon a time, her sisters, too, had been head over heels. But now they weren't happy with the monsters they'd created. Dani hoped she wouldn't ruin Tim by indulging his every whim before he even had a whim. "Tim's not the lazy type," she said out loud, assuring herself.

Tim had only asked to love her, and she'd known with their first kiss that the freight train they were on was unstoppable. She hadn't expected marriage and thought she'd never make that mistake again. But here she was.

She sat up and slipped to the edge of the bed, still hugging his pillow and daydreaming about him. It had been days since she'd thought about the ranches or the wineries and going back to work. After vacation, she'd get to it and make up for all the time she'd taken off. But not now, when all she wanted to think about was Tim's kisses.

FOUR

Senator Hershel "Buddy" Shearer stared at the ledger. His reelection campaign was already far behind his rival in fundraising—$5,700,000 behind to be precise. Worry squeezed at his stomach. He picked up his glass of Jim Beam and swirled the ice around. Ten in the morning was way too early to start drinking, but it calmed his nerves or made them worse; he couldn't decide. He couldn't lose now. He'd made promises to the party leaders, to his billionaire donors, to tech moguls. Those promises left unfulfilled would have consequences. Dire consequences. He desperately needed money. He needed to keep his power.

"What are we going to do about this? Sherm Rogers has more funds, and right now he's up in the polls." It was a razor-thin lead but a lead all the same. He narrowed his eyes at Charlie Hayes, his campaign manager, and slapped the ledger sheets down on the massive mahogany desk in front of him.

Charlie flinched and shrunk down into the chocolate-colored

leather chair placed at the forward edge of the desk. "You could always renew your friendship with Daniela St. Clair. I noticed the cleaning crew at her house yesterday. That means she'll be coming up for the holidays to ski," he offered.

Shearer contemplated the solution for a moment. The Shearer family met the St. Clair family years ago when the patriarchs of each clan had built these estates in the 1980s after the Vietnam War. They were cordial neighbors but never really friends. The homes were for vacations, and the families seldom occupied the places at the same time. He swiveled in his chair and looked through the window out to the snow-covered patio. "Daniela St. Clair," he whispered. In addition to her wealth and position in society, Daniela was stunning. She was one of America's princesses. Her father's wineries and cattle ranches made it big, and bottles of their best wine and their antibiotic-free natural Angus beef were featured in all the fine restaurants and grocery stores from coast to coast. And he'd read in *Forbes* that she was in charge of the businesses now that her father had passed away. Simon St. Clair had been a powerhouse in his day. His youngest daughter was said to have inherited her father's quick mind and business skills. The journo that penned the article estimated her net worth in the billions. Shearer could sure use that money now. He remembered her dressed in a designer suit on the cover of the magazine, her radiant smile welcoming everyone who saw it to the Seattle tasting room in the picture behind her. When he was president, she'd make good arm candy.

Shearer stood to his full six-foot height and grabbed up his whiskey glass from the desk. He strolled to the window overlooking the snow-covered grounds of his Schweitzer Mountain, Idaho, estate. Flames flickering in the fireplace at the other side of the room reflected orange and yellow on the window panes. In contrast to the warmth inside, a circular fountain at the edge of the brick patio was ice covered. Carved stone cherubs holding challises and pitchers poured water into the pond below. Drip by drip, the water froze on contact with the cold air, and low winter sunlight sparkled through the icy cascade. Across the two acres between, a snow-covered brick wall separated his property from Daniela's twenty-acre estate. He could see her house from his window. He almost opened the mahogany-stained French doors to the patio and let the music of the outdoors in. But there would be no scent of fresh mowed grass and roses mixing on the slight breeze—only stillness and cold.

After his wife passed of cancer four years ago, Shearer floundered a bit. MaryAnne had been a steady compass, always leading him in the right direction to keeping his senate seat. Now he relied on Charlie. There was no doubt he needed a good woman in his life. He loved the friendship and love of a woman, and the public expected their leaders to be married.

Finally, after seeing Miss St. Clair at a hospital fundraiser two years ago, he had approached her. He was a widower, she a divorcee; they'd be perfect together. Charlie was sure she would fall for him. Charlie had declared Shearer a handsome man in his own right. His full brown hair was streaked with silver at the temples; his dark eyes were expressive and bright. He was exceptionally fit and hadn't let himself gain the fat belly of most men in their midforties.

Power, Charlie had assured him, was an elixer most women couldn't resist. Shearer knew the St. Clair fortune was medicine a politician couldn't pass up. If Charlie's assertions were true, they should meet each other's needs. He recalled how their one date had ended amiably but not romantically—a handshake rather than a kiss. He had promised to call. Then campaign issues intervened, and he hadn't. In the world of dating, it was an unforgivable breach. But then she hadn't called him either.

Two years ago, he hadn't needed the money . . . but now was a different story.

"I thought I'd read somewhere that she'd married. Verify that for me, Charlie." For a moment, he faced his aide, then slowly turned back to take in the icy garden. "What else have you got?"

"You could *evolve* on your stand on late-term abortion. Family Planning is willing to donate a million in exchange for your support," Charlie suggested, lifting his eyebrows, hopeful. "It's a women's right to choose what she does with her body," Charlie said offering up the talking point.

Shearer whirled, and his stare pierced Charlie's insides. "In today's world, with birth control available everywhere for less than ten dollars a month, and with Family Planning offering the pills for free, right to choose my ass." He hated thinking about such realities. He hadn't ever before. MaryAnne had been for abortion during the first stages of pregnancy, and he hadn't given it much thought. He didn't know; he'd never been in that situation. MaryAnne's cervical cancer forced childlessness upon them.

One sleepless night after she died, he was channel surfing. He happened on a National Geographic series called *In the Womb*. He'd binge-watched the whole series until six in the morning. He reasoned, if dogs were dogs, elephants elephants, and dolphins dolphins in the womb, he could no longer think of a human as an undifferentiated clump of cells. It was a human, a baby. Since then, he made sure Charlie reminded him to take a sleeping pill every night.

He gulped his whiskey and ignited fire in his belly. He had always toed the party line in all his votes on abortion legislation. He still did, but now, not without guilt. The party amended their stand on late-term to mean even up to the moment of birth. Though he'd abandoned his religion long ago, words of a Bible verse swirled in his head. *What does it profit a man to gain the whole world, but lose his own soul?* The Sunday school lesson of days gone by wouldn't leave him and now had actual meaning. The thought of killing full-term babies and taking Family Planning's money made him feel cold, lifeless, a shell, one of the real-life walking dead. But he would take it. The feeling would pass. It always did. He shook his head and shuddered with a laugh of irony. If he wanted the party's endorsement, he would be pro-choice no matter what his aching conscience told him. He'd come too far. Losing his senate seat wasn't an option. He owed favors. He'd sold out country and constituents for money—lots of it. Money from the pharmaceutical lobbies, money from the energy lobbies, and, worst of all, money from foreign governments if their contribution was large enough. Charlie was the only one who knew.

Hell, he'd done so much wrong now, what was one more sin added to the pile? He justified himself and breathed out the guilt.

"All right. I've *evolved*. Get that donation and their endorsement." He again clinked the ice cubes around in his glass and swallowed the remaining whiskey. "Now, I only need four million seven hundred thousand, and I'll be even in fundraising." His voice rang with sarcasm. He turned back to look out the window facing the patio.

"You will get closer in the polls with Family Planning behind you. Besides, money isn't all there is to winning an election. Didn't that rude, uncivilized lump, Woolsey, win in California, District 4, with less money in the coffers?"

Shearer answered with a tip of his head, not turning back to look at Charlie's face. Once he was reelected, he'd leapfrog right into the presidency. Just yesterday, he was named in the *New York Times* as the party's favorite. The party needed fresh, young talent. He was only forty-five. He spun and faced

Charlie. "Has that worthless private detective done his job yet? Rogers has to have done *something—anything*," he grumbled.

"Clean as a whistle. Might as well be sainted," Charlie complained.

"We've paid your detective enough money. Tell him to make something up, something we can't prove and Rogers can't possibly defend against." Shearer's eyes were black slits.

Charlie returned a grin, and his voice brightened. "Sexual misconduct of some sort? Works every time. The evangelical voters are so stupid. They are in a huff with just the suggestion of wrongdoing."

Shearer knew. Lately, the voters were on to this trick. "We need money." He pressed his palms onto the wooden desk and leaned menacingly into Charlie's face. "You can do better."

"There is money with the Citizens Against Gun Violence." Charlie shrank into his chair as if wishing to disappear. He'd broached this group with him before. Shearer refused to politicize a workplace or school shooting. It infuriated him that the party tried to capitalize on tragedy. Charlie knew how to round up campaign cash, but he had to understand there were bridges that even Shearer wouldn't cross. Besides, he'd heard the group had staged events to stir up the public's fear of gun violence. It was ruthless, but they held to the philosophy of using all means to achieve their end of gun confiscation. Would Shearer have to ask for their help? He didn't relish the option. He'd wait on that decision.

Poor Charlie, Shearer suddenly thought. He was the only one Shearer could confide in. The only one who knew all his secrets. The only one who accepted him and all his faults. He walked over to the cowering man and scrubbed his hand through his dark hair. "Charlie, you know I don't mean any of this. I'm just frustrated." Shearer's whole demeanor changed, and he became the smiling glad-handed, ever-concerned, ever-helpful man of the people again. The one he knew Charlie adored and emulated.

"I know. We could always—" Charlie started and then peeked up at him. "I know of a secret group. They will give you every dime you need and more for ..."

Shearer waved his hand to silence him. "Don't tell me. I don't want to know. Just do it." He swallowed back his disgust. There was a light in Charlie's eyes. Shearer had heard the rumors about Charlie's dark side and wondered if they were true. Long ago, he had decided not to concern himself with his staff's private time, as long as it didn't interfere with his aspirations. But the rumors about Charlie were dark, disturbing. Briefly, he worried about what Charlie was planning to do. If it came to light, Rogers would have a heyday. Shearer should fire him. But he was the best campaign manager he'd ever had. He knew his way around Washington, DC, better than anyone. Charlie would be able to close the gap, both in fundraising and poll numbers, for him. He patted Charlie on the shoulder.

"Shall we let the rest of the campaign committee in for the meeting now?" Charlie asked.

Shearer agreed with a slight tip of his head.

FIVE

Tim didn't say a word; he just gasped in a breath as he ducked his six-foot-two frame through the main cabin door to Dani's private Gulfstream G650 and saw the belly of the beast for the first time. It was a mistake. He could tell by the frown forming on Dani's brow that she was stressed about disappointing him. But he couldn't take back his gasp now. He tried to cover up by nodding a greeting to Dani's pilot, Mitch Brady, and his wife, Shannon, seated past the open cockpit door.

The lavishness was beyond anything Tim had ever seen. All he could think of was a movie set. The cabin's leather seating even smelled like money. It was yet another reminder that this jet was one of the things that only Dani's wealth could buy. It would cement the nagging accusations from friends and family that he married Dani for her money. It impugned his character, and he resented it. And their assumption was the furthest thing from the truth. His motives weren't pure; he admitted that to himself. He'd been overwhelmed by her beauty and the way she moved, and when she caught him staring—her smile—her gorgeous smile. Mesmerized and smitten when he first saw her, he didn't have a clue about her financial circumstances, nor had he cared. He'd known at that moment he had to meet her. Ah, hell, he was lying to himself again. What he had known at that moment was that he had to have her. And that hadn't changed; the feeling only intensified with each day.

He gazed down into Dani's face, trying to make up for his overreaction to the jet. She was so excited about this trip. If he expressed his concern for how much this was costing her, he'd ruin the magic. She would laugh it off and jog his memory about the miserable trips he'd taken flying commercially, but she'd be hurt. It was his family's tradition for the man to be the breadwinner. Old-fashioned as it might be, that was the way he was raised. In his mind, he could hear his mother's complaint: his brothers were doing life right, why couldn't he?

He had to squelch these thoughts quickly before they became a spoiler. A hint of sadness colored the curve of her smile. *Damn it!* He loved her more than anything in the world and didn't want to hurt her. Tim reached his arm around Dani and squeezed her to him. He couldn't imagine his life without her by his side. It was true; the luxury of her wealth made him uncomfortable, and that made her defensive. In time, he'd get over it. He'd have to. So far, it was the only thorn in their otherwise perfect marriage, and it was all his fault.

The other reason for his blue mood was the tense conversation he'd had with Paul Goddard right before boarding. His invitation to coffee had been misconstrued, and Goddard didn't mask his disappointment when Tim didn't announce he was staying with the DA's office. Despite the pressure, Tim still hadn't decided what he was going to do once his leave was up.

Frustrated by his own indecisiveness, he hated being in career limbo but couldn't seem to find the door out.

Scott and Kathy weren't bound by the same silliness and were exuberant about flying in the opulence of Dani's private jet.

"Wow!" Kathy turned in a circle, taking in the gorgeous interior like a little girl. Kathy was entirely comfortable and was going to take every advantage. But as ever, her keen mind perceived Tim's anguish, and she chastised him with a concerned look.

"Knock it off, Tim. Be happy!" she whispered to him as she slipped past on the way to her seat in the cabin.

He tossed her a half-hearted smile.

"I let the interior designer supplied by Gulfstream do the décor. Do you think it's a little over the top? My sisters love it. I'm not so sure." Dani addressed Kathy with a laugh in her voice. It was way over the top in Tim's opinion. All the seats were buttery soft, cream-colored leather, and rather than standard airline wool throws and paper-covered pillows, the decorator had chosen faux mink in sable brown and creamy white. The galley was done up in stainless steel, and all countertops were finished in cream and brown polished granite. Three-quarters of the way through the cabin, behind an arched bulkhead, there was a sofa that converted to a queen-sized bed with the push of a button. Briefly, he thought about taking Dani to the back and using that bed. He chuckled to himself. Similar to the ones found in fancy motor homes, the lavatory included a luxurious shower wrapped in smokey glass. Dani had explained she'd wanted the jet to get from one place to the other comfortably, without the hassle of commercial flying—but this was more than just comfortable. It was a palace.

"It's beautiful!" Kathy exclaimed. "I love it." She slid into one of the leather seats in a grouping of four around a small table. She squirmed comfortably down into the cushions. Scott sat next to her and took her hand in his.

"Are you okay?" Dani gently set her head on Tim's shoulder before they took their seats.

"Of course," he answered. But when she wasn't looking, he felt the seriousness come flooding back.

"Did you talk to Goddard?" Scott asked, fooling with the armrest between his and Kathy's seats, finally lowering it and looking up with a smile of accomplishment.

"Goddard? You met with Goddard?" Dani seemed pleased. Maybe she wanted him to stay with the DA's office. He'd do it if that's what she wanted. It would be so easy then. But instead, she'd insisted the decision was his to make. She wasn't going to take the heat if everything went sideways. He watched as she sat down into the chair across from Kathy.

Tim plopped down in the remaining seat. "We had coffee," Tim answered, lovingly brushing a stray curl from Dani's cheek. He turned to Scott. "Your investigation has Goddard's blessing, and he'll see to it you get everything you need on the twins."

"Thanks, man." Scott grinned.

Dani looked at Tim, anticipating more information. Tim knew they shouldn't involve her in an active investigation. Hell, he probably shouldn't be involved either since he was on leave. But after Scott had talked Dani into wearing a wire and confirming their suspicions on his last case, he figured she was part of their team. She was his wife, and he trusted her completely.

"Anything new on your end? We haven't had a chance to talk." Kathy covered Scott's hand with hers and stared into his eyes.

"I assigned my team the task of finding all the security cameras in a ten-mile radius around the hospital. They collected and viewed all the video. We hoped we might find a frame with a better picture of the Beamer. At least we have his direction of travel. Can you believe there are no surveillance cameras on Northeast Fifty-Fifth across from Ravenna Park?" Scott reported.

"Didn't know that. Why does that matter?" Tim asked and sat forward, leaning toward the small table. His curiosity was piqued. This case might make his decision for him about staying with the DA. He wanted to see the twins get justice. When he remembered the picture Kathy showed him, anger began to smolder again.

"The Beamer was headed west on Northeast Fifty-Fifth. We caught him leaving Seattle Children's on Sand Point Way, then north on Fortieth Avenue northeast to Northeast Fifty-Fifth. We lost him at the park. At first, I guessed he probably intended to take I-5 South at the Fifth Avenue ramp," Scott answered.

Dani inclined forward, and Tim was intrigued by her interest in the case.

"We caught the car on video up to the park, but it was grainy and completely unusable. We couldn't make out the license plate or identify the driver. Very discouraging. After that point, the car vanished. It was late; traffic was light, so we knew we didn't miss it. I've sent patrol units to scour the park to see if the car was ditched there. Haven't heard back. I expected there to be video of the perp driving along the street when surveillance video resumed past the park. But no. No luck. There was only one other vehicle on the road—a light green Mercedes van. We had that vehicle traveling about fifteen seconds behind the Beamer; it made it through the blind spot because we picked it up on the other side of the park, turning on Roosevelt Way and moving south, then merging onto the freeway at the Fifth Avenue ramp. Same crappy film quality. Couldn't get a license plate or driver ID on that one either. Great, right? I'd sure like to interview the van's driver to see if he or she might've witnessed anything of value. I put out a BOLO to all police and sheriff's offices in Washington. A pale green Mercedes van is unique. I'd sure like to talk to the driver. It's probably a dead end. But that's all we have," Scott answered, looking up as the flight attendant Dani had hired arrived at the table to offer drinks. He asked for a shot of Pendleton whiskey and water.

Tim signaled that he'd have the same. Dani ordered plain water, and Kathy a white wine.

"We can worry about this when we get back from vacation," Kathy stated, after accepting her wine from the attendant.

"I have to worry about it now," Scott said. "I instructed my team to keep me updated no matter what. Don't worry; I won't spoil vacation for everyone else. I can catch a commercial flight back if I need to."

"No. Mitch will fly you back if it comes to that," Dani offered. Tim loved Dani's generosity. She would provide whatever she could to help them. The jet's engines started to whine. "Time to buckle up."

They all complied. The attendant gathered up the glasses and took her seat.

The Gulfstream rolled onto the active runway. Tim placed his left hand on Dani's right on the armrest between them. He felt the g's from the takeoff pressing him softly against his seat, and he surrendered to the force. He turned and looked at Dani. Suddenly, when she smiled at him, for some reason, he thought of her on their wedding day, walking down the aisle to take his hand. All the emotion of that moment flooded over him. He didn't deserve her. It was just dumb luck that they were even together. He'd never been with a woman that he wanted with every cell in his body. The good news was the same chains seemed to bind her to him.

Dani squeezed his hand, and then her attention gravitated

to the couple across from them. "I have a thought. What if ... what if the guy in the van was in on it?" Dani broke into Tim's thoughts of love, bringing him back to the twin's murder. "What if they dumped the car in the park, and the van picked up the Beamer's driver? What was the time interval on the surveillance video between losing the vehicles in the blind spot and picking up only the van?"

Scott stared at Dani, and then he laughed. "You should be on my team. I have my partner checking out that very thing. Let's see if she's got an answer." He picked up his cell phone, pressed the speaker function, and set it on the table between them, dialing Anna Marringe, his partner.

"Hey, Anna," he said when she answered her phone. "I've got a question for ya."

SIX

Beebe Knoll stood in front of Myra's desk, waiting for Tim's secretary to look up and acknowledge her. The door to Tim's small office behind Myra's desk was open, but the room was dark. Beebe straightened her bright gold SBC News badge on her turquoise suitcoat lapel. Her patience was at its end. She'd been here for at least two minutes. Earlier, she'd wheedled information out of some of the newer ADAs about the older woman. It was evident: Myra was her adversary. She ran blockade for Tim as a good secretary should. It annoyed Beebe to distraction. Myra had been with the district attorney's office for more than twenty years, spending the last four as McAndrews's assistant. Attractive for an older, overweight woman, Myra handled it by dressing modestly in classy, businesslike suits. Long ago, she'd stopped coloring her hair and now wore the silver strands pulled neatly into a French roll.

"Good morning, Beebe," Myra said with irritation in her voice.

"Morning. Is Jackass in yet?"

Myra narrowed her eyes. "Mr. McAndrews is on leave for two more weeks—and stop calling him Jackass. I hate it, and I'm sure he does too."

Beebe flicked her shoulders. She couldn't care less. She wasn't here to be polite or do anything McAndrews wanted to be done. To her, Jackass was appropriate. Obstinate as a damned mule, he refused to give her the news stories she wanted and needed to keep her job. She would've given up on him entirely—if he weren't so dreamboat handsome. She imagined him dressed to the nines in a gray suit, blue shirt matching his eyes, coordinated tie, presenting his argument to an enthralled jury. She'd snuck into the courtroom before to watch him work. He was perfect. At least in her imagination, he was perfect. In real life, he was a frustrating jerk. He didn't bend to her will and wasn't moved at all when she poured on the charm, unlike the other men she dealt with.

"Leave? Where? He said he would give me a lead on one of his cases this week," Beebe complained, a dramatic, exaggerated pout turning down the corners of her mouth. He'd never said such a thing. He told her to get her news stories from the district attorney's community liaison, but she might be able to trick Myra into telling her where he'd gone. For the last few days, he hadn't even been at the Seven's Club Gym or McTavish's Bar with his usual friends.

Myra laughed. "Sorry, Miss Knoll. I want to keep my job."

Beebe scowled at her. Myra was too perceptive. "Will you tell him I stopped by?" she cooed in her sweetest tone. But that didn't defrost Myra's cold expression either.

"Yes. I'll tell him, but, Miss Knoll, I think he's made himself quite clear. Don't you?"

Beebe sassily jiggled her head and felt her blonde ringlets bounce against her cheek. The left side of her upper lip curled angrily. Yeah, McAndrews had made it clear. Even though her television station had assigned her the crime beat, he'd told her concisely, and in an aggravated tone, that he wasn't obligated to give her anything—and furthermore that he wasn't going to. He didn't try his cases in the media. Her only revenge had been to write her "Alice Carroll" articles for the *National Globe*, a grocery store tabloid, all about his courtroom trials and life, complete with photos in living color. It thoroughly infuriated him, and she enjoyed seeing his annoyed smile when she brought him a copy of the paper with her latest article in it and tossed it on his desk. He should be grateful; after all, she'd made him out to be the prosecutorial version of F. Lee Bailey, even when the case he'd just won was a simple DUII. He'd asked her to knock it off, stop writing about him, and she'd countered with the First Amendment. But freedom of the press wasn't the real reason she was hanging around, and neither was her assignment from SBC News. She had a giant crush. She was in love with Tim McAndrews—had been from the first day she'd seen him at a press conference a month or so ago, about some serial killer the police had arrested. She'd deluded herself to believe she had a chance with him—until she found out he was married. Did she care? Not really. There was some guilt, of course. Would she want some newshound stalking him if she were the little wifey? Ah, nope!

But on the other hand, he was so irresistibly cute when angry about one of her tall tales. She especially loved to confront him when they were in a situation where he had to be polite. Watching him squirm was fun. It was mean and vengeful, but damn, he should be hers! She was determined to be in his life. No matter what.

Tim was always in the thick of "what's happening" in the criminal justice world. Just this morning when she searched through police reports, two cases set her intuition's alarm bells ringing. Unable to reach Tim for comment, she'd called his boss, Paul Goddard, about them. Tim would be assigned as lead prosecutor on both cases when he returned from vacation. Of course the police had to finish their investigations, but everybody knew Goddard was hands-on. His office knew everything about the police investigation. One case was the death of the sixteen-year-old son of a city councilman's brother by a hit-and-run. That was going to stir the pot of controversy and give her fodder for weeks. The other was the mysterious deaths of twin six-year-old boys found on the steps of Seattle's Children's Hospital. Two years ago, Tim won the conviction of a brutal couple on an abuse case. She knew just from that he'd be in the thick of the new investigation. The lack of information in the police report intrigued her. She used it in her presentation to Branson Holt, SBC's head of the news division and lead anchor. She convinced him she needed to get a statement from Tim and find out what was going on. What a great excuse to locate Tim wherever he was.

Besides, although Daniela St. Clair, Tim's wife, was wealthy and a looker, Beebe was just as pretty, wasn't she? And the most recent TV news ratings had her show just a point and a half behind Branson Holt and closing in. Couldn't McAndrews see what a great partnership they could have? He could keep her in crime stories, and she could make him a political star.

"Is there anything else I can help you with, Miss Knoll?" Myra asked, skepticism flashing from her gray eyes.

"Coffee?" Beebe hoped to get a look at Myra's computer appointment calendar. She'd bet Tim's whereabouts would be there. If only she could get her to leave her desk, she could confirm it.

"Break room is to your left." Myra didn't bite. It was almost as though she could read Beebe's mind. Beebe let a half smile tick across her lips. *Witch!* she thought as she spun on her heel and sauntered off toward the break room. She looked back once, only to see Myra's satisfied grin. Harumph! Myra thought she'd won this round. She stood in the coffee room's doorway for a moment.

"... ... Schweitzer. Skiing. Lucky guy!" Beebe heard James Rudolf say to the perky brunette next to him, and her mood picked up. Rudolf was often at the prosecutor's table with Tim. He'd know. She should've thought of Rudolf earlier and not wasted her time with Myra. She glanced back toward Myra's desk, and when Myra looked up, Beebe shot her a fake, placating smile.

"Yeah, that McAndrews, he has the life," she commented dismissively as she boldly walked into the break room. If Tim were at Schweitzer, Rudolf would spill it. Surprised by her appearance, he nodded agreement. Just what she needed.

"He sure does. Do I know you? I'm James Rudolf." He shoved his hand forward to shake hers. He gave Beebe the once over. She knew she looked fabulous. This morning, she'd dressed in the blue knit suit because it accentuated and hugged every curve, and the contrast with her blonde hair was camera perfect. Her intended target was McAndrews, but right now, Rudolf would do.

"Beebe Knoll," she answered coyly. "Coffee? Myra said it was in here."

James quickly rounded her up a mug and filled it with the steaming liquid. Beebe knew from the smell it was stale and slightly burned. Office coffee was the world's worst.

"Well, Beebe Knoll, are you new here?" James flirted. "You look so familiar."

"James, she's with SBC news," commented the cute brunette he'd been talking to before Beebe joined them.

His gaze landed on her SBC News name tag. "SBC News?

Oh, no. SBC News. Crap! You're that Beebe Knoll?" James swallowed. "Uh. Oh."

"I'm not as bad as all that!" Beebe laughed, studying his grimace. "I gather I'm on Tim's 'do not tell' list. He's at Schweitzer, right?"

James reluctantly agreed. "Everyone is on that list."

"Oopsy. But thanks for the coffee." She dumped the mug of its contents and set it in the sink. Quickly, Beebe turned, left the room, and headed for the elevator. She ripped her cell phone out of her purse and gave SIRI a voice command. "Alaska Airlines."

"Dialing Alaska Airlines," the iPhone assistant repeated.

SEVEN

The handoff was flawless. But instead of leaving immediately as he should've, Sam Graden lingered behind
the support post in the airport terminal lobby until
the couple approached the little girl. The tranquilizer made
her compliant. She stood obediently from the chair where he'd
placed her and went along when the woman picked up her
small school backpack and reached out her hand. He'd only
kept her for a little while, just over an hour, and she'd complied
with his instructions completely. This was the first time he had
ever followed to evaluate the client once he'd done his part and
delivered the child. If he hadn't liked the woman's looks, would
he have intervened and taken the girl back? Probably not.

Two nights ago, he'd started to question what he was doing,
after getting his contact's desperate midnight call. The idiot he'd
delivered twin boys to a week ago had dumped them in front of
Seattle's Children's Hospital. He was supposed to help with the
cleanup. He'd always suspected the clients who received the kids

weren't the desperate but wonderful childless couples who had paid for a babe rather than going through the hassle and expense of adoption. That was the bullshit story he had been given.

When he heard on the news the boys died, he knew he'd done the right thing. No child abuser was going to send him back to prison. But now, it wasn't just child trafficking; it was murder. And the whole operation was in jeopardy, and everyone was in cover-up mode. He hadn't signed on for this!

He made a quick calculation of the money in his bank accounts. Good news; he was only $300,000 away from his $2 million goal. He and Gina could retire comfortably on two million tax-free dollars. Live like a king and queen if they wanted to. Just not in America. Graden knew he couldn't stay in America anyway. He'd abducted too many children, and someone somewhere had to have seen something. And though he was good at his job, with the twins' abuse hitting the news, someone who did see something would connect the dots. Each time he took a child, he risked getting caught. And he'd be facing jail for life, or worse, now that the twin boys were dead. He had no control over what his buyers did with the kids once he delivered them, but what judge and jury would allow that as an excuse? Never get caught was his motto.

There was only one big glitch. Gina had begged him to share the work and the money with her brother and badgered him until he agreed. Now he had to worry about Georgie too. Though Georgie was help, he was also a big mouth, a braggart, and a drunk—a lethal combination that would eventually be big trouble if he couldn't keep him under control. Just two more, maybe three more jobs, and he was outta here, on his way to a tropical island. Gina hoped when he retired, he'd turn the operation over to Georgie. And that could be the plan if Georgie would settle down, put a sock in his pie hole, and do what he had to quickly, quietly, and very, very profitably.

After he watched the newly formed family pass through the gate to the Jetway, he walked briskly out of the terminal. He was almost to his car when his prepaid burner phone vibrated in his pocket.

"Yeah?" he answered. He never gave his name. Sure, they knew it, but if the NSA was listening, they wouldn't get his name. To law enforcement, he wanted to be a prepaid phone number on an untraceable throwaway. And at the end of each job, that's just what he did. He crushed the phone into pieces. He found a waterway, a river, a lake and tossed the pieces away, watching them float and sink out of sight. He played it as safe as possible, buying a new one periodically with cash.

"I have a job for you," the voice on the other end said mechanically. It was masked somehow. He knew there were devices out there that could perform that very function.

"Yeah?"

"I want to order plain vanilla cupcakes for four. Our client's favorite."

"Yeah?" He managed nothing more than a whisper. The cupcake order was code. But he understood clearly: plain vanilla cupcake meant blonde girl. "For four" meant she would be around four years old. And our client's favorite meant she would be a foster child buried deep in the system, and no one would care if she went missing and probably wouldn't even report her disappearance to the police. "How much?"

"One fifty." There was a long pause and then finally, "You in?"

"Where do I pick up the cupcake?"

"Idaho. Schweitzer Mountain. Family ski day."

They had already selected the prize. It would be easy. "I'm in." He opened the door handle to the Mercedes van.

"You know the routine. Call when you arrive at the destination."

EIGHT

Tim drew back the draperies covering the sliding glass door from their bedroom to the snow-covered deck outside. A clear sky greeted him, and the icicles hanging from the roof line sparkled full of rainbows in the rising sun. The expanse of yard yielding to the Selkirk Mountains beyond was blanketed in a new layer of white. His phone's weather app predicted seven inches of powder overnight, and it looked like the weatherman delivered. Dazzling glints of ice crystals shimmered in the sunlight, as if someone had taken a handful of glitter and scattered it on the icy breeze. The ponderosa and lodgepole pines and evergreen shrubberies in front of the house were thick with snow and resembled ghost trees. From the window, he could see over the valley of the Purcell Trench to the snow-covered Cabinet Mountains and the Bitterroots to his south and east.

So this was Dani's cabin. Cabin? A cabin in Tim's mind was like the one-room dumps he and his brothers stayed in on hunting trips with their father. This was no cabin; it was as big as a hotel in a whole neighborhood of similar estates. He wondered why Simon St. Clair had chosen this place for his retreat in the mountains. The northern Idaho Selkirk and Cabinet Mountains were listed on Wikipedia as the wildest and most unexplored in America. Maybe that was the answer. Simon had loved the wilderness. Tim had even read a warning in his internet search of the place, explaining what to do if you encountered caribou on a snowmobile trail.

The cabin was three stories, and the peaked roof constructed of blue metal prevented a buildup of snow. Underneath were bedroom suites and a massive, rustic living room, each with a fireplace and covered decks with spectacular views. Because they'd arrived so late, he hadn't had a chance to explore, but Dani explained a little about the layout. Simon St. Clair patterned the structure after a chalet in the French Alps. The rooms for the family and guests took up the first two floors. The help's quarters were located on the third.

Never in his life had he ever expected to live in a world where he had help for day-to-day chores—a full-time chef, a driver, a pilot, maids, gardeners. The list went on and on. Dani had even offered him a valet, if he wanted one. He could dress himself, thank you very much.

They'd had a serious discussion about it. He relented when she showed him the budgets. The St. Clair family and businesses employed thousands. They provided good salaries, bonuses, full medical, dental, and optical benefits, and generous retirement plans to all their employees. Dani didn't feel guilty in the least for the wealth her family had earned. Tim stretched. He had decided last night when they arrived that he wasn't going to worry over any of this stuff anymore. Kathy was right. He needed to enjoy himself.

It'd been several years since Tim had skied, and he looked

forward to it. He realized he was in for a tough go. Scott always managed to make everything a competition; a grin spread across his face. Scott was not going to win today. He imagined a race down the slopes and stretched his body right and left as if preparing for it.

As he stared out into the backyard, he felt Dani's warm hands wrap around his bare chest. She pressed her body against his back, and he felt a surge of desire sweep through him. He turned to face her, stared down into her blue eyes, and kissed her the way she liked it, his lips caressing hers, lightly and softly. They stood for a moment while passion broke over them in delicious waves. It was heady, almost overwhelming that she loved him and wanted him as much as he wanted her. Dani linked her arm through his and settled her head against his shoulder. Together they watched out the window as two Steller's jays pecked at the new snow, looking for a frozen meal.

"Beautiful morning, isn't it?" Tim asked, barely breathing, brushing the back of his fingers against her smooth cheek. She reflected his longing with her own. They kissed again. It was a tender kiss but full of a lusty hunger he could barely rein in.

"Want some coffee? I'll go get you some," Dani offered. Her eyes sparkled. She was up to something. A special breakfast maybe—one of the delicious omelets, or a big waffle filled with pecans and topped with bacon she'd treated him to in the past? He pretended he didn't notice. He'd play along and let her surprise him.

"Sure." He didn't want her to go, but there was more to life than this overwhelming craving he had for her, wasn't there? Dani rolled up onto her tiptoes and kissed his cheek. She unlinked her arm from his and headed for the stairs, then grabbed up her robe from a chair near the door and left on her mission. He watched her go and then slowly turned back to the window. A bundled figure appeared at the end of the driveway and acknowledged him with a cautious wave. The ornate, black, wrought iron gate was open. It alarmed him that anyone could see into his bedroom. He allowed the draperies to flow softly back across the window. Nosey neighbors!

Tim quickly shelved thoughts of the visitor and ripped back the covers to the bed, piled the pillows as backrests, peeled off his pajama bottoms, and slipped into bed. He loved the idea that Dani was bringing him coffee, waiting on him.

Tim listened to Dani padding quietly up the steps to their bedroom, and he pretended to be asleep as the door creaked open. But when she came close, he couldn't help but laugh.

"Coffee with cream." Dani smiled at him with curiosity in her eyes and started to set the mug on his nightstand. Instead, he took both cups from her hands and placed them on the bedside table. He pulled her on top of him. She giggled with surprise and delight. Within seconds, play melted to lust, and they made love.

NINE

W hat are you all smiles about?" Scott asked as Tim and Dani entered the vast dining room.

"Am I smiling? I didn't realize," Tim answered, glancing over at Kathy for affirmation.

"You're smiling," she said playfully.

"We're on vacation. There's new powder and lots of it." Tim grinned. He was ready to have breakfast and ready to ski.

Kathy and Scott, Mitch and Shannon, and a man he didn't recognize milled around an elegant, hand-hewn buffet set up with a choice of delicious breakfast items warming in silver chafing dishes. The rectangular room ended in double doors to the kitchen, where this morning's meal had been prepared. Tim could almost taste the bacon that wafted its maple-cured aroma through the room. Opposite the dining table, polished wood-framed windows and French doors opened into a large living room with massive fireplaces on either end.

Everyone was dressed casually, blue jeans and long sleeves

of various colors, ready to go out into the snow after the morning meal.

He couldn't keep his happiness from showing. He slipped his arm over Dani's shoulder and hugged her against his side.

"Miguel! Miguel Gonzales!" Dani wriggled away from Tim's embrace and quickly made her way to the handsome man standing at the buffet table, filling his plate. "You're here?"

"Hi, baby girl," he said, setting his plate down on the buffet table and sweeping her into his arms and twirling in a circle. He stood back from her, still holding her hands. "Let me look at you. All grown-up and just—*muy bonita!*"

"I can't believe you're here," Dani repeated with delight. She grabbed Miguel's hand and led him to where Tim stood, speechless, his wariness piqued. "Miguel, this is my husband, Tim McAndrews. Tim, this is Miguel Gonzales."

Miguel was a good-looking man. Tall and fit, his strong, olive-skinned face was clean-shaven, and his raven hair in a neat military cut. His eyes were big and dark and full of intelligence. Tim shook his hand, but it didn't keep his concern at bay.

"I'm on Senator Shearer's private security detail." He gestured with a tip of his head toward the estate next door. "Are Rachel and Liz here? When I saw the cleaning service come to set up your place, I couldn't wait to see you all." Miguel turned his attention to Dani, and Tim noticed melancholy, a longing, barely masked in his eyes.

"Rachel isn't coming. I'm sorry." Dani took hold of both Miguel's hands, and they shared a moment Tim didn't understand. Miguel was a little older; Tim speculated he was in his early thirties, the same age as Dani's older sister, Rachel. Tim hadn't met Dani's sisters yet, and the dashing Miguel had him intrigued. Rachel was married to another. How did Miguel figure in?

"Are you skiing today? It's a day off for me, and I thought maybe I could join you." Miguel directed his attention to Tim and then back to Dani. "None of the others in our detail ski. Can you imagine?"

"Yeah, sure. Join us," Tim answered with reserved enthusiasm.

"We aren't skiing today," Dani said, biting at her bottom lip, a tease sparkling from her eyes. Tim had been right. Dani had something planned as a surprise. "But you are welcome to join us, Miguel. Andy Wall from Bright Star Polaris is letting us test out some new snowmobiles. Come see." After motioning to Scott and Kathy to come, Dani took both men by their hands, Tim the right, Miguel the left, and pulled them toward the closed door to the hallway and the study.

The large room looked like it had been turned into a motorsports shop. The rustic settee and chairs were loaded with snow gear. A selection of HJC, Freedcom, and TORC Bluetooth-integrated snowmobile helmets covered the coffee table. Each helmet was equipped with a top-mounted GoPro camera video system. Jackets in all colors, with POLARIS emblazoned across the back, and protective bibs of different sizes hung on a store rack. Lining the north wall, a selection of Baffin, Joe Rocket, Castle X, and Sorrel snowmobile boots, still in their boxes, were stacked in a line. Tim glanced at Dani, and she beamed. She did this for him, and he was speechless. He and Scott had gone snowmobiling before, but it was an expensive sport they hadn't been able to budget for just starting in their careers.

"Wow!" Scott exclaimed and headed straight for the technology-laden helmets. "Communication and music all in one package."

"Wait until you look outside!" Kathy stood in front of the large paned window to the front lawn below. Tim joined her. Four brand-new, top-of-the-line, Pro-RMK Polaris snowmobiles, equipped with 850cc Patriot Clean-Fire engines and 174-inch-long tracks, and four RMKs, equipped with 600cc engines and 155-inch tracks, were parked side by side as if the yard was a showroom. Ever cautious, Dani had hired Andy to give them lessons today to minimize potential mishaps. She'd explained to Tim days ago when they discussed snowmobiling that you could get away from civilization in short order, and a minimum of riding skill would be required if trouble ensued.

Dani slipped up beside Tim, and a smile crept over his face.

"I made the right decision. You're ready to play," she said, laughing. She hooked her arm in his, leaned into him, and whispered, "Don't worry; this is just part of Andy's new rental fleet. I'm not buying unless you fall in love with one."

Tim breathed out. "There's at least a hundred thousand dollars' worth of snowmobiles out front, and if I add the gear inside, the tab has got to be more than I make in a year."

"Today, we test out the different machines. I'm renting sleds for the full two weeks for everyone who likes it. And we need to know which one you enjoy most." Tim was uncomfortable; she would have to be blind not to read it on his face. "Tim, what's the use of having money if I can't spend it on you and what I want?" she quietly asked, waiting for his response while staring into his eyes.

"Good point. But, Dani, I don't need all this to be happy. You're all I need." His smile reflected a sweet sincerity.

"You're all I need too. But all of this ..." She swept her arm in front of her. "We need it to go snowmobiling, so ... " She tossed her head and bit at her bottom lip with a tease. "You'll feel differently when we're on the snow." She hugged him. "Tomorrow, we ski."

TEN

Tim felt like a kid at Christmas as he leaned against his poles, sliding the new K2 skis Dani had talked him into trying back and forth in the smooth snow at the top of the steep run. The skis were rated number one for powder, and he'd promised he'd try them. The scent of pine filled the crisp, cold, morning air. The view of Lake Pend Oreille (pronounced Pond-er-ay) far below was spectacular. The mirror surface reflected deep blue back up to the sky. Tim read that the lake was 1,150 feet deep in places, and the southern tip was home of the Farragut Naval Training Center during World War II. The US Navy base was still active and rumored to be conducting acoustical submarine research to this day.

Yesterday, the snowmobiling was incredible. He was surprised by how quickly he learned to make the machine do what he wanted. The RMK was easily flickable. With a simple weight transfer and little effort, the sled moved from a left-hand turn to a right, gliding over the snow as if he were riding on clouds, not the earth. The experience was different than he'd imagined it would be: fast, soft, floaty, thrilling, as waves of icy white spray showered him in each turn. Pure fun. A day later, he still laughed at the memory.

Today, though, was a ski day and going to be just as fun. Dani was right to plan this trip. His mood lifted and improved with every passing minute. As he waited on the guys, he was reminded how much he loved to ski. At the top of the run, the black diamond sign warned of the difficulty ahead. As he looked down the mogul-covered slope of the White Lightning Trail, he guessed the group of men might have taken on more than they could handle. When they chose this trail at morning coffee, he wondered if it was more bravado than brains guiding their decision.

"Oh, crap!" Scott laughed, his eyes wide as he stopped at the crest of the hill next to Tim and viewed the run.

"Can't handle it?" Tim chuckled, knowing in their younger days they could make short work of this. It was all football in their high school years, until the snow began to fly around Thanksgiving, and then it was all skiing. Sometimes well into April. In college, they'd dropped football altogether and skied when the resorts opened. Tim loved the way it made him feel; muscles working, cold air rushing against his cheeks as he sped down mountainsides, the smell of pine, and the feeling of stepping into a Christmas card, even long after the holiday had passed.

"Me? Yeah, I can handle it. You? Not so sure," Scott teased him back.

While waiting for Miguel and Dani's pilot, Mitch, to catch up, Tim evaluated the different lines between the moguls. The top half of the run was steep and then leveled out to a narrow bench in about two thousand yards. They would rest there and then glide down the remainder of the way on groomed snow to the chairlift and do it all again. He decided on his course. Scott's grin made it a contest. *Last one down buys beer!* Scott didn't have to say it; they both understood.

Tim launched his weight forward when he saw Scott move off the imaginary starting line. Committed now, Tim couldn't turn back. He felt the edges of his skis chatter against the ice. They should've waited and taken this trail in the afternoon once the sun had softened the hard snow that had iced up overnight. *Don't hesitate!* He scolded himself and regained his balance and downward momentum. He picked up the forced rhythm carved out by the skiers who'd ventured down this run before him. Right, left, right, left, he off weighted his downhill ski; arms, shoulders, body core, and thighs all worked in harmony. Tim skied the zipper line.

He had learned early on not to worry where his opponent was and concentrate forward and down the hill. When he reached the bench, he spun, creating a rooster tail of white as he stopped.

"You're buying beer!" Tim laughed. He'd beat Scott down by mere seconds. Mitch and Miguel were close behind. When they all reached the resting spot, they broke out in laughter.

"We lived!" Tim said.

"Ah, ha! Part of the fun," Scott answered. Miguel stabbed his poles into the snow and wrestled off his backpack. He produced a silver flask, opened the screw cap, and took a swig. Tim could smell the peppermint schnapps on the cold air. Miguel passed him the container. Nothing ever changed, Tim thought, wiping the rim and taking a tiny sip, then passing it on. They should never drink and ski, but they always drank and skied.

After everyone had taken their traditional share of the schnapps, Miguel returned the flask to his backpack and readied himself to continue down the trail. Tim looked up the mountain behind him. At the top of the mogul run, a solitary figure stood poised to begin down the slope, faltered clumsily, lost control, and skidded in a full snowplow forward as if trying to stop. The skier struggled, caught an edge, and went down. With arms flailing, body tumbling headfirst, the skier bounced and slammed on each mogul. Tim sucked a breath through his teeth, almost feeling each nosedive. Skis, poles, hat, and gloves scattered on the slope above the poor soul sliding out of control and headfirst at full speed toward the men.

Tim immediately recognized that the skier was a woman and could be hurt. He shot into action. If it had been Dani, he'd want someone to help her. He snapped the quick release on his bindings and removed his skis as the small body spun to rest ten feet from him. Quickly, he stuck his boards into the snow and rushed over the short distance to her.

"Are you all right, miss?" He dropped to his knees beside her sprawled-out frame.

She moaned. Worried glances passed between the men. Miguel, Scott, and Mitch now crouched at her side too.

"Careful. Don't move until we make sure you're not hurt," Miguel commanded. At least both he and Mitch had some first aid training from the military, Tim thought. If she had broken something, they'd know what to do.

"I'm fine. Embarrassed but fine." She was flat on her back and lifted her snow-filled goggles from her face, wiping ice crystals from her eyes and nose. Snow-caked strings of blonde hair framed her head.

"Beebe?" Tim felt his jaw tighten, and his whole body tensed with amazement. "Beebe Knoll? What the ...?" His mind began whirring through the possibilities. He quickly surveyed the area around them, looking for her cameraman. Finding no one, he asked, "Are you hurt?"

"No. Embarrassed but not hurt," she answered, leaning

her weight onto Tim's arm as he helped her sit up. She flinched with pain.

"Careful, miss. You may be hurt and not know it." Miguel dropped down on the other side of her to help.

She sighed.

"Can I call someone for you?" Tim asked, reaching into his jacket pocket for his iPhone. He was amazed that anyone would try a difficult run like this alone. But then he'd skied similar ones many times without any consequences.

"I'm alone," she answered, and she stared at him with a helplessness he'd never associated with Beebe. But then, even a rattlesnake got into trouble sometimes. They'd still bite you once the rescue was over. Instantly ashamed of the thought, he pushed it aside. But why was she here?

Tim sat back on his heels, studying her. He could see her posture turn defensive, and his mind began to race. What were the chances he'd *accidentally* run into Beebe skiing at Schweitzer? It was a long way from Seattle, and there were plenty of local ski areas in Washington. Were this a bet, no one in their right mind would've taken those odds. Especially since she'd hounded him daily for information on his cases. Damn! He could feel irritation smoldering from his eyes. He looked around again for her cameraman, expecting to see him hiding in the trees. Beebe was here to snoop through his life. She was intent on writing gossip rag stories about Dani. Early on, in one of their heated discussions at the DA's office, she'd told him Dani was fair game because she was rich and the public was interested in her. She'd kept yammering at him about Dani's vulnerability to the press as he firmly escorted her from his office to the elevator, barely keeping his anger in check. He'd waited until the doors slid closed and the elevator headed for the lobby floor to go back to his office. He had to make sure she stayed on it.

Myra would never give his location away, so how did she find them? Double damn!

"Don't look at me like that! I could be hurt, you know, Jackass!" she complained, peeking at Tim sideways and brushing snow from her hair. A smile that begged forgiveness curved her lips.

"So, you two know each other?" Miguel glanced Tim's way. Tim knew his expression was evident. He knew her and wished he didn't.

"Yeah," he said. "Beebe Knoll, meet Miguel Gonzales."

Miguel tipped his head with curiosity. There would be questions later. "Miss Knoll, may I determine if anything's broken?" When she motioned her agreement, Miguel coursed his hands carefully down her legs. Miguel's worried look wasn't lost on Tim. Beebe could have broken her leg, severely twisted her knee, or at the very least sustained a nasty sprain. A concussion wasn't out of the question either, with the way she'd crashed down the mountain.

"I need to loosen your ski boot, and it may hurt, maybe a lot," Miguel reported. Tim knew he had to get ski patrol, so he stood and made his way to his skis. When he snapped into his bindings, he heard Beebe cry out. If she had been following him, she deserved it. Again, he pushed those thoughts away. But still, he had a hard time wrapping his head around it. Was she stalking them like paparazzi?

"I'll get the ski patrol. Miss Knoll won't be getting down on her own." Tim stabbed his poles into the snow and launched down the mountain.

ELEVEN

Tim relaxed against the turned pine spindles in the back of his chair. Every muscle in his body reminded him it had been years since he'd skied. He was ready for a drink to take the edge off and relax. He looked over at Scott and watched him roll muscle fatigue out of his shoulders. At least he wasn't the only one who'd pushed his body too hard. Hungry, Tim wondered what kind of fabulous meal Dani had planned for them. As far as he was concerned, a hamburger would do.

Packed with chatty customers, the Summit House Bar was the most popular on the mountain. The bar owners had taken pains to add flourishes to mimic an old-time ski lodge. A massive stone and mortar fireplace covered the western wall, and occasionally, over the constant din of bar noise, he could hear the seasoned oak logs pop and crackle behind an ornate safety screen. Whiskey, a trace of wood smoke, and the delicious scent of charbroiled beef mingled on the air, intensifying his hunger. Light flickering from the fireplace bathed the room with an incandescent warmth. Crossed vintage carved skis hung on the rough fir walls. There was a promise, unspoken, hinted at: *fun and romance are possible here.* He glanced at the tables around him. The customers believed that promise; it echoed through their laughter and happy talk. Tim believed it too. And he was ready to jump in, headfirst, as soon as Dani finished her day skiing. He'd missed her today. Though he'd had fun skiing with the guys, he still longed to see her. Tomorrow, he would spend the whole day with her. After today, he needed something far less daring.

He, Scott, and Mitch took their day-ending run a few minutes ago. Miguel had gone with Beebe and the ski patrol to the in-house clinic hours ago and hadn't reconnected with them. Miguel chose to stay with Beebe. Tim remembered feeling bad about his ill wishes for her when he saw her wrapped in blankets and transported down the mountain in the rescue sled. Still, he couldn't imagine her being here by chance. At least with Beebe in the ski patrol clinic, she wasn't out chasing Dani and him and making up whoppers about them for her gossip column. He wondered if SBC News knew about her sideline. Tim forgot Beebe soon enough as he, Scott, and Mitch finished out their day racing one another like a bunch of kids. Tim admitted every muscle in his body ached with exhaustion because of their alpha male rivalry. They had only one task left. Mitch had drawn the duty of driving the ski gear down the mountain to the cabin in the truck, and everyone else would make the four-mile trek on snowmobiles. Since the trail was not used by tourist traffic, it would be a fun dash to finish off their day.

Tim stretched and looked around the bar. *Dani should be here any minute,* he thought. But she'd already warned him that she skied up to the last possible second, sometimes taking the final lift before closing time.

Scott sat across the table from Tim, his chair slightly away from the table so he could rest his arm on the back of Kathy's seat. She'd spent the day in the lodge reading since she didn't ski. Scott recounted all the times he had beat Tim down the mountain and several of their more dramatic wrecks. Tim laughed at the wildly embellished stories.

"Good book?" Tim asked, trying to include Kathy in their day, as he motioned to the waitress. She glanced up and swiped a hand through her wheat-blonde hair.

"Great book," Kathy answered, a tease on her lips. "How to determine ligature strangulation."

"Uh, I thought you were going to read fiction this trip!" He frowned at her, then turned and watched the door again. Suddenly he sat back, scooting his chair as he did. Miguel strolled toward their table, helping a crippled Beebe with her new wooden crutches clomping against the floor, broadcasting each step. Judging by her Ace-bandaged lower-right leg, Tim surmised her fall was worse than he expected. Mitch stood and pulled out a chair for her. Scott stood too, trying to impress Beebe with a gentlemanly gesture. Tim remained stubbornly seated. He didn't trust her and let his mind regurgitate her excuse. She just happened to be here, *alone,* skiing at Schweitzer, on the very week he and Dani were here. *What luck!* From Beebe's tumble down the mogul run this morning, he doubted she knew how to ski at all. She was lucky she didn't break her damned neck. As he studied her, he was sure he heard her mumble "Jackass" under her breath. Tim stifled the sarcastic smile he felt pressing to be free. Glaring at him the whole time, she plopped heavily into Scott's seat directly across from Tim, garnering a surprised stare from Kathy. Beebe scooted her chair to the table so it lined up.

"Hi, guys," Miguel started. A big grin swept across his face. "You remember Miss Knoll?" He helped her by taking her backpack and hanging it on her chair and arranging her crutches so they would be easily accessible. When he'd situated everything for Beebe, Miguel pulled out a chair for himself and sat. A misplaced Scott grabbed an empty chair from a neighboring table and sat on Kathy's other side.

Tim greeted them with caution. "How could I ever forget Miss Knoll?"

Beebe shot him a nasty scowl. He laughed to himself.

The animosity between them was palpable. Beebe lied to him before to get a story for her gossip column, and he already knew she believed Dani was fair game for articles. Tim didn't know for a fact but suspected Beebe had a hand in all the media controversy surrounding his shooting of Gary Warden. She showed up at his office without appointments, shoved microphones in his face after every court case, relentlessly badgered him for crime stories, and when he wouldn't give her anything, she'd make something up and publish it as truth. Now, here she was, uninvited, on his dream vacation. Coincidence, of course. Yeah, right! He was pretty sure he knew what she was after, and it pissed him off. He'd had enough of Beebe's *National Globe* articles to last a lifetime. He looked toward the door to see if Dani was back yet.

"How bad are you hurt?" Scott asked cordially, leaning forward and across Kathy.

"Bad. The doctor said I have a sprained ankle and that I won't be able to ski the rest of my trip," Beebe explained. She stared at Tim when he turned back around.

"Too bad. You should go back to Seattle," Tim said. He didn't want her here. Especially if she was going to write about Dani.

Miguel tipped his head inquisitively. Tim knew he'd have to explain his hostility. Not now though.

"She's famous. Don't you recognize her, Miguel? Beebe

Knoll, SBC News, Seattle. Right?" Scott grinned as if he were starstruck.

"Famous? Right here? Well, I'll be." Miguel was smitten. Tim could see it. Miguel was the only single in the group, and Beebe was pretty and celebrated. Why wouldn't he be? Tim needed to warn him; Beebe was no prize. Dangerous and deceptive were the operative words.

"May I order you a drink? The waitress should be back in a moment," Scott offered.

"Sure, I'll have a Bombay Sapphire Martini, dirty." She flashed Tim a fake, sassy smile, letting him know she was staying, at least for drinks. Her challenge was clear. He wasn't going for it. He sat deep into his chair and contemplated her for a moment.

"Miss Knoll, you may join us as long as you understand everything said and done here is off the record. Not for print, not for broadcast, no pictures. Are we clear?" Tim was harsh, but he knew she'd do what she wanted to anyway. Even Mitch joined with the others at the table in an expression of surprise. They had no idea she'd use anything and everything said for news if they let her. Instead, they questioned Tim with their looks.

"Do you think I'd do something like that? Try to gain your trust and then ..." Beebe finished with a sigh, trying to gain sympathy from the others at the table.

"You? Yes. I do." Tim slowly shook his head. She'd divulged so much false, over-the-top, pure rubbish about him without his consent; he couldn't count the times. He knew Dani would want him to be civil. He could hardly look at Beebe without irritation bubbling up. He rested his elbow on the table and leaned into his hand, waiting for her to offer her explanation. Several seconds ticked by. He shook his head and then turned toward the door. Beebe would do what she had to to make a buck. She'd betray them in a heartbeat, and Tim knew it.

Daniela St. Clair. *Bitch!* Beebe watched Tim react to the woman entering the bar. He stood and pulled out a chair for her. All the scorn disappeared from his face. His whole countenance changed in Daniela's presence. His smile was stunningly handsome, and Beebe caught her breath. Did that woman even get what a total jackass he was?

"Well, well, you can be a gentleman after all," Beebe quipped.

"To a lady," he retorted without looking at her or changing his focus from his wife. Beebe felt jealousy raging beneath the surface and huffed out a breath. Everyone at the table seemed to snicker at their war of words. This was all going in the wrong direction.

How did Daniela St. Clair look so pretty after a whole day of skiing? Her light brown hair cascaded around her face and down her shoulders in soft ringlets, as if she'd spent hours on it. Daniela's skin was radiant; cheeks painted pink from the cold. Beebe caught her reflection in a window. Oh! Ugh! All her makeup was washed away because of her giant face-plant in the snow, and her blonde hair was a mass of disheveled strings, as if someone had plopped matted straw on top of her head. She ran her fingers through it as if that would help. And if that weren't enough, her roots were showing. She hadn't taken the time to do a touch-up before sprinting here as fast as she could, and now she was going to pay. She was competing for Tim and losing on day one! She knew she was glaring at Daniela, but she couldn't stop it. To make things worse, when Daniela reached the table, she greeted everyone graciously. Then Tim kissed her. Not a peck on the cheek either. A tender kiss—right smack on the mouth and right in front of Beebe. As they each sat down, Tim looked as though he savored a whole body rush. *It should be me!* Beebe needed to be the one he wanted. And now he leaned forward, rested an elbow on the table, and gazed, sickeningly lovestruck, into Daniela's eyes. Beebe was ready to scream.

"So, Goddard says you will be lead prosecutor on the murder case of the twins dumped in front of Seattle's Children's. What's new on that?" Beebe asked, looking toward Scott. Mission accomplished. Tim whipped his gaze to her, surprised. As she suspected, he knew about the case, but maybe he hadn't heard he was assigned as lead prosecutor. Scott dropped his empty glass on the table, scrambling to right it before the small remainder of beer spilled out. Tim and Scott stared at each other. Beebe bet they wondered who had leaked to the press, but they knew police reports were part of the public record. Beebe loved it. She had just become the center of attention.

"Off the record, of course." She leveled her gaze on Tim.

After a long pause, Tim grinned at her. "Off the record?" He waited until she acquiesced. Her heart started to pump blood. She was just about to get an exclusive. Why had she agreed to an off-the-record account? No way she was going to honor that. Not now.

"No comment." Tim stood and motioned to the waitress for the check. Everyone at the table began to gather their belongings. Beebe felt her mouth drop open, but no words came out. Après-ski was over.

TWELVE

Tim dropped his ski bag into the back of the pickup truck. He now understood Beebe's presence here at Schweitzer. For some mistaken reason, she assumed he would give her news stories here when he refused to back home in Seattle. *Good luck with that!* He laughed to himself. All she'd managed to do was infuriate him and make him even more wary of her. He grabbed his helmet and straddled his snowmobile.

The parking lot was full of people, finished with skiing and snacks and impatient to go home. Tim, too, was looking forward to the ride home. The few wispy clouds in the sky were colored pink by the setting sun. Tim was famished, and the bar snacks hadn't satisfied. Scott was all ready. He looked like something out of the 1950s' movie *The Thing*. All in black, coldproof bibs and jacket, gloves, boots, and helmet doubling his size. When he caught Tim laughing at him, Scott made a monster gesture. Tim knew he looked the same, so he shouldn't laugh. Tim could hear Scott testing out the communication equipment through the Bluetooth system as he pressed the earbuds into his ears. Scott loved nothing better than to talk during their ride. Tim guessed it was from being in constant communication while in his police car. Tim had to agree; it was pretty cool. If one wanted, they could drown out the snowmobile engine noise with music. And there was the real reason for the equipment: safety. No one could get in trouble without the others knowing about it and coming to their aid.

Miguel had taken Dani aside and was speaking to her in hushed tones. Tim felt a twinge. He wasn't sure he trusted Miguel. He'd been *Mr. Helpful* when Beebe was in trouble, which Tim would've begrudging done had he had to—but not without the impulse to leave her to freeze first flashing though his mind.

Still, Tim needed to understand from Dani where Miguel fit in. Tonight when they were alone, he would ask about him. Did Tim have a valid reason to be jealous? It would be good to get that settled. He and Dani had married so quickly after meeting, there were a lot of things they didn't know about each other. That was his fault, not hers. When he looked over at her now though, he didn't care. He loved her. As he watched, Dani slowly nodded, agreeing to whatever Miguel was saying. Then she turned, smiled at Tim, gave him a thumbs-up, and started to put on her gear.

Before he slipped his helmet on, Tim noticed Beebe climbing, with effort and Miguel's help, into the passenger's side of the truck that Mitch would drive back to the house. She'd begged for a ride to her hotel. *Good riddance*, Tim thought. He adjusted his helmet, making sure his communication gear worked.

Impatient, Scott stood on his snowmobile's running

boards. "Getting you guys ready to go is like herding cats!" he squawked over the radio.

"Meow!" Tim laughed into his helmet's microphone.

"Hey! Hey! What the heck is that guy doing? Do you see this?" Scott started his engine.

"What?" Tim asked.

"That guy—son of a bitch—he's snatching that little girl. What the hell!" Scott screamed. Tim turned and saw the scene unfolding. A man on a snowmobile grabbed hold of a child dressed in pink snow gear under both her arms and fought with a woman for control. The man was successful. He wrestled the girl around the waist and forced her in front of him on his snowmobile—so fast it was shocking. When Tim realized what was happening, the girl fell forward, bent at her waist and slumped against the front of the seat and gas tank. The kidnapper took off up the mountain trail, where the tourists began their snowmobile tours.

Without hesitation, Tim stood on his machine's running boards and started the engine with one pull of the starter cord. He pressed the throttle, and the snowmobile shot forward. He backed off a bit as he wound through the crowd in the parking lot. Over the sound of Scott cursing and shouting for people to get out of the way, still shocked at what he'd seen, he could hear the girl's mother wailing. He glanced over his shoulder, and Mitch was out of the truck and taking over his wife, Shannon's, snowmobile.

"Tim! Miguel! Mitch! Are you mounted up?" Scott came over the radio.

"Affirmative!" Miguel answered.

"Let's go get 'em," Scott said.

Tim glanced over at Dani and Kathy. They each stood next to their snowmobiles and held their helmets, both stunned by what was happening.

"Stay here, Dani," Tim commanded. He didn't wait for an acknowledgment from her and wove through the parking lot crowd to the trailhead. Clear of the skiers, Tim squeezed the gas and raced out ahead of the others. About one hundred yards in front of him, he could see the kidnapper's machine kicking out rooster tails of snow, colored pink by his taillight. He was moving fast. But the sleds Dani had provided were incomparable. They had the power and maneuverability to win this contest.

The chase was on. Tim formulated a plan. They didn't have the means to force the guy to pull over. He wouldn't be able to bump him. He might injure the child. Right now, all he could do was keep up, keep the guy in sight. He gripped his throttle, asking for more speed, and the Polaris delivered. Tim gained on the outlaw's machine. He glanced at his speedometer: seventy-five miles an hour. He was grateful for the introductory lesson Dani had forced them to take yesterday, or he'd be questioning his capabilities.

How do I stop him? He glanced at the control panel on his sled, and the answer hit him. On the right handlebar, he saw the bright red engine kill switch. Push down, and the engine quit. All he had to do now was maneuver in close enough, reach over, push the perp's kill switch, and Scott could catch up and arrest the creep.

THIRTEEN

Beebe couldn't believe her eyes. Right here, right now, she was witnessing a brazen kidnapping. All activity suddenly changed to slow motion. People all around the parking lot were now taking out cell phones and recording. Some, she hoped, were calling the police. But more than that, she was watching Tim McAndrews and his friends stage a daring rescue. She struggled to get her cell phone out of her jacket pocket. The fates had just turned the tables, and with any luck at all, she would make the man famous. She pressed the camera feature on her phone, then video, and pointed the camera at the men on snowmobiles. *Top that, Daniela St. Clair!*

She shot video with her phone, and when the rescuers were out of sight, she dialed SBC News Seattle.

"Breaking news desk. Branson Holt please." She waited while the operator clicked the call through to the station's news anchor and department head.

"Branson, Beebe."

"Where are you? You're breaking up."

"Oh, shut up, Branson, and listen," she fired back. "I'm at Schweitzer Mountain in Idaho. At this very second, there is a kidnapping going down. I have an iPhone. I have video. I'm sending it to you. Get me a camera crew, the works, right now. I know we have an affiliate station out of Sandpoint. I want to catch this. Branson, it's big!"

Branson stammered for a second.

"Did you hear me? We have breaking news, and I'm here to get it all. Get me a crew! Now!"

FOURTEEN

S cott, what if I can get to kidnapper's right, reach over, and push down the engine kill switch?" Tim asked over his Bluetooth mic as he leaned his weight to the right to start the tactic. The Polaris responded—solid, stable, fast.

"Go for it. We're right behind you." Tim didn't know who answered. The straightaway in the road made it possible for him to close in on the perp, but the space on the narrow road to the right of the getaway snowmobile was going to be tight. His mind raced to find a way. The side hills created when the Forest Service carved out this road might give him the room he needed. He could power up the incline in a gentle arc and drop down right beside the kidnapper, maybe even push the kill switch with his boot. It was worth a try. Though the perp was speeding along, Tim was sure he hadn't figured out he was subject of a police chase. The element of surprise would be in Tim's favor, and he was going to take every advantage. He'd bring back the little girl safe and unharmed.

Tim was within ten feet of the unsub when the perfect side hill came into view. He grabbed the throttle and powered the sled up the incline, arching with the flow of the hill. His speed was perfect. He could see the other sled's handlebars and the kill switch. As he started his descent, he would be side by side and a little higher than the kidnapper. Tim readied his body. He was close now. He took in a deep breath. In an instant, the perp realized he had company. He veered slightly left, which Tim had anticipated. Tim stretched as far as he could and kept his speed even. He reached for the kill switch. Not close enough! To stop Tim, the man would have to take his hand off the throttle, which Tim suspected he wasn't going to be willing to do. Besides, he couldn't possibly know Tim's intentions. Again, he extended his arm, his fingers just inches from the red button. Damn! The abductor swerved left and gave the snow machine every ounce of gas it had in reserve, burying Tim in the pelting snow kicked up by his track. He spurted ahead. Tim let off the gas a bit and shook his helmet's face mask clear of snow. He had to try again, this time without the element of surprise. He eased his throttle, and the Polaris responded, leaping forward with seemingly limitless power. Once again, he caught up, angled up a side hill, and ended his arch right beside the kidnapper, closer this time. But the man was prepared. When Tim was ready to touch the shut-off, the man threw his body weight into Tim's arm, shoving him off balance. But it had unbalanced them both. The kidnapper veered left, and Tim right. Football had prepared Tim for that kind of hit, and he recovered and squared himself for the next blow. But it didn't come. Tim realized then that off the left shoulder of the road was a ravine, a sheer drop full of trees that even a stunt rider wouldn't try.

Tim positioned himself for the third time. Though the other man wasn't ready for Tim's steady and relentless assault, he fought back. He wasn't going to let Tim bring his sled to a full stop. Tim looked behind him. He needed help, but the other three men were too far back; he couldn't even see their headlights. He renewed his focus, making certain he did nothing to hurt the baby. Tim extended his reach again for the red kill switch. He missed. He steadied his snowmobile and tried again. This time, he slammed his palm down against the handlebars, hitting the switch. All hell broke loose. He heard the other snowmobile's engine momentarily choke and then sputter back to life. The kidnapper had pulled the switch back up before it could do its work. He shoved the little girl off his sled to the left, and she dropped limp and lifeless into the snow in the roadway. Without her to hinder him, he made his getaway. Tim immediately let off his throttle and watched the limp girl tumble in the soft snow. He needed to save the girl. Quickly, he turned his sled around to get her. He knew Scott and the guys were close behind him.

"Careful, he's thrown the girl off, and she's in the middle of the road. Don't hit her!" Tim reported through his microphone. He stopped his snowmobile next to the child's body, ripped off his helmet, and tossed it into the space between the handlebars and windshield. He grabbed the earbuds and mic out of the helmet for communication, as well as an emergency blanket from the snowmobile's boot, and dropped down beside her.

He heard the roar of accelerating engines on both sides of him. Tim leaned forward and shielded the child with his body from the snow spray thrust-up as the speeding cavalry thundered past. His friends were still in the game and would bring the scumbag to justice. Without the safety of the little girl to worry about, they were free to do whatever they had to do. That stupid jerk picked the wrong place and time to pull this stunt.

Turning back to attend to the girl, quickly and carefully, with gloved hands, Tim peeled the duct tape with a cotton ball stuck to it from under her nose. He carefully brushed snow from her face. She was pale, almost as white as the snow in the rising moonlight. He bent down to listen to her breathing. Still alive! He let out a steady sigh of relief. He worried about moving her. She'd been thrown off the sled at high speed. He opened the plastic bag and unfolded the mylar blanket and covered her, tucking it around her as best he could. He didn't have a way to stabilize her if her neck was broken. Anxiety churned in his stomach. There wasn't a way for medics to get out here with an ambulance. He was going to have to call for an airlift.

"Dani? Dani? Do you copy?" he called out, but only static returned. Even the guys didn't respond. His heart sank as he realized he was out of range. "Dani, if you copy, I need medics and maybe an airlift."

No answer. He was on his own. He let the earbuds dangle around his neck. If they did hear him, at least he would know if they replied.

The little girl had most likely lost body heat and could be on the verge of hypothermia, even though dressed in snow gear. He had to get her warm and quickly. Making a fire was the only option. It could serve two purposes, warmth and a signal for the helicopter. The snowmobile had been equipped with a small folding saw and waterproof matches. He worried though; would she freeze before he could get that together? But just as he started toward a stand of trees, the little girl began to move; she seemed to thrash against the space blanket. He rushed back to her side. She blinked and sat up.

"Are you okay? Do you hurt?"

Sleepy eyed, she lifted her hand to rub her eyes. Whatever drug the kidnapper had used was wearing off. She looked at him and started to cry.

"You're okay, sweetheart. I've got you," he tried to reassure her. He plopped down to his knees beside her. She couldn't possibly know he was her rescuer and not the boogeyman. But then she stood, and when she slipped into his arms, he let her, gently pulling her close. "You're okay. I've got you," he whispered.

"Cold," she said in a tiny voice. He guessed she was about four years old. Anger stirred in the bottom of his stomach. He didn't have time for it now. He had to get her to safety and warmth.

He sat back and adjusted the mylar blanket around her like a cocoon. He stood, picked up the little girl, and carried her to the snowmobile. He held her next to the front of the sled, pulled off his gloves, and felt the hood. Warmth radiated from the engine.

"Can you sit here?"

She said, "Yes."

He carefully helped her onto the hood. She could walk; she could talk. That didn't mean she was out of trouble, but it was a good start. He remembered his mother telling him little kids were resilient. He hoped she was right. He had to plan for transport. He assumed Dani had called the sheriff. But he knew he had to get the girl out long before any public assets could arrive. He could feel the air temperature dropping, now that the sun had set. Even with a fire, they'd be in trouble if they had to survive overnight. The temperature was predicted to fall into the negative teens. It was up to him to get her back to the ski lodge. He picked up the communication equipment hanging around his neck and pressed the earbuds into his ears.

"Dani, Dani, do you copy?" Static. The truck was equipped as a base station, but with all the commotion, would they remember? "Dani? Kathy? Tim here. Do you copy?" The little girl started to move from the snowmobile hood. To reassure her, he placed a hand on her arm.

"Tim. It's Dani." Finally, an answer.

"I'm here. I've got you," Tim said softly and helped the child slip down the hood and back into his arms. She was so tiny. So helpless. And scared. "You're okay. I've got you." She wrestled her body out of the mylar and hugged him as tightly as she could.

"Dani? I've got the girl. Scott is still in pursuit. Call the sheriff, if you haven't already. Get an ambulance. I don't know how far out I am. But I'll be heading back in a few. Over."

"Sheriff is on the way. Is the little girl okay?"

"She's okay. On my way."

Oh, thank God, Tim. Be careful."

"On my way," he repeated into the radio. He disengaged and concentrated on the child. "Hey, hey, sweetie. Are you okay?" He shifted so he could look at her face. Her eyes were clear, and both pupils were the same size. Because she could walk and talk, he assumed she'd survived her fall much better than he expected.

"Are you my angel?" she asked sleepily, wiping her eyes with her fists. He wasn't sure if it was a concussion or the lingering effects of the drug.

He chuckled. *Angel?* "No. Just a guy who wants to get you back to your mom. What's your name? Mine's Tim."

"Chloe."

"Are you ready to go back to your mom, Chloe?"

"Stay with you?" She looked down at the snow, rubbing her gloved hands against her nose and sniffed. When she looked back up at him, she won him over. What a little doll! Now he understood how his brothers' daughters had them so wrapped.

"Sure. You stay with me until we get back to your mom. Okay?" he answered. "Ready?"

"Okay." She put two fingers in her mouth, gloves and all.

He picked her up and positioned her on the snowmobile seat, wrapping the mylar around her to make sure it was a windbreak. He put on his gloves and started to climb on behind her, but he remembered the tape and cotton he'd discarded when seeing if she was still alive. *Evidence*, he thought. Kathy would kick his butt if he left evidence and it was lost. The tape and the cotton ball could be the one thing that kept this creep from ever doing anything like this again. First, he took a picture of the discarded duct tape and cotton in its current location. Then, carefully, he picked it up and dropped it into the ziplock bag that used to house the mylar blanket. He stuffed it all into his pocket. He hoped it would be enough.

He began to put on his helmet but hesitated. "You know, I bet if you sit facing me, we can block that cold wind. Want to do that?"

"Okay."

When she turned around, she nestled sleepily against his chest. Before he put on his helmet, he admonished her, "Hold on tight."

He started the engine. He hadn't paid any attention to his location until now. He took a moment to set the snowmobile's on-board GPS, first to mark this spot for a crime scene team the sheriff would want to send and then to guide them to the lodge. He took a picture of the coordinates on the GPS screen. He tried to think of everything the DA would need when this case went to court—assuming, of course, that it would go to court. Satisfied, he closed the helmet vizor. Carefully, he pressed the throttle and slowly started back.

The moon had crested the mountaintops, illuminating the trail curving before him, and as they glided along, blue-white ice jewels sparkled in the snow.

FIFTEEN

Tim spotted all the lights well before he pulled into the Selkirk Lodge parking lot. Red and blue beacons flashed from the top of police cars, splashing color all over the clean white canvas of snow. In front of the lodge building, a gang of reporters waited for the hot story. Tim cringed. He hated media interviews and was going to defer to the sheriff.

Before he could avoid some of the hoopla, he was surrounded. It seemed that when the abduction went down, many of the skiers stayed to witness the outcome. He squared his jaw, picked up Chloe, and muscled his way through the crowd to the restaurant, ignoring all the shouted questions.

The sheriff posted deputies by the door, keeping the press and lookie-loos at bay. They helped part the crowd and let Tim pass through. The police had commandeered the inside for a base of operation. Dani greeted Tim and Chloe right inside the big carved wooden doors, and as if on cue, Chloe reached for her and slipped from his arms into hers. Before they separated,

Dani caught Tim's gaze and smiled at him with admiration. She mouthed *I love you* as she walked away in the direction of the vast stone fireplace. The hearth was warm and would help Chloe.

Tim didn't expect the strange rush of emotion. *Why here and why now?* Transfixed and staring after them, he didn't think he'd ever seen anything more beautiful in his life: Dani with Chloe in her arms. Thoughts of mother, child, and family hit him like an avalanche. He took in a deep breath.

"Tim McAndrews?"

Tim turned and faced John Woband, sheriff. Tim read the brass name tag above his star. The man was stiff and somewhat pompous, dressed in full uniform. He shook his hand. "Yes. I'm McAndrews."

"The press is hounding me for a statement. I've only got a mother's frantic one. Just wondered what you know." The sheriff smiled, still standoffish, as if being cordial would diminish the seriousness of the situation. "Start from the beginning. Don't leave anything out."

"My friends and I are here skiing. We are on vacation."

The sheriff raised both of his eyebrows, as if surprised by their willingness to stage a rescue.

Tim continued, "Scott Renton observed the abduction going down. We gave chase. Scott's a detective with Seattle PD."

"And you?"

"Assistant DA in King County, Washington. There are two others, Mitch Bradley, Mrs. McAndrews's pilot, and Miguel Gonzales. Miguel's with Senator Shearer's security detail. They are still out there running down the bad guy."

The sheriff slid his tongue over his teeth. "Usually, we appreciate it if an out-of-state detective lets us know— ..."

"Sorry, sir. We only arrived two days ago, and we didn't intend any of this." Tim tried to cover for Scott. If he had to visit the local cop shop every time he went on vacation, that would be a burden. And right now, he didn't have the patience to worry about jurisdiction or stepping on someone's toes. "Listen, the perp was headed out into the forest. If we could look at a map, we might be able to figure out which snow park he used and where he's headed. He had a plan. We need to guess his and make one of our own."

Woband flinched as if he'd been slapped. He should've thought of it, true enough. Tim wasn't going to judge the man. Unfortunately, rivalry was part of the game. Every cop he knew would want credit for the collar when it went down. Tim continued, "We still have a chance to catch this guy. You all know the area far better than I do. The guy shot out of here like a bat out of hell. There was a fork in the trail about five or six miles out, and he took the left fork. He knows his way around."

The sheriff motioned for two deputies to join the conversation. "Jeff Mantan and Bob Caldwell, this is Tim McAndrews. He's the guy that brought the girl back."

They shook hands. Both deputies were dressed in full uniform, clean and neatly pressed. Tim guessed the sheriff ran a tight department. The four walked to a bar table that had been converted into a command center and spread out a large map.

"Are you thinking he might be a local?" the sheriff asked.

"Anyone know what kind of problems the mom and dad are having? Any prior arrests? Was it the father?" Tim asked. Family feuds were usually the reason for abductions. Tim decided to eliminate easy motives first. Stranger abductions were rare but had far worse outcomes.

"Chloe is a foster. They aren't the actual parents." Woband tipped his head once in the direction of the couple standing next to Dani and Chloe, close to the fireplace.

"So, maybe the real parents want their daughter back," Tim suggested.

"Real mom's dead. Father did it and is in prison for the rest of his life. I know. I put him there."

"Oh." Tim swallowed hard. It was a stranger abduction. Thank God they'd been there to stop it. Chloe was one lucky girl. He breathed out. Tim remembered the duct tape and cotton in the ziplock in his pocket. He pulled out the evidence and set it on the table. "This was stretched across Chloe's mouth, just under her nose. I suspect chloroform. Sign for it, and I'll sign that I delivered it to you. We find this guy, and we have a record of the chain of custody. Your DA will appreciate that. I also have GPS coordinates and a picture of where I found the tape and cotton ball for your CSI team. The King County medical examiner is one of my friends in our skiing party if you need help. She's outstanding."

The sheriff blinked at Tim. "Do you bring a whole crime scene team with you on vacation too?"

Tim felt a grin tickle his lips. Suddenly, he remembered something Kathy asked him days ago about colored duct tape. He snatched up the plastic bag and studied the contents. Coincidence? When it came to crime, Tim didn't believe in coincidences. He swiped his right hand over his lips.

"I've already decided to interview other relatives. And I've dispatched deputies to Priest Lake and up here to Tenmile snow park." Woband pointed it out on the map. "The fork you think he took winds around the mountain here and ends up at Priest Lake." Woband clicked the point back into the ballpoint he'd pulled from his pocket and traced the route on the map. "It's a good seventy-mile trek. The local snowmobile club keeps the trails groomed. Bob thinks that the groomer may be out on the trail tonight."

"Seventy miles—we hit speeds over seventy miles an hour. And that was before he realized he was being chased. He could be close to the snow park by now. If Scott didn't get his hands on him first. Can we reach the groomer by radio?" Tim asked, peeling off his jacket. "My friends are out of range. We could communicate between ourselves, but I don't think much past five or six miles. I lost contact a while back."

Tim motioned for Dani. She still had Chloe on her hip. They were chatting with Chloe's guardian, but the child was clinging to Dani almost as if she was afraid to let go. When Dani looked at him, he could hardly believe the rush of feeling again. It stopped all other thoughts cold. They were so beautiful together.

"Dani, I need to take the truck to Priest Lake. And I need to get into radio contact with Scott and the guys. We are pretty sure that's where the perp is headed."

"Of course." She handed him the keys. "I don't think the radio's range is more than a couple of miles," she said, cringing a little as if she should've done more. "If it's okay, I'd like to wait for the ambulance. We, Chloe's mother, and I decided it would be best to have a doctor check her out and watch her overnight."

"I agree. How will you get home?"

"Kathy, Shannon, and I have two snowmobiles. We can double up on one. It's only four miles.

"Be careful. Gotta go. Bye, girls." He kissed Dani's cheek and brushed the back of his fingers along Chloe's. The little girl giggled and pressed her face into Dani's shoulder.

"All right, let's go," Tim said. The two deputies joined him, and they headed for the heavy doors. Tim turned back. "Oh, Sheriff, there's press outside. They want a statement. If you give them something, we can slip out of here unnoticed." His voice was hopeful.

"Yep. I'll do it." Woband grinned. "But if you want to avoid the press, you can sneak out the back."

"Show me the way!" Tim said.

SIXTEEN

Sam Graden flew along far faster than he'd ever gone before on a snowmobile. Each time he stole a look behind him, he saw headlights. The cops were tight to his tail, and they weren't giving up. He felt panic rising to his throat. But keeping cool was imperative now. The trail curved to the right. If they couldn't see him, he might be able to get off the path and into the forest. Did they have night vision? Infrared?

Up ahead, he saw his chance. A set of snowmobile tracks led off the road and into the trees. He followed the trail, making sure to keep beside the existing tracks. When he was far enough off the road, he shut his machine down. He pushed the kill switch, the one that cop was so intent on hitting earlier. It had taken him three tries before Sam understood what he was trying to do. The asshole almost sent him off the road twice—with no concern for the little girl. He'd had no choice but to abandon his plan. He just hadn't realized there was more than one cop.

In the distance, he heard the engine noise of the approaching snowmobiles. He dismounted and crept deeper into the trees. The gibbous moon cast long shadows all around him. He looked back at his sled. Luck was with him; it was parked in darkness. But still, wisps of steam rose from the warm engine compartment. If they had infrared, they would see his signature in a hot second. When he took the side trail, he'd kicked snow up onto the hood. He hoped that would help. If they passed him by, he was safe. They would go to the snow park.

Little did the cops know they'd planned for this eventuality. Instead of parking at Priest Lake, he'd taken a trail to an empty summer home his boss had given him the use of. He'd had to chain up to get in. He'd cursed it then, but now it was a blessing and would keep him from being caught.

Suddenly, the snowmobiles were on him. Engines growling, they were taking the curve in the trail and passing right by. Three of them. He didn't even breathe.

He let his mind race. He was sure he'd seen these men in the Summit House Bar when he'd given the foster mother the signal he was ready. He remembered thinking to himself at the time that they were cops, young recruits. Probably just out of the military. He could peg an off-duty cop in his sleep. They were cookie-cutter men—square jawed, buffed by exercise, military haircuts, clean-shaven, even on their days off.

He guessed the mother had had second thoughts. She was supposed to grieve and cry but not to fight him when he grabbed the girl. Her little drama called too much attention to the abduction. And cops, hell, they couldn't resist a good police chase, even if it was on snow. He lifted the cuff of his gloves and looked at his watch. The cops would make Priest Lake in twenty minutes. He'd wait for ten, to make sure they didn't head back his way. Then he'd take the turn he'd passed two minutes ago that wound through the trees to the summer house below.

His contact was going to be pissed. But it wasn't his fault. He'd done his part. It was the momma who decided acting was her forte rather than following the plan. For this breach, she would pay.

SEVENTEEN

Tim pressed the touch bar, and the back door opened. Without warning, portable lights TV stations used in remote locations blinded him. It was Beebe Knoll.

"Well, well. I figured you'd try to pull something like this, Jackass." Beebe came into view, stood next to him, fluffed her hair, signaled for her cameraman to roll, and then shoved a microphone in his face.

"Not now, Beebe." Tim blocked the light with his hand and kept moving toward the truck. Beebe followed, struggling along with her newly acquired crutches, like a crippled crane. She motioned for her crew to keep up.

"Wait, just a sec. You know I'm injured. Come on, Tim. I just want a quick statement for my viewers. Will it hurt you to give me a second?" she asked breathlessly, sliding a little on the packed snow.

Tim didn't want to be responsible for a fall. He stopped and let out an exasperated breath. "All right. The kidnap victim has been rescued. That's all, folks," he said in his best rendition of Bugs Bunny. He restarted his brisk pace away from her.

"And what's your name for the record?" She faltered dramatically. And it worked. Tim slowed.

"Come on, Beebe, you know my name." He laughed, shoving the microphone away. "You're missing the real news. The sheriff's giving a briefing in the front of the lodge, and here you are chasing me."

He pressed the door unlock button on the key fob. The deputies quickly loaded, one in the front seat and the other in the back.

"You're the real news. I saw you bring the little girl in," she challenged him, twisting the microphone toward him to collect his response.

"Did you? Are you sure?" he asked. For a moment, it looked as if Beebe questioned herself. Of course, she'd seen him. But he'd distracted her long enough to get in his truck, close the door, and start the engine.

"McAndrews! You jackass!" she yelled as he started to drive away. He waved bye to her, making sure she could see it in his sideview mirror.

Infuriated, Beebe threw the microphone after him.

She turned and looked at her startled crew. "What the hell are you gawking at?"

EIGHTEEN

Hungry, tired, and grateful to be home, Tim stripped off his gloves and stuffed them in his jacket pocket, then peeled off the jacket and removed his snow boots, setting them upside down on the electric boot dryer. He hung his bibs on the coat rack in the entry, next to his jacket. In sock feet, he made his way to the kitchen. He could smell bacon, and it made his stomach grumble.

As he entered, he saw the whole gang—Kathy and Scott, Mitch and Shannon, Dani and Miguel. All five sat around the chocolate-colored granite-topped kitchen island, while Dani cooked at the gas range across the room. The guys still wore their snowmobile bibs, but the girls had changed into their nightwear and robes. Dani even wore the silly pink unicorn slippers he'd bought her as a joke. Dani stopped cooking and hugged him. The clock on the wall read 1:37 a.m. His hopes of an early end to the evening were shattered. He pecked her cheek. Whatever she was whipping up smelled wonderful.

"How was the drive?" Scott asked.

"Miserable. It's snowing. Hard," Tim answered.

"Take a seat." Kathy shoved her chair aside to give him room.

"Thanks." He sat down heavily. The kidnapper had escaped. He wasn't going to complain. He wasn't there when the guy got away and didn't know what his friends had faced. Little Chloe was safe, and that was the main thing. He wasn't even going to ask for an explanation; they didn't owe him one. If his stupid plan had been successful in the first place, they would've been able to stop him *and* save the girl. He should've known it wouldn't work. Plans made on the fly seldom do. He'd rehashed it over and over in his mind on his drive home from Priest Lake. With time to think things through, now he realized the four of them could've boxed the guy in a snowmobile version of a rolling roadblock. If they'd thought of that, the bad guy would be housed in accommodations courtesy of the Bonner County sheriff, waiting for arraignment, rather than escaping to another state. Tim suspected that was precisely what he was doing at this very moment. Dani set a plate of scrambled eggs in front of him. He searched for a fork, finally taking the one in front of Kathy's place. He took a bite. Perfect.

"Sheriff wants to see us in the morning," Scott said, then sipped from a mug. "Wants our statements."

"Yep," Tim answered. As he drove home, he'd decided to wait until morning to tell them about the evidence he'd found. But seeing them all together, he quickly changed his mind. They needed to know, even if after finding out, they wouldn't be able to sleep. "I think this abduction attempt is connected to the twins."

"You do?" Kathy's lifted both eyebrows. She raised both hands, gesturing for him to explain.

"What twins?" Miguel asked. He perked up and searched their faces one after the other. He was alarmed.

"Just before we left, two little boys were found abused and murdered in Seattle. Twins," Scott answered.

"Why do you think they are connected?" Miguel asked, standing from his stool.

"Rainbow-colored duct tape," Tim said and after was intrigued by Miguel's response. The man stood perfectly still when the tape was mentioned. They were all waiting for Tim to explain. He pulled his phone from his pocket, scrolled through some screens, and set it in the center of the marble counter. He had taken a picture of the tape and the drug-soaked cotton ball. "This is how he controlled Chloe."

Miguel leaned across the counter and looked. He rocked back. Tim could see he was making some sort of calculation. Miguel wasn't going to share his thoughts, and that made Tim suspicious. He held on to Miguel's gaze.

"Kathy always assumes I don't listen to her. Do you remember you said you recovered duct tape from one of the twins? You asked if there was such a thing as rainbow-colored duct tape. I had no idea, so I looked it up on the internet. And there it was. The brand is Duck Tape, spelled with a *k* not a *t*. Play on words, I guess. Anyway, our unsub used rainbow Duck Tape on Chloe, and if this tape and the piece from the twin match, that's our connection." Tim took another bite of eggs. They were delicious, or he was so hungry he'd eat anything.

"Do you have it with you right now?" Kathy was almost breathless. He knew she wouldn't be able to keep her hands off that kind of evidence.

"Passed it on to the sheriff." Fumbling through his jeans pocket, he pulled out an evidence receipt and some light blue lint. The receipt, he placed next to his phone in the center of the counter; the lint, he brushed away and watched as it drifted to the floor.

"But, Tim!" Kathy cried. "I need that for my case."

"Kathy, we're visitors here. This part is Bonner County's case. Evidence belongs to them."

She sat forward and placed her face in her hands.

Tim grinned at her and wiped his fingers along the outside of his lips. "I've already called Goddard. He was none too pleased about being rousted out of bed. I asked him to fill out the paperwork and start a collaboration between the two counties. You'll get to do all the tests you want with the forensics lab here."

Kathy perked up. "My hero!" She threw her arms around his neck and planted a big, wet kiss on his cheek. "Sorry, Dani. I just had to."

Dani laughed as Tim wiped it away.

"I have to wonder why. Why would the unsub try to do this at such a crowded place? He had to know someone would make him," Miguel stated. A perplexed frown furrowed his brow.

"Did you make him?" Tim challenged, studying Miguel's face. "No. You didn't, because it's the perfect place." Tim offered his argument. "Tons of confusion. People are in a hurry to leave, traffic everywhere. People are putting away skis, changing clothes, and snowmobiles are running here and there. Perfect for a quick grab and go. He didn't count on there being an off-duty detective in the parking lot. And you know how cops are, with their bad-guy radar always turned on. Scott sees things that don't fit before anyone else." Tim sat deep in the back of his barstool. "All we know is some guy grabbed a little girl and took off with her on a snowmobile."

"Arctic Cat," Scott said.

"Okay, a guy on an Arctic Cat snowmobile," Tim corrected. "Sheriff is pulling the bar's surveillance video. Maybe he was inside before the abduction, and we can pick him out from that. But snowmobile gear is a complete disguise."

Miguel stared at him. Tim knew he was wrong to challenge the man, but he needed to know how he fit into Dani's life before he could fully accept him.

Scott finished his eggs, got up, rinsed his plate in the sink, and put it in the dishwasher. He walked to Tim and patted him on the back. "I'm turning in. Good job. Sorry I let the bastard give me the slip."

"My guess: he's local, or he scoped out the trails for days," Tim said.

"How do you figure?" Scott asked.

"I was lost. I had to use GPS to get back to the lodge. I had no idea where I was. But he knew exactly where he was. We were disadvantaged from the start," Tim said.

"At least you saved the kid," Miguel added.

"He tossed her. He knew I'd stop for her or guessed I would. I didn't do anything that any of you wouldn't have done," Tim said. "If I'd been smart, I would've continued after him, knowing one of you would help the girl. I was the closest to him. I could've body-slammed him and knocked him off his sled once the baby was out of the picture. I didn't think of it," Tim said.

Scott intervened. "Tim, I'm not sure I would've continued the chase at that point either. You needed to make sure the child was safe."

"Stop it!" Kathy raised her voice. "We are going to get this guy. Just not tonight and certainly not by second-guessing what happened." Tim could tell Kathy was already running through all the tests she wanted to do on the tape. She wasn't going to be able to sleep.

Miguel stood. "Time for me to get back to the senator's. See you first thing." He looked over at Dani. "Remember your promise. And thanks for the food. Good night."

Promise? What promise? Tim searched her face for a clue. He didn't find one there and was too tired to pursue it.

"Are you going to be able to sleep?" Scott asked, taking hold of Kathy's hand.

"I can try."

"Let's go." He pointed to Tim, saying good night.

Mitch and Shannon excused themselves too. Dani cleared all the dishes away. Silence followed. They were alone at last.

Tim watched her, turning in his chair. "Did I tell you how beautiful you are today?"

She stopped cleaning and walked to where he sat and kissed his cheek.

He held onto her. "God, you looked so fetching, so gorgeous, with Chloe cuddled up on your lap. I realized why my brothers' girls are all so spoiled. You could've asked for anything, and I would've gotten it for you. You women wrap us around your fingers."

"Are you telling me the McAndrews boys are cursed?"

"I guess," he said, laughing. "Loving you is a pretty good curse."

She stroked her hand down the side of his face. "You aren't just Kathy's hero. You are *my* hero. When you brought Chloe back, I was so overwhelmed. I—I am so in love with you. No matter what you say, you're my hero." Her gaze took in his eyes and his lips as if she wanted nothing more than to kiss him. Desire was contagious. Their lips met, soft, barely touching, fueling excitement and need. They kissed long and slowly. Tim didn't care what anyone else thought; it was Dani's opinion that mattered most. He stood, picked her up, and set her on the counter in front of him. He kissed her over and over until they were lost in pleasure. He untied her robe. The sheer gown didn't hide her nudity underneath. Tim took in a deep breath. He wanted her, here, now. Without hesitation, he started to open the top button on his jeans. She reclined, inviting him to make love to her. He undid the zipper. Why he glanced at the kitchen doorway, he couldn't recall. But like getting a glass of ice water thrown in his face, the moment was shattered. Beebe stood there with a big, nasty grin on her face and hands on her hips, her wooden crutches leaning against the doorjamb. Dani quickly sat up and slipped the robe back around her shoulders.

"What the—what are you doing here?" Embarrassed, he turned away from Beebe's stare and refastened his jeans.

Dani reached for his arm. "I forgot to tell you. There was so much going on. Beebe is staying here for the next couple of days." Dani pulled her robe together and tied the sash.

"Am I interrupting something?" Beebe asked, a smart-ass tone in her voice as she hobbled into the kitchen.

"Ya think?" Tim matched her tone as he helped Dani by lifting her down from the counter. He stared at Dani. "Why? Why would you let her stay here?" Beebe had published terrible pictures and written such ridiculous things about them; he couldn't imagine why. Incredulity was giving way to annoyance. But then he remembered Miguel asking Dani to keep her promise. Was this the promise?

"I was invited." Beebe made her way to the refrigerator, opened the door, took out a Lime-a-Rita, and popped the tab.

"Miguel said she didn't have a place to stay and asked if she could stay here. We have six suites to spare."

"I have such great timing! Don't you love my timing?" Beebe took a swig from the can, staring hard at Tim. "The light was on, I heard voices, so I figured someone was up. I just didn't realize someone was really—up," she sputtered, trying to contain her snickers.

Dani gasped and covered her mouth with her hand. Her eyes sparkled with laughter.

"Beebe, do you ever think before you let rubbish spill out of your mouth?" It was funny but at his expense, and Tim wasn't going to give her any credit or satisfaction by laughing. "No censor button?"

"What are you, my dad now?" Beebe took another drink.

"My fault. I should've warned you or put up a sign: Newlyweds, proceed with caution," Dani chirped. She tried her best to keep things light. She took hold of Tim's hand and winked at him. McAndrews's curse. She had him wrapped around her little finger. Exactly where he wanted to be. He'd have a talk with Miguel in the morning.

"One night. You find a hotel tomorrow," Tim said sternly as he started out of the kitchen. "Are you coming, Dani?"

"Yes. I'll show Miss Knoll to her room, and I'll be right there." Dani was holding back. He could tell she wanted to laugh. He did too. He wouldn't give Beebe the satisfaction. Dani walked out into the hall. Tim passed by Beebe, frowning at her.

"Oh, McAndrews, I just tested my censor button. It does work, after all." Beebe looked him up and down with such intensity he almost felt undressed and flinched. When he arrived at his bedroom, he made sure he'd buttoned all he'd undone on his jeans. Beebe made him shudder to his core. She was one crude woman.

NINETEEN

Beebe felt hot tears forming in her eyes. Why had she said that? Why couldn't she keep her thoughts inside? Words seemed to flood without control. But only where Tim McAndrews was concerned. Jealousy had swamped her when she opened the kitchen door and realized Tim was making love to his wife. That's why she'd slammed the door so hard against the stop. Not as a warning that she was there but to break them apart. This wasn't going at all like she'd imagined it would! She'd lost all control.

Beebe followed behind Dani wishing she would die. How about a terrible skiing accident, or a snowmobile ride right off a cliff? Dani opened the door to the guest room. It was beautifully decorated, but to Beebe, everything was black and gray. At least she had a place to stay for the night. But damn, she'd already worn out her welcome. She had to fix this somehow. Tomorrow morning, when her news report hit the morning shows and McAndrews was made the hero, he'd forgive her, she reasoned.

"I hope this room will be satisfactory," Dani said. Beebe read something else in her eyes. Curiosity? A question?

"It will be fine," Beebe said.

"Miss Knoll, may I ask you something?"

"Sure, ask away." Beebe couldn't fix what she'd broken tonight; tomorrow she could start again.

"Are you in love with my husband?"

The question was so off the wall and yet so pertinent; she was briefly shocked to silence. "I—no. No, I'm not," Beebe lied. She swallowed hard, and her breathing rate increased. Was she that obvious? Oh, Lordy! Did Tim know? "You caught me a little off guard with that one!"

"I see. And is he in love with you?" Dani asked. She was utterly sincere. There was no guile. Beebe felt horrible.

"No. No, he's not. Hate would be a better word for it." That answer was, unfortunately, true. Beebe sat heavily on the bed. It was only a dream, the love Tim had for her. A figment of her imagination.

"Ah, I see. For your sake, for his, and for mine, do you think you could stop—um—what's the right word for this—throwing yourself at him?"

That was the most polite keep-your-hands-off-my-man request she'd ever heard. "Is that what you think I'm doing?" she asked.

"Yes."

"Is that what Tim thinks I'm doing?"

"No. He doesn't understand you. He thinks you're after news stories. But I'm not so sure."

"Well, you're wrong. I'm after news stories," Beebe lied. But hell, how could she admit to the little wifey she had been throwing herself at her husband at every available opportunity, and if there were none, she'd been making excuses on her own. She'd followed him here.

"I think Tim sees it this way: he's had a good run at the single life. He is married because he's chosen to be. He can't imagine anyone not honoring that choice."

Dani's voice was soft, kind. She wasn't judging Beebe as immoral and ruthless. She should be, Beebe thought. She was going to lie to Dani tonight. But give up on her dream of Tim? Nope. "Good to know," Beebe said, pursing her lips.

"Good night then, Beebe."

"Yeah, you too. Have a good night." When Dani left and Beebe heard the door click closed, she let her emotions go and cried.

TWENTY

E lias Cain?" Tim was intrigued to see the giant of a man from the FBI's behavioral science unit in the Bonner County sheriff's office. Cain's extreme height accentuated the commonness of the cinderblock, no-frills building. Behind a small lobby, desks filled an open area. A pathetic, scarcely decorated Christmas tree leaned precariously next to the counter where the duty officer handled walk-ins. The clutter everywhere reminded Tim there was always more crime than officers to solve it. Along the west wall, three interview rooms with two-way glass waited, doors open, a step up from the main floor. The fourth office belonged to the sheriff. Tim assumed the jail was in the back. "What brings you to Idaho?" Tim asked.

Elias broke off his discussion with an attractive, brunette, female special agent and headed across the small lobby. A big grin covered his face.

"McAndrews, I heard you rescued our kidnap victim. You are all over the morning news."

He'd given no interviews last night, except his pithy one-liner to Beebe. That wasn't enough for a story, was it? Tim dismissed it.

Cain traversed the distance between them in two strides, his large black hand reaching out to shake Tim's. Elias, wearing the FBI's classic uniform of a dark three-piece suit and tie, still sported his signature handlebar mustache, and his brown eyes sparkled with affection. The feeling was mutual. Tim admired the older man. Cain had earned a reputation for his almost paranormal ability to envision a perpetrator from the evidence left at a crime scene. He was one of this nation's most valuable crime scene investigation assets.

"Have you met my wife, Dani McAndrews? This is Elias Cain. Elias, Dani. And you remember Scott Renton from Seattle PD? It was Scott's suspicion that sent us off on our wild excursion last night." Tim grinned as Elias reached to shake Dani's hand and then Scott's. The group scrunched together in the small lobby to let people pass by. "And this is Miguel Gonzales, with Blackhawk Security. He's on the detail protecting Senator Shearer while he's here for the holidays. Kathy Hope is here too. She's in giving her statement to one of the sheriff's detectives."

"Scott, nice to see you again. And it's Miguel, right?" Cain acknowledged him with a slight dip of his head. There was a look, an acknowledgment between the two men, that Tim was sure he wasn't supposed to see. But he did see it. They knew each other and well. Immediately, his mind spun off in a crazy direction. Was Miguel FBI? And undercover? At least that was the read Tim got. If he was right, why? Did it have something to do with Chloe's attempted abduction? Miguel's reaction last night to the duct tape triggered this suspicion. Tim lifted his shoulders. The why would be revealed soon enough.

"We're giving our statements on the abduction this morning," Tim said, still wondering about the Cain and Gonzales connection.

"Looks like it's my turn." Dani excused herself, and Tim watched as she went to talk to the sheriff's detective, who had called out her name.

"So, how'd you get sucked into this mess?" Cain asked. Tim knew Cain was here to help the sheriff. He would profile the kidnapper.

"We'd just finished a day of skiing when some jerk decided to snatch a little girl. Right in front of us," Scott said.

"I'm guessing this is bigger than one kidnapped little girl at the ski lodge?" Tim lifted a quizzical eyebrow.

Cain sighed. "Third—third in less than a month." He moved forward to let a deputy walk past.

"In a little town like this?" Tim was stunned.

"Not just here and not just little girls. We put out a bulletin two weeks ago. There's been an alarming uptick in the number of child abductions lately. When this went down last night, the Bonner County sheriff called us. We flew in this morning," Elias explained. "Earlier this month, there were two boys from Renton, Virginia. They were biking home from school. Disappeared into thin air. Vanished in broad daylight, no witnesses, very little trace evidence at the abduction site, except the boys' bicycles."

"Twin boys?" Tim asked. He stared at Cain, then rebalanced his stance as a receptionist brushed his arm with one of her files. "Blond and about six or seven years old?"

"Yes." Cain paused. "You have something for me?" he asked.

"I might. But Renton, Virginia, to Seattle, Washington, is

a long way." Tim filled Cain in on the twins and the rainbow tape connection.

Cain stood for a moment, mouth agape.

Tim continued, "We couldn't identify the twins. There's nothing in missing persons. You'd think the parents would be frantic—unless of course they are involved. Kathy Hope, our medical examiner, determined the twins were tied up and held captive for several days. We suspected the parents until we found the tape last night." Tim sucked in a breath and let it out.

"Twins weren't from Washington. Your state's database wouldn't have any information. That's why you couldn't identify them," Cain said.

"Scott did a nationwide search. Still, nothing." The two men looked at each other. Tim had the distinct feeling Cain had entered the boys' information personally and was startled that it couldn't be found. Tim couldn't keep his mind from racing. Had someone higher up *disappeared* the missing person's record?

"Maybe you searched incorrectly, Scott," Cain explained and reached into the breast pocket of his suit coat. Worry still sat heavily on his brow. He pulled out a playing card–sized photo and handed it to Tim. Two boys were dressed in matching shirts and shorts, each holding a miniature sailboat in front of them. Their family—a mother, a father, and a sister—stood behind the boys. They were in a park, with trees in full summer bloom, and a bright blue lake shimmered behind them. The boys had a family; they were important to someone. They were loved once. But their happy lives were cut short by a crazy, sick, selfish reprobate. Tim handed the photo to Scott for a look.

"Are these boys the victims you found?" Cain asked.

Tim struggled to wrap his mind around it. He remembered his childhood. He, Scott, and Kathy running free and wild without a care, and no fear. It was a different world today.

Tim slowly shook his head. "I can't tell. They look like it, but I can't say for sure. Kathy Hope would be able to." He looked around the cinderblock station for Kathy again. Scott handed the photo to Tim. He gave it back to Cain as if, if he did it quickly enough, he wouldn't feel the crushing sadness. No luck. No matter how many of these horrible humans he put in jail, more surfaced. There were always more.

"Now, we're not just consulting on a profile. It's kidnapping, and the perp has crossed state lines." Cain pulled his iPhone from his pocket, turned his back to Tim, and walked out of earshot for a moment. Tim guessed he was calling the Boise field office for help. When he disengaged from his call and returned, his eyes were black with anger.

"The boys were from a foster home. The foster parents didn't realize they were missing until bedtime. They waited a full seventy-two hours before reporting the boys missing to the police. Someone from Child Services told them they had to wait." Cain swiped his fingers down the outside of his mustache. Staying detached was almost impossible, but they had to keep perspective and clear heads.

"That's crazy! Seventy-two hours! We have different rules for children," Scott complained. Another nagging unanswered *why*. Tim was compiling quite a list.

"From a foster home? Chloe was a foster child too. What the hell is going on here?" This was bigger than Tim imagined.

"Sex trafficking, kiddy porn, a ring?" Scott asked. The ugliness was emerging, and the portrait of evil was beginning to take shape. Tim's emotion had coalesced to anger. A cold blue fire burned in his belly. He felt his nostrils flare, adding oxygen to it. His argument before the jury was already forming. The words evoking the pain and suffering of the victims and the righteous passion he read in the investigator's eyes had to be conveyed with all their weight to a jury. He knew he had to be on the prosecutorial team that brought this unsub to justice. Tim ran his index finger along the bottom of his chin, thoughts racing through his mind.

"Makes you good and angry, doesn't it?" Cain asked, taking a moment to stare into Tim's eyes. Tim nodded once. "McAndrews, you need to be on my team at Quantico."

The four men were interrupted when the sheriff emerged from his office with a man in a pricey navy blue Brooks Brother's suit. Tim recognized him from his many media appearances: Senator Buddy Shearer, the handsome and popular senator from California. There were rumors that Shearer would run for president in two years. Cain noticeably bristled.

"Don't like Shearer?" Tim asked aside to Elias.

"Solid gold prick," Cain said quietly since the men were headed in their direction. Tim felt a smile briefly cross his lips. He couldn't wait to hear Cain's explanation.

"I want to shake your hand, young man. Are you Tim McAndrews?" Shearer gushed. When he reached to shake hands, Shearer's eighteen-karat gold Rolex glittered in the light from overhead fluorescents. He smelled as though he'd spilled a whole bottle of expensive cologne on himself, and Tim backed up a step. First impression: what a fraud! Tim guessed he could care less about the victim from his smile, and this was all about facetime on the news.

Tim noticed the population in the sheriff's office was steadily increasing. Press from all over the state of Idaho crowded in. Now, several national correspondents from the various alphabet networks had arrived as well, flooding the tiny office with cameras, microphone booms, and floodlights. This was going to be a regular circus. Speaking of a spectacle, Beebe suddenly came to mind. She'd be in the middle of this fray. He was still steamed about her walking in on him and Dani last night. Tim glanced around and saw Beebe leaning against one of the concrete support pillars holding up the roof of the old building. She watched him and acknowledged him with a nasty little smile. At that moment, he vowed he would make love to Dani on the kitchen island later today so that he could win. Unexpectedly, the thought made him catch his breath and softened his anger. Right on cue, Beebe, even with crutches, was ready to get her story. She hadn't confronted him at the cabin this morning. What was up with that? He had a sinking feeling she was about to embarrass the hell out of him. He shook the senator's hand.

"Can we do this again for the cameras over there?" Shearer asked, pointing to a stage set up for the sheriff's news conference.

"Senator, I wasn't alone. Detective Renton recognized that a crime was going down, and we just pitched in to help. I'm not the guy you should be congratulating." Tim gestured toward Scott.

"Then this morning's news report was wrong? Miss Knoll had nothing but good to say about you," Shearer stated, and acknowledged Beebe with a small flick of his hand.

"I'm sorry; I haven't seen the news this morning." Tim narrowed his eyes at Beebe. She'd done it to him again. What kind of BS had she manufactured this time? "Sometimes, Miss Knoll has been known to be a little loose with the truth."

"Want to see it?" Elias asked. "I can get the recorded SBC newsfeed on YouTube." Elias pulled out his phone.

"Jerk or Superman?" Tim asked. It was always one of the two when Beebe made up stories about him. To defend himself, he knew he was going to have to look at it.

"Superman." Elias chuckled and handed him the phone. He watched the video unfold. The first scene was of Beebe, her affiliation with SBC News, followed by the narrative. Beebe read a voiceover while in the background a video played of Tim riding up to the ski lodge on his RMK, picking up Chloe, wrapped in the mylar blanket, avoiding questions from the press, and muscling his way into the lodge's front doors. The next scene was his one-line quip, "The kidnap victim has been rescued," before he and the deputies headed for Priest Lake to search for the perpetrator. At least she'd edited out his smart-ass, "That's all folks," and his attitude toward her. He'd give her credit for that. She finished with a stock reference to them as heroes. Scott's photo was from the paper when he was promoted to detective, a rather dashing picture of Mitch disembarking in captain's uniform from Dani's jet was next, and finally, Tim's official photo from the district attorney's office flashed by in a slideshow behind Beebe. She'd done a commendable job editing her report. But Miguel was conspicuously missing. Tim glanced over to the spot where Miguel was earlier standing. He was gone. Another *why* lengthened the list.

"Well, you shouldn't be shy. You rescued a little girl from who knows what. Let me congratulate you for the whole nation," Shearer said.

The whole nation? That was over the top. "Senator, I'd feel better about this if we'd caught the perpetrator," Tim said.

"I'm not going to force you, son. But I want you to know how much we appreciate your bravery. Most people would have walked away, hoping someone else would deal with it."

"We in law enforcement know we are that someone else," Tim said.

"Are you a police officer?"

"Assistant DA."

"Here in Bonner County? Why haven't I met you before this? I started my career here. I have a home up on Schweitzer Mountain. I visit every time I'm in the state." Shearer was acting as if they were alumni from a college fraternity.

"No. I'm in King County, Washington." Tim smiled at Shearer. But he realized that underneath the you're-my-new-best-friend act, the wheels were turning. Shearer was evaluating Tim's every move. It was almost as if he could determine whether Tim could be bought, just by looks. Tim wondered what his blue jeans and long-sleeved Henley said about him. He decided to test his theory.

"Can you do something for me, Senator?" Tim asked.

"Anything." Shearer smiled with his lips but not his eyes. Tim guessed Shearer was hoping he wouldn't ask for money.

"Last night, I called my boss, Paul Goddard, King County district attorney. We have a case that might be linked to this one. With your influence, you could expedite a collaboration between police departments and DA offices. That would be the best help we could get."

"If you think it will help, of course. I'll do it immediately." He turned as if he were looking for someone. Tim had noticed Charlie Hayes, Shearer's campaign manager, skulking around earlier, directing news anchor traffic. He'd seen Charlie from time to time on TV. Charlie was a small man that reminded Tim of a beady-eyed collaborator from a 1940s' spy movie. He had disappeared. Shearer's eyes suddenly lit up. Tim followed his gaze, and it rested on Dani. "Daniela St. Clair. Daniela St. Clair is here? Have you met her? Lovely young woman." Behind Shearer's eyes, the cash register was ca-chinging totals.

"McAndrews. Daniela McAndrews," Tim corrected, watching to see if Shearer made the connections. He only returned a blank stare.

"I'll get that collaboration going. Count on it. Excuse me, gentlemen." Shearer hustled away from the men to hit a more lucrative note. Tim watched. Shearer was angling for dollars. Tim felt sorry for Dani. Her money made her a target for every politician and shyster. Shearer was going to pitch Dani for all he was worth. Tim could never be a politician. Begging for money didn't work for him. Politicians started *for the people,* making a crappy government salary, but somehow ended up filthy rich. He'd rather prosecute that kind of corruption than be a part of it. But sadly, it was the state of politics in America these days. He caught Dani's annoyed glance as Shearer trapped her. Tim knew he needed to rescue her. They had long ago established a signal for circumstances like this, and she'd just given it. He headed for her, picking his way through reporters, politicians, police, and all the television equipment. When he was halfway there, Beebe stepped out from behind a pillar and pulled him back behind it with her.

"What the hell, Beebe? Must you always blindside me?" He brushed her grip away from his arm and scowled at her.

"Morning, McAndrews." She had a big grin on her lips.

"Not Jackass this morning?" he asked. She hadn't used her favorite name for him, and that was a first. He looked past her and checked to see if Dani was okay, but he couldn't find her in the crowd. He caught a glance from Scott, who had both eyebrows peaked in curiosity. Tim rolled his eyes at him, took in a breath, and let it out, exasperated. More and more reporters arrived for the news conference, and the crowd swirled around the small station house like a wind-driven eddy.

"What can I do for you, Beebe?" He'd lost sight of Dani and returned a distracted gaze in Beebe's direction.

"I'm trying to be nice. Anyway, did you see my story this morning? You were the star." She'd added a sultry spice to her voice. She got his attention. He liked the smart-ass Beebe better. This Beebe left him suspicious. She was up to something.

"Why start being nice now?" Tim dismissed her. He wanted no part of Beebe today. Or any day for that matter. "Yeah, I saw it." She momentarily stalled. She'd wanted a compliment; Tim knew it and wasn't about to give her one. "Excuse me, will you?" He tipped his head in Dani's direction and started to leave.

"Well, did you like it?" Beebe slipped her arm under his and started to turn him away from his mission of saving Dani from the senator.

"No. We've had this conversation before. I don't want to star in any more of your stories. And Dani doesn't want to either." He narrowed his eyes at her, emphasizing his point. When she acknowledged him, he started to leave, knowing she wasn't going to honor his wishes no matter what he wanted.

"Don't go yet. I want to talk to you." Her demeanor was different somehow. She seemed to be playing at something he couldn't figure. They had always had an adversarial relationship. But now it was like she was attempting to be seductive. She reached for him.

He moved to discourage her touch. He chuckled. "Now I really know you're after something. Be upfront for once, Beebe. What do you want?"

"What makes you so sure I want anything?" She tossed her hair back and parted her lips. Her body language was loud and clear. Or was it? He had to be reading her wrong. They didn't like each other. But he recalled the days before Dani. When a woman acted like this back then, she wanted to take him home. Why would Beebe think he'd do that? He stepped away from her. Nothing on earth could make him go there.

"Oh, I don't know, maybe because you're grabbing me to keep my attention," he replied. He knew his expression was cynical; he could feel his frown.

Slowly, she traced a finger along her lips. The tease was too obvious. He retreated one more step.

"What do you think I want?" she asked. She leaned back against the post, bending her knee, so she showed plenty of thigh from her already too-short skirt. He shook his head. Beebe was dressed inappropriately for the weather.

He tried to catch himself before he laughed at her. But he

was too shocked by disbelief to respond in any other way. "I'm guessing you want a news story. But your act is novel. Is this how you lobby for breaking news these days?" he finally asked, displeasure puckering his brow. "Stop the crap, Beebe. This isn't high school. What do you want?"

Beebe bit at her bottom lip and gazed up at his face through a long, slow blink. He shook his head and started to walk away, grinning to himself. What a player she was. But she seized his bicep. He turned back, glaring at her hand on his arm and then at her face.

"I don't want a news story." She fussed with her blonde hair, then slowly lifted her gaze to his eyes. Then it dropped to his mouth.

Why was she trying to lead him to a path he was never going to take? Dani had changed everything for him. "Am I supposed to guess? Are we playing twenty questions? I'm rubbish at that game." He waited for a beat for her answer. She didn't say a word; she just stood there smiling at him with a come-kiss-me look on her face. "I don't know what you're playing at. But knock it off. You've got me all wrong." He had to put an end to this and right now.

Instantly, her whole performance changed. Her shoulders dropped, she stood square, and the regular old combative Beebe was back. "You are so arrogant. What an ego! Not every woman on the planet is in love with you."

She'd made her play. It was the wrong play. Now she was turning the tables, suggesting it was his fault. He chuckled. "Well, yeah. The only woman I assume loves me is Dani. So, I'm still not getting what you're after."

"So, Jackass, are you going to give me an exclusive or not?" she huffed.

"You don't have to demean yourself, Beebe. This flirting

thing is unbecoming and could be a dangerous game. Some guy might take you up on it."

"But not you, Mr. Wonderful?" Her tone was hateful—the usual Beebe.

"Of course not me. I'm married," he scolded. He realized he was a bit self-righteous, but he couldn't help himself. Beebe had always gotten under his skin. At their first encounter, she'd accused him of being a cad. She didn't even know him.

A flush colored her cheeks. She was mad but trying not to show it. If she'd been a cartoon character, steam would be shooting out of her ears. "McAndrews. In. Your. Dreams. As if I would ever try to seduce you!"

"Perfect. We're all clear on the ground rules." Joking aside, he made sure she understood he was serious. He changed the subject to news stories. "Now, as for your exclusive, this isn't King County's case. It's Bonner County's. Talk to the sheriff. Talk to the Bonner County DA. I couldn't give you an exclusive even if I wanted to, and you know it."

"You could give me your point of view as a witness." She recovered quickly, a pout forming on her lips.

"You know me better than that. No."

"Jackass!" Her fists tightened into balls. Apparently, her first impulse had been to hit him. She softened. "Come on, Tim. Please?"

If looks could kill, Tim thought. He shook his head. "Beebe, no." He walked away and made his way through the crowd to find Dani.

"I was looking for you," Dani said as he strolled up to her. "I want to run over to the hospital and check on Chloe."

"Miguel wants to have breakfast. I assumed he meant with you too."

"No. Apologize for me. I'm going to see Chloe. I'm worried about her."

"Okay. But I'll miss you." Tim kissed her cheek. "We could have breakfast with Miguel and then go see Chloe together."

"And Beebe, what did she want?"

Tim was set back a bit by her tone. If Beebe caused him a problem with Dani, he'd be more aggravated with her than usual, if that was even possible. "She wants an exclusive. I said no. She needs to get that from the sheriff." Tim noticed Dani wouldn't look at him. It puzzled him. Was she jealous? He tipped up her chin gently with his fingertips. "Did I do something?"

Dani smiled and shook her head no. "Beebe's in love with you. I'm a little jealous."

Tim chuckled. "Baby, Beebe's in love with Beebe. She wants to be a media star. If an exclusive would help her, she'd do anything to get it. And besides, I love you, no one else," he said. He put his arm around her shoulder and pulled her close against his body. He closed his eyes briefly; just that touch swamped him with desire. Didn't Dani know how she made him feel? Tonight, before sleep, they would talk this out. He wondered if he even had the verbal skills to express his love for her, when so often Dani left him speechless.

Tim felt a touch on his shoulder. He turned, and Senator Shearer was standing in front of them.

"So, not only are you a rescuer of helpless children, I just learned you are Daniela St. Clair's new husband." Once again, Shearer had a smile on his lips but not in his eyes. It was off-putting.

"Dani's husband, yes," Tim answered.

"Well, congratulations. I'm envious." He winked. "Anyway, I wanted to ask you both over to a small gathering I'm having in my home Friday night for the equinox. We are neighbors. My place is next door to you to the west. I don't want to miss the opportunity to get to know you both better."

The equinox? Was that a new age politically correct reference to the Christmas holidays? Tim stifled his desire to say *you mean you want to get to know Dani's money better.* He deferred to Dani. He didn't want anything to do with Shearer. He was going to take the opportunity to ask for campaign donations, and Tim didn't agree with his politics. But he'd be neighborly if that's what Dani wanted.

"Yes. Sure, Buddy. Friday would be fine," Dani answered, and Tim dipped his head in agreement. "And I'll see you at the hospital." She kissed Tim's cheek. Both men watched her go.

"Wow. You are one lucky man," Shearer said to Tim.

"I know," Tim answered.

TWENTY-ONE

Dani sat behind the steering wheel of the jeep in the sheriff's parking lot, watching a snow shower drop a new blanket of white on the dark asphalt. She leaned forward and set her forehead against the steering wheel. When she watched Beebe grab Tim and pull him behind the building pillar, jealousy had hit instantly. She still breathed out, trying to calm her heartbeat. All the sickening feelings she remembered when she'd caught Carl, her ex-husband, cheating came rushing back. And God, she dreaded them.

At that moment, she thought if Tim was betraying her, she had to find out. Now, not later. She'd have to prepare herself for heartbreak, for all those terrible stories in the tabloid press about another failed relationship and for ruin. Ashamed of her mistrustfulness but still suspicious, she had taken two steps forward in the sheriff's office so she could spy on their conversation. She had cringed before opening her eyes to look at them, afraid she'd catch Beebe and Tim in a steamy embrace, kissing.

Instead, Tim was backing away from Beebe, jaw tight, with that blank, noncommittal expression on his face Dani had seen him wear in the courtroom when the opposing attorney proposed an outlandish defense theory or accused him of prosecutorial malfeasance. When she'd described *the look* to him, he'd laughed and explained it as his poker bluff face. *Can't let them see they're getting to you,* he'd said. So, was Beebe getting to him?

Beebe had been flirting outrageously. Dani remembered wanting to run, to get away, but her feet wouldn't obey her brain, and she stood there, heart pounding in her ears, staring at them across the room. She'd even toyed with the idea of storming up to them and being the jealous wife and intervening. But her pride wouldn't let her. *You're a St. Clair. You're better than that.* She could hear her father's words.

And now she remembered the day she'd given her heart to Tim despite her fears. She'd been so swept up in his heroism. When he saved her and Mark's boys from the serial killer, she'd been so overwhelmed with love; trusting him was just natural. He'd given her every reason to trust him. Why couldn't she? She hated herself for it. Tim didn't deserve to pay for Carl's transgressions.

Dani sat back in the seat, putting her hands on the steering wheel. She adored Tim. Losing him would be a heartbreak she would be hard-pressed to survive. She was disappointed her talk with Beebe last night hadn't been effective. The woman wasn't going to leave Tim alone. Beebe was so pretty and successful, and Dani wondered how long he—or any man for that matter—could resist her if the flirtation persisted.

She felt helpless. She wasn't going to be able to stop Beebe's pursuit of Tim. The only thing she could control was her reaction to it. She let breath fill her lungs. She lifted her chin with resolve. She was better than this. No matter what came, she would get through it. She was a St. Clair after all.

TWENTY-TWO

Miguel slid into the restaurant booth across from Tim, setting a mug of coffee in front of him and keeping one for himself. They had chosen this place because it was within walking distance of the sheriff's office. They sat in the corner booth for its distance from the other patrons. Tim expressed his thanks with a tip of his head but said nothing. He was still sizing Miguel up as he fingered through the packages of fake cream in a small glass rectangle on the left side of the table. He swept a hand over his black hair, brown eyes sparkling with intrigue. He wrestled off his down jacket.

"You are wondering how I am connected to the St. Clairs, aren't you?" Miguel asked, adjusting himself in the red leather seat. Tim was curious. He figured Dani would tell him when the time was right. Miguel was FBI; Tim had picked that up from the way he and Elias Cain greeted each other at the sheriff's office. But he'd also surmised that Miguel was undercover. Otherwise, Elias would have readily introduced him as Special

Agent Gonzales, instead of accepting Tim's introduction and pretending they'd never met. This was one of the questions on Tim's long list of whys.

"Yes. So, how are you related to the St. Clairs?" Tim hadn't warmed up to Miguel. There was more to him than he understood. He'd imagined Miguel as Dani's ex-Latin-lover, a childhood sweetheart, and hated to admit to himself that it wasn't sitting well. He was downright jealous, especially after seeing how her face lit up upon seeing him at breakfast the other day.

The buzz of the other patrons' conversations and the clang and clatter of dishes seemed exceptionally loud and accentuated the silence between the men. The waitress appeared with their breakfast dishes, and the smell of grease assaulted Tim. What had he expected? It was the local greasy spoon after all.

"First, let's get some facts out of the way to ease your mind. I was never romantically involved with Dani," Miguel started, his expression shining with confidence that he'd correctly addressed Tim's major concern. Tim didn't flinch. He was right, but Tim wasn't about to let him know it. "It always was—still is—her sister Rachel who is *mi asunto de Corazon,* my matter of the heart. We were sixteen when I fell in love with her." Miguel took in a deep breath and let it out with a wan smile. A flush of color raced into his cheeks as if from the thought of her. When Dani told Tim about her sisters, she'd reported Rachel had married twelve years ago. So, if Miguel was still carrying a torch for her, his love was misplaced. But man to man, Tim realized Miguel wasn't over it, even now—all these years later. That had to be rough. Tim stirred his fork through the undercooked omelet he'd ordered. He didn't eat it. That was it? He was connected to the St. Clairs through a juvenile affair.

"Our families met showing Arabian horses," Miguel continued, as if he'd read Tim's mind. "Venezuela was oil rich back then. My father was the owner of what now is Petro'leas de

Venezuela. In the old days, gas and oil were in private hands. Chavez had only started to steal the oil profits through excessive taxation. He would fully nationalize the oil companies a few years later." Miguel ate a bite of his toast. There was a darkening, a sadness in his brown eyes. "We were the lucky ones. Somehow, Simon St. Clair saw tragedy coming. Old Simon—he hated socialism and communism in all of its forms with passion." Miguel shook his head slowly. "Simon had contacts in the CIA. You didn't know that, did you? Anyway, he learned that the Chavez government intended to arrest my father, our family. Chavez knew that if the oil company owners banded together, there would be blood in the streets. He had to eliminate us and all those clinging to the hope of a true democratic republic.

"Just hours before the Chavistas came to take my father, we were warned. Simon St. Clair had sent help." Miguel sipped his coffee, then looked straight into Tim's eyes. "Sometimes I still feel the terror racing along my spine and twisting my stomach in knots. I wake up drenched in sweat. *Mal sueños*, bad dreams, haunt me. I think of my fear, especially when my mother or sister stumbled as we ran—my mind repeating a constant prayer that they wouldn't catch us." He crossed himself. Suddenly, a smile curved the corners of his lips. "When we thought all was lost, we stumbled into a clearing less than a mile over the border with Colombia. Simon had arranged a private plane, and they waited for us on that remote airstrip.

"He saved us. Simon St. Clair let us taste freedom. My father wept that day." Miguel stared out into space. "The first time I'd ever seen him cry. Leaving his Arabian horses and the winery he'd built with his own hands broke his heart. If it hadn't been for Simon—helping us, sponsoring us to become citizens, and hiring my father as his premier vintner—I'm not sure my father would've survived. He still manages the Walla

Walla winery, at sixty-one, to this day. He refuses to retire. He claims gaining his freedom is a debt he can never repay." Miguel took a sip of his coffee. "And now, under Maduro, look at what's happened to Venezuela. A million percent inflation, no food, no necessities. I read some men broke into the Caracas zoo and killed the animals for food.

"Oil rich to eating out of garbage cans. That's socialism. In sixteen years. In the beginning, we wanted it. They promised everything for free. We didn't know it was a lie. Or more realistically, we didn't want to believe it was a lie."

Tim had no words. The challenges he'd met in his life were small compared to Miguel's. He shoved the greasy omelet aside, set his elbows on the table, and folded his hands together. He rubbed his chin along his index finger, studying Miguel's eyes.

"Now, I must bore you with my story of Dani's sister."

"You won't bore me," Tim said.

"Rachel and I were sixteen when we met. As I said before, I fell for her instantly. Their father had assigned Rachel to coach me with my English. Foolish man. Didn't he know that around Rachel I could barely think? She took my breath away. How could I concentrate on the homework? When I wanted— Rachel was—is—so beautiful." Miguel laughed. Tim understood. He felt the same about Dani. Did the St. Clair girls have a magic, a sorcery that held men captive? "Have you met Rachel yet?"

"No. I haven't," Tim answered. That day had to come. Dani had been dropping hints for weeks.

"Dani was only twelve, and she had the most tender, sweet heart. Dani looks so like her but even more beautiful than Rachel, now that she's grown," Miguel said wistfully. Tim felt a flash of jealousy. Dani belonged to him, and he to her. Tim knew he would never want another. He guessed that's the way Miguel felt about Rachel. "She was a child, but she seemed to know Rachel and I were in love. She always looked out for us. She sometimes stood guard when Rachel and I would sneak up to the hayloft to kiss. Ah, those kisses. I remember them to this day." Miguel closed his eyes for a moment. "Dani always said she couldn't wait until I was her brother. I am her brother anyway, even if Rachel ..."

"What happened? Why didn't it work out between you and Rachel?" Tim asked, watching the vacant stare return to Miguel's face. He was looking back into a painful past. "America rescued my family and took us in, welcomed us, saved us. When I was eighteen, I joined the navy. I was going to give back. This was my country now. I was determined to make it into the SEAL program, and I worked hard to do it. I had to serve the country that had saved my family and me. I was so grateful."

Tim felt a sense of awe race through his system. Miguel was a SEAL and a real hero. He encouraged Miguel to continue. The café noise seemed to fade away.

"Rachel couldn't wait for her life to begin. She wanted so much; she wanted everything. After I had been in the service for two years, she married Robert Shaw, after dating him for only three months. I always hated Shaw. Even when we were in school, he was a real arrogant ass. When I came home for leave, Dani met me at the airport. I assume she hoped to defuse my jealousy and anger before I could confront Rachel. We had dreams: a wine label of our own, a home, children.

"Dani had the courage Rachel never had. Rachael just stopped writing to me, no explanation. When I found out she married Rob, I signed up for six more years. Even now, Rachel won't confront her feelings. I want to see her. I want her to look at me. I want her to tell me she doesn't love me."

Tim grabbed in a breath through his teeth. "Sorry, man."

"When I saw the service come and set up the house, I hoped

I could see Rachel, talk to her. Tell her I understood. That I didn't expect her to wait for me, though we had promised each other. I want her to know I forgive her." Tim could tell by his tone that Miguel wasn't going to be satisfied with anything less than a reconciliation.

"Have you talked to Dani? Would she arrange a meeting?" Tim asked.

"I have. But she loves her sister too. She says I should find someone new. But how can I?" There was forgiveness in his words but not his eyes. He was still in love, ego bruised, and angry. Tim could see why Dani had avoided getting involved.

"I have no answers," Tim explained. "I've spent my share of time fumbling around in the dark when it comes to women." Tim was somber. "Dani changed all that. When I first saw Dani, I knew, given the chance, I would marry her."

"So, you do love Dani. This isn't about money?"

"I adore her. It was never about money. When I first met Dani, I thought she was a secretary or the boss's assistant. It never occurred to me that she was the boss. I make my own money, nothing like she's used to but enough to get by."

"I needed to know you loved her. If we could pick siblings, she'd be my little sister." Miguel smiled and paused. "One question, though. What about Miss Knoll?"

"Miss Knoll? That's an odd question." Tim was perplexed.

"I was thinking that perhaps something was going on with you and Beebe Knoll?"

Tim shook his head. "No. Not a chance."

"Just a casual observation. She seems to want to be where you are. It's one-sided then?"

"She's decided Dani and I are breaking news. She's after stories," Tim said coldly.

"Shall I take her off your hands?" Miguel asked. It was an unusual request. Tim felt a smile rising.

"Go for it; she's all yours. But be warned. She isn't a very nice girl. All for Beebe, none for you, if you know the type," Tim answered matter-of-factly.

Miguel stared at him across the table, raised his eyebrows, and laughed. "We'll be perfect for each other then; I know just how to look out for myself."

"I guess you'd have to, or you could get in trouble pretty fast. Covert FBI. Interesting work. Who's the target? Senator Shearer or someone on his staff?" Tim thought of the weasel Charlie Hayes and shuddered inside. The man gave him the creeps, even though other than today he'd only seen him on TV.

Miguel took a sip of coffee, looking at Tim over the rim of his mug. He was assessing him and working out his reply. "I've never had anyone make me as FBI before. Was I obvious? Or is Elias right when he said you are uncanny smart."

The compliment was a ploy meant to throw Tim off balance. Instead, his curiosity grew stronger. "Obvious to a cautious observer. Not to the public at large," Tim reassured him. "First, I noticed you and Elias knew each other. Not casually but very well, and you didn't want anyone to know it." Miguel's face at first was deadpan. But then a crooked smile curved half his lips.

"There has to be a reason," Tim continued. "Shearer hasn't announced his bid for president; it's only rumored. So he doesn't have Secret Service protection yet. He has hired private security. You're on that detail, no problem. But when Beebe produced her news story about the kidnapping and rescue, she used all of us in her piece except you. She flashed our pictures on the TV screen but not yours. Now, why was that? My guess—you asked her not to expose you. That is a risk I wouldn't take if I were you. As unreliable as Beebe is, I'm amazed you were able to work that out. But then if your boss,

Cain, went to her editor, omitting you was a snap. The real tell was that when the senator emerged from the sheriff's private office, you went missing. You couldn't let Shearer know you were with us last night. You needed him to think you were out on your regular days off but nowhere near the kidnapping scene. I figure it this way; either you're undercover, investigating the senator or someone on his staff, or a real shy guy. Now, for the bad news. You went to all that trouble for nothing. Last night, I inadvertently told Woband you were with us when he asked why we got involved." Tim added some cream into his coffee. "My question: what's the relationship between you working undercover on the senator's security detail and the kidnappings?" Tim savored a sip of coffee.

Miguel's smile reflected surprise with a dash of amusement stirred in. He wasn't going to admit to anything. Miguel's cell phone chimed. He stared at Tim almost without blinking.

He took out his phone, pressed the button to accept the call, and paused briefly while the person on the other end spoke. Miguel replied, "Yes, and waiting on you." He disengaged.

Tim watched as Elias Cain strolled through the café's door, dropped his cell phone into his jacket pocket, and headed straight for their table.

TWENTY-THREE

May I join you?" Elias asked with his smile showing white teeth under the black mustache like piano ivories. He removed his wool tweed overcoat and slung it over the back of the booth.

Miguel slid over, and without waiting for consent from Tim, Elias sat down. He motioned for the waitress to bring him coffee and stared at Tim until the coffee was in front of him.

Tim suddenly felt like a buyer at a notorious car dealership. They were double-teaming him. Briefly, he was flattered. Only briefly.

"So, Tim. I've been talking to Paul Goddard about you this morning." Elias paused, expecting a reaction from Tim. Tim didn't know how to react. He'd asked for the law enforcement agencies to collaborate, but he didn't think they'd be able to put anything together in less than twelve hours. Usually, a whole hell of a lot more convincing was required.

"That was fast. I thought it would take longer to get a team effort going," Tim replied and looked around the café. They were still well separated from the rest of the customers. He wasn't sure they should be talking police business for just anyone to hear.

"Yes. Surprisingly fast." Cain lifted his coffee mug to his lips and sipped. "But that's not what Paul and I were talking about. Before you get defensive, let me explain." Cain lifted his palm, and Tim stopped his protest while still a thought.

"As you know, Goddard wants you back in the King County DA's office, and I'd sure like you to join the FBI. We know there are probably other offers, and we know we can't match the salary of a firm like Hollingsrow and Meagan."

"You know about the offer from Hollingsrow and Meagan?" Tim felt a little shaken. He'd read about government surveillance of candidates for clandestine work by the CIA, but that was in a Vince Flynn novel, not reality. Did the FBI do that? He had his first contact with the FBI as a third-year law student. They were recruiting athletes and law students out of school. Both he and Scott were approached and had seriously considered it. But now there was no way he was a prospect for undercover work, especially since Beebe had sensationalized his prosecutorial victories, even the smallest ones, in her gossip column in the *National Globe* with pictures. As if anyone would be interested in the life and times of Tim McAndrews.

"Just a guess. But you know it's my job to try to figure out what people are thinking. And you figured out Miguel in minutes, and so I ..."

Tim knew shock was drawn all over his face. "Is Miguel wearing a wire? What the hell?" Tim shifted uncomfortably in the booth. Miguel's smile said yes.

"It wasn't meant for you. Not at first anyway. But when I saw the wheels turning when you introduced us back at the sheriff's office, I knew I had to see if Miguel had blown his cover."

"Elias, I would never expose an operation without first consulting you."

"I had to know that for sure. You understand?"

Tim didn't understand. He couldn't imagine he was the subject of this investigation. Something wasn't right. "Where are you going with this?"

Elias sat back deep in the booth. He took in a deep breath. "Goddard has agreed to loan you to the FBI Behavioral Science Unit for at least six months. Even though you're cleared by the King County Commissioners and the Ethics Review Board for the shooting of Gary Warden, they aren't ready to let you go back to work. I already have approval from Director Chadwell. If you want the position, it's yours."

Tim was stunned. "Six months? They aren't going to let me go back to work for six months." He gulped. Maybe he should've gone to their stupid therapy sessions after all. How was he going to explain this to Dani?

Elias's expression was expectant. "Tim, you're an intuitive investigator, whether or not you believe it. I've been keeping tabs on you. You follow up on all the evidence in your cases. You even investigate on your own. That's why your percentages are so high. I know you would make a great profiler. We need more men like you. So, what do you think?"

"Did you think I could answer you right here, right now? Dani—I'm married."

"Tim, you are already ahead of us on this child abduction case. You've tied together the latest pieces before we even knew about them," Miguel said.

"Why are you undercover at Shearer's?" he asked. His mind was reeling with questions. "Do you think he's involved with the kidnappings?"

"Not now," Elias warned.

Tim felt his jaw drop as his thoughts spun through the possibilities.

"Are you on board?" Elias continued.

Mixed emotions made him hesitate. He needed a job. He'd always been intrigued with the science of profiling. He'd be acquiring a new skill. Weeks ago, when they'd discussed his options, Dani had consented to any one he might choose. She didn't know what she was getting into. Hell, neither did he. He set his elbows on the table and leaned his chin into his hands.

Elias held his gaze. "Around two hundred fifty-nine thousand children go missing in the United States in a year. That's approximately seven hundred a day," he said. "Sixty percent of all kids in the foster care system end up sex trafficked for various reasons."

Tim hadn't realized the statistics but had tried a few cases in the last four years. Usually, a kidnapping was due to a custody dispute with the parent, not awarded custody by the court, snatching the children. The foster care stat he hadn't known. It was disheartening. Tim gave Elias his complete attention.

Elias continued, "Around one hundred fifteen abductions per year are nonfamily member—what we call stranger abductions. Most of these children are sexually assaulted or molested."

Tim shook his head, both with dismay and with deep sorrow. He'd had a childhood full of love. The other option was hard to imagine.

Encouraged, Elias went on. "Only 20 percent of these kids are returned, escape, or found alive. Tim, that's twenty-three out of one hundred fifteen. The other ninety are never found, or only their bodies are located. In the last year, this number skyrocketed. There has recently been a push to normalize pedophilia as a sexual preference." Elias struggled with the words. "Consenting adults—I don't give a fuck what they do in their private lives. But children can't give consent. They don't know what it means."

Elias reached into the inside pocket of his wool tweed overcoat and took out a small stack of what looked like playing cards. He removed the rubber band that held them in place.

"I had these cards made up to remind me of why I do this job," Cain started. "Letisha Watson, age five." He set the picture down in front of Tim. "She was riding her bicycle down the block when she was taken in broad daylight. Her mother was waiting for her in the driveway; she only turned her back for a second to answer her cell phone. When she turned back around, Letisha was gone."

Tim glanced at the photograph. Letisha's big, innocent smile looked up at him. He felt the heartache and anger simmering inside.

"Bret Grath, age seven. He went to the toy aisle in the grocery store when his father realized he'd forgotten to pick up a dozen eggs and rushed back to dairy to get them. When Dad went to the toy aisle to collect Bret, he was gone."

Elias peeled the card off the deck, setting it on top of Letisha's like he was dealing a hand of blackjack.

"Robbie Wentlock, age six. He went to the park to throw a ball for his dog. His mom was with him. He threw the ball too hard, and it landed in some bushes. He went after it and never came out."

He set this card on the stack.

"You want more?"

Tim was shaking his head. "No." He looked up at Elias. "Are these children connected to the twins and Chloe?"

"We believe they are. We've narrowed each kidnapping down to a stranger abduction, and all the children were in foster care, under the age of eight, and vulnerable. After Letisha's kidnapping, we found a used-up roll of duct tape in the gutter. We weren't sure if it was connected or trash on the street, but because you never know, we collected it as possible evidence. The roll had only about a quarter-inch of tape left on it. Rainbow tape. No fingerprints. You tied up this link for us, Tim, with the twins and last night's little girl," Cain said.

"I'm in," Tim answered. He knew it was on impulse and knew it was fueled by a rush of disgust and his strong personal feelings that children should be protected, nurtured, and cared for by loving families. He felt a buzz of excitement. It wouldn't hurt him either to have FBI profiling on his resume. "Won't I have to go through ..."

"Under ordinary circumstances, you'd go to Quantico and through the field agent training. Yes. But these are not ordinary circumstances."

Tim had often gone to the police academy with Scott on the weekends and tested himself on the training course when Scott went to refresh his skills and wanted company. Goddard had also insisted that his attorneys have firearms training, just in case they needed to defend themselves. Still, he did not feel prepared.

"Good to have you, Tim," Elias said, reaching across the table to shake his hand. Elias snapped the rubber band back around the cards to keep them secure, just as Scott Renton slid into the booth next to Tim. Surprised, he quickly made room.

"We found the silver Beamer in Seattle," Scott announced, almost breathlessly. At the station, he'd brought Cain up to speed on the twins. He let the new information sink in. "It was shoved into and buried in some deep brush about a quarter-mile from the parking lot at Ravenna Park. And that's not all. You ready?" Scott searched the eager faces at the table. Tim gestured for him to spill it. "The driver was shot dead, right through the left temple. My partner, Anna, says a .40-caliber pistol was used. No gun, no shell casings were found at the scene. It's not a suicide. Dani has arranged for Mitch to take Kathy and me back to Seattle this afternoon."

"Do we know who the driver is?"

"Anna is running his plates now. There was no ID on the body. She'll let me know as soon as she confirms it."

"That's why you never saw him emerge on the other side of the park in the video," Tim mused, then sat forward, turning slightly to face Scott. "What was the time interval for the light green Mercedes van leaving surveillance by the park and re-emerging?" Tim asked, remembering Dani's question on the jet. The van had been the only other traffic on video. What if the van's driver was also the shooter?

"One minute and thirty seconds. Enough time to commit murder and shove the Beamer into the brush," Scott answered. "They probably had agreed to meet in the park. If this is a trafficking ring, as we suspect, I'm thinking the shooter didn't like the risk the vic took dumping the twins in front of the emergency room. The killer in the van walks up to the driver's side window. Beamer man rolls it down. Bang! You're dead. Then the shooter puts the car in neutral, releases the parking brake, rams the car off the trail and into the brush. He may have even guessed it would take us several days to find it. If ever."

"Any paint transfer on the bumper? Tire tracks?" Tim asked.

"CSI is at the scene now. They'll take the car to the lab, go over every inch, and let us know."

"When are you leaving?" Tim asked suddenly.

"This afternoon, after we see if we can find our kidnapper," Scott answered.

"The sheriff has the snowmobile trail cordoned off. We need to ride that and see if we can find where last night's kidnapper turned off. He never showed up at Priest Lake. You went all the way there on the forest service road, and we were there before you arrived by taking the main highway. Those are the only ways in or out. We could've missed him, but that's unlikely." Tim mulled it over.

"What are you thinking?" Elias asked.

"Just a hunch. What if our mystery snowmobiler's regular car is a green Mercedes van?" Tim let out a breath and stroked the blond stubble on his chin.

"That deserves a follow-up." Miguel grinned.

"And you think the sheriff hasn't gone over that trail with a fine-toothed comb by now?" Elias asked, twisting one end and then the other of his handlebar.

Tim thrummed his fingers against the tabletop. "No. No, I don't. He hasn't got the manpower. That's why he called you, Elias. Let's ride that trail. I'll meet you at Dani's house in an hour. I have one thing to do." Tim prodded Scott out of the booth. "You in, Elias?"

TWENTY-FOUR

After three soft raps on the hospital room door and then the metal clicking as the door handle's tongue released from its receptacle, Tim softly shouldered the door open, trying to keep the huge, stuffed white unicorn behind his back. Dani sat in a chair by Chloe's bedside with a storybook open on her lap. She looked over her shoulder and beamed a smile. Once again, all the feelings he'd first experienced last night flooded over him. Mother. Child. Family. Beautiful. He took in a deep breath and almost choked on the medicinal smell of the hospital room.

Dani shifted in her seat to face him. "I thought you had things you had to do?"

"All done," he answered. "Sort of."

"Hi!" Chloe said, bouncing with joy as she sat up. Her blonde hair fell forward in ringlets. Her eyes were round and blue. She was trying to see what he had behind his back. Smart.

She'd guessed the gift was for her. Tim wondered if she remembered him.

"Hi, Chloe. I brought you something." He walked forward into the room and set the toy on the bed, backed up a step, and placed his left hand on Dani's shoulder. When she looked up at him, another wave of emotion crested over him. Dani took hold of his hand and kissed his fingertips. She'd done it to reassure him, but it made his speechlessness acute.

Chloe grabbed the unicorn and hugged it. It was bigger than she was.

"I'm gonna name him Tim," she announced.

Tim chuckled. Dani squeezed his hand. "That's my name too," he said.

"I know." Chloe then looked up at him with horror at her breach of etiquette. "Thank you," she said before burying her face in the plush fur. "Thank you. Thank you. He's so pretty."

"You're welcome. How do you feel?" Tim asked. He looked at Dani for an answer.

"Fine. Can I ride him?" Chloe asked. She scrambled out of the covers and sat on the toy as if she were riding a horse.

"Look at that. She's a natural." Tim grinned at Dani, knowing how much she loved horses. "What does the doctor say?"

"She's doing great. She had a touch of hypothermia and a headache from the chloroform. He'd like to keep her overnight to make sure she doesn't get pneumonia, but after that, she's good to go home," Dani reported, watching Chloe play with the stuffed toy. Chloe pulled on the unicorn's white satin wings, opening them.

"We're flying up in the clouds," she said with glee. "Giddyap."

"Don't fall off then," Tim chimed in. Dani stood, took hold of his arm, and pulled him aside. "What is it?"

"She can't go back to that foster home. Tim, she can't." Dani begged him as if he could do something. His thoughts raced. Schweitzer Mountain was kid friendly. Along with the steep and deep for adults, they had an area dedicated to kids. If the parents had taken Chloe to Schweitzer for the day, how bad could they be? Sandpoint was only a few miles away, and skiing was great fun. He could request a new home with the Bonner County DA. He wasn't sure what effect it would have or even why he needed to.

"What's wrong?" He studied her eyes, breathed in, and held it. He readied himself for the words he feared were coming. Tim could feel his jaw tighten. Anger smoldered as he released his breath. He glanced at Chloe; she was an innocent four-year-old flying to the sky, in a dream world, on the back of a pure white unicorn.

"The doctor said there are indications—there is evidence of recent abuse," Dani said softly. She set her hand on his arm and closed her eyes against the pain. When she opened them, she had crushed the sleeve of his jacket in her fingers. Tim stared down into Dani's face.

"How did you get the doctor to tell you that? That's against HIPPA privacy rules, isn't it?"

Dani looked at the ground for a long beat and back up to his eyes.

"You lied. You convinced the doc and staff you're related. Wait. No." He wagged his finger in the air. "You paid the bill." Tim chuckled, shaking his head. "Dani? If the doctor suspected abuse, he would've already reported it to Child Services. That's how she gets a new family."

"Okay. So what? I paid the bill. The parents haven't even come by since last night. They haven't even called," she explained, a pout on her full lips.

"Not at all?" He was incredulous. This didn't bode well.

The assumption would be, of course, that the parents were the abusers.

She shook her head—no. Tim licked his lips. His list of whys just exploded. They abandoned her. What the fuck! She wasn't an unwanted puppy you could leave at the vet's when you couldn't pay the bill. The county welfare system would pick up the tab anyway. It only confirmed their culpability. "I can—I don't want to believe it. Not Chloe."

Dani stared in his eyes. "It's true."

Instinctively, he knew it was true. It happened. Every. Damn. Day. What she said next was not a surprise.

"She should come home with us," Dani insisted.

Tim gulped and rubbed his brow. He knew it didn't work that way. Child Services would have to approve of them. There was a process: paperwork, background checks, court hearings. He remembered the sheriff saying there was family around. But they hadn't been granted custody. They could protest. But more than all that, he wasn't sure he was ready. He loved having Dani all to himself. Maybe he could compromise for a few days. Maybe he could get temporary custody on an emergency basis. He could try. "I'll see what I can do."

Dani was in his arms, hugging him, kissing his throat, making him lose track of his thoughts, transporting him to places he shouldn't go right now. No way he was ready for kids. Not when Dani's simplest touch could send him to the moon. Besides, he couldn't be assured he could fulfill what she wanted. He gently pushed her back so she would have to look at him and tipped her face up, forcing her to contain her hope momentarily. "Dani. Dani. Don't. I can try. I can't promise. Do you understand?"

She smiled that she understood. But it was understood only for a second, and then he could see the Tim-can-do-anything look wash away her reason. He didn't want to disappoint her.

She sat on the bed next to Chloe and the unicorn and began petting his nose. Chloe started a story in her happy little girl voice. She and Tim the unicorn were flying through the snow. Tim suspected she remembered the snowmobile ride when he rescued her last night.

Dani engaged him, pressing her lips together in an optimistic smile. Now, he had no choice. He had to make it happen; whether he wanted to or could would be a different story.

"You girls—you have me wrapped around your little fingers." *McAndrews curse*, he thought.

But the real reason he stopped by the hospital interrupted his tease. "Dani, Scott and I need to ride the snowmobile trail. We want to see if we can find more evidence." He didn't tell her they hoped to find the kidnapper. He didn't want her to worry.

"Of course. Whatever you need." Dani stroked Chloe's hair. "Mitch will be ready when Scott and Kathy are too. To go back to Seattle. You aren't going back, are you?" Dani didn't want him to.

"No. I'm staying here. Goddard loaned me to the FBI."

"He did what? Can he do that?" She was standing now.

"Not without my consent. Okay to talk about this later? I should go." Tim glanced at his watch and moved forward to kiss Dani goodbye. She readily slipped into his arms, but apprehension creased her brow. He cringed inside. This might not be as easy as he hoped.

"Don't forget about Chloe," Dani whispered against his lips.

"How can I when you ask like this?" They parted, lingering for a second longer, touching fingertips.

"Love you," Dani said.

"Me too."

TWENTY-FIVE

The far west meeting room at the Selkirk Lodge was still under the control of the sheriff's office. The giant river rock fireplace crackled with a seasoned oak fire, and a faint hint of wood smoke lingered on the air. The forest-green walls diminished the daylight, so the small electric lamps on the tables gave off a romantic glow. Tim thought of Dani. Soft incandescent light always made him think of her, her honey hair shimmering when she moved, her blue eyes sparkling with love, and that freckle, that beautiful, kissable freckle at the top curve of her lip.

He hoped she hadn't done something to keep them from getting temporary custody of Chloe by lying to the doctor and paying the bill. On his way here, he'd called their friend and attorney, Brad Hollingsrow. Brad's new judicial appointment to the superior court might give him the clout they would need to circumvent the usual bureaucratic gauntlet. But Brad practiced in Washington, and this was Idaho. They might not appreciate the interference.

Not really wanting to, he turned back to the task at hand. The sheriff had suggested they meet here before heading out to see if they could find the kidnapper.

Maps of the Forest Service roads, snowmobile trails, and county roads were still spread out on one of the oblong tables, from last night. The two deputies he'd driven with to Priest Lake the previous night were here, sipping coffee, dressed in snowmobile gear and waiting for instructions. They both had served in the department for ten years, joining as recruits within months of each other. Jeff "Grey Wolf" Montan was a tall, striking man. His face bore the high cheekbones and strong, straight nose and full lips characteristic of his heritage. Tim had enjoyed his sense of humor and the quick wit that flashed from the man's brown eyes as they'd talked on the way to Priest Lake last night in pursuit of the kidnapper. Deputy Jeff, he'd discovered, had used his experience with the Nez Perce tribal police to transfer to the Bonner County sheriff's office when he hit his twentieth birthday. The sheriff had allowed him to continue to wear his long black hair in a braid down his back.

His partner, Bob Caldwell, was a more serious and reserved guy. He was big and burly like a linebacker. He was from a family of cattle ranchers and was often teased for covering his thick, short-cropped brown hair with a cowboy hat, his green eyes with Ray-Bans, and wearing expensive Tony Lama snakeskin boots. The deputies told Tim they were best friends. Counting on each other for your life did that. Their families spent a lot of their off time together, as they all enjoyed rodeo and horseback riding. Together they had come up with a name for their partnership: Tonto and the Lone Ranger. But they begged Tim not to repeat it in front of the sheriff. A female deputy, Cheryl

Raymond, had been triggered by their good-natured joke and had taken great offense. She complained to the sheriff. They'd been admonished and had to endure sensitivity training for six weeks.

Sheriff Woband walked toward Tim with a highly annoyed snowmobile tour concessionaire following behind. The man was dressed in black snow bibs and boots and wore an uptight, frustrated look on his narrow face. Obviously, he wanted access to the trails for his afternoon tour group.

"Listen, Jay. With your help, we can get you back up and going quickly," Sheriff Woband said as he approached Tim. "Jay Worth, this is Tim McAndrews, Elias Cain with the FBI, Scott Renton, Seattle PD. Jeff and Bob, you know," he said as he stopped in front of the map table.

Tim tipped his head in greeting. The men shook hands.

"Thank you for helping us, Jay. It's Jay, isn't it?" Tim held the man's gaze long enough to get an acknowledgment. "You know the trails up here better than anyone. We are looking for a turnoff from the main Forest Service road between here and Priest Lake that might have a house or cabin where someone could hole up overnight. We need to figure out how the unsub eluded us last night, if he's found a place to hide out and is still here." Tim traced a finger along the road on the map. "Here's approximately where he abandoned his captive last night." Tim pointed to a spot just west of a fork in the trail where he'd stopped his pursuit to help Chloe. Tim realized Jay had little interest in the investigation and just wanted the trails reopened. His narrow face was stone, and a tight-lipped grin curved his mouth.

"His victim was four years old. She wasn't his first. He's suspected of abducting two six-year-old boys too. The boys were found severely abused and died from their injuries." Tim held the man's gaze until that point sunk in and hoped the man could find some empathy.

Jay's jaw dropped with shock, his face softened, and he quickly leaned forward and studied the map. "I'm not an insensitive guy. I'm just trying to make a living," he said to counter Tim's guilt trip. "This map doesn't show it, but the topography changes. The steep canyon levels out, and the national forest gives way to land in private ownership. There is one property, about a hundred fifty acres, right in this area." He drew a circle with his finger. "There are some great meadows down in there. They get deep drifts of snow. We pay the owner to use them for some of our more advanced riders. Great powder riding," Jay explained.

"It looks like this property is bordered on the north by the snowmobile trail and the south by Highway 57," Tim stated more as a question. "That would make a getaway easy."

"Yep. It's the Bransons' place. Gorgeous spot. They're snowbirds. Go south for the winter. Arizona, I understand." Jay smiled. "They love to ATV during the summer but say it's too cold for them when the snow flies. I've tried to sell them snowmobiles for years.

"It's an ATVer's paradise. You can take Highway 57 to the house, unload your trailer, and hit the Forest Service road in about a half hour. There's a narrow road up the mountainside, lots of switchbacks. It takes you up to the gravel Forest Service road here from the house." He traced the route for Tim to see.

Tim looked over to the sheriff, expecting input. Woband returned a noncommittal, almost bored stare.

"We'd better get going before we lose daylight," Scott said with urgency in his voice. He slipped his arms through the sleeves of his jacket. Tim agreed. It was almost noon. In winter, before the equinox, the sun set around three thirty in the afternoon.

"What else is down there? Anything closer to Priest Lake?" Tim asked, also putting on his outerwear. He slipped into the black vest with POLICE emblazoned on the back in bold yellow letters, as did the others.

"Two small summer cabins. But the Branson house is the most secluded. You can't see the house from either road," Deputy Jeff said. "The owners of the cabins pay us to patrol their places once a week. They're snowbirds too, and it's a service we offer to keep down home burglaries. We don't patrol the Bransons' place. They supposedly have some fancy-dancy alarm system," he explained in response to Tim's questioning look.

"Sheriff, do you think you can get the Bransons' permission to go onto their property?" Tim asked. "We don't have enough evidence to convince a judge to grant a warrant." The sheriff pulled his cell phone out and called to make arrangements.

After hanging up, Woband said, "Let's get going."

Tim looked over at Elias. The man looked twice his size in snowmobile gear, and Tim shot him a big smile. Tim was surprised he'd decided to go, but after he'd sent his two agents with the deputy doing the well-check on Chloe's foster parents, Elias was the only other representative of the FBI. Tim didn't think he qualified as a special agent. Not yet anyway. Elias grinned at him in anticipation. He'd never been snowmobiling, and maybe he was happy to get out of the desk work.

The men rode their snowmobiles up to the edge of the Forest Service road they'd cordoned off last night with yellow crime scene tape. Tim pushed the kill switch on his sled's engine, removed his helmet, and set it between the windscreen and the handlebars. His stomach turned over. With disgust, he studied the trail. The snow on the road was scored with the corduroy lines typically made by a groomer. He was speechless. He whipped his gaze around until it fell on Sheriff Woband.

"I thought you stopped the groomer last night. The snow-mobile tracks are erased. What the hell?" Tim complained. *What a colossal fuck-up.* He glanced around until he found Scott's face and bit at his bottom lip. Tim realized that they both wondered, *Was it intentional?* It was a policeman's nature to be suspicious, but should they go down that road?

"Couldn't reach him," the sheriff explained offhandedly. He was too casual about it. Tim stood on the sideboards of his snowmobile, evaluating the damage, and looked over at Elias. His demeanor changed, confirming he shared their suspicion. He didn't vocalize it. There was a reason. How many kidnappings did Bonner County have in a year? He hadn't asked that question, but when he did his computer research tonight, he'd find out. Was it inexperience? Duplicity? Was Sheriff Woband lazy? Incompetent? Or dirty? Tim pushed the information to simmer on the back burner. Right now, he wanted to catch their unsub. The groomer erased all snowmobile tracks in the snow on the road but wouldn't bother to take out the off-road ones. They would find those.

"All right. What we are searching for is snowmobile tracks beside the main trail, tracks that lead to a hiding place," Elias jumped in, booming the instruction in his bass voice.

The men put their helmets back on, started their engines, and ducked under the yellow tape.

Tim left his visor up and looked out through a pair of wrap-around goggles with yellow-tinted lenses. They brightened his view and as a bonus would help him avoid the ever-present problem of visor fog-up. He breathed in the cold air and the fresh scent of pine. It was pristine here. It was like he'd stepped out of the real world and into a sparkling white fantasy land. Ponderosa pine and Douglas fir were mixed in a snow-covered forest. If he wasn't investigating a kidnapping, this might be fun. As they rode along, he realized that the groomer had gifted them with a consolation prize. Though the big machine had erased all last night's snowmobile tracks, the ride was sweet, like floating above the earth on clouds of glittering white. All the bumps and washboard created by the daily tours were gone. Tim had an overwhelming urge to play, to race ahead at full speed and take the side hills in daylight he'd struggled with in his pursuit of the kidnapper last night. "I'm on vacation!" He shouted, knowing it was drowned out in the braaaappp of the snowmobile engines. He quickly tamped down his frustration. He knew if they had it all to do over, he and Scott would do the same thing. There was no way they would let a four-year-old child be kidnapped in front of them, even if it wasn't their watch.

When he came to the spot where he'd rescued Chloe, he slowed. The pack slowed too. Rather than stop their progress, he used the Bluetooth headset in his helmet and spoke over his microphone.

"Here's where I picked up the little girl. We need to be vigilant from here on," he said, standing up on his sideboards so he could see along the sides of the Forest Service road.

After crawling along for ten minutes, it seemed like they were on the wrong page. They had gone miles, and there wasn't a single track off to the left, as he'd anticipated from reading the map. He felt discouraged. But as they rounded a curve to the right, they came upon a small level clearing. A set of tracks were imprinted into a shallow embankment leading to the field. Once up and over the lip of the bank, Tim followed the impressions in the snow. Scott and Jeff kept right with him. The rest of the men stopped in a line on the road and watched. Tim turned back and concentrated on the trail left in the snow. It led him back into the trees. He came to a stop and closed his eyes, trying to put himself in the position of being a kidnapper on the run. He let his imagination go. Had the perp turned into this field, ridden back here into the trees, turned off his engine, and let Scott, Miguel, and Mitch race past him last night? That's what Tim would've done. He dismounted his sled and studied the impressions. The rider got off here and walked briskly to a fallen log. Had he hidden there, on his knees? That's what the remaining prints looked like. Jeff and Tim both took pictures.

The rider that left these tracks looped back toward the road. When he resumed his travel, the sled dug into the snow as it made initial traction. The marks led back to the main road, but the angle of entry to the road was not forward toward Priest Lake but back the way they'd come. Did he miss seeing the turnoff? Did they all? Tim couldn't believe it. Slowly, he retraced his path. Then he saw it. The sun reflecting off the snow had disguised the trail that was clearly visible in this direction. Tim looked behind him. The others were catching up. He turned off his sled, removed his helmet, and searched in his jacket pocket for his cell phone. He swung his leg over and walked to a trail that wound down the steep mountainside and looked over the edge. The elements of a snowmobile's passing were there—the smooth indentations of the front skis and the churned middle made by the lugs on the track. Jeff rushed up beside him and dropped a numbered yellow triangle next to the prints. They both took pictures from all angles. He could erase them if this turned out to be a dead end. Before they started, Tim made a mental list of the evidence he'd like to have in hand, as if preparing for court. He didn't know if snowmobile tracks were as unique as tires, but a good forensics lab might be able to match them to a specific sled. He could only hope.

"This snow is too powdery to cast any prints. Just like the ones in the meadow," Jeff said. Tim knew the sheriff's deputies brought some things with them because a crime scene van would never make it up here on the snowmobile trail without getting stuck until spring.

"Damn. I hate losing this evidence when we drive over it," Tim worried aloud.

"If it is evidence," the sheriff commented.

Tim cautiously smiled his agreement. "If it is evidence," he repeated.

"We could go straight down through the trees," Jeff commented. But his face said it all.

"We could. But should we? I don't think I'm that good a rider," Tim chided.

"I am that good." Jeff laughed. "And we shouldn't unless we want to die."

Tim sighed. "I say we take the trail. I'm planning to make love to my wife tonight. I need to make it home."

Jeff grinned big. "Evidence be damned then?"

"If it is evidence." Tim chuckled to himself.

The men mounted up and slowly descended. Big ponderosa pines lined both sides of the narrow path, and a sprinkling of dead needles littered the snow, deposited by an eastward breeze. The low winter sunlight glittered on the white when it broke through the tree shadows. In a few minutes, the route opened to a clearing, and they stopped. The main house, a new log home, surrounded by decks, took up the most significant part of the clearing. To the north side, there was a matching three-bay barn. The bays were enclosed, and automatic garage doors were centered in each. Fresh snowmobile tracks led to the bay closest to the men and the mountainside trail. The Bransons told Jay they didn't want to buy snowmobiles because winter was too cold for them. A lie? Tim wondered.

From the third bay, a set of tire tracks led past the house and onto a road or driveway that Tim assumed met up with the paved highway. He recalled the map. He lifted his palm to keep the group from proceeding any farther on snow machines. He stared at the house. The place was dark. No movement stirred past the windows. From here, they would continue on foot and with caution. The Bransons explained to the sheriff that the house was unoccupied, but the prints said otherwise. Tim again scrutinized the house. They had obtained permission to search the outbuildings but not the house, unless they suspected a break-in. No matter what the Bransons said, someone had been here. Were they still?

He removed his helmet and motioned to Jeff. "Let's document these tracks, just in case."

Jeff concurred.

Tim walked beside the snowmobile tracks. Scott joined him. They smiled at each other. When they arrived at the garage door, Scott pressed in the code the Bransons had given them on the pad mounted there and ducked away as the door began to move. Tim realized the person who'd been here had the code. Strike two. The Bransons were lying. Why?

"Proceed with caution. This could be a setup. An ambush," Tim said just above a whisper.

The door ground open. Inside the bay were three ATVs parked side by side and one Arctic Cat snowmobile pulled forward as if to disguise that it had been recently ridden. Arctic Cat was a popular brand. The fact that the kidnapper rode the same brand last night could be nothing more than coincidence. Tim thought.

"Well, well. Lookie here, an Arctic Cat," Scott said, grinning.

Tim knew he needed more. "We have to connect this particular Arctic Cat to the kidnapping." The sheriff, deputies, and Elias Cain joined in inspecting the snowmobile.

Before joining the others, Tim cautiously observed the house again. Still dark and silent. He hoped it stayed that way. It didn't necessarily mean it was empty. The occupant could be watching them right now; he felt a chill race down the muscles in his back. For some reason, in this unspoiled, snow-covered landscape, a shadow hovered, menacing and evil.

At first glance, the snowmobile looked clean. On closer inspection, Tim noticed snow was packed into the undercarriage and was still frozen. The puddle that formed under the engine was now solid ice. The garage wasn't heated. The temperature had been below freezing for days, and this didn't mean much unless they could find something else to connect it to the kidnapping. Tim breathed out a sigh of disappointment. Maybe there were fingerprints. A CSI team could determine that, but so far, they didn't have a reason to call in CSI. Yet. He ambled around the snowmobile, carefully inspecting it one more time. He was ready to leave the bay when something caught his eye. In the uppermost part of the snowmobile's running board, up under the hood that sheltered the rider's legs from the icy wind, a small wad of what looked like crumpled paper was smashed against the side of the snowmobile. Tim moved in for a closer look.

"What's this?" he asked, leaning forward and moving the wad with a small stick he'd found on the floor.

"What?" The sheriff came over to look and started to reach for the paper. Tim blocked his hand.

"Don't touch. Call in your CSI team," Tim exclaimed. "It's duct tape. It's rainbow-colored duct tape, and if anyone's in that house, arrest them. We have our probable cause."

TWENTY-SIX

"Everything is evidence. Everything," the sheriff instructed his men. They were all inside the bay now, carefully observing the house.

"The snowmobile engine noise alone has alerted anyone in the house that we are here," Tim said.

Scott, the sheriff, and the deputies had already put together an entry plan and unholstered their pistols and chambered rounds. Tim dismissed the worries he had about a search warrant. He could easily persuade a judge that any reasonable police officer would believe their suspect might be in the house based on the duct tape. They had an excuse to enter the house without a warrant.

The house was still dark. If the perp was inside, he would keep it that way. Light would give his presence away, and with six men wearing vests with POLICE emblazoned on their backs, walking around, hiding would be the kidnapper's priority. If he was here, he kept an eye on them. The question was, Was he armed?

Scott snuck up beside him. "Damn, wish I had my Kevlar," he whispered.

Tim dipped his head once in agreement. He rubbed his gloved hand across his brow, deep in thought. He was an amateur when it came to arrest tactics. His wars were fought in three-piece suits in the courtroom. Kevlar wasn't part of his wardrobe. "I haven't seen any movement in the house," he said quietly.

"Me either," Scott added. "If he's in there, it's time to find out." He lifted both eyebrows and smiled in anticipation.

Tim took hold of Scott's arm. "Be careful."

"You know me," Scott answered.

"I do. That's why I'll repeat it. Be careful."

Tim knew Scott loved this. He thrived on the adrenaline, ate and drank the excitement. Tim could easily get caught up in the thrill of it; he had been swept up before. But his inexperience made him worry he'd be a liability in the end.

"Stay here," Scott commanded. Scott and Deputy Bob would take the back; the sheriff and Jeff would take front entry. It was his jurisdiction, after all. Though they'd called for backup, apparently they weren't going to wait. Scott took two deep breaths and spun into the driveway, dropping low as he dashed around to the back of the house. The deputy followed.

Elias crept up beside Tim and watched with him as the police officers did what they did best.

"Jesus, it's cold," Elias complained, stomping his feet on the concrete floor. It was a reasonable observation, but Tim hadn't noticed. He breathed out the tension building in his chest as Scott disappeared around the back of the house. Tim ducked back against the wall as he heard the sheriff knock on the door. This was the moment of truth. Tim sucked in a breath, whispered a prayer for their safety, and waited. He smiled at Elias, standing beside him against the wall in the bay.

Nothing. No sound.

The sheriff knocked again. "Police, open up."

Silence.

Tim heard the *cla-clink* as Elias armed his .40-caliber semi-automatic Sig Sauer. Tim chambered a hollow point in his weapon.

Elias flicked his head in the direction of the house. Tim once again peered around the corner, observing the front of the house. The sheriff slowly turned the front doorknob. The door soundlessly opened an inch. The unlocked door was a bad sign. Tim glanced at Elias and swallowed. He slipped out of the bay, dropped low, so his profile was lower than the deck railing, and made his way quickly to the bottom of the porch steps. The sheriff kicked the door open, and Tim heard it slam against the stop.

"We wait here," Elias commanded, coming up behind him and grabbing hold of the back of his jacket. "We go in once the house is cleared."

"That's pretty chickenshit." Tim glared at Elias.

"Profiling is a special skill, son. Not everyone can do it," he explained just above a whisper. "We need to stay alive."

He understood. But instead of waiting, Tim crept up the three stairs to the porch. He listened and looked into the house through the open door. The room oozed with shadowy purple darkness. In the living room's corner, next to the fireplace, stood a nearly life-sized statue. Tim froze for a moment. The bronze reminded him of some pictures he'd seen in one of his history classes in college. It conjured thoughts of Moloch, the bullheaded, ancient Canaanite god. Not exactly the decor he'd want in his home, but maybe the Bransons collected Middle Eastern artifacts. He stepped inside. The rest of the room was decorated in western-themed furniture. He chuckled to himself. Perhaps the statue wasn't Moloch at all but just a bull rearing on its hind legs. He dismissed it.

"Clear. All clear."

Tim was interrupted by Scott's voice, and with it, he relaxed. He returned outside and leaned against the porch rail. He emptied his pistol's firing chamber and shoved it back into his jacket pocket but left the zipper open in case the gun was needed later. He scanned out over the snow, letting his mind calm. An icy breeze murmured through the pine needles, tickled up some loose powder, and redeposited glittering crystals in a new place.

In the quiet, Tim thought of Chloe and her unicorn. He thought of her sparkling eyes and innocence. What had the kidnapper planned to do with her—or worse, to her? He felt an icy finger run down his spine and shuddered. But most of all, he thought of Dani. So much love flowed from her heart. She was all aglow at the hospital when near the little girl. Dani had given up on the dream of children, moved on with her life, but Chloe—Chloe had brought hints of that dream back. Even if she didn't realize it yet, he'd seen it in Dani's eyes. But was he ready? He'd seen himself in many roles—district attorney, corporate lawyer, even FBI special agent—but he'd never thought of himself in the persona of father before.

Elias tapped his shoulder and nodded in the direction of the barn. Tim forced himself back on task. Thinking about what their next steps in the investigation should be, he went back to the barn. When he reached the garage bay, Tim pressed the code into the opener. He heard the door begin to hum. Without any warning, he felt a full body slam into his back. He tumbled forward face-first into the snow. Sprawled out from the experienced tackle, he fought against the weight on top of his back.

"Damn it, Tim!" Scott cried out. "Don't fight me!"

"What the hell?"

Scott held him down for a few more seconds. "Damn it. You could've been killed. You enter the code and then move away from the door! You don't stand right in front of it!" Scott rolled off and sat in the snow, shaking his head and laughing. "If the perp had been in there and armed, you'd be history."

Tim sat up, brushing the snow from his face and the front of his jacket. He'd allowed himself to become distracted. Shit!

"Definitely sending you to Quantico." Elias chuckled as he reached for Tim's hand and helped him to his feet. The sheriff and deputies turned away and covered up their laughter too.

"Lawyers." Jeff grinned at Tim.

He shrugged. "That's my excuse, and I'm sticking to it." Tim laughed. He spun and investigated the empty bay. Tim realized that the one thing he'd left off his mental list of to-do's for the prosecution was staying alive.

TWENTY-SEVEN

The last two bays were empty. The van they'd hoped to find was not here. The perp was gone. Tim walked forward. In the center of the bay, speckles of paint spray outlined a rectangular shape in blue. In the corner, next to a half steel barrel used as a trash can, several spray paint cans were tossed haphazardly, as if the container had been used as a basketball hoop by a man who didn't play. The sharp chemical smell of oil-based paint still filled the air. He picked up one of the cans. He could hear the mixing ball rattle in the bottom but knew by the weight it was empty. As he started to set it down, he saw the dark blue paint smeared across the palm of his right glove. He leaned down, studying the contents of the barrel. Inside were more empty spray cans and a set of tan leather gloves you could buy at any hardware store for around six bucks. The tan gloves were used as an outer layer. Inside each was a plastic surgical glove. Tim was encouraged. He'd tried a case recently where the forensic team had recovered both fingerprints and DNA inside surgical gloves. He smiled to himself. Jeff walked over and dropped another evidence tag beside the barrel.

Tim lifted his palm, showing Jeff the blue paint smeared across his glove. He ran his tongue over his teeth and let his thoughts roll. Questions immediately came to mind. Was the van recently here and spray-painted, the Mercedes van they were searching for? Did the perp know they were looking for the light-colored van that followed seconds behind the BMW from the hospital in Seattle? Did he have a police scanner? Did he know about the BOLO? Is that why he disguised the color? Or was the perp tipped off by a crooked cop? Tim looked around the bay at the men with him. He knew for a fact that it wasn't Scott or Elias, but the others?

Newspaper edged with masking tape was crinkled in a messy pile in the front left corner of the bay. It was soiled with a fine blue mist. The perp had used it to cover the windows. Tim turned back and walked along the rectangle outlined by pixels of paint. It was the size of a van. Deputy Jeff scraped a boot and smeared some of the droplets together. His gaze snapped up to meet Tim's.

"This hasn't dried." Jeff dropped an evidence triangle near the spray and started shooting pictures. Tim knew the freezing temperatures would affect the drying time of the oil-based paint. CSI could tell them what to expect. Like the rainbow duct tape, a van with wet blue paint would be irrefutable evidence. The perp was panicking. He was making mistakes.

The sheriff radioed the new color information to the department. They were now looking for a dark blue van. He sent out an updated BOLO and asked that it be forwarded on to other police departments. He decided to set up a roadblock on Highway 95 both north to Canada and south to Coeur d' Alene and on Highway 90 east to Montana and west to Spokane. If the unsub was still in Idaho, they were going to catch him.

Tim followed the tire prints out into the snow. Jeff walked with him. "He backed out here, spun the tires on ice when making his turn, and took off in a big hurry up the driveway."

"Are you thinking what I am?" Jeff asked.

"Depends, but if you're thinking he heard us coming down the trail and got the hell outta here, then maybe." Tim breathed in. "We may have missed him by minutes, maybe seconds. Or on the other hand, by a day." Then he saw it, an elongated drop of paint, its tail showing the direction of travel in the snow. "Over here." He motioned to Jeff. "Let's see if we can find more of these." Tim pointed to the blue frozen to the snow. "And we should stop CSI from coming down this driveway until they can process all of this."

"Want to see if we can find more blue paint drops on the main road?" Jeff asked.

"We have snowmobiles. Can't ride in regular traffic. Isn't backup on its way? We can send a patrol car on that mission."

The two men walked along the imprint of tire tread on the driveway, marking each blue spatter of paint as they went. The driveway was around a half a mile long, and when they reached the road, they met the CSI van just as it started its turn.

TWENTY-EIGHT

They started their ride back to the Selkirk Lodge at three o'clock in the afternoon. The winter sun dipped low on the horizon and painted the underbelly of the clouds brilliant flame. The reflection from the sky, in turn, washed the snow in soft coppery pinks. The sky was breathtaking.

Tim felt some of the stress of gathering evidence wane. Putting the puzzle pieces together on paper for court was the easy part compared to finding them in the three dimensions of the physical world. But even after all they'd uncovered today, they still didn't have the identity of their elusive kidnapper. Who was he? Why was he doing it? Was he getting ready to do it again? Would he come back for Chloe? His stomach twisted at the thought.

Suddenly, frustration gripped him, and Tim grabbed hold of the throttle of his snowmobile. The sled responded instantly. He felt the jerk upward of rapid acceleration and power in his hand. What a rush! It was like a wheelie on a motorcycle, only on snow. He raced ahead, leaving the others behind on the trail. The groomed snow underneath his snowmobile's track whipped up into a contrail behind him. He wanted more, wanted to go faster. The RMK delivered. He couldn't resist and jumped his sled up over the lip on the side of the road created by the groomer. He danced his machine in the clear, untracked powder, by standing on the rails and shifting his weight from one side to the other. He felt like he was floating, as if no longer earthbound but riding in the clouds. As he blasted through deeper drifts, snow sprayed and splashed over the windshield and into his face, taking his breath away. He executed a series of sweeping turns, and as the sled rolled into each, snow washed over him in a flood of white like a breaking wave. It was exhilarating.

At the end of the clearing, he reentered the road and throttled up. He nosed the skis up a sidehill, shifting his body to the uphill side of the sled. When he crested, he rebalanced and let the engine weight pull him downward in an arch toward the trail. The excitement of speed, maneuverability, and centrifugal force pumped adrenaline through his blood with every heartbeat. When he hit the edge of the road, the lip left by the groomer launched the sled upward. Airborne for a second, he gasped for breath. When the snowmobile settled back down onto the road, he clutched the throttle and headed full on for the next sidehill. He heard the roar of an accelerating engine next to him. Scott joined the game and signaled he'd follow. For the next few miles, they played, each sidehill giving a new thrill like riding a roller coaster. He could feel the icy wind on his cheeks, and the white landscape blurred as he rushed by. Finally, they had to slow down at the trailhead and the lodge parking lot. Tim thought the speed would help settle down his feelings of frustration, and for a moment, it did. But now the worry was back. How was he going to stop the kidnapper from striking again?

Scott dismounted and walked over to Tim, laughing as he removed his helmet. "That was crazy!"

In the far distance, they could hear the engines of deputies, Elias Cain, and the sheriff racing to catch up.

In the middle of one of Scott's stories of how he'd almost crashed, he became very serious. "What do you think is going on here?" he asked.

"Me? I think our perp heard us coming down the trail from the Forest Service road. He glassed us and saw the police vests and hit the streets running. He didn't even take time to clean up or cover up his tracks," Tim said.

"One theory. Mine is he was tipped off," Scott said.

Tim whipped his gaze to Scott's face. Scott thought it too. "Makes me sick to think of that kind of corruption is here. It's possible, but who?"

"I haven't gotten that far. But the thought has crossed my mind. Doesn't matter. The roadblocks will net the perp anyway." Scott scrubbed a hand through his matted hair. "And then we will know for sure. These kiddy things can be nasty. Like an octopus, tentacles reaching everywhere."

Tim waited for more. Scott didn't offer anything. They just stared at each other. Tim wasn't so sure about the roadblocks or that he had even left the area. He could have found another place to hide.

"So, Annie called while we were at the Branson house. Guess who Beamer man in Seattle is—I guess that's *was* now. Dr. Rudy Van Hatten. It's now confirmed he was shot through the left temple at close range with a forty-caliber. What a fricking mess," Scott said, his eyes seeming to darken. "And CSI found a used condom under the seat, marinated in Nonoxyl 9 and full of Van Hatten's DNA. During the autopsy, Kathy found what looks like drug tracks on the inside of Van Hatten's left arm. I sent Anna out to his house and office to find what drug he was shooting up."

Van Hatten had been a rich political player, always donating to one cause or another with plenty of notoriety and aplomb. Tim knew what the man was. Just out of college, his shiny new law license hanging on the wall of his office, and still on employment probation, Tim had worked up a file for Goddard. He'd recommended that Van Hatten be brought up on charges: four counts of sexual abuse of a minor. After much wrangling, Goddard ended up negotiating a deal. A judge, no jury, would hear his case. Tim remembered how angry he was when he realized Van Hatten's crimes would never see the light of day.

Tim had been so mad about the outcome he stormed into Goddard's office, only to get Goddard's lecture: *Grow the hell up. This is a tough business. We get most of the bad guys; some get to walk. Get over it.* That night, Tim had hiked the Seattle waterfront until sunrise. He'd gone so far along the coast he had to call an Uber to take him home. Where was Beebe Knoll when Van Hatten needed to be exposed? It would've been unethical; he would've been fired and disbarred had he leaked to the press, but seeing Van Hatten's crimes out in the open, in big, bold headlines, would've been sweet.

"You helped when he was arrested a few years ago, didn't you?" Scott asked.

"Worked up the file for court." Tim felt his abdominal muscles tighten, and his jaw harden at the thought. "I always suspected I'd get that scumbag one day. Guess someone with a forty-caliber had the same idea."

"So, was doctor PhD or MD?" Scott asked.

"MD," Tim answered.

"So much for 'do no harm.'"

"This is on Judge Morganstein and Goddard for taking that crappy deal. I knew by looking at the weasel he'd repeat offend. I was afraid the sick bastard would escalate to murder. But Morganstein agreed with the defense and decided it was a misunderstanding. Yeah, I guess Van Hatten misunderstood that eight-year-old Julio Garza didn't want his dick in his mouth. If the maid hadn't walked in when she did, who knows what would've happened." Tim shook his head and swept a gloved hand across his forehead, brushing away a blob of snow that had dropped from a tree branch. "Wish I'd been wrong. Wish they'd listened to me. Those twin boys would be alive today. At least he'll never have the chance to touch a child again."

Scott just nodded. His lips were tight with disgust.

"I almost quit. I was on probation. I was so pissed. What's the point of being DA if you can't bring the bad guys to justice?" Tim asked.

"Now Goddard is whining like a baby because you might not stay." Scott laughed. "What are you going to do, by the way? Have you decided?"

"No. Not really. Still thinking about it. But for now, I'm on loan to the FBI. I'm working with Elias for a while."

Scott gulped down his surprise.

"Don't look at me like that. I agreed to do it. I guess the county commissioners haven't decided whether or not I'm their kind of guy." Tim laughed.

"You were cleared," Scott said sternly.

"Yeah, but the commissioners thought it would have been better for me to let Warden succeed the night he broke in and tried to kill Dani and me. We supposedly had a duty to flee. I want to work with Cain," Tim said with a healthy measure of sarcasm. He exhaled a big breath.

"Why am I not convinced? So, that's what Cain meant about sending you to Quantico? What are Kathy and I going to do? Kathy's going to freak. What does Dani have to say?" Scott continued the barrage until Tim lifted his palm to stop him.

"Dani and I are discussing it tonight."

Elias, the sheriff, and the two deputies rode up beside them. Stillness returned when they turned off their engines, except for the breeze whipping through the pines and dropping more snow bombs on them from the branches. Tim knew he was going to get his rear end handed to him for racing ahead full speed and leaving the rest of the crew. He removed the police vest the sheriff had made him wear and handed it over.

"McAndrews," Elias started, "what the hell were you doing, taking off like that?" Elias looked from Scott's face to Tim's. His scowl was clearly expressing his displeasure.

Tim gave back a big smile. "Playing. I'm on vacation."

TWENTY-NINE

All afternoon, Beebe looked for Tim. She'd gone to the ski lodge and had even risked her life by taking the damned scary gondola to the Mid Mountain Bar. It was no easy feat to hobble along in the snow with her crutches. Just after she'd given up on finding him and struggled to take the stupid gondola back down the mountain, she was unlocking the door of her rental car in the main lodge parking lot. That was when she saw Tim. He, Scott, the FBI guy Elias Cain, the sheriff, and two deputies rode up to the Selkirk Lodge parking lot on snowmobiles. She ducked behind her car so they wouldn't see her and suspect she spied on them—which, of course, was exactly what she was doing.

As she waited for them to pass by, thoroughly annoyed, her feet and fingertips aching with the cold, she wondered, *What on earth made these men think they could go snowmobile riding in the middle of a kidnap investigation? Didn't it occur to them they needed to catch the bad guy?* Well, if they weren't going to look for the guy, she'd have to expose their incompetence.

She trailed a distance behind them, watching as they entered the small bar off the meeting room they'd used last night as a base. They took a table in the darkest corner and ordered drinks. Now, they were drinking beer. She pulled her hood up and walked to the end of the bar closest to their table. She made sure she could see most of their faces in the mirror behind the liquor shelves that ran the whole length of the bar. It was very dark in here. Small lamps on the tables gave off very little light. She slipped onto one of the barstools, hoping to eavesdrop. But all she heard were hushed baritone whispers and laughter. Lots of laughter. Didn't they care about that little girl? What if the kidnapper tried again?

She wanted to march up to their table and remind them they should look for the bad guy. But now she was stuck. Her need for a good story conflicted with her desire to be with, at least near, Tim. Even now as she studied him in the mirror, she felt her heart beat faster. They would be so perfect together. She was obsessed. And she didn't know how to change it. She should've made her presence known long before now. But Tim would think she was following him. She had to gulp down her margarita and sneak out of here.

The men finished their beers, paid, and stood to go. She tugged her hood tighter around her face. They didn't notice her and walked out of the bar. She tossed down a ten-dollar bill on the counter and shadowed them. Nothing interesting happened. The cops loaded their snowmobiles into the enclosed trailer emblazoned with Bonner County Sheriff on the side. Tim was on a phone call, probably with the little wifey, and when he disengaged, he and Scott rode their snowmobiles off toward the house. Gradually, as she climbed into her car, it occurred to her that she couldn't follow. She had a car and would have to drive halfway down the mountain to get to the turnoff to Snow Country Lane. From the intersection, she had almost a fifteen-minute drive back up on that winding, ice-covered road. If she survived, she'd arrive at the chalet in about twenty minutes.

When she reached the house, she was scared half to death and furious. She hated driving on snow. Twice she almost slid into the curb, and when she slowed down, she slipped backward as her tires lost traction. Her heart was racing in her chest. She was glad she had on her ski jacket because her pits were drenched in a nervous sweat and would freeze to her sides when she stepped out of the car.

Tim was in the front driveway putting covers on all the snowmobiles. He looked so handsome. Fascinated, she watched as he rocked out to some music playing in his earbuds from his phone. What kind of music did Tim like? Beebe realized she didn't even know.

Scott, Kathy, and Mitch tossed overnight bags in the jeep and left. So, she waited out of sight for a few minutes before pulling up and parking in front of the house.

She hung back until Tim walked into the house. She snuck in after him. So distracted by his music, he didn't seem to notice her. Once inside, she saw him place a small blue thumb drive in the desk in the office off the entryway. He locked the drawer and slipped the key into a red and gold oriental jar and closed the lid. *What a stupid place to hide a key*, she thought.

She scrambled to get to the sofa in the living room before he could see her spying on him. She made sure she was still in a place where she could watch everything he did. When he walked into the living room, he hummed to the music playing through the earbuds. He looked so gorgeous, so endearing, so sexy, while unaware of her presence. She pretended to read the evening paper, even though she could barely catch her breath.

She was never going to forget Tim's expression when he saw her, though. It wasn't exactly what she'd hoped for. He stopped cold and she saw the muscles in his jaw twitch tight. He didn't say a word, just stared and slowly pulled the earbuds out of his ears.

"The hotels are all booked. Sorry. It looks like I'm here one more night. Dani said you wouldn't mind," she explained. That wasn't exactly true. The hotels up here on the mountain were booked. She could stay in Sandpoint. But Tim was crazy if he thought for a second that she was going to stay somewhere far away from the action.

He didn't respond. He didn't even offer an afternoon greeting to be polite. He just walked away down the hallway.

THIRTY

Tim found Dani reading in the private living room that was connected to their bedroom suite by an almost-hidden staircase. The drapes were open, and the snowfall outside past the covered deck was heavy, almost like a solid blanket, making the light from the lamps and fireplace inviting and warm. He sat on the log-framed sofa next to her but remained on the edge.

"Beebe is still here." He took in a deep breath and exhaled it. He was perturbed. All the way home from the mountain, he'd daydreamed about being alone with Dani. Once again, Beebe trashed his plans.

"Please don't be mad at me. She said the hotels are all booked. I couldn't just throw her out in the snow." She snuggled up against him.

"Why not? She's just going to write trash about us."

Dani laughed. "Meanie!" she teased. "To make up for it, I've asked Winona to serve our dinner in here. We will be

166

dining alone, just the two of us." She took hold of his hand and was toying with his fingers. She brought them to her soft lips, and she was instantly forgiven.

"Tim, Chloe's parents never came to see her." Dani's face filled with concern. "I tried their phone number, and it just goes to voice mail."

Tim sank into the sofa cushions. He nodded.

"I called Brad after we talked at the hospital. He let me know late this afternoon that he'd pulled some strings and got the court to grant us temporary custody of Chloe until a new foster family can be arranged. We can bring her home as soon as the doctor releases her. The hospital has a court order that she isn't to be released to anyone but you, in case the missing parents show up," he said.

"Do you think something has happened to Chloe's parents?" She sat forward, turned sideways, and looked into his face. "Why haven't they come to see her?"

Tim wiped his fingers along the outside of his lips. He had his suspicions. "The cops went to their house for a well-check. It was empty. Cleaned out. There wasn't even a used gum wrapper on the floor. We suspect they have abandoned her." Tim let out the breath he didn't realize he'd held. Dani stared at him in shock. The parents had dumped Chloe, or they'd met with foul play. He scrubbed his hand through his short hair and didn't share that fear. Tim reached for her and pulled her close. "It's all okay, baby." He said it; he wasn't sure he believed it. She settled back down into the crook of his arm. He smoothed her hair. "The police are searching for the parents now. They've put out a bulletin about them and their car."

All the worry on Dani's face softened. "You did it. You made it happen. Chloe is staying with us." She picked up his hand and whispered against his fingertips. There was an emotion bordering on worship in her eyes. It both aroused and terrified him. He was lucky this time, but somehow, he had to lower the bar; he didn't ever want to fail her. Not ever. And there was something deeply disturbing and surreptitious about this case. He was on edge. Foster parents sometimes had a financial motive rather than an altruistic one when it came to taking on helpless children. What would stop an uncaring couple from selling the unfortunates for the right price?

THIRTY-ONE

Tim and Dani had their dinner off somewhere alone and left Beebe with Shannon, the pilot's wife, as company. They had their meal in silence, on the kitchen island. It was apparent that Shannon didn't care for her. The feeling was mutual. She didn't initiate any conversation either.

Beebe laughed to herself, remembering the almost love scene she'd witnessed last night. She let her mind wander into daydreams. What she really wished was that *she* was the one Tim was undressing. That *she* was the one he was going to make love to. *Damn you, Jackass! You have to love me,* her thoughts whispered. She needed to figure out how to make it happen.

Still scheming, after dinner, she wandered through the chalet. The rooms were all decorated perfectly, rustic log furniture, paintings of the mountains, wildlife, and horses. She'd looked into log furniture once back in Seattle. It was expensive. Not something she'd buy on a whim. But for this place, it was perfect.

When she became a national news anchor, she'd have a place

like this. She suspected she'd be promoted to Branson Holt's job after she finished this kidnapping story. He'd never done anything like it and couldn't possibly compete. McAndrews would fall for her then. She imagined him overwhelmed with respect and admiration, sinking to his knees, professing undying love for her and kissing her hand as if she were a princess. She laughed at her fantasy. It was silly.

She continued her exploration. So far, each room on the downstairs level was for a family's normal living: Tim's office at the foyer, the living room, and the dining room where the fabulous breakfast buffet was served this morning. Down the hallway, an in-home theater was to her left. She walked in and sat in one of the cushy leather recliners for a moment to get the full experience. What else was down this hallway? Upstairs there were eight bedroom suites, each with its own luxurious bathroom. The master had a downstairs and separate living room that could be accessed down this hall. She'd perused the rooms this morning after they'd all given their statements to the sheriff and the house was empty.

She heard music muffled by a closed door a little way down at the end of the hall. Listening for a moment, she decided to investigate, even against her better judgment. The music came from the master suites living area. Carefully, she turned the doorknob. She pressed the door open a crack. Tim and Dani were in the center of a beautifully decorated parlor, dancing to a dreamy Richard Marx love song. A rock fireplace along the west wall bathed the room in warm flickering light, and a bank of sliding glass doors revealed a deck with views to the south. It was snowing now, but Beebe bet on a clear night she'd be able to see the black outline of Lake Pend Oreille and maybe the lights of Sandpoint below.

In front of an upholstered sofa and matching love seat, on an ornate, claw-footed coffee table, a silver ice bucket chilled an open bottle of Schaumburg's Blanc de Blanc champagne. Two half-filled champagne glasses were on the table next to it.

Music. Fireplace. Champagne. How romantic. She shook her head in surprise and giggled silently to herself. McAndrews, a romantic? She'd never really thought of him that way. Passionate, lusty, raw, the kind of man who picked his wife up and took her roughly on the kitchen island, sure, but this? She could barely hold back her sigh.

He held Dani tenderly, swaying with her, moving with her as if the melody from the Echo was washing over them. They occasionally parted from their embrace to whisper and laugh at the sweet secrets they shared; that she couldn't hear. Beebe pretended Tim whispered to her. Was he telling Dani that he loved her? Jealousy sprung to life and started to simmer. If she could get Tim alone, if she could show him how good it could be, he would leave Dani. She knew it. She almost gave in to the impulse to walk in and put a stop to their dancing. But she decided she needed to make a plan. Be subtle. Tim had to come to her. He had to think it was his idea to leave Dani or he never would.

The music changed to a Motown oldy she recognized. One of the Jackson's—Germaine, she thought. His mellow voice crooned, "Do what you do when you did what you did to me ..."

What was this? McAndrews a fricking Fred Astaire? He twirled Dani, and they moved rhythmically to the beat for a few seconds, and then he engaged her back into his arms. There was so much she didn't know about him. So much to learn. In her imagination, she drifted on the notes as if she were dancing with him instead of Dani.

They stopped, but the music still played. They gazed wistfully into each other's eyes. Beebe realized she had never in her life had a man look at her the way Tim was looking at Dani. His breath quickened, and they kissed. Beebe could almost taste it.

Silky, tender but sending pulses of aching desire through every cell. Tim picked Dani up and braced her against the wall, kissing, kissing. Dani surrendered to him and fueled the exploding passion. Tim held Dani against his body in a way that made Beebe audibly moan. Shit! Were they going to do it right here, right now? Beebe panicked. She couldn't be caught watching them in the act. Not again!

She scrambled, looking around her for a way to silently escape. But she paused before limping away. She looked at Tim and Dani one more time. She had to make sure they hadn't seen her. She discovered they were so immersed in each other she'd gone unnoticed. Cringing, she quietly pulled the door closed, barely wanting to let go of the knob in case it made noise. Then she hobbled on her tiptoes and crutches as quickly as she could down the hall to the living room. She fell into the sofa cushions, picked up one of the throw pillows, and screamed into it to muffle the sound.

How was she going to turn this around? At the sheriff's station, Tim had said, with his straight-arrow voice, "You've got me all wrong." Beebe rolled her eyes. Under the right circumstances, every man was a cheater. Besides, she was a reporter. If there was one characteristic that made a reporter good, it was persistence. She was going to find McAndrews's weak little underbelly. He was going to cheat. He was going to fall in love with her. He was going to leave Dani. She was going to see to it. Feeling refreshed with new purpose, she practically skipped up the stairs to her bedroom. Well, she would've skipped if she wasn't on these darn crutches anyway. Sitting on her bed, she started to formulate a plan to get Tim alone. She had to get him alone. Her mistake this morning was the crowd.

Wait. That thumb drive Tim had brought home. Was there anything on it that would help her bring about the right circumstances?

THIRTY-TWO

He was forced to kill them. That was all there was to it. Forced. In his mind, Sam Graden justified the act he would soon commit. He sat behind the wheel of the van watching the couple gas up the U-Haul truck. She was the only one who could identify him. Stupid woman. Why had she changed her mind? She was supposed to pretend like it was a real kidnapping, not fight him. The setup only worked if the fosters played their assigned roles. But she alerted that whole table full of off-duty snowmobiling cops with her overacting. He shook his head and rolled his eyes in disgust. Now, he wasn't going to get paid, and she and her husband were dead, though they didn't know it yet.

Last night, after he escaped from the cops, he drove to their rental house, parked two houses down, walked along the white picket fence, and hid behind the solid snow-covered spruce in the front yard. He snickered to himself as he watched them clean all their furniture and belongings out of the house as fast as they could. He was coming for them. They knew it.

He didn't kill them right away. Maybe he should've. He followed them for hours and postponed it for the right time and place. He studied the road map on his GPS as he waited for them to finish filling up. They decided to take every damned winding, snow-clogged, back road they could find. They were running, covering their tracks. He realized they were headed south through the Sawtooths. He knew this road as well as he knew Gina's body. He'd gone home to California this way countless times in his drug-running days. He tried his best to avoid it in winter, but this time, the bodies and buried U-Haul truck would be lost under feet of snow until spring.

They started their engine, and the truck pulled out onto the icy highway. There was no other traffic. A big, moisture-laden storm had arrived from the west, and only the very brave or the very stupid ventured out. The swirling mass on his iPhone's weather radar app showed him how bad this storm was going to be. A real bitch. He turned on his van's engine and followed. Five miles ahead, the narrow road plunged into a dangerous stretch, especially in these conditions. In three miles, the "chains required" warning sign would be flashing in big gold letters. Traction tires wouldn't do. A rare 10 percent downgrade along a steep canyon wall saw to that. One way or the other, they would have to stop in the brake-check area before the most treacherous part of the road. When they were off to the side, he would pull in behind them and offer to help them chain up. He'd kill them. One bullet each to the brain. Fast and simple. Then shove the truck down the near-vertical canyon wall to the rocks below. The snowstorm would do the rest. He glanced at his .40-caliber Glock 23 on the seat beside him and breathed out a sigh. Stupid woman.

THIRTY-THREE

This was one of Tim's favorite times of the day. He collapsed back against the stack of pillows at the headboard of their bed. A light sheen of sweat covered his body from the excitement of making love to Dani, and he closed his eyes, still awash in waves of pleasure as she snuggled up against his side. Outside their bedroom, the wind had grown fierce. Crystals of snow tinkled against the glass slider. In between the gusts, a veil of white, lacey snowflakes flowed across the windowpanes. Good thing they'd gathered their evidence before the storm broke this afternoon. Still, there was no word if their roadblocks had netted the kidnapper. But the kidnapper may have had as much as a full twelve-hour start on them. Tim struggled to think of that now as Dani softly nibbled at his shoulder.

"I love you, baby," he whispered against her hair. He combed his fingers through the strands.

"I love you too," she confirmed, wriggling closer still.

In a few minutes, the dreaminess of bliss would recede like an outgoing tide, and they would talk. He so enjoyed their talks. He loved holding her, warm against his skin and the scent of their lovemaking perfuming the air. When he married her, he'd never expected it to get better and better every day. His older brothers had told him many things about love and marriage, but they'd never told him about this part—this delicious, dreamy sweetness.

He loved the soft tone of her voice as they shared the events of their day. Dani was everything. She approached life with intelligence and humor. She grounded him. And rocketed him to the moon.

"Are you mad at me over Beebe staying on?" she asked.

"I'm never mad at you. Never." He kissed her hair. "I get it. I didn't expect you to turn her out in the cold," he said, chuckling.

"Would you? Turn her out?"

"I'd consider it. But no. Probably not. Still, I don't like or trust her. She's going to write another story about you. You know that, don't you? I hate seeing it. It isn't fair. And there are plenty of hotels around here and in Sandpoint," he said.

Tim sighed with pleasure as Dani caressed his abdominal muscles with her fingertips. She kissed the nipple of his left breast, and he shuddered with a wave of pleasure. "Dani, baby, I want you again," he whispered. "So, if you want to talk, you have to stop kissing me."

Dani repositioned her body and rested on an elbow, looking down into his blue eyes. She traced a finger over his smile. He closed his eyes and felt his whole body relax into the deep memory foam mattress. Any lingering stress from today disappeared like a wisp of steam. He let all the evidence they'd found today, all the complexities of the case, swirl away. The twelve abduction cases Elias had given him to review would have to remain locked in the drawer of his desk until morning. He was even going to let thoughts of Chloe's missing parents drift down to the recesses of his mind. This time was his. He wanted to cherish these precious hours with Dani.

"Thank you for letting Chloe stay with us." He opened his eyes, and Dani was aglow. "You are the best man in the whole world. I know it's a sacrifice. You said you didn't want kids." She snuggled back against his shoulder and started to kiss his throat.

"Did I?" He stroked her hair. He remembered telling her he was okay with the fact that she couldn't have children. In his mind, he hadn't dismissed the other options. But this longing for a family was new and confusing to him. He'd never thought he would want that. It started the minute he saw Dani comforting Chloe after the kidnapping. He knew it would be a lifelong responsibility and commitment. But he'd had a happy childhood and an engaged mom and dad. He had learned by example what it meant to be a good father. It was an obligation he wasn't afraid to take on. His brothers were happy. "Can I change my mind?"

"Of course." He could hear the melody of joy in her voice. "I'll arrange for Mark's sister to come in the morning. And Chloe can have the room next to ours. A door connects it in case she gets frightened at night." She tenderly kissed his chin, and her fingers, soft as a summer breeze, swept across his chest. He felt a surge of desire.

He drifted deeper into longing, his breath quickening with every touch. He had to tell Dani about agreeing to work with Elias and the FBI, but she kept kissing him, and he was drunk with her. He had to tell her. Had to.

"Remember, I told you I'm on loan to the FBI?" he asked her quietly, savoring her caress.

"Yes." There was a hesitant edge to her voice, and she withdrew her touch.

"That lacked enthusiasm," he said with a hint of sarcastic amusement. "You don't have to stop touching me."

"I'm sorry. It scares me a little. Will we need to go to Quantico?"

He turned on his side so he could look at her. "What do you want, Dani? What do you want for us?" If she demanded a direction, he wouldn't have to make a choice. But she was too wise. She would never do that and let him blame her for his unhappiness if what she chose was the wrong thing.

"I want you. I want us to be together no matter what life hands us. I want you to be happy. I have the resources to make anything work," she answered honestly. That was true enough. He'd never thought of it that way.

"We have Chloe to consider now too," he said.

She brushed her hair away from her face, moved so her lips were touching his. "Are you saying we should adopt her?"

"Whoa, slow down here. We only have temporary custody." Tim frowned. He certainly knew he could do temporary custody. He loved where he and Dani were right now. And his brothers had warned him that kids changed all that.

"And you think we can just send her back if it doesn't work out?" Dani laughed. "She's not a stray puppy. I called Brad, just in case."

"Wait. You called Brad without talking to me?" His biggest fear about marrying Dani was rearing its ugly head. Was he going to lose all of himself? "I haven't thought that far ahead," he lied. He had; he just hadn't had the time to follow through. It was a decision they needed to make together.

She chuckled at him and reached to pull him into her arms. "You know it would never be like a normal family, Tim. She'd have a full-time nanny and tutors, and then there are schools to consider. She could travel with me, of course, until she's old enough; I still have to run the family businesses. But if you take the FBI job full-time, you may be away a lot." She kissed away his frown.

He hadn't thought about Dani's money. He'd only imagined Dani at home as his mother had been. He thought of tree-lined streets, neighborhood kids playing together after school, Mom in the kitchen, baking cookies and waiting for Dad to come home for dinner after work. Middle-class dreams might collide badly with their ultrarich reality. Family had never meant nannies and tutors to him, and yet—it would mean someone would always be there to love Chloe, even when their careers needed them to be away.

"I can still take the position with Brad," he said and briefly wondered if he'd miss the excitement of criminal law or if he could settle for corporate law. "If we adopt Chloe, we will be giving her a chance at having a loving family. However that plays out, it will be better than what she has now." He couldn't believe he was arguing for adoption. "Wow, where did that come from? Did you put something in the champagne?" he teased, hugging her tightly.

"I love you," Dani whispered. Her expression told him he'd said the right thing. He said it. Now he had to decide if he believed it.

THIRTY-FOUR

Tim woke with a start. Was that a creak on the stairs? He listened. He waited to see if the sound repeated or if it was just a house noise, caused by the fierce wind blowing outside. Once again, the sound repeated—like a person taking careful steps. Ever since the night Gary Warden broke into his home, he'd locked their bedroom door. He felt it gave him a few seconds to get ready. If some asshole wanted to breach his private space in the middle of the night, the idiot wasn't coming out of the encounter unscathed. He peeled the covers back, and Dani stirred awake.

"What is it?" she asked sleepily.

"Someone's on the stairs." Tim quietly reached in the top drawer of the bedside table and set his hand on the fingerprint lock on his gun safe. When it opened, he took out his Walther, inserted the clip, and chambered a hollow-point round. The safety was still on, but that could easily be remedied by a swipe of his thumb when or if the time came. He carefully set the pistol on the table and pulled on the sweatpants he always left on the floor next to his side of the bed. He slipped the gun back into his palm.

"Get dressed, baby."

Dani hurried to her side of the bed and obeyed his command. "Tim, it might be Shannon or Beebe going to the kitchen for water." She dressed anyway.

"Why? They have bathrooms in their suites. They don't need to be skulking around the house," he whispered and swallowed down the anger that was sliding up his throat. He'd had enough of Beebe. The thought that she was still here after he'd demanded she leave infuriated him. If Beebe was sneaking around the house at night, he'd be madder yet.

He looked at Dani. She bit her bottom lip with worry.

"Take out your gun. Get ready. If I don't come back, get down behind your side of the bed and call the cops. Don't let anyone in unless it's me or the police. If it's neither, don't let him come through this doorway. If he opens the door, unload your clip. Don't hesitate for a second. It takes less than two to cross this room," he said, anxiety making his voice gravelly and his throat dry.

"And if it's Beebe?"

"She packs it up and is out. I don't care if she has to sleep in her damned car and it's minus twenty," he growled.

"Tim." It was all Dani had to say, and he softened, just looking at her.

He breathed out. "You win. But I'll still be pissed."

Tim had a sinking feeling it wasn't Beebe. He would be lucky if it was Beebe. He crept to the door and unlocked it. "Lock this door as soon as I'm out," he whispered. He stepped into the hallway and let his eyes adjust to the semidarkness. He conjured up a plan. If he turned on the lights, that would warn the intruder and give them time to prepare. He would leave the lights off until the last possible second. As he passed by the bedroom Shannon and Mitch used, he quietly twisted the doorknob. It was locked. So, the creeper wasn't Shannon. Tim sucked a breath in through his teeth. He checked Beebe's door the same way. Locked too. That answered that question. He grimaced to himself as a wave of anxiety crawled under his skin. He slid along the wall, finally making his way to the top stair landing. He studied the living room below him. He was grateful for the little nightlights placed here and there in electric sockets. Still, the oversized furniture cast strange shadows in the soft glow throughout the room. There was no movement.

Before proceeding, he leaned over the railing and checked that the green light indicating the alarm system was armed radiated from the keypad in the entryway. The doors to the outside had not been breached. He ran his left hand over the stubble on his chin. He was dealing with someone with the alarm code, someone who knew how to defeat his system, or an insider. The uneasy feeling he'd had earlier in the day and that Scott had shared, that the kidnapper was tipped off, sent a cold shudder across the top of his shoulders.

He quickly let his mind run through his impressions of the sheriff and his deputies. He had eliminated Scott and Elias long ago. A dirty cop would be a tough adversary. They'd be armed, wary, motivated, and, unfortunately, a good shot. If someone from the sheriff's office was involved in a child-trafficking scheme, they'd want to see what Elias had given Tim. Elias had passed the information, conspicuously, in full view of everyone who had gone to the kidnapper's lair. A corrupt cop would want to see what the FBI had and if it differed from the public record. Tim readied himself for the worst case. He was no hero; he should just let them have the file. But he wasn't going to let anyone hurt Dani.

He grabbed a breath, pushing fear and dread out of his

mind. But once again, the image of Gary Warden surfaced. Dani holding on and pressing her face against his back, Warden stabbing the bed until fluffs of pillow stuffing and mattress floated on the air. And then charging, knife held high. The realization that to survive, he had to shoot and kill another human being had made nausea gag up into his throat after he'd pulled the trigger. He had three women in this house he needed to protect. He steeled himself.

On tiptoes, Tim crept down the stairs and through the living room. He paused briefly and checked to see if light filtered from under the kitchen door—only blackness. No snackers were raiding the fridge. One theory down, one to go. He felt anxiety wring knots in his stomach. He quietly blew out a breath.

As he turned to go down the hall, the light in his office flicked on. He braced himself against the wall. A sliver of light outlined his office door. Whoever it was had to be looking for the FBI thumb drive or a file on his computer. Dread forced beads of sweat to form at his temples and on his upper lip. He wiped it away with the back of his hand and slipped closer. He slid his thumb down the side of the pistol, releasing the safety.

He found the door ajar about an inch. The lamp on his desk spilled light into the room. The computer was up, the welcome screen open, and the password box blinking. The blue flash drive was in the USB port on the side of the machine. The middle desk drawer was open as if the intruder was searching through papers for something. The password? *Good luck with that*, Tim thought. He couldn't see who was in the room though.

His jaw tightened; his teeth clenched tight. He sucked in a breath and counted: one, two, three. He kicked the door open. In the doorway, he took a shooter's stance, legs apart, shoulders square, both hands steadying the pistol, finger on the trigger.

Beebe stumbled backward, shoving the office chair rolling back against the wall with a slam. She grabbed the thumb drive as she started to sit in the chair. But the chair was gone. Tim lowered his pistol and watched in amazement. She fell hard and took a little bounce when her butt hit the floor. Her legs were straight out in front of her. Both of her crutches clattered to the hardwood, making enough noise to raise the dead. She looked up at him, holding the little blue drive to her chest.

"Damn it, Jackass! Don't shoot me!" she yelled.

THIRTY-FIVE

The deed was done. Graden had dispatched the couple by blowing their brains all over inside the front windshield. They hadn't even had a chance to scream. And the woman didn't recognize him until he'd already done the guy. Too late for excuses or apologies then.

He'd pushed their rental truck easily over the cliff. The icy ground in the brake-check area had helped with that. Once the truck started sliding, it couldn't stop, no matter what. His luck held; there wasn't a single other vehicle on the road. As he watched the truck plunge, he felt safe again. No stupid woman was sending him back to prison.

He'd driven back the five miles to the gas station, gassed up, and grabbed a big cup of coffee to keep him going. California and home were miles away to the south. He was tired, but he couldn't rest until he hit McCall. There was a little roadside motel with crisp, clean sheets and black-out curtains waiting for him. He would park around back, and his van couldn't be seen from the highway. He couldn't wait.

He gulped the coffee. It was stale and lukewarm but loaded with caffeine. As he set the paper cup into his middle console, his burner phone began to ring. He huffed out a breath. He recognized the number. He knew he had to explain what had happened. They couldn't possibly blame him for things beyond his control. He debated for a second. Then answered.

"Yeah?" he growled defensively.

The masked electronic voice started to speak. "Sam, our client still wants his cupcake."

"It was delivered to the cops by mistake," he reported sullenly. "Can't get it back now."

"It was delivered to Sandpoint Hospital. It's still there, completely intact. And our client wants that cupcake and only that one. He's agreed to pay double for it."

"Double?" He thought about it for a second. He was so close to his goal. He could visualize swaying palms, warm breezes, the sound of lagoon waves swishing softly against a white-sand shore. But he was a realist. The cops were on this one, and bars and cold cement blocks weren't the paradise he dreamed of. "Too hot, man. Way too hot."

"Triple," the mechanical, emotionless voice said.

Graden sat speechless for a moment. He could feel his breath quicken, his heart pounding. His dream waited just a few miles back up that snow-covered road.

"Triple," he agreed.

THIRTY-SIX

Tim spun into the hall and leaned against the wall outside his office. He burst out laughing. A small part was relief. He didn't have to face down a fully armed, crooked cop. That theory was put to rest. For tonight anyway. He tried to be sober, but the image of Beebe hit him again. Her feet were splayed out in front of her, her terry cloth robe open, revealing the flower print of a flannel granny nightgown underneath. The fuzzy slippers made her feet too large for the rest of her, and her head was covered in brightly colored rollers that brought to mind Medusa's snakes. He knew she was going to be bruised. He shouldn't laugh, but once again it hit him. He tried, but he couldn't stop. She deserved it for rifling through his things.

He had to force himself to be a grown-up. He needed to see if Beebe was hurt. He heard a noise at the top of stairway landing and turned. Dani was there, in contrast to Beebe, a vision in a beautiful, wispy blue nightgown and robe, the momentum of her run to the landing making the fabric swirl softly around her legs as she stopped. She held her pistol in her right hand, pointed to the floor. All the crashing and clatter had brought her out of the bedroom to help. Shannon was behind her, peeking over her shoulder.

"It's all good. All clear," he called to them, calming the chuckles. They headed back to bed. He cleared his pistol's firing chamber, flicked on the safety, turned back, and entered his office. He set the pistol on his desk.

"Damn it. Beebe, what the hell are you doing in here? Are you hurt?" He failed to hold back snickers that kept erupting out of control. She was sitting against the wall exactly as he'd left her.

"Yes, I'm hurt—and quit laughing at me."

"Sorry. I don't mean to laugh, but ..." He pressed his lips tight, trying to hold back. She reached for him as if expecting him to help her up. Instead, he took the thumb drive out of her hand. He scolded her with an icy stare and shook his head, but he knew there was mirth in his eyes.

Beebe sighed.

"Key, please," he said, holding his hand out toward her. Beebe reached into her left robe pocket and slapped the key she'd stolen from the red oriental jar into his palm. Mocking her, he dramatically showed her the key and the thumb drive, twisting it like a magician would for a disappearing act, and then slipped both into the wedge pocket in his sweatpants. Finally, he went to her and offered his hand to help her up. When he thought she had her footing, he let go and picked up her crutches. She hopped on her good leg, and he helped her steady herself. She slowly blinked, looking up into his face. An expression he couldn't interpret flashed briefly in her eyes. Her fingers barely touched his bicep, almost a caress. It was clearly sexual. He felt a quick surge of exasperation. He was a prosecutor. Beebe had to realize he'd been here before. Better women than she, professional women who knew all the games, had tried this gambit. She knew she was in deep doo-doo and was going to try to play him. He took hold of her wrist and firmly pressed the crutches into her hand. He glared at her and stepped back two steps.

"Okay, let's hear it. Care to explain?" Tim asked, tapping his fingers impatiently on the desk. This, of course, was no mystery. Breaking news was Beebe's priority.

"I was—I was—no." She looked down at the ground and then back up to his face, leaning her weight onto the crutches, acting helpless. "What are you going to do?"

Tim took in a deep breath, still fighting to keep the grin down. "This is bad. Really bad," he lied. Even if she'd been able to open it, everything on the small blue thumb drive was public record. She could've gotten all the information on her own computer if she'd taken the time to search and had known what to look for. Of course, Beebe thought stealing the info would be so much easier, and it would've been. It was all neatly organized case by case. But she hadn't even gotten beyond the password screen. Still, going into his office and opening the locked drawer was breaking and entering. He considered charging her. She'd be out of his hair. But it was two in the morning and minus eight degrees outside. Dragging the sheriff up here would be a waste of their time when he could handle this himself.

Then he wondered, would their abduction and murder investigation be hurt or helped by a little media exposure? He wasn't above using the press when he needed to. But the compilation of police reports belonged to Elias. What would he want to do? Tim wasn't going to wake the man at two in the morning for an answer.

"I didn't see anything. I didn't have time to read. I—I ..."
She stopped. "Is snooping a crime?"

"You broke into my private office, unlocked a drawer. Yeah,
breaking and entering is a crime."

"I am an invited guest here though," she argued, her voice
unsure.

"That makes it worse. Dani trusted you. You weren't invited to look through my private office, Beebe. You know and
I know you were going to steal any information you found for
a news story."

"I wasn't—okay, I was. But I couldn't get your computer
open. Does that count?"

Tim licked his lips and let a barely perceptible smile tick up.
"Huh, just means covert activity's not your strong suit. Don't
sign up to work at the CIA."

He watched a bolt of anger zip across her face. Her pause
told him she had thought better of saying something sassy.
"Are you going to toss me out tonight?" she asked, looking
defeated and desperate. She had no place to go.

"You know I want to. God, I want to."

She squinted her eyes at him. "But Dani won't let you?"

A small gasp stuck in his throat. He would never admit to
that. And she had just affronted his manhood. She questioned
whether he wore the big-boy pants in his family. Beebe couldn't
know he was struggling with that very thought after learning
Dani had called their attorney about adopting Chloe without
consulting him.

Tim remembered that this was part of the usual pattern.
When caught in the act, a female perp will first try sex, and
when that fails, go for the insults. Textbook. He was on to her.

"It's too late and too cold. Besides, we'll need to see if Elias
Cain wants to charge you in the morning with—snooping,"
he retorted.

"Are you arresting me?" Her voice rang with panic. She imagined herself in a jail cell, and he left her in that moment of torture. He enjoyed it.

"House arrest," he finally stated, running his tongue over his teeth to keep from snickering. It was a lie.

"Wait? *Wait?* Elias Cain? Those are FBI files? Do you have FBI files? Why do you have FBI files?" She tipped her body forward and looked owl-eyed into his face, almost stumbling over her crutches.

He didn't answer her. He couldn't let her know he was on loan to the FBI. She'd make a front-page story of that. "Time for you to go back to your room." He picked up his pistol and slipped it into his pocket.

She blinked at him. "Why do you have FBI files?" she asked again.

"Beebe. Bed." He took hold of her arm, pulled her forward, turned her body to face the door, and gently shoved her toward the opening. Her crutches hung up on the doorjamb, and she wrestled to free them. When she was loose, she resisted, walking as slowly as possible. He was confused and annoyed by their constant war. But he didn't know how to end it. He remembered Goddard telling him that every public figure, be it the president of the United States or a lowly assistant district attorney on loan to the FBI, had a media nemesis. President Trenton had Branson Holt; he had Beebe Knoll. He sighed and locked the door behind him, then deposited the key into his pocket.

Beebe kept turning back to him as he coaxed her through the living room and up the stairs. At the door of her room, she asked again, "Why do you have FBI files?"

"Good night, Beebe." He reached past her to open her door for her. It was locked.

She fumbled around in her robe's pocket and retrieved the key and unlocked the door. "Tim?"

"No, Beebe. Just no," he said. He drew her door closed after she went through and laughed as he heard her turn the deadbolt. She couldn't possibly think he'd break in. He walked away, shaking his head.

THIRTY-SEVEN

Earlier, Tim transferred the police reports Elias had given him to his laptop computer and studied them with his morning coffee in the dining room. He'd grabbed a yellow legal pad and made notes as he went through the files case by case.

He looked up as Winona, the St. Clair's chef, brought in a tray of cinnamon pecan sticky buns, hot from the oven.

"Good morning, Mr. McAndrews. How are you this morning, sir?"

"Winona, it's Tim. You don't have to be so formal with me." He grinned as he took the small plate and napkin from her hand before she could set it in front of him. She used a set of tongs to place a sweet roll on it.

She blushed. "Yes, sir, Mr. McAndrews."

That worked, he thought, laughing inside. "Thank you for making these this morning. They smell delicious." He didn't think she could turn any more red-faced, but she did. She didn't wait for him to taste the treat; instead, she scurried from the room. He took a bite. The buttery, sugary bun practically melted on his tongue. He licked the frosting off his fingers. Winona was a great cook.

He wiped his hands on the cloth napkin before scrolling through the reports on his computer screen. Taking another bite, this time with a fork, he leaned back in his chair. Dani was in the office planning for Mitch to pick up the trusted babysitter she'd hired. She also had a call into Dr. Nathan to see when Chloe was going to be released so that they could bring her home.

Tim couldn't believe how much joy it was giving Dani to take in this little girl. He still had his reservations. Now that Dani had talked with Hollingsrow, he finally allowed himself to think of the three of them as a family. He was pretty sure temporary custody was going to morph into adoption. Dani seemed to be all prepared for it. He, on the other hand, wasn't. Later today, if he had time, he would call his brother Tony and talk to him about being a dad. Any pointers would be welcome since he was going to be thrust into the role without the benefit of a pregnancy giving him time to get used to the idea. He blew out a breath.

Dani had become a whirlwind. She pulled every string her money could buy. For once, he didn't mind. Deliveries of furniture, clothes, and toys were already on the way. By the time they picked up Chloe, her new room would be complete, and her new life was just waiting for her to begin.

First thing, though, he had one grim task to perform. He'd made a reservation for Beebe at the Selkirk Lodge. He'd even paid for the rest of the week, just to be rid of her. He wanted her out before Chloe arrived. He wasn't going to tolerate any news stories about Chloe. Not. One. Word. This wasn't some stunt; it was his life. He had to keep Beebe out of it.

He also had to meet with Elias this afternoon to go over the profile they were developing of the kidnapper. Thankfully, Elias had agreed to come to the house. Tim wanted to be here for Dani and Chloe on her first day.

Still, it worried him. The sheriff and his deputies were not invited. Elias had assured him they developed the profile first and presented the finished product to the cops to aid in their search. It left him with the uneasy feeling that Elias shared Scott's and his opinion that a cop on the take might be in their midst.

Tim also wondered what Elias expected. He had zero experience with developing profiles. None. But he'd decided to work with Elias and was willing to learn the craft. Tim chuckled to himself. This could end up being a real cluster. He still had to tell Dani about his decision. Last night, he'd left her believing he might take Brad Hollingsrow's offer to join his firm. But after just a cursory look at Elias's cases, he knew he had to help save these kids first. He started to reread the case files.

He picked up his coffee and sipped. He sat back deep into his chair. He set his mug down and closed his eyes. What kind of person would do this? Each child was taken in broad daylight; one or both parents were close by; they were all foster children, vulnerable children; they were all under eight years old. The rainbow Duck Tape linked at least three cases together, and the MO tied them all together. Usually, a child predator operated within a small radius from his home. The FBI could often map out where the kids were taken, triangulate, and project the monster's operating base. Tim mapped the missing children from Elias's files and added the twins and Chloe to the mix. He sat back heavily in his chair. This guy was all over the place. He was working coast to coast but not in a line, allowing them to guess where he might strike next. As far as Tim could tell, he was abducting a child once every two weeks. But those were reported abductions. How many children among the thousands trafficked across the border illegally were also in the mix? How many from developing countries in crisis? They would be easy prey. No one would report them missing to US police. He opened his eyes and listed these observations in a column on his yellow legal pad. He was staring at his notes when it came to him. The victims weren't random. These weren't crimes of opportunity. The kids were chosen. Chloe was chosen. He felt sick. The pictures Kathy had handed him of the abused twins kept replaying on a loop even when he tried to shove it from his mind. They had been chosen. Chosen by whom and for what? Horrific abuse, like the twins?

He swallowed down his nausea. What did the kidnapper look like? He tried to focus, to force a picture of the perp to come forth as if by magic. Profiling was going to be hard. The only image he could muster was of a person all in black, helmeted, and hunkered down on a snowmobile. No age, sex, race, height, weight, or background surfaced.

His mind wandered. Why hadn't the roadblocks netted their kidnapper? *Simple*, he answered himself. He made it out before they set it up. He was long gone. Tim didn't like that theory, but it was the most plausible one. The bad guy had been tipped off and fled. He took another sip of coffee and started back through the reports.

He looked up as Beebe noisily hobbled in. She had her crutches, but he noticed she was wearing a blue walking cast now. Tim was reminded once again of her fall in his office last night and smiled at her. He had to admit she looked pretty this morning. At least compared to the previous night. Her blonde hair curled softly around her face, the result of wearing the Medusa curlers, he guessed. Her brown sweater brought out the vibrant chocolate color of her eyes. And the sweater's clean lines accented her figure. She was an attractive woman.

He wondered briefly why she was alone. She wasn't his type, but she might be someone's. And he wondered why she had rejected Miguel's attentions. He was a great guy. Fun. Good-looking. Gainfully employed. *None of my business,* he decided. He didn't care.

Beebe took a cup of coffee and left her crutches at the end of the buffet; she limped to a chair at his end of the table. She seemed to be practicing walking with her soft cast. She sat to his right side at the corner of the long table. She leaned forward as if trying to read his notes. Annoyed, he turned over his yellow legal pad. He closed his laptop. She gave him a skeptical look as if wondering why he was hiding the information from her.

"Am I still under arrest?" she asked, sipping her coffee.

"You never were," Tim answered.

"You shit! I worried all night," she complained, smiling and looking at him over the rim of her coffee mug. She knew better.

He stared at her and decided he wasn't going to engage in their usual sparring. The police reports had taken all the humor out of the morning. And thoughts of the kidnapped children pressed in on him. He wanted to find them, find them all, and bring them back to safety. It wasn't realistic. There would be bodies. His spirit sank a bit. He rubbed his fingers across his brow.

"Elias will want to talk to you." He paused, but what he was going to say next had to be said. He braced himself for the confrontation. "And I've arranged a room for you at the Selkirk Lodge." He tore a piece off the top page of his yellow pad and flipped it back over. He pushed the scrap toward her. "Here's the confirmation number. Just talk to the clerk at the desk when you get there. They'll fix you up."

She nearly dropped her mug. "Tim, please. I'm sorry. I ..."

He lifted his right palm to stop her. "I get it; you couldn't resist a good story, I know. It's your job," he said softly and seriously. "It's mine to get bad guys off the streets. If yours interferes with mine, I sacrifice yours. That's the way it works," he explained, very no-nonsense. "No offense intended."

"It doesn't have to be that way. We could work together."

He chuckled. "Come on, Beebe. I work behind the scenes. I have tactics that need to be kept quiet until trial. I have strategies that need to play out in the courtroom. People's rights and reputations are at stake. Your job is to expose all that. And to be honest, we can't work together. Most of the time, our purposes are one-eighty out from each other."

"I want the bad guys caught too."

"Sure, but you don't care who you hurt. You've made it your mission to dig into Dani's life, my life. And you keep shoveling. I need you to leave us alone. Let us live." He immobilized her with an icy stare.

After seconds, she squirmed in her seat. "So, you're saying we can't work together, not ever?"

"The DA's office gives you stories all the time when that time is right. You always want it before. And when you don't get what you want when you want it, you make it up, spin the truth—or like last night, steal," he answered.

"You make me sound like the bad guy here."

"It is what it is."

"You hate me, don't you?"

He kept his face wholly noncommittal. "As I said, it is what it is." Tim hoped she'd just leave. He pushed the reservation toward her again. There was a quiet moment, and then she reached out. But instead of taking the scrap of paper, she covered his hand with hers. It was an intimate gesture that set him back. He quickly moved his hand away. His eyes narrowed with suspicion. "I thought we established the ground rules yesterday morning. No games," he reminded her.

She fussed with her blonde waves. "It's not a game. Do you think I'm pretty, Tim?" she asked, fixing her gaze on his eyes. She lightly skipped her fingers on the reservation, moving it ever so slowly toward her side of the table.

He scowled at her. That question meant trouble, no matter how he answered. "What does that have to do with anything?" He sat back in his chair. "Okay, sure. You're pretty."

"Do you want me?"

For a moment, he was stunned to silence. Where the hell did that come from? "Incomplete question. Want you for what exactly?"

"Go ahead. Play dumb; play coy." She lifted both elbows to the table, wove her fingers together, and set her chin on her hands. "You know exactly what I mean."

"No. I don't want you," he said coldly. He didn't care if she was hurt by it.

"Liar." She let a sly smile cross her lips.

He contemplated her, wondering if he'd somehow contributed to this confusion. He had to set the record straight. It was past time. He stood. He picked up his mug and went to the buffet table, refilled it with coffee, and sloshed a measure of cream into it. He came back to his chair, set his coffee on the table. He spun his chair around, straddled it, and crossed his arms along the top rung. He decided to do this task as gently as he could.

"If I've given you a wrong impression, I didn't intend to. I'm married, and I chose to be. Don't get me wrong; I had a great run at being single. Lots of fun. My share of pretty girls." He was struggling. He seldom revealed his innermost feelings with anyone except Dani. "The day I saw Dani for the first time, she was it. At that moment, I realized, if she'd have me, my single days were over. I love her. She's what I want."

The silence between them was breathless. It seemed as if seconds ticked into minutes. Different emotions colored her eyes: anger, embarrassment, disappointment, more anger. He wasn't sure which.

"Lucky her," Beebe said heatedly, standing and pacing in a tight circle behind her chair.

She had no right to be mad. Not at him, not at Dani. His jaw tightened, and he could feel his frown. He stood and turned his chair back around.

"You think I don't know what that's like? You think loving someone is unique to only you?" she asked—no, demanded. Of course, he didn't think that. But she'd rendered him speechless, importing and projecting emotions and thoughts he didn't have, making him a strawman she could knock down. Annoyance flushed warmth into his cheeks.

"I feel that way about you. I love you, Tim. I have from the first day I saw you," Beebe said quietly, suddenly leaning across the table toward him—expecting what?

He stood perfectly still in open-mouthed shock. Their eyes locked. "Well, don't. Don't love me." He shoved the paper with the hotel information on it toward her. "You need to go."

She snatched up the paper and crumpled it into a ball. He barely flinched when she threw it in his face. He let her have her little victory. Storming out of the room, she grabbed her crutches as she passed by the end of the buffet. He sank into his chair. He had to admit her declaration of love was an unwanted surprise. He turned his legal pad over and started back over his notes.

"Out of my way," Beebe snipped at Dani, shoving her as she met her at the doorway, making Tim immediately stand to defend Dani if need be. They passed each other without incident.

Dani watched Beebe leave and then sat down in the chair next to Tim that Beebe had previously occupied. It was still warm. Tim fingered his legal pad. He smiled but was distressed. She covered his hand with hers, as she'd earlier seen Beebe do. He didn't pull away.

Tim was tough when he needed to be but gentle and kind too. Dani was concerned. Beebe's confession had him in a contemplative mood.

"Beebe can't help it, you know. You're so easy to love," she said, waiting for him to smile. He did.

"You heard? That was crazy. I didn't see it. Should I have?"

She shook her head no and pressed a finger to her lips to hush him. "Am I really your *it* girl?"

"You are." His face softened; his eyes radiated love.

Dani bit her bottom lip. "I didn't mean to listen. I didn't. But then when I realized what she was telling you, I had to. That old green-eyed monster grabbed me and wouldn't let me leave. Bad, huh?"

"Not really. I'm glad you're jealous, at least a little bit. I adore you. You know that, don't you?" His voice was soft; his expression matched his words. He stroked her fingers with his. Dani so wanted to kiss him. "Did I tell you it took me seven months to screw up the courage to come to you with roses that day I introduced myself? For seven months, I watched you from the window at Jake's Deli as you came down the parking garage steps every morning. You took my breath away. Left me speechless."

"Seven months? Am I that scary?" Laughter turned the corners of her mouth. She took hold of his hand in both of hers across the table. No wonder Beebe was crazy about him. She loved the way the morning sun spilled across his strong jaw and glistened in the tousle of short blond hair. Dani remembered watching him in the courtroom when she'd secretly slipped in sometimes. Confident, well researched, and smart, he could sway a jury in a snap, especially when he went in for the kill on a lying witness on cross. And here he was trying to explain what he shouldn't have to. But thank God he was. She needed his reassurance.

"I didn't know what I was going to do if you turned me down for that first date. Become a hermit? A sad, lonely recluse? One of those bachelors that his best friend's wife invites to dinner because he's so pitiful," he teased, grinning big.

She stood, went to him, and began rubbing his shoulders. "We don't have to find out how pathetic you'd be without me or how wretched I'd be without you. We have each other." She leaned forward and kissed his cheek.

"Do you think Beebe followed us here? I kept wondering, what are the odds she'd be skiing here when there are so many places closer to Seattle? Now, that's scary."

"Yes," Dani said softly. She wrapped her arms around him, and he rested his head against her breasts.

"I think she manipulated Miguel into asking you if she could stay here."

"Yes." She kissed him behind his ear. He immediately turned. Her next kiss found his lips. He rose and took her in his arms. "Are you upset about hurting Beebe?" she asked, with hesitation in her voice.

"I don't care about Beebe. What on earth did she expect? It pisses me off that she thought I would cheat, that I would dishonor my love and promise to you. Who'd want a guy like that, anyway? She'll get over it. She'll write some mean shit about me in her tabloid column for revenge and then fall for someone new. Beebe's too in love with Beebe to be upset for long." He laughed, but then seriousness returned to his eyes. He took hold of both her hands and waited a beat until she gazed up into his eyes. "Dani, I—I'm not going with Hollingsrow's firm."

Dani felt her lips part with disappointment. She quickly tried to cover it up with a small smile. Tim took a breath in through his teeth. He'd read her.

"Are you going to be okay with that?" he asked.

"Of course. I told you I would be. Whatever you decide." Dani could tell by his expression she had failed to convince him. She wasn't going to interfere with this part of his life. She was going to support him, even if it frightened her.

He pulled her into his arms, kissed the top of her head, and explained, "There are these kids—kids like Chloe, fosters, that have gone missing." He tipped her chin up so she would look at him. "I'm going to help Elias find them and get them back to safety."

"Oh," she whispered. Dani knew her face radiated the wonder she felt for him. He was a good guy, and good guys did heroic things. "I'll find a Realtor in Virginia," she said. She reached for him and pulled his face down so his lips met hers. The touch was heady.

"Okay. Don't stop doing that." He kissed her long and slowly.

"Doctor Nathan called; we can go get Chloe now," she whispered against his lips. "That's what I was coming to tell you when I stumbled on your conversation with Beebe."

He chuckled. "I'm not sure I'm going to like this fatherhood thing if it means I have to wait until the kids are in bed to have you."

"Does that mean you want me?" Dani asked, mirroring Beebe's question.

"So much. So much, baby," he said.

"But just think how good it will be tonight when, finally, we are alone."

"Umm." He grabbed a breath. "I can't wait." He kissed her again. When he finished his kiss, they reluctantly parted.

"Time to go," she said. "Are you sure you want to do this?"

He picked up his briefcase and set it on the table. He stuffed his work and his laptop inside and locked it. He took in a breath and let it out. "Yes. I'm sure. Let's go get our little girl."

THIRTY-EIGHT

The hospital corridor spread out before him, cold, gray, and sterile. He held his breath as the memory of prison hit him. One institution seemed like another in the fog of his ugly memories. He held on tight to the brown teddy bear until his knuckles turned white. When he realized it, he forced himself to relax and unzipped his gray down jacket. It had suddenly become exceptionally hot in here. Graden felt beads of sweat forming along his hairline under his ball cap. He changed direction and followed the signs to the restroom. Once inside, he flipped off the hat and stared at himself in the mirror. He set the bear down on the counter beside him and sloshed cold water over his face. Dripping with water, he observed the image staring back at him. His brown eyes were tired and bloodshot, and the scruff from the two-day growth of beard created a dark shadow along his jawline and upper lip. He needed a haircut. His brown mop was just cresting over the tops of his ears. He quickly raked his fingers through his hair, trying to tame the wild curls spilling down the left side of his broad forehead.

This is just recon, he told himself. *Once he figured the layout, he'd figure how to grab the girl.*

Once again, he splashed cold water over his face, then pulled two paper towels from the dispenser and dried. He straightened and tucked his shirt into his jeans. With one last glance in the mirror, he settled the ball cap down over his hair and then snatched the bear.

The hospital check-in counter was a semicircle and had five stations. He loitered in the roped-off corridor behind the Wait Here sign for his turn. He smiled at the little gray-haired woman standing close behind him. She harrumphed her disapproval. He was the one who should be annoyed; she crowded him. He smirked at her when one of the check-in monitors motioned for him to come forward.

"Chloe Jeffers. She's my niece. I just heard she was here only a few hours ago. I would've come earlier. Excuse my appearance. I just got off work and rushed over," Graden explained, leaning forward, trying to read the computer screen as the attendant typed.

The attendant was a prissy man and didn't care about his excuses. His gaunt face gave the impression that everyone was beneath him. He looked Graden up and down. Graden wanted to reach over the counter and string him up by his prudish tie. But he smiled nicely instead.

"Do you have ID?"

"Sure," Graden said as he fumbled in his jacket pocket. He'd anticipated this and produced a false Idaho driver's license.

The jerk pulled down a pair of reading glasses from their perch on his balding head. He studied the license, comparing it with Graden's face. "Sign here." He pushed a sheet on a clipboard toward him. "Chloe Jeffers is in room 315. You take the elevator to the third floor, Pediatrics, then left."

Graden scribbled some letters by the typed entry of Jeffers, Chloe, and the date and time as required. After grabbing up the teddy bear, he walked toward the bank of elevators. He looked around and took the elevator labeled Staff Only in red. Once inside, he pressed the button for the second floor. The car had a door on either side. Some hospitals had lifts with this feature. One door was to accommodate the staff. The other would lead to operating theaters, x-ray and imagining machines, the laundry, maintenance hatches and doorways, and the kitchen.

When the elevator stopped, he pushed the button to open that inner door. It noisily rolled open. He stepped into the hallway. It was just as he imagined, darkened, empty, icy cold. Two passengers who rode up with him acknowledged him with a nod as the door slid closed. They didn't seem to be alarmed by his presence. He assumed the third-floor layout would be a duplicate. As he started to his left, automatic motion sensor lights illuminated his path a few feet in front of his steps. It was a power-saving measure he'd seen before. That was a bummer. If he were forced to use this avenue to escape, the light trail would give him away. Carefully, he noted the location of surveillance cameras. He didn't have the time or the wherewithal to disable them.

He had to take Chloe tonight. The drop-off point had been arranged. When he got the girl, if necessity forced him to go this route, he'd have to make certain all the branches off the main corridor lit up. Otherwise, his escape path would be easy to follow. And now he knew he'd need a balaclava or mask to hide his face.

He explored down the hallway and found the clean laundry cubby. Various sizes of green surgical scrubs were stacked in layers by size on built-in shelves. He took a pair in extra-large and stuffed them under his jacket next to his body inside his shirt. The custodian's closet was right next door. He tested the knob to see if it was locked. It was. He reversed and headed back toward the elevator. As he went along, he casually parked a wheelchair next to the wall at the entry of each passageway off the main. It was insurance. When he took the child, he'd shove a wheelchair down each, making sure the motion sensor lights turned on, disguising his movements. They would pick him up in the surveillance video but only after he was long gone, not in real time.

As he passed by the elevator, he pressed the call button. While he waited, he noted the set of emergency stairs on the left side past the elevator. Warily, he pushed the touch bar to open the door. He flinched, expecting a loud warning alarm to sound.

Silence.

Satisfied, he reentered the elevator just as the doors started to close. He pushed the button for the third floor. He didn't acknowledge the other passengers and straightened the bright red bow around the teddy bear's neck.

The elevator doors opened on the third floor. Graden disembarked. He stood quietly in the hall, orienting himself by the numbers on the patient rooms to guide him in the direction he needed to go. He turned the corner toward 315.

He glanced at the first door he came to, 317. Two doors to go. He took a bold step. The door to the little girl's room burst open. A doctor in a white coat stepped into the hallway, holding it open. A wheelchair with the child in it rolled through, pushed by a stunningly beautiful woman. He was stopped cold. She and the doctor discussed the little girl's treatment. But he was spellbound and studied the woman. From her perfectly fitted jeans, the dainty snow boots, the fur-lined jacket, the way her light brown hair caught the overhead light and shimmered around her shoulders, her kind blue eyes, and her full kissable, very kissable, lips, everything about the woman spelled money. She caught his stare, and a smile passed gently across her lips and was gone. He didn't think it was possible, but his mind whispered, *I think I'm in love.* He entertained a brief thought of making love to her, by force if need be. He glanced from the wheelchair to the woman and back again. The little girl in the wheelchair was Chloe, his mark, and could easily be mistaken for the woman's very own. Ironic. Plan B was taking shape. What was the woman's interest in the child? Was she a new foster?

He was brought back to the real world when he thought he heard the doc say, "Watch for pneumonia." There was a twinge of guilt but not for long.

And then Graden's heart skipped a beat. One of the cops, the blond one that almost caught him on the mountain, walked through the door carrying a great big stuffed horse. He was one of the fucking snowmobiling cops that had ruined this whole operation in the first place. He'd know him anywhere.

The thing about these young cops was that they weren't the fat, doughnut-gobbling wannabes he associated with most cops. Many these days were military trained. That made them more frightening. He assumed the blond one was the new, scary kind of pig: fit, athletic, smart, and meaner than shit. He remembered his tenacity and his moves that night on the trail. Their eyes locked. Graden's first impulse was to run, but he'd learned not to follow that first rush. He watched for a spark of recognition to flash from the man's ocean blue eyes. It wasn't there. He understood that by the time they'd realized a kidnapping was going down, he was fully covered in his snowmobile gear. And that was a perfect disguise. They had no reason to look through the bar's surveillance tape. And if they did, they would never be able to pick him out in the crowd. A great advantage. He recognized the cop, but the lawman didn't remember him.

He had to make the best of this encounter. He turned and stood in front of the door to the patient room in front of him. He calmed his pounding heart and trembling fingers.

He put on his best confused act and asked, "Is this 314?"

"Next one down," the blond cop said, tipping his head in the direction of the door past him with a friendly grin. That was the police: your best friend and your worst enemy. Fuck him.

"Yeah? Thanks. Excuse me." Graden brushed the cop's shoulder as he squeezed by, getting a good look at the guy's face and sizing up his adversary. "Oh, sorry. Thanks again," he said. This guy would be formidable. His muscles were lean and rock hard. Tangling with him might be a big mistake—but he'd do what needed to be done.

THIRTY-NINE

Tim felt the hair on the back of his neck stand up as the burly man crowded through the traffic jam they'd caused in the hospital hallway, brushing his shoulder as he pushed by. He watched the man enter the patient room just one down from Chloe's. The man held out the brown teddy bear toward the room's occupant and disappeared behind the automatic door as it quietly closed.

Tim stood for a moment. Had he seen that man before? Not here; he would've remembered him if it had been here at the hospital. But somewhere. Somewhere.

Possession of a controlled substance and with intent to distribute flashed to his mind. That was it. Poor schmuck reminded him of one of the many drug dealers he'd prosecuted when first assigned to try cases four years ago. What he did know is that it wasn't one of his cases. He'd memorized his perp's faces. Drug dealers were a dangerous group. They'd been known to hold prosecutors personally responsible for their incarceration and to hunt them down once they'd served their sentences. None of Tim's would be out of jail yet. Not even for good behavior. All the same, Tim felt he'd seen him before. But where?

He shook it off. Chloe reached for her unicorn. They were ready to get out of here. He knelt and positioned the stuffed toy across her lap.

"Hang onto him. He might fly away," he teased. Chloe wrapped her arms tightly around the unicorn's neck, burying her face in his fur. Tim stood and slipped his arm over Dani's shoulder. He could tell Dani was ready for this. Ready for motherhood. She was beaming, glowing, and more beautiful than she was five minutes ago—if that was even possible. He pushed the wheelchair toward the elevator.

"What do you say we get a Christmas tree on our way home," he suggested. Christmas was only five days away, and he hadn't thought much about it. He'd picked out his gifts for Dani in the Ski Shoppe at the lodge but wished Kathy was still here to confirm that his purchase of the diamond tennis bracelet and matching stud earrings were the right choice. Kathy had warned him early on when he was first dating Dani that kitchen appliances were *not* appropriate gifts. Jewelry, expensive perfume, and lingerie were right. He tried to stick to that.

Dani agreed with the Christmas tree idea, and Chloe said in her shy little voice, "A big one. Can we have a big one? Tim says he wants a big one too."

Dani and Tim looked at each other, and both chuckled.

He pushed the wheelchair into the elevator. As the doors closed, he said, "Can we ask Tim if we can change his name? Sometimes when you talk to him, I might think you're talking to me."

Chloe wrinkled her brow. Then she whispered in the unicorn's ear. "He says yes. What should we call him?"

"We can think about it for a while and then talk about it later," Dani offered.

"Okay."

On the ground floor at the main hospital doors, Tim left the wheelchair and picked Chloe up and carried her and the unicorn out to the car. Dani helped him figure out the car seat, and they loaded up and started out of the parking lot. He was following the exit signs when he noticed a mint-green Mercedes van. It had navy blue lettering—Bonner Bakery—on its side and a big dark swirl along the bottom half of the body that looped around to look like a cresting wave. He stopped, reversed, and pulled into a parking space. He looked at Dani.

"The van," he said. Dani knew what he was talking about.

"Tim, no." She grabbed his arm. He squinted at her. She had to know it was like holding back a racehorse at the starting gate.

He seized his iPhone from the cup holder in the middle console. He flipped to camera and shot pictures of the van and the license plate.

"Let's go," she said. "Call it in. We have Chloe with us." Dani was scared. She was right to be.

Just as he started to dial the sheriff, a young woman opened the van's driver-side door. He watched as she dashed around to the back and removed a sheet cake packed in a big pink box. Tim could see the rear of the van was full of baker's racks. Bread, packages of fresh cookies, and various other baked goods filled the cargo area. The girl wore a long-sleeve mint-colored shirt, blue jeans, and a navy blue apron under her winter puff coat. She had earbuds in her ears and pranced away with her cake delivery. Logic told him this wasn't the van he was looking for. Just from observing the paint, he knew this wasn't a skimpy hardware store spray-on job. The surface was glossy and smooth, as if the color was under a professional, clear coat.

"Sorry, girls. False alarm," he said as he put the Jeep in reverse, backed out of the space, and went on their way. But he realized that the van, the real suspect van, could be partially painted, not fully painted, as they had assumed. He called Elias and relayed that information.

FORTY

Graden ducked behind a concrete pillar when he saw the cop pull into a parking space. On top of having possession of his triple-whammy kid, the pig obviously knew about his van and the navy blue paint. Somehow, somewhere, law enforcement had made that connection. Graden clenched his fists in frustration. It wasn't his van; he parked his two blocks away behind the liquor store next to the dumpster in the back. But watching this told him all he needed to know.

He'd misjudged them. The cops weren't the Keystones after all. They had found the house at Priest Lake. He couldn't believe it. He purposely timed the kidnapping on one of the nights the SnoCat groomed the trails for the tours. He had hoped any snowmobile tracks would be obliterated by the machine's rototiller-like teeth. He scrambled to remember if he'd wiped all the surfaces in the house and the outdoor bays. If they had indeed been to the Priest Lake house, and if he'd left prints, he was going back to prison. They had his prints, his DNA, in the police and FBI databases. He'd need to finish his work, quickly collect Gina, and get the heck out of Dodge.

But if his instincts were still working, the beauty that accompanied the cop was filthy rich. That fact made him hesitate. Maybe he could more than triple his take. Perhaps he could extort a ransom *in addition* to his fee. He had to find out.

As the blond was taking pictures of the bakery van, he started through the parking lot, checking for a vehicle left unlocked, preferably with the keys in it—but unlocked would be enough. He'd cut his teeth by jacking cars. He kept a casual eye on his adversary while he checked through the first row. It didn't take long; there was always someone who tested fate. He could see the silver link of a keychain dangling from the driver-side visor from the passenger-side window. He examined the door of the small gray Honda. It opened. He slipped into the seat, and when he pulled the visor down, the ignition key dropped into his lap. Quickly, he cranked the engine over. Within seconds, he exited the hospital parking lot only five cars behind the snowmobiling policeman's Jeep.

FORTY-ONE

Just a few blocks from the hospital, Tim found a Christmas tree lot. Two men unloaded a truck of fresh trees. They'd have a good selection. Chloe and Dani were thinking up names for the unicorn and bantering them back and forth.

"Satin wings? Satin for short?" Dani asked.

"No," Chloe said, shaking her head furiously.

"TimmyTwo? That way, you can still call him Tim, but he'll be number two, and the real Tim can be number one," Dani suggested.

As Tim watched in the rearview mirror, Chloe seemed to be concentrating and heavily weighing this option. "TimTwo," she offered in her little-girl voice.

"How about this place for a tree, girls?" Tim interrupted. Dani grinned her consent, and Chloe bounced happily in her car seat.

"A big one, a really big one, please. This big." Chloe spread her arms as wide as she could. Tim found himself glancing at Dani and laughing.

He pulled into the customer parking and stopped. "A really big one it is."

Tim helped Chloe from her car seat, and Dani took hold of her hand. "Now, Chloe, you always hold onto one of our hands. No running off. Okay?" He knelt to be at eye level and held onto her until she acknowledged him with an affirmative nod. He was going to be an overprotective father, he guessed.

"Okay," she answered, and tugged Dani toward a row of trees.

"That's my girl," he reassured her.

Tim couldn't say why he suddenly felt uneasy. Perhaps it was the strange, lost man at the hospital, or maybe it was his new role as father and the responsibility that brought with it, but whatever the reason, he felt he needed to be armed. He went back to the front of the Jeep, unlocked it, took his Walther PK 380 from the glove compartment, and tucked it into the waistband of his jeans, quickly covering it with his jacket. He pressed the lock button on the key fob and glanced around the parking area and back to the street. A gray Honda decelerated significantly and crawled past the lot, much slower than traffic demanded. The driver wasn't recognizable, just a shadowy shape. Tim could tell the driver was looking in their direction. But was he observing his small family or the Christmas tree offload? He straightened and watched as the Honda turned right at the street corner. If the Honda came back around the block, he was pretty sure he'd have his answer. The driver would either stop for a Christmas tree, or he'd slow for another look. Tim caught up with Dani and Chloe.

As Dani and Chloe judged the trees, out of the corner of his eye, Tim saw the Honda drive past the lot a second time. The thought that Chloe's kidnapper might be swooping in for a second shot at abducting her made his jaw tighten with resolve. He knew the kidnapper was not afraid to take a child in broad daylight, with the parents only yards away and, in Chloe's case, inches away. He tightened the grip on her small hand. Suspecting the perp wouldn't make his move here on the Christmas tree lot, Tim watched as the Honda inched by for the third time. He'd know soon enough if his fears were overactive imagination or the real deal. His tenacity and toughness surprised even him. He hadn't realized he would feel this way. No one was going to mess with his girls. No one was going to get to his family. Following the Honda with his stare, teeth clenched, and reactions on a hair trigger, Tim watched as it turned the corner once more. *Try it, asshole. I dare you.* He wished he could see the man's face. He had to plan, set a trap.

Finally, after the Honda didn't return for a fourth go, Tim felt Chloe's tug on the hem of his jacket. "This one. We want this one," she said joyfully. Dani stared at him, her brow fraught with worry. He wondered if they'd been trying to get his attention for a while.

"Sorry, this one?" He pointed out a beautiful, full, symmetrical tree.

"Are you all right?" Dani asked.

"Yeah." He tried to reassure her with a kiss on the cheek. At this moment, he didn't want to alarm her. "This one it is," he said cheerfully. He picked up the tree to carry it to the cashier. Chloe began to dash ahead. Tim dropped the tree and grabbed up the little girl around her waist. She giggled as if it were a game.

"I told you to hold onto my hand or Dani's. You have to do that. Okay?" Tim realized his tone was sharp. Alarmed, Dani gawked at him with fear in her eyes.

"Tim, you're scaring me. What is it?" Dani grabbed hold of his bicep.

He set Chloe down on her feet, took her hand and Dani's, and pressed their hands together. "Hold on," he scolded softly.

"Tim?"

He shook his head. "Just feeling uneasy. Let's get this tree and get home." He picked up the tree and directed them to walk ahead of him. When he arrived at the cashier, he set the tree down and did a quick scan around him. There was no one along the street, and the worrisome Honda was not in view. Tim paid for the tree and, with the help of one of the concessionaires, tied the tree to the roof racks. Wary now, he kept scanning the surroundings. Dani and Chloe already waited in the Jeep when Tim slipped into the driver's side. He backed out of the parking lot, looking around carefully for anything suspicious. He saw nothing and no one. But the eerie, uneasy feeling lingered.

FORTY-TWO

Tim smiled at Elias and studied the two special agents he'd brought with him. Before closing the door to the chalet's dining room, he looked around the corner and watched Dani and Chloe choosing decorations for the seven-foot tree they'd brought home. He'd put the mini LED lights on earlier, before Elias and his crew arrived. It had always been his family's tradition. It was Dad's duty to string the lights, and the ladies completed the finishing touches. The warm, sweet feelings of home made him happy. Tim had to repack family life into its sacred compartment. He had work to do and closed the door.

"Have a seat." Tim gestured toward the dining table. *Let the profiling begin,* he thought. Everyone brought their copies of the police reports with them, and four laptops sat open on the inlaid dining table. Tim retrieved his legal pad with the notes he'd made this morning. It still didn't make him a profiler.

Dani had asked Winona to set up the buffet with a Keurig

coffee machine. Various coffee flavor pods were stacked in a special lazy Susan. Coffee mugs, cream, sugar, and a gorgeous tray of home-baked cookies were neatly arranged on the mahogany buffet.

Elias unfolded a portable screen he'd unpacked from his briefcase. It connected to his laptop. As he typed, it would memorialize their thoughts on the screen, and they would draw a character picture of the kidnapper.

The FBI agents, Betsy Lamphere and Kandar Singh, had worked with Elias for years. Tim remembered them from two other cases they'd worked together over the last four years in King County. Betsy was a good-looking woman in her forties. She wore her shiny brown hair in a smooth pageboy style. Neatly put together, she dressed in a crisp white blouse and navy blue suit. She had compromised and worn ankle-length fur-lined boots with her navy skirt rather than pumps. But here on the mountain, she should've worn snow gear. Kandar was more practical. Like Tim, he wore blue jeans. But instead of Tim's royal blue turtleneck and matching sweater, Kandar wore a pale pink oxford button-down and a wool tweed blazer. Elias, as ever, was in a dark brown tweed wool suit and tie.

"Help yourself to refreshments," Tim offered, and the two agents quickly went for the cookies. They wouldn't be disappointed. They settled back down in a few minutes and were ready to get to work.

"Shall we get started?" Elias asked but didn't wait for an answer. "Here's what we do know." He read as he typed the list, and it printed in bold black letters on the screen. "One: the kidnap victims are all under eight years old; our youngest is four. Two: they are all from foster families. Three: they were all taken in broad daylight. Four: the foster parents were close by when they were taken." All these bullet points were on Tim's list too. Elias breathed out a sigh and pulled his kid cards out of the inside pocket of his brown tweed jacket. He dealt the deck of pictures out in front of him, his eyes filled with a deep sadness. "Anyone have anything else?" he asked, engaging each of his agents around the table one at a time.

Tim looked at the two special agents. They had nothing. But he did. Significant? Maybe.

"He uses chloroform on cotton balls as the tranquilizing agent. He uses rainbow-colored duct tape; brand name: Duck, with a *k*, Tape," Tim added. He set his elbows on the table and folded his fingers together. "I don't think the kidnapper is involved much beyond the initial assault. I think he's selling them, trafficking them." Tim rubbed his temples. "These are not crimes of opportunity; the children are chosen. Maybe they're chosen for appearance. I can't figure out the criteria. I can't come up with the answer to why," Tim said.

"Okay. Good," Elias said. "The why is important. We need that piece. Any ideas?"

Becky asked. "Why do you think they are chosen?" She stared at Tim, obviously not impressed by his theory.

"Geography. I'll send you this map from my computer." He sent an email to Elias, and after a minute, Elias opened it up on his computer and displayed it on his folding screen so that everyone could see. Rather than a city, it was a map of the United States, each abduction location marked by a red star with the date listed underneath. He generated the map this morning as he'd read Elias's files and made notes. "As you can see, the kidnappings aren't around a base of operation or linear; the perp's not following a route, like say a truck driver or a package delivery service guy would. His selection of children is random, scattered, chaotic. On May 30, he took a kid from Dayton, Ohio. June 15, Tampa, Florida. June 28, Austin, Texas. So, I think the criteria is something unique, specific. I can't figure what." Tim tented his hands in front of his brow and then ran his fingers up through his short blond hair, trying to stimulate the thoughts. "We have connected Letisha Watson, abducted in Ohio, and the twins, abducted in Virginia, with Chloe, abducted here, by the tape. The others we haven't linked with direct evidence but from circumstances. Same MO. The rest of the children are still missing."

"Why do you think he uses rainbow-colored tape? Any ideas?" Elias asked.

"He secures the cotton ball soaked in chloroform with the tape. But why rainbow-colored—I haven't the slightest. It's so odd; he has to know it's a giveaway. Does he want to be caught?" Tim asked, throwing up one hand in surrender. "Maybe it's something simple like it was on sale."

"He has a kid of his own," Kandar offered. "He thinks the kids will like it."

Elias typed, and a new column appeared on his screen: 1. Married or in a relationship. 2. Has a child or children. 3. May want to be caught/stopped.

"He's thirty-five to forty-five. Works in a trade, construction maybe," Betsy added.

Tim could see that they suspected he was driving a van, pale green, Mercedes, now with blue embellishments. But he wanted more explanation from Betsy. He needed it if he was going to learn his craft. "I get that the guy's in the construction trade by the van, but what are you basing your age on?" he asked, genuinely wanting to know.

"Statistics." She gave her one-word answer with a dismissive look. Tim knitted his brow. He forced himself not to take offense. *Solve the problem. Don't get involved in the pettiness of personalities,* he admonished himself.

Without prompting, the image of the man in the hospital hallway skimmed across his mind. He found himself wondering about him. He was thirty-five to forty. He was dressed like a tradesman. Tim stifled himself from describing him to the others. There was no evidence he'd done anything but walk into the hospital hallway and visit the patient next to Chloe's room. Even though it had been an ordinary encounter, an uneasy feeling nagged him each time he thought about the man. The drug charges scrolled through his mind again. Where had he seen the man before? Damn it. Uneasy feelings weren't evidence. Was he the person in the Honda slowly driving by the Christmas tree lot? Scott's suspicion of everyone might be rubbing off. He smiled to himself. He missed Scott and Kathy and their crime-solving skills. There was never any ego or emotion when they started one of their sessions. Disagreements from time to time, yes, but their longtime friendship always kept them on target. They worked together with pure logic, reason, teamwork, and an inexplicable dash of intuition. Tim remembered reading books by John Douglas, one of the fathers of criminal profiling, and thinking to himself the man had ESP; he didn't realize it, but he had it. Tim had prosecuted many cases solved by the investigator's hunch.

This team had not accepted him. Elias had but not the others. Tim looked at each of them briefly. He wasn't going to let resentfulness interfere now. They needed to keep on task if they wanted to catch this guy. If the man at the hospital was the kidnapper, they still needed to find the ultimate buyers to stop the entire ring. He remembered Dr. Van Hatten. His mouth curled into a sneer of disgust.

"The kidnapper is a middleman. The twins were ultimately sold to Dr. Van Hatten. They were raped, tortured, and exsanguinated. Why would anyone do that?" Tim said, returning their attention to the mystery.

"Vampires?" Kandar said. He looked around the room. "Well, it fits."

"At least people who are playing vampire, perhaps," Betsy offered.

Tim felt his eyebrows shoot up with incredulity. *Vampires? You watch too much TV.* He wanted to break out laughing and dismiss the thought but stifled himself. As a prosecutor, he of all people knew humans were capable of evil beyond imagination. Dr. Van Hatten was one of the most evil men he'd ever encountered.

"A blood cult, Satan worshippers?" Betsy threw it out, and it lingered like a rotten smell.

Tim rolled his shoulders to relieve the tension there. The statue in the Bransons' living room flashed in his mind. He tried to recall the history of the Canaanites who worshipped the bronze god but couldn't. Had some crazy whacko resurrected a past evil and built a cult around it?

Suddenly Tim remembered his conversation with Scott at the end of their snowmobile excursion. Tim lifted a finger and wrestled his iPhone from his pocket. He punched in Kathy's number. When she answered, he said, "Kath, would you email me your autopsy notes on Van Hatten and the twins? To my new address, McAndrewsT@gmail.com. Thanks." Tim hung up and leaned back in his chair for a moment. He sat forward, set his elbows on the table, and massaged his temples. Were the drug track marks Scott mentioned yesterday on Van Hatten's arm IV transfusion marks instead?

"Vampires," he said quietly.

FORTY-THREE

Tim sipped on the eggnog from the small mug Dani handed him. He watched as Chloe hung a little star on one of the bottom branches of the Christmas tree. Mitch and Shannon sat together on the sofa in front of the fire, and Dani helped finish up the tree decorations. Outside, the snow had started to fall again. At first, one or two lacey flakes drifted lazily by the window; now, a curtain of white blocked the view. Skiing was going to be amazing tomorrow. Tim let himself engage in a daydream of muscling through light, dry powder. He could almost feel the rhythm.

Marta, the new nanny, looked very much like her gruff brother, Mark, Dani's ranch manager. She was tall and lanky, her salt and pepper hair pulled back into a severe bun at the nape of her neck, her thin lips tight with worry. But her kind blue eyes softened all her sharp edges. Marta's connection with Chloe had been instant. Love at first sight. Tim smiled, watching them interact. Chloe seemed to affect everyone with love.

She was a confident child, downright bold, and friendly with strangers, in spite of all that happened to her. Tim couldn't help but think she was going to be a force to be reckoned with when she grew up. She was a little doll; her blonde ringlets framed her face and accented her blue eyes and pink bow lips. She looked surprisingly like a combination of Dani and him. She would be easily mistaken for their very own. That would probably make life easier if—and it was a big *if*—they settled on adoption.

Marta was immediately included in the family. Dani told Tim that Marta had helped both her sisters when their little ones came along. She was as trusted with the St. Clair brood as Mark, her brother, was with the ranches.

Tim sat on the hearth and let the fire warm his back. He caught Dani looking at him from where she sat on the floor at the base of the Christmas tree. Chloe showed her an ornament and chattered away. But Dani's attention remained on him. He held her gaze as long as he could. She raked her fingers through her hair and then traced an index finger along her bottom lip. Enjoying thoughts of kissing her, he caught his breath. He took another sip of eggnog. He was content with his new family but couldn't wait until he had Dani alone. He was slow to respond when he felt his iPhone vibrate with a call in his shirt pocket. He sat forward and set his eggnog next to him on the hearth.

He answered, "McAndrews." A pause. "What? What did you say?" Tim shook off the trance of daydreams and was instantly on his feet.

Tim pointed to Mitch and motioned for him to follow. Mitch was immediately alert and complied. They'd been here before. All of Mitch's military training would get a refresher. When they were out of earshot of the women, Tim engaged the speaker function on his phone.

"I'm putting you on speaker. Say again."

"Okay. It's Miguel. I'm on Senator Shearer's deck. I'm look-ing at your place through my night vision and infrared goggles. Are you expecting anyone? I'm watching a man jimmy open the electrical box at your gate."

"No. Not expecting anyone." Tim was emphatic. His gaze settled on Mitch's face. He mirrored Tim's concern. "If he thinks he can cut the power, he's mistaken. We have a whole house backup generator; it will kick on in no more than thirty seconds after the power goes down."

"Yeah? Well, let's give this guy the surprise of his life," Miguel said, his voice challenging him. "Call me back when you're in gear. I'll keep eyes on."

Tim and Mitch quickly slipped into their snow bibs, donned their snow boots, and grabbed gloves and hats in preparation for the outdoors. He and Mitch pressed earbuds into their ears. Tim dialed Miguel. All the equipment Dani had bought for their snowmobiling adventure was getting a workout tonight.

Miguel emailed a link to his night/infrared vision to both men. The screens on their iPhones would show them precisely what Miguel was seeing. Tim paced as he waited for the down-load. Though all the tactical equipment was going to give them the advantage, he still felt adrenaline racing through his system and his anger building. No doubt about it now, Tim was sure the kidnapper had come back for a second try for Chloe. It con-firmed his theory that each child was chosen. He knew it just as sure as he was standing in the foyer of Dani's Schweitzer man-sion. Even though he'd been extra careful when driving back to the house after getting the Christmas tree and wound through Sandpoint, making sure he wasn't followed, the kidnapper found them. And as determined as the would-be intruder was to take the child, Tim was determined to keep him from her.

Gradually, as he realized the kidnapper was here, he was filled with a cold, calculating calm. He'd had this feeling before.

His senses became sharp, his vision crystal, his reason and logic like a precision machine. Underneath all his civilized guise, at his core, Tim understood he was a warrior after all. No one was going to harm his girls. No one.

Tim and Mitch made eye contact. They had decided to surprise the intruder. Miguel would guide them through the woods and the snow. They would circle behind him. Tim threaded his shoulder holster over his bibs. For a moment, he studied his pistol and chambered a hollow-point round by pulling back the slide. The semiauto had a seven-round clip. He pocketed a second. He watched as Mitch holstered his revolver.

"I've called the sheriff. And I have a rifle bead on him," Miguel informed them. "Sheriff has dispatched a cruiser—no lights or sirens but about twenty minutes out. You should be on the guy just about the time the deputy arrives to take custody. I haven't seen any weapons," he reported.

Tim walked back through the living room, sliding his arms in his jacket sleeves as he went.

Stunned by his behavior, Dani grabbed Chloe, bringing her onto her lap. Shannon moved from the sofa and sat down on the floor next to them. Tim knew Dani wanted an explanation by the look on her face, but there was no time. He caught her glance and gave her a brief smile. He could see the worry.

"Stay here. Lock the doors after us," Tim commanded. He headed for the kitchen door to the outside. Mitch was only a few steps behind. Tim slipped his hands into his gloves. It was good luck that Miguel and all his sophisticated surveillance equipment were right next door at the senator's. The high-priced infrared could see through the blanket of snow. The heat signature of the intruder glowed brightly on Tim's iPhone screen. He studied it to orient himself.

With the cell phone nexus, they would communicate as if this were a military operation. Tim could see Mitch's eyes shining with the same excitement he heard in Miguel's voice. This was a chance to use their fighting skills.

Once at the back door, Tim pointed to the left as an instruction to Mitch, and he indicated he was going to head right. The plan was to circle to the street and confront the intruder from behind unless he ran. Then all bets were off.

Dani's twenty acres was longer than it was wide. The house was set back about a half mile from the paved road. Snow-covered lawn stretched on either side. On each side of the property, she had installed an ornamental iron gate in the solid brick wall, to allow access to the neighbors. The gates were locked now and half-buried in snow. Tim knew it was going to be a slog to reach them. Inches of snow had accumulated on the stone walkways, and the gardener hadn't been able to use the snowblower to clear it for days. Tim wished for snowshoes.

"Adjust right, ten steps, Tim," Miguel directed in a whisper from his perch high on Shearer's deck. "On target, Mitch. Keep straight." The advantage of headsets was that they could hear Miguel and communicate, and the intruder couldn't hear them.

The snow had drifted against the rock wall surrounding the chalet, and Tim struggled through the deepest drifts as he reached the gate on his side. He vaulted to the top of the gate. His heart pounded, and his breath was ragged as he dropped to the other side of the wall. He was in good shape, but the deep snow was more work than he expected. He rested for a few seconds before edging along the brick wall.

"How far to the target?" he asked Miguel, pressing the throat mic against his skin.

"Tim, one hundred yards and closing, adjust left two feet. Mitch, one fifty and closing. Adjust right ten feet." Tim guessed Miguel's instructions were like an IFR landing to Mitch. "It's affirmative. Unsub's tampering with the electronics in the gate-opener box. I just saw sparks," Miguel whispered.

Tim flushed with a controlled rage. This guy meant his girls harm. He increased his pace. Any earlier muscle fatigue disappeared in a rush of adrenaline.

The wall was the boundary between Dani's property and the senator's. A thicket of trees lined a small creek on the senator's side that still hadn't frozen. Under the blanket of snow, Tim could hear water gurgle over the rocks on its way beneath the road. On the other side, a waterfall spilled from a concrete pipe and traced a serpentine path through the forest to the river far below. The plan was to creep along the senator's side of the wall, steal onto the street between two parked cars, slip up behind, and surprise the perp. Mitch would come down the hill in a similar maneuver.

The half-moon hid behind scurrying snow clouds, casting long, shifting tree shadows across the snow, camouflaging their movements. They had only minutes before the clouds closed and a snow squall would obscure their view. A huge hoot owl took flight from a low tree branch, calling out a warning and startling him. Tim froze in place and took in an icy breath, hoping he hadn't given their offensive away. When there was no report from Miguel, he started up the incline to the street. The climb took longer than he anticipated, but finally he stood between two cars hidden from the intruder's view.

"Mitch, what's your twenty?" Tim asked.

"Coming up on the street," Mitch panted into his mike.

"Any shift in the target?" Tim let his gaze drift to the senator's deck, where Miguel coached their movements from his vantage point. He could see him, a black shape, backlit by lights from inside the house.

"Gate just opened. Tango is on the move. Headed on the driveway northwest. Fifty paces," Miguel reported.

Before entering the road, Tim looked down the street. He noticed a gray Honda parked another hundred feet down the hill. His stomach tightened. He swallowed hard. He'd been right at the Christmas tree lot. The person in the Honda *was* tailing them.

"Sheriff on the way?" Tim asked.

"Jeep making the turn now," Miguel recounted.

"I'm ready," Tim heard Mitch whisper.

Tim pulled his knit hat out of his pocket and slipped it on, covering his hair and ears. If this was the kidnapper, he couldn't allow him to identify him before he sprung the trap.

Tim stepped from between the cars onto the street. He adjusted his pace to that of a jogger out for an evening run. He observed Mitch coming onto the road up the hill. As he moved forward, he could make out the perp's silhouette against the white. Closing the distance now, he increased his speed. He noted that the unsub wasn't dressed for this weather. He wore a down jacket but no hat, only blue jeans and tennis shoes. The intruder intended a grab and go. The man had no intention of being in the cold for long. His hands were stuffed in his pockets. Slowly, he turned and started down the driveway.

"Tim, you're made. Tango is running up the driveway. He's turned left into the trees." Miguel's direction came across loud and clear.

Tim sprinted after the man. He followed the deep prints where the guy left the driveway into the forest. When he was in sight, Tim gauged the distance, readied his body, and launched as he used to when tackling an opposing player in a football game.

"Wait, Tim! I think I see a knife," Miguel screamed.

Too late. Tim couldn't stop his momentum now. The contact was violent. Locked in hand-to-hand combat, Tim and the kidnapper tumbled headlong into a drift. At the last moment, Tim had seen the man raise his hand to spear him, and he'd grabbed his wrist. They wrestled for control of the weapon. The world was white. Blinded, snow filled his eyes, nose, and mouth, but Tim held on, keeping the knife away. As they struggled, Tim came to rest against a small tree. The unsub overpowered him. He was pinned. With everything he had, he rolled and forced the perp's hand against the tree. Over and over, Tim slammed the man's right hand and the knife against the trunk, hoping to jar the weapon loose. He could feel the man's left hand flailing against his face, almost as if he were scratching for his eyes. The man wasn't wearing gloves, and soon the cold would take its toll. Tim pinned the intruder's knife hand against the tree and threw all his weight behind it as he scraped the skin on the back of his hand down the rough bark. The man yelped in pain, and Tim watched the knife drop from his fingers. Blood oozed from the scrape on the back of the man's hand, dark red against his pale skin. With his left hand, he punched at Tim's head. He missed. Tim hit back as hard as he could. The man fell forward, and snow caked into eyes, nose, and mouth. But despite being buried in the drift and dazed, the perp kept fighting. When the two men surfaced, gasping for breath, the kidnapper started to crawl on his hands and knees away from Tim. Tim grabbed for his legs and feet, pulling one of the man's shoes off. Running now would be excruciating as the man's flesh met the frozen ground. The man kicked out, just missing Tim's jaw. He scrambled after him on all fours. He wasn't going to let this guy get away. He seized his ankles and held on. The kidnapper doubled up, trying to swat Tim's grip away. As the man bent forward, Tim reached out blindly for the man's balaclava. He fingers found purchase and poked through the knit. He ripped the covering off the man's head together with a handful of hair. The man screamed in pain and spun away right into Mitch's legs.

"Don't move, motherfucker," Mitch growled as he pressed the ice-cold barrel of his Colt 45 onto the man's temple.

FORTY-FOUR

Y ou?" Tim boomed as he sat back in the snow. Tim removed his hat and slapped it against his thigh to dust off
the snow. He swept his hand through his hair, brushing
the ice away. He looked at the kidnapper at Mitch's feet, kneel-
ing now, with his hands on his head. "You?" It was all he could
say. The intruder's sullen face was painted alternately in red
then blue as the lights from the sheriff's Jeep flashed across the
snow. Tim wanted to punch the smug grin right off his face. He
recognized him. He was the man from the hospital corridor.
Tim slowly stood.

Deputy Jeff bounded down the small slope, kicking off tiny
avalanches in front of him as he went. He cuffed the perp and
lifted him to his feet by the handcuffs. He roughly shoved him
up the rise toward the four-wheel drive. Tim watched Mitch
clear the bullet from his firing chamber and replace his gun
into its holster. Tim gathered up his earbuds and iPhone that
had fallen in the scuffle. He wondered if the phone was ruined

as he brushed ice from its face. He felt for his pistol, making certain it was still in its holster. Finally, he sifted carefully through the snow for the knife. The sheriff would want it for evidence. He made sure Bob was helping when he found it. He pointed it out and let the deputy pick it up.

Tim shook his head. His instincts had been right. Maybe as time went on, he'd stop second-guessing himself. The man from the hospital corridor glared at him, his faced twisted into a snarl. He shivered, and his thick brown hair was wet. Melting snow dripped down into the man's eyes. Tim slowly brushed the snow from his bibs and jacket, taking the time to let his anger and heart rate slow. When Jeff reached the roadway, he jostled the man against the hood of the Jeep. He frisked him, removing a wallet, keys, and a plastic bag, and set them on the hood. Tim watched, wishing he could be the one administering the rough treatment. He made his way up the incline.

After putting the man in the back seat of the sheriff's rig, Jeff looked over at Tim before closing the door. "You pressing charges?"

Tim stared angrily at the captive. "Yes. He disabled our electric gate to get in here. He came at me with a knife."

"That was self-defense. You jumped me," the man growled through the open window.

"This isn't a neighborhood dispute. You disabled my electronic gate to get into my property. Why was that?" Tim snarled back. As he paced, still irate, he walked over to the hood of the car. He glanced at the items displayed there. It took every ounce of self-discipline Tim could find to keep from grabbing the man by the throat. In a gallon-sized plastic bag, he saw a small amber bottle, cotton balls, and a partial roll of duct tape. He lifted it, and the iridescent rainbows on the tape gleamed in the moonlight.

"You son of a bitch. You came back for Chloe!" Deputy

Bob restrained Tim from getting a hand on the perp. Tim could barely keep himself from losing it and going ballistic. Rage flared over him like striking the head of a match. Mitch set a calming hand on Tim's shoulder. Tim flinched away and glared at the man. Wanting to take him out with his bare hands, instead, he forced himself to breathe.

Jeff's mouth fell open. He made his way quickly to the Jeep's hood. He grabbed up the plastic bag studying the contents. He dumped out the wallet.

"Samuel Graden, Warren Winslow, Wendel James, James Samuel?" Jeff laughed. Jeff read the names from the four driver's licenses that spilled from the wallet to the hood. "Run these names," he said to his partner as Bob entered the information into the onboard computer. Jeff spun on his heel and jerked the back door all the way open. "Samuel Graden, or whatever your name is, you're under arrest for breaking into the St. Clair Estate, criminal trespass."

Tim walked away as Jeff finished explaining his constitutional rights to Graden. Mitch walked alongside Tim as he paced the length of the Jeep.

With a big grin on his face, Jeff said to Tim, "We got him. Meet you down at Sandpoint. Twenty minutes."

Calmer now, Tim agreed. "It's going to be a long night."

Tim and Mitch started to stroll up the driveway after the sheriff's Jeep made a three-point turn and drove toward town.

"You going?" Mitch asked.

"Yep." Tim knew his voice was as sharp as a shard of broken glass.

"You got him!" Tim heard a distant voice and realized Miguel was still connected. Tim fumbled with the earbuds and pushed them back in his ears. Despite all the punishment, the iPhone still worked. He pressed the mic against his throat. "Thanks to you. Thank you, Miguel," Tim answered.

"Gotta go. Later." Miguel quickly disengaged. There was something worrisome in his tone. But Tim was only interested in getting out of his snow gear and down to the Sandpoint station. He dialed Cain.

FORTY-FIVE

Charlie Hayes slammed open the sliding glass door out to the deck on the senator's mansion. Miguel disengaged his call with Tim. He studied the man and would have dismissed him entirely if the little puke hadn't brought backup. Two senior members of the senator's security guards stood on either side of Charlie as if they were *his* bodyguards. Miguel realized he was the new kid on the block, and they were still sizing him up.

"Russ, Rich, what's up?" Miguel asked. He intentionally bypassed Charlie. He'd never disguised his contempt for the weasel. Charlie was in charge of soliciting the major donors for Shearer. When he courted Rafael Houseman, the billionaire, for donations, Charlie had drawn FBI attention. Houseman had bought himself a lot of high-up political protection by his contributions, notwithstanding his penchant for underage girls. They knew he trafficked children internationally from his private island, but his island was not under FBI jurisdiction.

Once, months ago, Miguel was determined to get his SEAL team members back together for a surprise raid, but Cain had stopped him. He had reasoned that it was better to have patience than to become an international outlaw.

Charlie was suspicious, so Miguel played it cool, but the whole time, he observed his surroundings, mapping in his mind an avenue of escape if this suddenly turned to shit. He casually unbuttoned his overcoat, putting the .40-caliber Sig Sauer pistol stuffed into his waistband within easy reach. To cover, he reached into his shirt pocket and took out a square of gum from an Ice Cubes pack. He offered it all around. All three declined.

"Who were you talking to?" Charlie demanded. Risky, since he was a skinny, four-eyed, punk and Miguel was itching to kick his ass.

Miguel let a half smile slide across his lips. No reason to lie. "Our neighbor, Tim McAndrews. I noticed a guy jimmying open his gate while on my rounds and reported it to him." He motioned with his hand for them to look.

Charlie walked to the deck railing. Below on the St. Clair driveway, an arrest was playing out, and the red and blue lights from the sheriff's Jeep danced across the snow. Charlie's friends didn't bother to look. They just stared at Miguel, watched his every move. Miguel popped his gum, making sure it was plenty annoying. He knew it covered up his worry and added to his false image of careless bravado. Miguel was anything but careless and had a sinking feeling his status as undercover FBI was compromised. He began to size up his adversaries. Charlie was a gnat; one swat, and he'd be cowering in a corner. But these other guys, if this went south—Miguel began to prepare himself for some serious pain. He licked his lips. He would use the bigger guy's weight against him. He'd watched him long enough to know he lacked agility and intimidated with size alone. The other guy was close to Miguel's size and abilities and was practically vibrating with nervous energy. He felt he was looking at a hair trigger on a loaded gun. Cool heads needed to prevail.

"How do you have McAndrews's phone number?" Charlie didn't turn around. But his tone was wary and unsettling. Russ and Rich took one step closer. "Is he a friend of yours?"

Miguel heard the implication loud and clear. Charlie knew McAndrews was on Elias Cain's team. Had he made the small leap in logic to Miguel being an agent with the FBI? He forced himself to keep calm. They didn't trust him, and he needed to change that.

"McAndrews? He seems nice enough; I just met him. I'm longtime friends with Daniela St. Clair. Our fathers were friends," Miguel answered honestly and watched for a reaction. He hoped the money connection would ease the tension. Charlie Hayes was always grubbing for money and status. Dani St. Clair had both.

Charlie spun his face open with surprise. Better than he expected, Miguel mused.

"So, when I saw the guy messing with the gate, I called the sheriff and McAndrews. Just think of me as your local neighborhood watch." Miguel chuckled, drawing them in. "Besides, who knows what the guy was up to? With the party coming up tomorrow night, he could've been setting up shop next door with plans to do the senator harm. I thought it best to get rid of him."

Charlie stood blinking at Miguel. Miguel sensed the wheels were turning. Charlie was weighing this encounter; was Miguel FBI or was he genuinely private security? The scales were momentarily in balance, and then Miguel could see them tipping in his favor. A sly smile crossed Charlie's thin lips.

"Good job. Good thinking, Miguel." Charlie reached out

and patted him on the shoulder as he passed by. Russ relaxed and gifted him with a big smile. Rich, on the other hand, tipped his head slightly sideways and lifted one eyebrow.

"Watch your step," Rich warned when Charlie and Russ were out of earshot.

"Always," Miguel answered back, intentionally snapping his gum. Until Rich turned and walked away, Miguel allowed a congenial smile to remain planted on his face. When Rich was gone, Miguel knew he had to get a message to Cain. He wasn't convinced and suspected they were on to him. And Charlie, well, Charlie had just removed all doubt that he was guilty as hell—of something.

FORTY-SIX

Buddy Shearer looked up as Charlie zipped into his office, closed the door behind him, and slipped into the chair beside Shearer's desk. He didn't ask any questions but gave Charlie that what's-up stare he was very familiar with.

"Miguel caught a man trying to break into the St. Clair's estate. The police are there. He was concerned that the guy was setting up for a hit on the party tomorrow night," Charlie reported. He was skeptical of Miguel's story. There was something about Miguel he didn't like. The man was too self-assured, too professional, too competent, and too willing to prove his worth. None of the other guards had even noticed the attempted break-in next door. Why was he questioning the integrity of the one man doing the job he was hired to do? He knew he shouldn't be. It might be just that: Miguel was doing the job he was hired for.

"And what do you think?" Shearer leveled an icy gaze in his direction.

"We should double the security, just in case." Charlie was hesitant. Did he believe that the criminal breaking into the St. Clair estate meant them harm? No. But could it be true? Yes. There was so much political division; it was almost as if with minimal provocation, the whole country could erupt into a second civil war. And with the president attending the party to give Shearer his endorsement, it was critical to take everything seriously.

"But?"

"But I don't trust Miguel. There's something about him."

"He came highly recommended. Blackhawk Security said he's one of the best in the business," Shearer defended. Charlie knew Shearer was afraid. His politics made him fair game for all sorts of crazies. The baseball practice shooting of a Republican congressman had both parties acutely aware of the danger of not tolerating free speech and not allowing the free expression of opposing views. Gone were the days of civilized debate. Now it was a milieu of clearly drawn sides. Black and white, right and wrong, with both sides claiming the upper ground.

To be clear, the senator's upcoming equinox celebration was the perfect time and his mansion the perfect place to take out a whole bunch of people of the senator's political persuasion.

"He spotted and diffused potential danger without causing any commotion. That's a good thing, isn't it?" Shearer asked.

"Maybe. But he's in contact with McAndrews. And I just found out through sources that McAndrews is one of Cain's boys," Charlie said. Cain and Shearer detested each other. Especially when he didn't give one of Shearer's best contributors a break when charged in a child sex-abuse scandal. Cain didn't understand how much it cost Shearer emotionally to ask for it. And how much it cost him financially when he couldn't deliver on his promise.

"Cain's? McAndrews said he was an ADA with Goddard

in King County," Shearer protested, but not too strongly. Charlie could see he was worried.

"He is that too. But he's on a leave of absence after shooting and killing a man attempting a home invasion—his home. Goddard loaned him to Cain for several months, until the leave of absence is up. I confirmed it with Mo. Mo said McAndrews was a good prosecutor but too much by the book. The man still believes in God, family, and the American way." Charlie snickered at the thought and picked up on Shearer's smirk. Politics was a dirty business. Shearer used to believe in those things too. Probably when he was McAndrews's age, before reality and his obsession with the power of the presidency took hold. Charlie never did. He only ever believed in power.

Charlie stared at Buddy Shearer's handsome face. He had to admit he envied Shearer's camera-perfect, movie star, good looks. If he'd had his looks, he would've run for the senate himself and dropped his position as chief of staff. Shearer's looks were their only edge over the other candidates vying for the party's nomination. And after they won, he, Charlie Hayes, would be known as the real power behind a President Shearer.

"I understand through my sources that Cain's profiling team is working on some big case." He looked down at his fingernails and then back up to meet Shearer's glare.

"What big case? Should we know? It's not that attempted kidnapping, is it? Would it be useful? Better yet, can we make it useful?" Shearer asked, leaning forward across his desk. Charlie sat back in his chair, contemplating the questions. "Can we twist the information to our advantage and get the press to make us heroes?" Shearer added.

Of course, it would make a difference. To present Shearer as a hero, helping to break open a criminal case of national importance would make him unbeatable. But no one, not even his source, was talking about the subject of their investigation, which left Charlie wondering about the attempted kidnapping. It was all hush-hush. Briefly, he wondered if they'd linked it to him. He dismissed it. The FBI had looked into other child abductions carelessly linked to him and found nothing. He'd covered his tracks this time too. They could speculate all they wanted. But there was no direct evidence he'd ever done anything wrong.

"I'll find out. I have sources."

"What about Sheriff Woband? You have to remind him of how much money I've paid him. And how much money we've contributed to *his* reelection." Shearer scowled. "Get down to the sheriff's station and find out what this is all about," Shearer commanded.

"Woband's gone soft. He's not talking and said he wouldn't even if we cut our contributions. Something spooked him. McAndrews, perhaps? Mo claims he's like a dog with a juicy bone. Once on a case, he won't let it go," Charlie added.

"Smart, tenacious, and married to money. Makes him almost untouchable. Find something. And invite that reporter, Beebe Knoll, to our party tomorrow night. She strikes me as the ambitious type."

"As for Miss Knoll, ambitious?" Charlie repeated slowly. "She's ruthless and infinitely corruptible. But what about Miguel? I still don't trust him."

"Keep an eye on him. If he's doing something he shouldn't be, something against us, we'll find it soon enough."

"And then?"

"Then he can have a tragic accident, or he can find the stress of life to be too much, if you know what I mean," Shearer said. "And if they are big friends, Miguel and McAndrews, maybe they can have an accident together."

FORTY-SEVEN

Warm and dry, Tim stood in the small viewing space outside the main interrogation room in front of the two-way mirror at the Bonner County Sheriff's Office. Like the rest of the building, everything was gray-painted cinder block. Samuel Graden sat beside a battle-scarred table. The scuffed surface had been created by handcuffs raking across the wood as the police interviewed suspects. Still cuffed and wet from his wrestling match with Tim in the snow, Graden shivered. At least someone in the sheriff's department had the kindness and courtesy to throw a wool blanket around his shoulders. Tim almost enjoyed watching the man fidget impatiently. It was intentional—making him stew for a while. They wanted him to imagine what was coming his way.

Tim waited for the evidence report to come from the crime lab. They were matching all they'd gathered earlier in the investigation to what they'd collected this evening from Graden's pockets. Duct tape tied together the murder of the abused twins, the abduction of Letisha Watson, and Chloe's. Now all they had to do was link the physical evidence to Graden, and they had their man.

Tim looked forward to having Scott back from Seattle. Just after Graden's arrest, Mitch took the jet to pick him up. Scott was a master at interrogation and obtaining confessions. He'd made a reputation for himself in the first year with Seattle PD. They realized they wasted his talents by leaving him on patrol. Scott claimed it was one of the reasons he was promoted so quickly to detective—that and the fact that he'd aced the test.

Tim could use Scott's input. Cain's team members hadn't warmed up to him, and he and Scott had always bounced ideas off each other. They'd played at solving mysteries since they were kids. He remembered unraveling the mystery of who was poisoning the neighborhood pets when they were ten. The culprit was Johnny Mitigan, a crazy kid and bully who, as it turned out, was currently serving a life sentence for arson that resulted in the death of two unsuspecting teens.

Tim's confidence sagged as he stared at Graden, shifting around on the uncomfortable chair. Tim knew he was good at courtroom drama. He could play on the emotions of a jury and lead them where he needed them to go with the best of them, but interrogation was a little outside his circle of experience.

Jeff walked up to Tim and handed him the rap sheet he'd just pulled off the printer. Tim glanced through Graden's offenses. Felony possession of a controlled substance and felony intent to distribute, listed over and over. He remembered his first impression at the hospital. But half of the charges were in King County, Washington, the other half in Sonoma County, California. Tim bit at his bottom lip. He knew he'd seen this guy before; now the where was coming back to him. He looked for the ADA that tried each Washington case. Mo. His shoulders slumped slightly in disbelief. Mohammad Rashad had tried each King County case. So, why was this guy out? His last conviction was three years ago in King County, and he was sentenced to ten with no possibility of parole because he was a repeat. And yet here he was, cooling his heels in the Bonner County sheriff's interrogation room. Why was he out? Had he escaped? And when did he graduate to kidnapping? But more importantly, *why?*

Jeff parked himself next to Tim, studying his face and then joining him in observing Graden. Jeff crossed his arms in front of his chest.

Tim felt a tap on his right arm and turned to see Elias standing next to him. He handed him a venti Starbucks coffee.

"Evening." Cain smiled in greeting.

"Thanks, but don't you mean morning?" Tim noted the time on his watch. It was just after midnight. He took the coffee. Tim quickly got Cain up to speed.

"And this is the guy I saw yesterday at the hospital," Tim finished his report.

"Sandpoint PD found a Mercedes van behind a liquor store, near the hospital. Mint green with spray paint navy blue accents. One of the keys from Graden's pocket opened it. CSI is processing it now. The Honda he drove to your place—stolen," Cain said, watching Graden through the two-way.

Tim studied Cain's profile. He watched as a big grin passed quickly over his lips underneath the handlebar mustache.

"You didn't mention you'd seen anyone at the hospital at our meeting," Cain said, tipping his head slightly, almost scolding him.

Tim said matter-of-factly, "Can't exactly have a guy arrested for visiting a patient at a hospital."

"But he made you uneasy, didn't he?" Cain asked, turning and dropping his gaze directly into Tim's eyes.

"He did."

"Sometimes, you need to trust your gut." Cain rotated and watched the man behind the two-way. Graden began rattling the cuffs against the tabletop again.

"I don't think making me uneasy qualifies as a crime either."

"No. But when Betsy talked about the statistical age and the likelihood of the kidnapper being a construction worker, did you think of this guy?" Cain asked.

Tim turned and considered Cain. He wasn't accusing him of wrongdoing. Tim could tell by his slightly upturned lips. This was instruction in profiling instead.

Tim looked down at the floor and then back up, unflinchingly into Cain's eyes. "Yeah, I did."

A big grin broke out on Cain's face, and he nodded without explanation.

The sheriff walked up with sheets of paper in plastic protectors. "We have the prints back, and they are a match to Graden." He handed the plastic sheets to Tim. The first frames were color computer pictures of the prints found on the sticky side of the duct tape developed both by Sticky-Side Powder and Gentian Violet, followed by a page with the same images enhanced by the matching whorls, loops, and arches marked with red numbers. All three samples of duct tape possessed sticky-side prints. It was a common mistake Tim had seen before in more than one of his prosecution cases. Perps didn't realize they had touched the sticky side of the tape and that the police could get prints from the adhesive. And it was impossible to wipe down to remove them. Tim passed the picture on to Cain. Then the sheriff handed him a photo with three squares. The images were of the ends of the duct tape enlarged by the microscope. All the tape they had in evidence came from the same roll, and the ragged ends could be fitted together like pieces of a jigsaw puzzle. Tim's pulse throbbed up his carotid, and his heart pounded steady and hard in his chest. Graden was the kidnapper. No longer was there any doubt in Tim's mind; he'd come back for Chloe.

"We think he tore the tape with his teeth. CSI swabbed to collect DNA he might've left from his saliva." Cain lifted both eyebrows quickly as if hopeful. He took the sheet of evidence from Tim's hand.

Distracted, Tim stared at Graden. Why had he come back for Chloe? What was so important that he had to have this girl over any others? This unanswered question was the key to finding all the missing children.

"Let's confront him," Cain said to the sheriff. Tim started for the interrogation room door but paused.

"You aren't waiting for Scott?" Tim asked.

"Scott only has jurisdiction over the twins' case. He'll have plenty of time to get his questions answered."

Cain grabbed Tim's arm. He snapped his gaze to Cain's hand and then to his face. "Not you, Tim. You're too angry."

Tim felt his teeth clench together. He recognized Cain was right. It had become personal. Reluctantly, he stepped aside. He watched as the sheriff and Elias entered the room. He adjusted the volume on the speaker in the viewing area. He wasn't going to miss a word of this.

After they made introductions, Cain tossed a picture on the table. It was a picture from Dani's gate surveillance cameras of Graden disarming the electrical box. Graden sat back deep in his chair.

"So, Mr. Graden, I'm sure you understand why we have arrested you," Cain started, his deep voice rumbling calmly.

"All this for trespass?" he asked, lifting his cuffed hands for all to see, a superior grin on his face. He hadn't waited for the interrogators to ask the first question.

Cain set his elbows on the table between them and tented his fingers, tapping them slowly against his smile.

"Is that why you think you're here, trespassing?" There was an element of disbelief in Elias's tone.

Graden shifted. His smart-ass arrogance faded. He couldn't dispute the picture. Now, his mind was probably whirring through the other crimes he'd committed and compiling a mental list of other evidence they might have. He had to know they had him on the theft of the Honda.

"Mr. Graden, trust me, the FBI doesn't get involved with simple trespassing," Cain said softly.

Tim watched Graden's expression momentarily shift to apprehension, then return to smugness.

"The car keys we recovered from your jacket were to the Honda we found parked down the street from the St. Clair estate. Does that Honda belong to you, Mr. Graden?"

"I borrowed it from a friend."

"And that friend's name is?" Cain took out a small note pad and pen from his pocket. He looked across the table at Graden, expectant.

Silence.

Graden had no answer. He'd forgotten to look at the registration. He'd forgotten to cover his bases. Tim enjoyed watching the man's eyes darting back and forth as he tried to formulate a dodge.

"Joe Blow," Graden answered in an impertinent tone.

Cain lifted an eyebrow and twisted the corners of his black handlebar. "Joe Blow, huh. DMV records show that the car is owned by Candi Watts. My guess, Mr. Graden, is that when you saw the McAndrews leaving the hospital, you took Candi's car to follow them. Why did you do that?"

Cain was unaffected by Graden's attitude. He leveled a cold stare at Graden's face.

"Have you seen her? McAndrews, is that her name? She's one hottie."

Hearing Graden refer to Dani as a hottie made the simmering anger inside begin to boil. Tim shifted his stance and wiped his hands down his face.

"So, you followed her and broke into her place to do what?"

"I wanted to ask her for a date." Graden's disrespect was starting to grate on Cain. Tim could see it from the annoyance flashing from his eyes. Cain glanced at the sheriff.

Cain tossed a picture of a roll of duct tape on the table. "What were you going to use this for, Mr. Graden? Your date?"

Tim paced. The thought of Graden binding Dani or Chloe with duct tape made him sick. His heart rate and breathing had increased dramatically.

"Nothing. That's not mine."

Cain left his elbows on the table and rubbed his hands together, sliding them past each other palm to palm. He never let his gaze move from Graden's face. He waited until the man altered his weight against the back of his chair. He slapped the next picture onto the table. "Not yours? Then explain to me how we were able to recover your fingerprints from the tape. You want to know what I think?"

"Not really," Graden answered back.

"I'm not listening to your insolent answers anymore. You start telling us the truth," Woband warned. He stood and raised his arm to strike Graden across the face.

Cain stood and blocked the sheriff from assaulting Graden. "We don't do that in my interrogation room," Cain said heatedly, intimidating the sheriff with his size and deep voice. Cain shoved Woband toward the door as an amused Graden watched. "You want to stay in my interrogation, you keep it civil. Do you hear me?" Cain threatened. Woband lifted his arms in surrender. And just like that, the two seasoned professionals established a good cop, bad cop team. The sheriff sank back down into his seat. Tim chuckled. He wondered if they would be able to use the ruse tonight.

"Mr. Graden," Cain started again. "Do you understand how much trouble you are in?" Cain didn't wait for an answer. "Right now, you are under arrest for criminal trespass. That carries a penalty of six months in jail and up to a three-thousand-dollar fine." Graden shrugged his shoulders as if the sentence were nothing. Cain smiled and continued. "And grand theft for the stolen car. That carries a penalty of one to twenty years in the state pen. But when I found this baggie with duct tape, a piece of cotton, and a bottle of chloroform, I got the sinking feeling you were going to kidnap someone, not date them. Now you sit here telling me you were going to ask Mrs. McAndrews for a date." Cain's hard stare had Graden wriggling uncomfortably in his seat. "I think you were going to try to kidnap her or to try to retake Chloe Jeffers. That's what I think."

Graden shook his head no.

Cain tossed the next picture out, showing the microscopic match of the duct tape ends.

"See, we found this tape in your jacket pocket, and it matches the tape we found on an Arctic Cat snowmobile we located at a house belonging to Grace and Will Branson. And this tape is the piece you used to silence Chloe Jeffers, and with it, we discovered a cotton ball soaked in chloroform." The pieces were yin and yang to each other, a matching puzzle piece fitting exactly together. "The penalty in this state for kidnapping or conspiracy to kidnap is death." Cain left it there without explaining the other option of life without parole.

Through the two-way mirror, Tim watched Graden squirm

in his chair, his eyes darting back and forth as he tried to figure a way out. There was no escaping this. No way out.

"I want a lawyer," Graden demanded, his voice trembled with panic.

FORTY-EIGHT

Tim punched in the door code and heard the tumblers clicking open. He reset the lock and the alarm once through the door. The house was quiet except for the whir of the forced air heater pushing warm air and the light scent of cinnamon and baked apples through the vents around the house. The big clock in the foyer with a view of working gears moving the hands ticked off another minute. It was four fifteen in the morning. He removed his boots and walked in sock feet through the living room. The fireplace on the far wall glowed with a few remaining embers. Dani had left the Christmas tree's lights on to help him find his way. He tiptoed over to the small bar in a nook beside the dining room. He poured a shot of Pendleton Stampede whiskey and downed it in one burning swallow. He needed to take the edge off. The confession he'd hoped for from Graden didn't happen. It was always possible that a suspect would ask for a lawyer. They had prepared for that eventuality. He was disappointed but not deterred. Tomorrow the crime lab would send up their reports on the other evidence, and Scott would be here with his questions on the twins. *Patience*, Tim reminded himself. It was hard to have charity when they had so much evidence. But all of it still swirled without direction in his mind. There was more to this than they knew. Graden wasn't working alone. Besides the buyer, what was Dr. Van Hatten's role? Were the IV tracks on the inside of Van Hatten's left arm for drugs, or was the sick old pedophile playing at being some sort of vampire as Kandar had suggested?

And though Cain hadn't said a word, Tim wondered if he and Miguel believed Shearer was involved in child sex trafficking. Was that weasel Charlie Hayes involved? And how did Mo figure in? He had to have authorized Graden's release from prison. They had established he hadn't escaped. Tim needed sleep. He set the empty shot glass down on the bar, considered pouring another, but finally decided to pass. They would resume the interview once Graden's lawyer showed up later in the morning.

As he walked through the living room, he realized the girls had finished most of their decorating. The living room was glittery and magical, and it brought back memories of his childhood Christmases. He delighted in the thought that he and Dani would get to play Santa for Chloe. It chased all thoughts of Graden away. He could almost see the packages in bright paper stacked all around the base of the tree, waiting for Christmas morning.

Noiselessly, he ascended the carved log stairway to the second floor. For a moment, he hesitated. With care, he opened the door into the room Dani had given to Chloe as her own and peeked in. The light from the hallway illuminated the sweet scene. Chloe slept soundly on her queen-sized bed, snuggled down in her pink comforter. Her white-blonde locks spilled over the stuffed unicorn's back. She used TimTwo for her pillow. Tim wondered what she was going to do if she met up with Dani's real live horses. She'd be horse crazy. He snickered to himself. Maybe he could be a full-time father; the idea was growing on him. He slipped out of the room, not wanting to wake her, and went to his room.

Before he opened the door, he dialed down the brightness of the hall sconces at the switch by the bedroom until only a soft pink glow illuminated the passageway. He gently opened the door and let his eyes adjust to the darkness. The remaining embers in the fireplace barely tickled light on Dani's cheeks. For a moment, he didn't move. He wanted to stand there and look at her. She was nearly buried in the down comforter and hugged his pillow to her chest. Finally, exhaustion reminded him he needed rest, and his eyes were heavy. He undressed, leaving his clothes where they fell. He sat on the edge of the bed and carefully took the pillow from Dani. She moaned in protest and reached for it. He quickly slipped between the covers and scooted close to her. Briefly, she opened her eyes and smiled. She nestled up against his cool skin, bringing him her warmth. He was moved by emotion that left him in awe. He was so in love, and his girls were safe. Graden was behind bars. Still, this wasn't over. Tim slipped his arms around Dani and felt her kiss his shoulder. He closed his eyes and was instantly asleep.

Dani woke when Tim pulled his pillow away from her. Having him in person was so much better. She cuddled up to his side but was not surprised when he quickly fell asleep. Their vacation was in shambles. Tim was out until all hours chasing bad guys, but she was the mother she'd always wanted to be. Neither would be skiing in the coming daylight. She decided she'd extend their vacation for another week, if necessary.

The steady rise and fall of Tim's breathing comforted and

reassured her. She propped herself up on her elbow and studied his handsome face. His full lips were so kissable; if she wouldn't wake him, she'd do just that, kiss him. His face and body were sculpted with tough, masculine angles that left her feeling astonishingly feminine, even though she'd been the horsey one, the tomboy of her family. But what she admired at this moment was his confidence. He was self-assured but not arrogant. He was easy in his own skin. Once again, he'd stepped up to protect her, as he had every time he was needed. It was almost as if it were an innate duty Tim had willingly accepted. In this, he was a lot like her father had been. There were few men like Tim left. There were only soy boys that were so popular with her sisters and friends. No. Thanks. She'd take Tim. Tough and tender. All man. Pure sex.

She felt a twinge of guilt race through her system. She kept putting Tim in danger. She knew her wealth made her vulnerable to every kind of money-grubbing scum and villain on the planet. Finding out this new creep had followed them home reminded her she needed to hire full-time private security. She couldn't expect Tim to always rush to her aid, especially if he joined the FBI. He'd be out chasing bad guys all over the country. She had mixed emotions about that. On the one hand, she was proud of him. On the other, she was scared for him. Scared for herself. She never expected to feel this way about anyone. Needy and exposed, desperate for his love and touch, wanting to be his only one, and afraid of losing him; she fought her battles in silence. She knew what she promised. She was going to let him pursue the career of his choice by supporting him. She was going to let Tim be Tim. It was all of him she'd fallen for after all—all of him she adored.

Tim stirred and reached for her. And she surrendered, ready to let him envelop her against his warm skin and hold her in his protective arms.

FORTY-NINE

Graden shivered in the cold cell. The wool blankets didn't take away the chill or the disgusting smell of old, stale piss. He never wanted to be in a place like this again. But here he was. Sleep was impossible. He had a whopping case of the *you shouldn't haves*. Number one: he shouldn't have ever taken this gig in the first place. He could've served out his sentence and walked in four more years. Number two: he shouldn't have let what the doc did to the twins get to him. He'd always known this could happen to the children he'd taken, but still he wasn't ready for it. He'd reacted badly. He was pretty sure it wouldn't be long before the police connected him to Van Hatten's murder; they may have already. Number three: when this current kidnapping went south, he shouldn't have come back here to get the little girl, no matter if his employer offered him ten or twenty times his usual fee. No is a tiny word, easy to say; he should've said it. It would be a while before the cops found the second murders, but they'd be looking for the parents, once they figured out he'd done the doctor. Now, he sat here in the cold, in the dark, wondering what he was going to do.

He also knew his employers would find him. They had promised him that. But that wasn't necessarily a good thing. He didn't know who they were. They were rich and powerful; that much was obvious. And they would kill him in a heartbeat and in a way that couldn't be traced. He would be *suicided*. But sitting here against the wall, cold still seeping through the two wool blankets cocooning him and bars striping shadows across the floor, he could honestly say he wasn't ready to die. He kept dreaming of Gina, and the numbered bank account, and that tropical island. No. He wasn't prepared to die. He had to turn this around.

If the cops had found the keys to the stolen Honda, they'd found the keys to his van. And if they found the van, they'd find the gun, the bullet casings he'd collected at both murder scenes and deposited into the van's ashtray, and the burner phone. If the cops were smart, they'd be able to read the van's GPS and trace every single kidnapping he'd done in the last year since he bought the damned thing. He kept meaning to erase the history, but wishing he could was pointless now. What other evidence they'd find or had found, he couldn't imagine. It would be devastating, whatever it was. He sat, contemplating his fate for a good hour. He'd heard Idaho was one hard-ass state. They still had the death penalty for all sorts of crimes and weren't afraid to use it. He'd have to get his case moved to Washington. Inslee was as soft on crime as Newsom in California. He took in a deep breath. Maybe he could turn state's evidence and get witness protection. Did they do that kind of deal for murderers? The one thing he knew right now was this: if he was going down, he wasn't going down alone.

FIFTY

Beebe flipped through the channels on her hotel room TV one more time. At this hour in the morning, nothing was on. Sleepless, she'd broken down and watched the demonstration for the Copper Chef Indoor Grill twice. If she could've figured out how to charge it to her room, and McAndrews's credit card, she would've, twice.

Well, don't. Don't love me. His words kept repeating through her mind. Yeah, sure. Just turn off the love switch like flipping off a light. She remembered the look on his face. It was anger, it was surprise for sure, but what else was in the mix? Disgust? Disappointment? Shock that she'd say such a stupid thing as *I love you* to a happily married man. *Oh, God!* She covered her face with her pillow.

What was it about McAndrews anyway? So what if he was tall, blond, with Caribbean blue eyes, and a smile that stopped you in your tracks and left you speechless and quivering. So what if you could become the envy of all your college friends who had disparaged you throughout school, if they ever saw you walking along arm in arm with gorgeous Tim. So what if both of you could leapfrog your careers to the heights by working together. So what?

She threw the pillow off to the floor. She picked up the remote and flipped through the channels again. This was her life. She just found *another* demonstration of the Copper Chef Indoor Grill. She left the TV on that channel. She almost tossed the remote across the room, but it wasn't its fault. She turned and set it on the bedside table. It was then that she noticed the text message bubble on her phone. She must've been too enthralled with learning all about that damned grill. Was Tim telling her he'd changed his mind? Telling her he really did want her? She didn't recognize the number. He'd never texted her before, or called her for that matter, but it could be, couldn't it? Hope was one of the sickest emotions known in the human experience! Quickly, she opened her text message screen.

"Hi, Beebe, it's Charlie Hayes. If you have no plans tomorrow night, would you join us at a party at Senator Shearer's?"

The text was time-stamped at eleven o'clock last night. And she hadn't noticed it until now. Senator Shearer lived right next door to Tim. He'd be invited; well, Dani would be anyway, and Tim would tag along. And Miguel would be there. He was no slouch. He was quite good-looking, handsome, and fit—if she was honest with herself. She remembered his black hair, olive skin, big brown eyes, and beaming, white-teethed smile. Perfect jealousy material. Wasn't there a flashy, red, strapless, sequined gown in the Selkirk Lodge Ladies' Shop? And wasn't there also a pair of ruby red slippers to match? Yes. Maybe they were magic. She could try one night without the blue walking cast, couldn't she?

Beebe propped herself up in her king-sized bed. A plan was forming in her mind. A sparkling red dress that hugged every curve, and Miguel might make McAndrews jealous. It just might work.

Beebe typed in all caps in her text message box and pressed send.

"YES! I'D LOVE TO COME."

FIFTY-ONE

Scott waited for Tim at the Bonner County Sheriff's Office. When Tim walked behind the duty officer's counter and saw him sitting beside Bob's desk, he felt a wave of relief. He needed to bounce some of his theories off his best friend, to make certain he was on the right track. Tim carried the molded cardboard tray of six coffees from Starbucks he brought to share. He set it on the edge of the desk and wiped his fingers down his jeans, cleaning off the small dribble of spilled coffee. Jeff walked over and grabbed one.

"Morning," Tim greeted everyone, grinning, especially at Scott. The detective greeted him back with a slight bow of his head. "Elias here?" Tim asked as he looked around the busy office.

"Not yet," Bob said. "Graden is still in with counsel." He rolled his eyes.

Tim studied him. "That bad? Who's counsel?"

"Johnny Stiles. Public defender, extraordinaire." Jeff laughed. "Total idiot and arrogant."

"Great combination," Tim said, breathing out. "Anything new on the twins' case?" Scott flashed him an almost imperceptible no by a slight side-to-side of his head. He didn't want Tim to ask anything about the twins here in the station. Maybe Scott believed their dirty cop hypothesis was true.

"What twins' case?" Bob asked, interested.

"Oh, nothing. Just a murder back home in Seattle," Scott said dismissively. "You had breakfast?" Scott asked, holding Tim's gaze.

"No. Want to go?" Tim understood Scott trusted no one else. That set Tim on edge. Tim didn't want to suspect the deputies, but they had to be cautious. They couldn't trust anyone until they had proof otherwise. "Let's go then. There's a greasy spoon just a short walk from here."

"You guys can call us when Graden is ready to talk to us, right?" Scott asked.

"Sure," Jeff answered. "Oh, hey, can you bring me back one of Justine's glazed doughnuts? I love those things."

"Will do. Can you tell Elias where we are when he gets here? I don't want him thinking I'm slumming." Tim smiled. As the two men turned to go, Tim glanced up at the three interrogation rooms and Woband's private office elevated one step up from the main floor. Shearer and his weasel, Charlie Hayes, entered Woband's private office. Tim felt instant disquiet. Now, if something dirty was going down, there's where they'd find it. He glanced at his watch; it was eight thirty.

"What would a prominent senator and his top sycophant be doing here this early in the morning?" he asked quietly to Scott. *Interesting.*

As they continued walking toward the exit, Tim realized that Shearer had spotted him.

"Oh, hey, Tim," Shearer called out, disengaged with Hayes and the sheriff to stop him before he and Scott could leave.

"Senator," Tim greeted him. "You remember Detective Renton?"

"Yes, of course." He reached out and briefly clasped Scott's hand and pumped it once, then disregarded him, snaking his arm over Tim's shoulder and guiding him to an unoccupied part of the office near the last interrogation room. Tim looked back at Scott and caught his surprise. When he and the senator were out of earshot, Shearer started to stare at him with a big, fake-ass grin on his face. Tim couldn't help but recoil. "So, Tim, I hear you have been loaned to Elias Cain's criminal profiling unit."

Tim wasn't happy. Who'd leaked that? He glanced around the office, trying to peg the culprit. "Yes," he answered. Though Shearer's face begged for an explanation, Tim wasn't going to give him one. Charlie Hayes had surely researched him and left no stone unturned.

After a long pause, Shearer said, "I also understand you've had a break in the case I arranged the collaboration on with King County. Is that right?"

Graden's arrest was public record. Though it wasn't in the paper, it was on the department's media flyer. It would be in the paper when the editor decided it was news.

"Yes," Tim said. It was pointless to keep it to himself when the sheriff was going to tell Shearer in seconds anyway.

"Can you tell me what's going on?" Shearer asked, almost breathlessly. He set his hand on Tim's forearm as if they were friends. Tim looked down at his hand and back up to his face. Shearer immediately withdrew his hand.

"With all due respect, sir, shouldn't you be addressing this question to Sheriff Woband? I am an outsider." There was the issue of jurisdiction to consider. And Shearer hadn't gotten the memo. Tim kept all his cards very tight to the vest. He was no leaker.

"I hear that *you* were very much involved." He grinned, patting Tim on the shoulder. "Once again, you give the credit to others. This modesty of yours ..." Tim wondered where he'd heard that before talking to Woband.

"Sir, it's not modesty. I'm married to Dani St. Clair. For her sake, I'd prefer to keep her out of the press. The reporters seem always to attach me to her, and she's had more than her share of—unkind press. They tend to hound her. I'm sure you can understand." Tim looked boldly into Shearer's eyes, letting him know there would be no negotiation on the matter.

"Modest and noble. That's refreshing." Shearer didn't mean the compliment. He was pissed. The pupils of his eyes had tightened and were jet black with anger. Tim knew that what he was going to say next would add fuel to the smoldering fire. He also knew Shearer wouldn't explode. Not here, not now.

"In addition, sir, Elias Cain is my boss. He may have more information for you than I do. I'm only one member of his team. Looks like he's arriving now. I'm sure he'd be better suited to answer your questions." Tim watched as Elias stripped off his overcoat. Behind him though, Beebe brushed wet snow from her boot and walking cast and brushed her jacket hood from her hair. She casually looked around the station and caught sight of Tim. Their eyes met for a second. She did a double take, then shot an indignant glance his way, snapping her chin up haughtily. Tim had hoped to get away before he was forced to have unpleasant encounters with the press. But now Beebe stood in the only path out of the building.

Shearer noticed the simmering hostility and smiled slyly. "Ah, looks like Miss Knoll is here. She's a very ambitious news reporter. Have you met her? Charming woman." He flicked his fingers, asking her to join them. Tim decided to be adult about this. He wasn't in the wrong by protecting his marriage to Dani. Beebe was. It irked him that she assumed he'd be disloyal.

"Buddy Shearer, how are you?" Beebe linked her arm under the senator's. She snubbed Tim entirely.

"Beebe, darling," Shearer gushed, slipping his arm around her shoulder. "Do you know Tim McAndrews?" Politicians had an innate ability to read people, or they wouldn't be where they were. Shearer was going to stir this pot because he could. He knew they knew each other. He'd seen them talking at the press conference two days ago. Tim wondered what Shearer was getting out of this. Maybe he just wanted Tim to squirm.

"We've met," Tim said simply, his expression blank, noncommittal, and unreadable. He didn't offer to shake her hand.

"Have we? I don't remember. McAndrews, is it?" She flipped her wrist in his direction, brushing him off as if he were a mosquito. "So, Senator, what brings you to the sheriff's department?" She quickly took both of the senator's hands in hers and tried to change the subject. Still, hurt and anger sparked from her eyes when she looked at Tim.

From *undying love* to *do I know you?* in less than twenty-four hours. Tim stifled a laugh. He thought about coming up with a barbed retort, but he didn't care enough to think one up. Giving Shearer any ammunition to use against him with Dani was also dangerous. Tim had seen how the man wanted his wife. His best choice was to make himself scarce.

Tim smiled. "Well, if you'll excuse me, Senator, Miss Knoll, I have a meeting with Detective Renton."

"Will you and Dani be coming to my party tonight?" Shearer asked as Tim turned to leave. "At the last second, President Trenton has decided to attend, and I'm trying to coordinate with local law enforcement. It's going to be exciting. He'll be staying on a few days to ski." Shearer was beaming.

"Yes, sir. Thank you for the invitation." He shook hands with the senator. Tim couldn't get away fast enough. But now what was left of his ski vacation was going to be strained. He hoped the POTUS wasn't going to be skiing the same runs.

But as Tim spun on his heel to leave, he heard the senator say, "Miss Knoll, if you aren't doing anything tonight, why don't you come to our party?"

"I received Mr. Hayes's texted invite last night. I'd love to come," she answered.

Tim rolled his eyes. The senator's party just went from bad to unbearable, and it hadn't even started yet. As Tim approached Scott, Elias intervened.

"Morning, Tim."

"Elias. I was heading out to breakfast with Scott. Care to join us?" The two men shook hands.

"Is that Shearer?" Elias asked, gears grinding behind his eyes.

"It is," Tim answered, watching Elias's smile resolve to stone.

"Yes, I'll join you. I guess you've heard; the president will be attending tonight's party. I hear he'll be endorsing Shearer's reelection for Senate. The media is all abuzz."

"Just now." Tim wondered how that would affect their investigation. The media would be distracted, for one, but law enforcement in this small community would be stretched to the limit.

The three men walked out of the station the short block to Justine's Diner. The place was decorated as a late 1950s' early 1960s' malt shop and teen afterschool hangout and was rumored to have the best burgers in town. The front half of a turquoise 1957 Chevy Coup jutted from the wall at the end of the malt counter. Elias sat in the teal upholstered booth across the table from Tim and Scott. They ordered coffee.

"Aren't you having food?" Scott asked, turning the dial on the jukebox located at the far edge of the table under the window. "Is this thing real?"

Tim reached in his pocket and pulled out a couple of quarters and set them on the table. "Try it. I ate at home; I just needed to get out of there."

Scott deposited the quarters and selected an Elvis Presley tune. The lyrics to "Jail House Rock" began.

"We have the CSI report on the van," Elias said. "You're not going to believe this. We found a .40-caliber Glock 23 under the front seat and another phone."

"A burner?" Scott asked.

"I assume so. He had another phone on him when he was arrested. His fingerprints are all over both items. The Glock is not registered to him but one Gina Basqin and has been recently fired."

"What about the tire prints at the Branson house?" Tim asked.

"I sent an inked set of the van's tires down to our tire print expert last night. I should have an answer by this afternoon," Elias commented. "Betsy and Kandar are working with the phone carrier on the burner to see if they can get into its call log and contact lists. They are recharging it. We want to see if anyone calls. We'll trace it by cell tower pings."

"I Fed Ex-ed the paint chips you gave me this morning to the Washington State Police Crime Lab. If they match, Graden pushed Dr. Van Hatten's BMW off into the blackberry brambles with his van." Scott stopped scrolling through the jukebox menu and readjusted himself in the booth. "The slug Kathy recovered from Van Hatten's skull was from a forty-caliber.

But it's so deformed we may not be able to match the rifling to any gun."

"Three rounds are missing from his clip. It was a nine rounder, and there are six bullets left," Elias said. "We found three shell casings in an ashtray."

Tim sat back in the booth and ran his thumb and index finger down his jawline. Graden had used one bullet on Van Hatten. The pedophile doc sought medical attention for the boys that he, himself, couldn't give. That one act put the whole operation on law enforcement radar. Graden had to get rid of him. The gun found in Graden's van was the right caliber weapon. He knew they could match the shell casings to the gun, and if there were any striations left on the severely deformed bullet from Van Hatten, any at all, the state police crime lab would be able to find it and match it, now that they could get a test fire.

Suddenly, it hit him, and he asked, "Has anyone located Chloe's foster parents?"

Elias bit at his bottom lip. Scott turned to look at Tim, confused.

"Why would you ask that?" Scott wrapped his hand around his mug of coffee and lifted it to his lips. "Didn't they just abandon her?"

Tim answered, "Maybe, maybe not. If Graden killed Van Hatten, why wouldn't he kill again? We need an all-out search for them."

"Good point," Elias said.

"I think it's time you tell me why Miguel is undercover," Tim stated, staring into Elias's eyes.

Elias didn't blink. Tim knew he was considering the consequences, probably worried about leaks.

"Scott's safe. I trust him completely," Tim said, adding the needed reassurance.

Scott smiled.

Elias cleared his throat. "You're right. It's time. As you know, one of Shearer's megadonors is Rafael Houseman. I was just informed his jet landed in Spokane an hour ago. He and a small entourage are en route to the senator's mansion as we speak."

"*The* Rafael Houseman?" Scott's eyes widened in disbelief, and Tim sat forward. The man was a known billionaire and a suspected pedophile.

Elias bobbed his head in the affirmative. "The one and only. Anyway, Houseman owns a small island off South America. Isla de Casa Hombre. We've been investigating him for years. We know he's been using underage girls as prostitutes on his island. We suspect he's been providing these girls to high-profile government officials when he jets them to his island. We fear these high-profile officials have been compromised. They could be blackmailed for—who knows what. Then it's government secrets to the highest bidder?" Cain let the information stew for a second. Tim couldn't stop his stare from boring into Cain's eyes. His simple vacation had flipped from fun to international intrigue in the blink of an eye. "We get close to an arrest, and he slides off to his island, where we have no jurisdiction. In my opinion, he's bought protection from men like Shearer when they accept his donations, and he keeps them in line by the threat of exposure. Blackmail. We believe Hayes, at the very least, has been arranging the trafficking of children to Houseman. We suspect Houseman is picking up a load of kids to take to his island."

Tim had heard about Isla de Casa Hombre in rumor and conspiracy theories. But when linked up with Cain's pocketful of missing children cards, he felt dread sweep over him like a dark shadow following the flight of a carrion bird across a hayfield. One of the disturbing allegations was that many of the Haitian earthquake victims, young orphans, had ended up on the island as sex slaves. He looked at Scott swallowing back his disgust. Was that the end game they'd planned for Chloe? Every memory of the little girl safe in Dani's care looped through his mind. He whispered a prayer of thanksgiving.

"What about Shearer? Is he involved in this?" Tim asked incredulously.

"Maybe," Elias said.

"The president?" Tim felt sick, having to ask the question.

Elias gritted his teeth, drawing in a breath. "What better way to distract law enforcement than to have them all chasing their tails over the president?"

"Where are the kids being held? Do you know?" Tim asked.

"We don't know. We followed Hayes and two bodyguards to a little house in Sandpoint. But Miguel says there are rumors swirling amongst the bodyguards that there is a secret wine cellar in the senator's house. He hasn't been able to find it. They won't let him out of their sight. They don't trust him."

"Is he safe?" Tim asked, worried.

"So far." Elias sipped from his mug of coffee.

Just then, Elias's phone began to ring in his pocket. He scrambled to remove it. "Cain," he answered. As the voice on the other end spoke, his brow puckered, and he looked at the men across from him one at a time. Finally, he disengaged. "Graden's ready to talk with us. Let's go finish that interview."

The men left their food, paid, and walked back to the sheriff's station.

"Tim." Cain pulled him aside before going back in the Station. "You and Dani are going to the senator's party tonight, right?"

Tim nodded.

"I want you to give Miguel a hand. Keep your eyes and

ears wide open," Cain said in a throaty whisper. "Miguel will set you up once you're in the party with surveillance gear and a pistol. Because of the president, security will be extra tight. But if Houseman is transporting the children tonight, we've got to get him before he gets to the safety of his island."

Tim felt wholly inadequate. He'd never done any undercover work. But with the feelings of ineptitude was a thrill. He felt a small grin turn up his lips. His new job was going to be very exciting.

Tim joined Jeff outside of the interrogation room, handed him a white bag containing his doughnut, and watched as Scott, Woband, and Elias entered the room. Graden was a very different man this morning. The cockiness was gone. He leaned forward in his chair as if ready to negotiate. His attorney, Johnny Stiles, took a seat next to Graden. Stiles was the poster boy for public defenders: pasty white, curly, unkempt brown hair, horn-rimmed glasses, and a cheap brown suit. He looked confused, in over his head, a just-off-the-turnip-truck graduate from law school. Tim remembered feeling the way he looked. Just then, Aaron Raines rushed into the viewing room. He was the assistant DA assigned to the case from Bonner County. He was just as disheveled as Stiles. Tim was suddenly grateful for Scott and Kathy. This poor guy was scrambling to get up to speed, and Tim had always been in on his cases from the start.

The sheriff took care of the formalities and informed Graden his answers were going to be recorded and obtained consent.

"Good morning, Mr. Graden," Elias started. "I understand you wanted to talk to me?"

Stiles immediately waved his hand, silencing Graden. "My client is willing to tell you everything he knows; we understand the weight of the evidence you have against him. He will expect some leniency in exchange."

"Okay." Cain motioned for the DA to enter the interrogation room. "Shall we start at the beginning?" Elias smiled and seemed to radiate a genuine warmth that Graden didn't deserve.

"I was set up," Graden blurted out. *Sure,* Tim thought, *they all say that.* But he was still going to listen to the man's story.

"There was this prison guard, Steven Washburn." Graden spat his name with contempt. "He said he knew a way to get me out of jail." Graden looked up into Cain's eyes. Tim noticed something he seldom saw in jailhouse interviews. He scooted forward to the edge of his chair, resting his elbows on his knees. Graden had his full attention. The man was telling the truth.

FIFTY-TWO

Tim stood under the hot water in the shower, but no matter how many times he lathered up, he couldn't wash the filth of this case away. Graden had traded the innocence of children for a release from jail and money, lots of money. But after four long hours, they weren't much closer to busting up this trafficking ring. Tim knew they had a lot of work to do. Scott was on his way back to Seattle to pick up and interview Steven Washburn, the prison guard Graden had accused of setting up the whole thing. Tim didn't buy Washburn as the mastermind, but perhaps they could use him to go up the food chain.

Many of Tim's suspicions were confirmed. They, whoever they were, targeted foster children all under the age of eight. The foster parents were complicit. Elias notified the FBI field offices in each state where a kidnapping occurred, and the parents were going to be rounded up in simultaneous raids in the morning. Information from the parents would lead to other arrests.

Graden said he didn't know what the children were being used for. He was always instructed where to drop off the kids. Different each time. He didn't know of any central location where the children were being held. He did admit that more than once he'd delivered kids to Dr. Van Hatten. And dead men tell no tales.

Graden didn't confess to murdering Van Hatten, but there was so much circumstantial evidence, were Tim the DA, he could get a conviction without much effort.

But nothing they knew now answered the burning question: why? Why were these specific children targets of the ring? Graden divulged each child was prechosen, and he was given particulars on when and where to pick them up. Tim couldn't keep his thoughts from cycling through a litany of horrors. Were the kids all together? Could they be rescued? Was the ring local or international? Were the children being used as stars of kiddy porn? Sex slaves at Isla de Casa Hombre? Child brides or concubines for terrorist scum? Were the boys being used for Bacha Bazi? Tim was swept into waves of nausea. Childhood should be laughter, joy, riding bicycles down tree-lined streets, baseball, football, skiing, and after all the play, the kids should go home to loving and protective families. They should be secure knowing that they would be loved, fed, and cared for. That was the ideal. Tim knew reality was very different.

He had to find the children and set them free. He had to find out why; it was the key to everything.

Tim turned off the water and toweled himself dry. He shaved. Deep in thought, he slowly started to dress in the crisply pressed slacks, turtleneck, and sweater Dani had set out for him. He had no interest in going to tonight's party.

He wanted to stay home where he could protect his girls from all the terrors of this world. But Elias had pressed him to go. He was to wear a recording device that Miguel would supply. They needed to know what was happening at this party for two reasons. One, Rafael Houseman was attending. Was he also accepting delivery of the missing children? Two, the president of the United States was going and announcing his endorsement of Shearer this evening. If children were being trafficked by Shearer or any of his staff, it would reflect on the president, whose ratings were already in the toilet. He might even be implicated. Tim didn't care for the man, but this was even beyond imagining. All the same, if he was involved—no one was above the law. No one.

Overwhelmed by a sudden urge to make sure Chloe was safe, he tucked in his shirt, and as he did, he went to the end of the hallway, stood on the stair landing, and looked at the living room below. Chloe and Dani were sitting together in an overstuffed, oversized chair. Chloe was coloring in a unicorn book and making up stories about TimTwo. Marta, Mark's sister, sat across from them, fully engaged in Chloe's story, even adding snippets to it. Dani glanced up at him, held his gaze, and smiled.

"I guess I should go get ready for the party," Dani said, untangling herself and standing. She kissed Chloe on the top of her head and ran her fingers through her blonde hair. Tim felt the warmth of home and family all through him. The words of an old song played through his mind. *"Love was so good; it filled up all my needs."* For a moment, he wondered how he'd survived his single years. How did any man? When Dani reached the top of the stairs, he put his arm over her shoulder and walked with her back to the bedroom.

Tim sat on the edge of the bed, and as unbelievable as it seemed, it was just as sexy to watch her dress as undress. Maybe it was all in the knowing each layer he was going to get to take off her later.

"Do I look okay? You're staring." Dani made a runway turn in front of him. She was dressed in a pair of designer jeans covered with a spattering of glittering rhinestones, a Morganite pink cashmere turtleneck sweater that accented her curves in all the right places, and pink, ankle-high snow boots with a fluff of white fur at the top. She finished by putting on Morganite jewelry.

"I just like looking at you," he answered, grinning hungrily.

She sat down next to him. She brought her lips close to his, almost touching, as if she could say no to a kiss at any time. The tease was exquisite.

"Shall we go face the money grubbing?" she asked, laughter in her eyes.

"Let's skip it, stay here, and make love," he offered. Her lips barely touched his; he could feel the silky texture of her lip gloss sliding onto his mouth. It had the taste and scent of cherries. He could barely breathe; he wanted her so much. "Is that a yes we stay, or a let's go and get this over with?" he asked, hopefully.

"Stay," she said. This time the kiss was more profound, passionate. "But I promised."

"All right. Let's go and get this over with, quickly. Very quickly. I can't wait to get you home already," he said, laughing.

Dani agreed with a nod.

FIFTY-THREE

So this was what a room full of the beautiful people looked like. Tim recognized several of the senator's guests from their frequent appearances on cable news. Others he identified as tech moguls from Seattle and the Silicon Valley. Some were television and movie stars. The one-upmanship game was in full swing. Rich and powerful men paraded through the crowd with beautiful women and starlets on their arms, dripping with exquisite jewelry, wrinkle-free Botox smiles, and perfect, augmented breasts revealed by low-cleavage sweaters. Not to be outdone, older, wealthy, and powerful women were escorted by tan and buff young men, decked out in designer après-ski clothes, gold jewelry, and expensive watches. Everyone was armed with a drink in hand. Tim noticed he was garnering his share of stares. They all seemed to know Dani or at least who she was, as he expected. She was in their class, after all. And they were sizing him up because he was not.

A butler took their coats and hung them in an entryway

closet. Next up was a Secret Service pat-down and a stroll through a metal detector. The president would arrive soon. Press crews from all the major news networks milled around just outside the entryway in the cold.

Unlike Dani's cabin, the senator's mansion was decorated in a classical style. Antique, or at the very least Queen Anne re-production, chairs in pale green, printed silk lined the west wall of the ballroom. A table as long as the room was set up against the east wall full of every kind of hors d' oeuvres imaginable. Tuxedo-clad waiters with white gloves served champagne and mixed drinks off silver trays. At the end of the great hall, a mas-sive fireplace provided warmth and flickering romantic light that danced in reflection on the highly polished wood floor.

Tim grabbed a couple of glasses of champagne from a pass-ing waiter. He handed one to Dani. They clinked their glasses in a toast to each other and sipped, staring into each other's eyes a little too long. Dani linked her arm through his.

"I love you," she whispered.

Tim grinned. He guessed it didn't matter where he was if Dani was by his side. He noticed the small clique standing around with the senator suddenly turned and took notice of them. A couple of women looked him up and down. A hint of lust and evil mixed in their stares. Dani must've felt it too. She tightened her grasp on his arm. Shearer started toward them. But Miguel got there first.

"Hey, you came," Miguel said, pumping Tim's hand once in greeting. He pressed a small lapel pin discreetly into Tim's palm. Then he took both of Dani's and twirled her in a slow turn, positioning himself between Shearer and Tim. "You look beautiful."

Tim glanced at the pin. It looked like a Schweitzer Mountain tourist knickknack. He rolled the pin with his thumb and looked down. It wasn't solely a pin; it was a tiny digital camera and recording device. Tim forced himself not to react openly. Though Elias had told him about this, he got the feeling something had changed—changed for the worse.

"Want to see where I was when I noticed the guy breaking in last night?" Miguel asked, tipping his head toward the deck outside.

"Yeah," Tim answered. He knew Miguel would explain what was up with the camera. Tim took hold of Dani's hand, and the three headed out a set of French doors to the deck outside.

"Over here," Miguel said.

The deck was built from stone and surrounded by a four-foot solid-stone wall at least six inches thick. From the edge of the floor, Tim could see the main road to Dani's cabin, the driveway that meandered to the house through the copse of trees, and the electric gate. The men moved to the far end corner away from any view from inside or the surveillance cameras mounted under the eaves.

"Wow, thankfully you were on watch," Tim said, looking over the railing. What would've happened had Miguel not been there? Dani wandered off along the wall, looking over at her estate.

Miguel stood next to Tim and reached inside the pocket of his jacket. He slipped a small .380-caliber Colt semiauto into Tim's hand. It was in an ankle holster. In a low voice, Miguel said, "Something is going down, Tim. Going down and soon. Two white trucks arrived earlier. Looked like the caterer's trucks, but whatever they held as cargo wasn't off-loaded at the kitchen."

"The kids?" Tim asked.

"That's my guess. Either coming or going. I don't know which," Miguel whispered. "Vans are still here."

"Is the president involved?" Tim asked as he put his left

foot on a patio chair and strapped the gun into place inside his boot. He pulled his slacks down over it.

Miguel stared at Tim without words, his lips forming a tight line.

"What are they using the children for?" Tim asked quietly.

"Wish I knew. Maybe we can figure that out here, tonight." Miguel patted Tim's shoulder.

"Is that what you want me to do?" Tim asked. He needed direction.

"I've been here for days. Nothing out of the ordinary. One of the other guards reported that there's a wine cellar. I haven't been able to find it. Hayes doesn't trust me. Every time I try to explore, another guard shows up unannounced to help with my duties. Which leads me to believe there's something in that wine cellar—and it ain't priceless wine."

"Okay."

Suddenly, Miguel stiffened and pointed toward the tree. "And that's where you tackled that guy," he said at normal volume. Tim turned toward the door. Charlie Hayes stood there the shadow of suspicion constricting his pupils.

"Thank you again, Miguel," Tim said, catching Hayes's glare. "Dani, let's go back in. It's cold out here." Dani rejoined the men, and they started toward the ballroom. *Okay*, Tim thought. He could play a covert operator. Two mysterious white cargo vans, a hidden wine cellar, and a notorious pedo with a jet ready to transport the cargo to locations unknown— he was going to be busy during this party.

As a waiter passed by, he set his empty glass on the tray. He perused the room, and when he determined he was out of the view of the other guests, Tim positioned the pin just below the ribbed knit of the crew neck collar of his sweater. After a few seconds, he received a thumbs-up from Miguel. It was recording.

Dani started to say something but stopped short when Miguel made the *zip-it* sign by tracing an index finger quickly along his lips. Dani was smart and a cool customer when she needed to be. She grinned at him, then at Tim. Tim turned just as the senator approached his group.

"Tim, Dani, so good of you to come." Shearer beamed. The men shook hands. "You know Miguel? He's on my security detail." His dark glare immediately put Miguel in his place.

"I do," Dani said icily, letting Shearer know he'd just blundered. "Miguel's father is CEO of my Walla Walla Vineyards. We have been friends since we were kids. Miguel and I used to show horses together."

"Ah, I'm sorry, excuse me. They are signaling that President Trenton has arrived." The senator was distracted by the sizeable entourage at the entryway to his house. "May I catch up with you later? Duty calls."

"Of course," Dani said cheerfully and politely. After he left, the three stood staring at one another, almost as if stunned.

The moment of awkward silence was interrupted by the brazen entrance of Beebe. She shoved her way past Dani and into the circle of friends. She aggressively wrapped her arms around Miguel's neck and planted a big, wet kiss on his lips. Amused, Tim stepped back, allowing her room, and slipped his arm around Dani's shoulders. He read the surprise in Miguel's eyes. He wasn't expecting Beebe's show of affection. He put a stop to it after enjoying several seconds.

"Beebe, I'm on duty," Miguel scolded her playfully.

"Me too, darling. I've lined up an interview with the president later," Beebe said, wiggling her shoulders as if she were top dog. She jerked her chin up at Tim. He wasn't impressed.

"Can I find you another drink?" Tim asked Dani.

"Okay."

"Want to stick with champagne, or do you want something harder?"

A sly smile passed quickly over her lips. "Champagne for now, something hard later," she whispered to him. He briefly closed his eyes as a rush of desire surged.

"Okay, it's a deal," he promised. Dani tantalized him to distraction, only upping his need to get this party over with and go home.

"You're on duty, so nothing for you," he said to Miguel, laughing. "How about you, Beebe? Can I bring you a drink?" Tim offered, pleased that Beebe appeared to be moving on. Miguel was a great guy, though Tim had his reservations about Beebe.

"I'll have a Bombay Sapphire martini, *dirty*." Her glower challenged him to question her inference. He didn't.

Tim headed toward the bar at the far end of the room. He wove his way through the crowd. There were familiar faces, but he realized that he only recognized them from television interviews. He didn't travel in this circle, and neither did Dani. She was their equal but not a friend. As he moved close to the bar, a man turned with drinks in his hands. Tim decided to take his spot. It was Mo. He felt a chill run across his shoulders as they stood face-to-face. The fact that he was here set every suspicion whirling through Tim's mind.

"Hey, Mo." Tim cordially offered his hand. Mo set his drinks down on the bar and shook Tim's hand. "This is a surprise."

Mo retrieved his drinks. "McAndrews," he greeted him coldly, warily.

Tim read the reception for what it was. Mo didn't care for anyone at the office. The feeling was mutual. Tim knew Shearer was running for president in two years, even though he hadn't announced. Was Mo looking for a position in a Shearer administration? Undoubtedly. And now Mo presumed Tim was in the running for a job too. It couldn't be further from the truth.

"The surprise is actually that you are here. I didn't realize you followed politics. Especially Shearer's brand of politics." Mo didn't smile.

"I don't. We were invited because we're neighbors. My wife owns the house next door." Not that he owed Mo an explanation for his appearance at the party. "Well, I'd better get the drinks I promised. Good to see you."

"We'll catch up back in Seattle at the office," Mo offered, an interesting expression in his eyes. Tim nodded and watched as Mo walked away. Tim couldn't help but wonder if Mo's appearance had anything to do with Graden's arrest. Mo was the only ADA that could've negotiated his early release. Would he now be pulling strings to lessen the charges? He tried to squash the thought but couldn't. If Mo was involved, was Goddard? He didn't want to believe it of his mentor. He scrubbed his hand through his hair, trying to chase his apprehension away.

"Well, that was awkward. Mo is not your bestie I take it. Am I right, handsome?" Tim didn't recognize the voice and turned. "I'm Anita Brustow, and you are?"

"Tim McAndrews," he answered, automatically extending his hand to shake hers. She set her fingers gingerly on his palm and softly tickled his skin as she withdrew. The woman facing him from the barstool was the anchor of a highly successful cable news program: *Anita's America*. She was beautiful for a woman in her fifties. Her bottle-blonde hair curled softly at her chin line. Her brown eyes were intelligent and curious. Cosmetic surgery had kept most of the facial wrinkles away, but if she wanted to cover her age altogether, she should never have worn the low-cut sweater.

"McAndrews—ah, yes, you're Daniela St. Clair's

latest husband," she said in a dismissive tone, suggesting Dani changed husbands as regularly as he changed his socks. Anita lifted an eyebrow as she studied him, letting her gaze wander down his body and back up.

Tim hated women looking at him that way. He let a warning frown cross his lips and turned to the bartender. "Bombay Sapphire martini, dirty, and two glasses of champagne," he said. Then he turned back to Anita. "Yes. That's me. Dani's *new* husband." He handed her tone back to her.

She accused him by pointing a perfectly manicured index finger at him. The red glitter polish sparkled like flame under the soft lights. "You're the one who shot that serial killer, aren't you?" She parted her lips and closed her eyes with an expression that reminded him of tasting a perfect whiskey and knowing the harsh edges of a bad day were going to soon mellow. "What was it like—to kill a man?" Her eyes flashed hungrily.

Taken back, he said, "Not good, ma'am. If you'll excuse me." He lifted a palm and retreated.

"Don't get your feelings hurt. Why don't you come on my show? I'll interview you, and you can tell me and my audience all about it." She reached out, and he flinched back. Anita stole the olive from Beebe's martini and stirred the drink with the toothpick. Then, before taking a bite, she touched the olive to her lips, and they glistened, wet with gin. Had Dani done that, it would've driven him wild, but it was a turnoff coming from Anita.

"I'll give that some serious thought," he said with a measure of sarcasm, carefully juggling the three drinks in both hands.

She was not affected by his reply. "You do that, McAndrews. I'll be waiting with bated breath." She stood and flicked a card out of the pocket of her tight jeans. She started to give it to him and grinned as she noticed his hands were full. Slowly, she slipped the card into the front pocket of his sweater while watching his eyes. "Call me. Um, um, um, you are just delicious, aren't you? That Daniela St. Clair really can pick them." She sat back on her stool, tipped her head back, and laughed. "By the way, what brings you to this party? The treatments or the celebration?"

"Treatments?" Tim asked, suddenly curious.

"Parabiosis. The latest best thing next to Botox parties," Anita said.

"We're just neighbors, celebrating Christmas."

"Christmas? Not here, darlin'." She looked at him with a darkness that made his whole body recoil. "Be careful of what they offer you to drink at the celebration." Her eyes fluttered as if she were anticipating sex.

"You passing out roofies?" Tim asked cynically.

"I'll never tell. Whatever they pass out, find me if you take it." She laughed again.

Tim had never done drugs, and he wasn't going to start now. "Right. Excuse me."

Tim shook his head in disgust, turned, and headed back for Dani. Somehow, his path was suddenly blocked by a crowd of about ten women. They ogled him as though he was on the menu. He deliberately turned a three-sixty. Each woman leered hungrily at him as he met their gazes. What the hell did they do at these parties? *This is creepy*, he thought. The circle of women tightened around him. They didn't touch, but he felt they had undressed him.

After a few seconds, they parted, giving him a path out of their circle. He looked at the drinks in his hands and noticed that Anita had put the half-eaten olive back in Beebe's martini.

He quickly made his way back to Dani, Beebe, and Miguel. He handed out the drinks. He stared back at the crowd. It was almost as if a dark veil separated them from the rest of the party.

"What the hell, Jackass? Are you that hungry? You ate half my damn olive. There's a whole buffet table of food," Beebe complained. Deep in thought, Tim barely heard her.

"Are you all right?" Dani asked, running the back of her fingers down his cheek. He felt himself soften at her touch. He took a swallow of champagne and let his gaze drift to her eyes.

"Odd party," he answered.

"Odd people," Miguel said. "I've got to get back to work."

"Meet you for skiing in the morning? Nine o'clock?" Tim asked.

"You're on." Miguel went out of a French door to the deck outside.

"Can you ladies excuse me? Nature calls. Meet you at the buffet?" Tim asked cheerfully, leaning forward and kissing Dani on the cheek. He didn't exactly know where he was going, but questions swirled in his mind, and he needed quiet to answer them.

He pushed through the crowd and found a stairway up to the second floor. He set his empty champagne glass on the end circle of the dark cherry banister. He took two steps up and observed the crowd below him. The room was alive with chatter, laughter, and the clang and clatter of silverware against china. No one would notice his absence.

FIFTY-FOUR

Tim slipped the rest of the way up the stairs. When he reached the upper hall, all the doors along the way were closed. He carefully opened the first door. The dimly lit room was a vast library. He crept inside and silently pressed the door closed with his weight. He let his eyes adjust. At the far wall, there was a fireplace like most homes up here in the mountains. Bright orange and yellow flames played along the logs behind an etched glass screen. The whole wall on the east side of the room was filled with dark wood bookshelves and a collection of leather-bound volumes. The scent of leather and dust mixed on the air. In the center of the room, a grouping of a sofa, love seat, and matching chair, upholstered in a floral pattern in jewel tones, were all tied together by an antique oriental rug. Heavy, blood red, velvet drapes hung in pleats across the windows. He continued to explore. At the opposite end from the fireplace, he found another door. He opened it. It was an elegantly appointed bathroom. There was a sink, toilet, and a shower stall enclosed by an etched glass surround that matched the fireplace screen. He went in and closed the door and locked it. He shut the lid to the toilet, sat down, and took out his iPhone. He pressed the call button.

"Elias, I know you're listening. Put your ears on and turn up the volume," Tim said aloud, knowing the microphone would pick up the call. When his party answered, he quickly said, "Kathy, it's Tim." He put it on speaker. He wished he had earbuds, but he hadn't thought about bringing them to a party.

"Hey, how's vacation?"

"I'm at a party. Okay. Listen, I have a couple of questions. Tell me, what's parabiosis?" he asked, skipping the usual pleasantries.

"I thought you said you were at a party. Why? What kind of party is this?"

"I overheard a woman talking about it. Figured I should know what she was talking about."

"What made you think I'd know anything?"

"Sounded like a medical term to me. You're the smartest doctor I know." Flattery would get him what he needed. He truly believed she was the smartest doctor he knew.

"How much time do you have?"

"I've locked myself in a bathroom, so make it the CliffsNotes version. Someone might need to use it."

"All right. Give me a second. I'll need to think," Kathy said. She sighed and then continued. "Where to begin. Where to—okay. In 1864, physiologist Paul Bert paired the circulatory systems of two mice together: one old and one young. After he published the positive results in the medical journals of the time, rich, older elites began to take blood infusions from young people, mainly servants and the poor. Problem was they didn't understand blood typing at the time, and of course, that was a disaster. The intermingling of blood types caused so much death the practice was abandoned.

"But in the 1950s, the experiments were revived. Young mice and old mice were paired. Like today, people were searching for ways to extend life, maybe seeking eternal life. Anyway, the results were dramatic. All the failing systems of the older mice began to improve. Whether it was because the organs in the young mice were doing the heavy lifting for the failing organs in the old mice or whether the hormones, enzymes, and nutrients in the young mice blood were benefitting the old mice wasn't clear. Scientists discovered that it worked best when blood was extensively crossed and matched, and the donor and the recipient were genetically related. Less rejection. Since life was the goal rather than death. The work tapered off in the 1970s when it didn't produce the kind of results in humans they were hoping for.

"But like most bad ideas, the idea of parabiosis has been resurrected by rich moguls in Silicon Valley, politicians, movie stars, and anyone who can afford the treatments. Nowadays, the treatment is young blood plasma, rather than a whole blood transfusion. High-dollar pseudomedicine," Kathy finished.

"That was the short version?" He puffed out a breath. "Sounds like vampirism to me. Elizabeth Bathory stuff. What's the cost per treatment?" Tim asked. As fanciful as Kandar's *vampire* theory was, it was fleshing out. He shook off the shudder.

"I've heard about ten to fifty thou per treatment," Kathy answered.

Tim whistled. "Does it work?" He was curious.

"Jury is still out on that. There is no empirical evidence in humans—no clinical trials. Evidence is mostly anecdotal. But that hasn't stopped people from saying it's the latest, greatest, new cure-all—and relieving the desperate or delusional of their money. The positive results could be psychosomatic. You feel better because they tell you that you feel better, and you think you feel better," Kathy reported. "A couple of boutique clinics have sprouted."

"How much blood would you need for a treatment?"

"That's the problem. No one knows. The mice were paired by joining circulatory systems. That meant *all* of the young mouse's blood served the old mouse," Kathy answered. "As I said, these new clinics offer young blood plasma, not whole blood and certainly not circulatory system pairing. That would be unethical. See, though the old mice's lives were lengthened, the young mice's lives were shortened in the animal studies."

"What else? What else do I need to know?"

Kathy paused. She was thinking. "Ah, better results were obtained from younger mice. They had to be mature enough to accommodate the old mouse, but the younger, the better."

"How do the clinics guarantee the age of the plasma donor?" Tim asked. "So, if you want a four-year-old's blood versus a twelve-year-old's, do you pay more?"

"Now you're getting into the weeds. I have no idea. See, giving plasma is not illegal, but there are rules. You can donate plasma if you are eighteen and weigh one hundred ten pounds and are in good health. Whole blood is sixteen in some states; others require parental consent. One hundred to one hundred ten pounds is the norm, and of course, you must be in good health. I guess it all depends on how ethical the clinic is since the younger the donor, the better the outcomes—in theory, not proven."

"There's a black market for this. There has to be," Tim said, letting his thoughts spill out uncensored.

"Plasma has to be processed. The red cells, platelets, cryo, and such are separated. If it's black market, I think they'd use whole blood, or they'd have to have a laboratory to do the processing," Kathy answered.

"Can blood be transfused directly from the donor?"

"It can be; that's the way it was done in the past—donor artery to recipient's vein—but not so much anymore," she answered.

"How much blood does a child have inside compared to an adult? Does that make sense? Jesus, Kath, I don't even know what to ask," Tim said, frustrated. "If you were to guess, which works best, whole blood or plasma?"

"It's called blood volume," she teased. "I get what you're asking. Remember, I helped you and Scott get through physiology. A child around six will have a blood volume of about seven pints. An adult eight to thirteen pints," she answered. "My guess: whole blood would be best. You get the benefit of the hormones, nutrients, and enzymes carried in the plasma, plus the benefit of highly oxygenated young red blood cells. But that would only last for as long as the red cells live, about one hundred twenty days."

"So, you'd need a constant supply of young blood—children. And if they were already typed and cross-matched, the better. Do they blood type foster kids?" Tim could barely get the words out. He felt dizzy.

"Not a question I know the answer to. Tim, what's going on?"

"Say you donate blood. How long does it take to regenerate?" Tim asked.

"Twenty-four to forty-eight hours for plasma, four to six weeks for the red blood cells to recover. Tim, tell me what's going on."

"I wish I knew. My suspicions are horrible," he said. Could they be abducting children and using them over and over, holding on to them until their blood regenerated? Or are they just throwaways? "Now we're back to the question of how much blood does one treatment consist of?" he asked, mostly to himself.

"There is no—no one knows. The mice systems were paired; the old mouse was using it *all.* Where are you going with this, Tim? I don't think I like where you're going with this." Tim could hear a tremor in her voice. "What kind of party is this? What's going on?"

"Kath, don't fall apart on me. I need you to help me think this through."

"The twins, do you think ...? Wait, are you asking me if the twins could've been used for this? My God!" She paused momentarily. "Of course they could've been used for this. My God! That's what those vein punctures were. I thought they—I assumed the twins were given IV drugs. I think I'm going to be sick." She panted into the phone. He could hear her sniff. Tim felt heaviness in his chest. He knew her eyes were filling. He could visualize her fighting back the tears. The thought was unimaginable. When he put Chloe in the twins' stead—he swallowed hard. He took in a deep breath, forcing control, and let anger make him man up.

"Kath, you okay? I have to ask one more question."

"No. I'm not. But go ahead and ask away," she said. The tremble in her voice was acute.

"Is there a way you can test Van Hatten's blood and see if it mixed with the twins' blood?"

"It's tricky. Red cells have no nucleus, so no DNA, but if he received whole, unprocessed blood, maybe."

"Test it. If we get nothing, we get nothing. If we get something, then that's what I need to know," Tim said with urgency. They agreed to talk as soon as she had results and disengaged. Tim realized he needed to get back to the party. And if they were doing what he feared, he wanted to get Dani the hell out of here. He stood and started to leave, turned back, and flushed the toilet in case someone was out in the study and had found his self-made SCIF, his sensitive compartmented information facility.

Once back in the library, he glanced around again. The fire had reduced to embers. He noticed a shadowy shape behind some draperies. It looked like a figure standing in the corner of the room with outstretched arms. He walked closer and pulled back the dark red velvet curtain. The same statue he'd seen at the Bransons' stared back at him with glowing ruby-red eyes. The pieces were fitting together. No doubt now. It was a statue of Moloch. After seeing the first statue, he'd extensively researched the Canaanite god on the internet. The ancient people had brutally sacrificed their children to the insatiable god.

Tim rubbed his brow. So, this is how it worked. He began to review his theory. Mo negotiated Graden's release in exchange for his agreement to kidnap the foster children. Graden handed the kids over to complicit doctors or techs, who then arranged to take their blood and sell it to waiting elites, hoping to gain eternal life or good health through parabiosis treatments. The kids could be used for other purposes too. Whatever brought the best price. The abducted children were, in theory, sacrificed to Moloch. Their young lives cut short to fill someone's insatiable lust and greed for the fountain of youth. His premise was so crazy he could hardly believe he was even thinking it. Scott's words resounded in his mind. *These kiddy things can be nasty. Like an octopus, tentacles reaching everywhere.*

Tim heard the door rattle behind him. He quickly ducked behind the curtain covering the bronze statue. Carefully, quietly, his eyes straining in the semidarkness, barely breathing, he watched as Charlie Hayes and two bodyguards entered the room. Charlie approached the bookshelves and pulled a book forward from the third shelf from the top. Tim counted it intentionally. He heard the whir of an electric motor. The bookcase rolled open, one shelf sliding behind the other. Charlie looked around the room, slipped inside, and disappeared with the two bodyguards following behind.

FIFTY-FIVE

Tim knew the tiny camera was recording everything for Elias. He imagined it even had infrared and night vision. Tim had to see where they were going and what was behind the secret door. He crept forward and observed the passageway. A concrete stairway spiraled downward. At first, he wanted to dash down the stairs to see if the children were kept somewhere below. But doing this alone would be incredibly dangerous. He could give his life for nothing, be caught, and not save the children. He had to slow down. Think. He had to get Miguel.

When he heard the scrape of footsteps on concrete stairs, he silently returned to his hiding place behind the statue and waited. Seconds passed. Charlie and the bodyguards emerged. They had a handcart full of wine and other liquor. It was a passageway to the wine cellar. Relief washed over him. He'd found the hidden wine cellar. He imagined the senator kept the room secret because he had a costly wine collection. After giving it some thought, he decided to explore anyway. He had to know if it was full of wine or held something else.

Tim counted thirty seconds, the way his father had taught him as a kid to tally the seconds between the flash of lightning and the sound of thunder. *One thousand one. One thousand two. One thousand three.* When assured Charlie Hayes wasn't returning, he slipped out from behind the bronze statue.

Carefully, he stole across the polished wood floor to the bookshelves. He calculated which book on the third shelf was the lever and touched the book he assumed would open the passageway. He tapped it with his fingers, not sure the electric motor could be heard and give him away. He hadn't noticed any security cameras but knew full well they could be hidden anywhere. When new out of college, he'd bought two for his place, one in a digital clock and one in a picture frame. They connected to his iPhone with a simple app. He could tell if anyone entered his place at any time. Curiosity had the better of him. No matter the danger, he had to explore. He placed his hands on the book's spine and pulled forward. If they caught him, he'd deal with that when or if it happened. In any case, if the children were here, he had to get them out. He would figure out how and when if that time came.

The motor quietly began to whir and slide the shelves, one behind the other, opening the passageway. Tim took a breath and entered. He determined how to open and close the entryway from the inside and then carefully proceeded down the gloomy stairs. At the bottom, a long hallway stretched out in front of him. There were doors on either side. To his left, he saw stainless steel ones that were reminiscent of a walk-in freezer; to the right directly across were saloon doors to the wine cellar. In the semidarkness, he saw countless bottles stacked in wine racks floor to ceiling. At first, he felt foolish but then began to wonder why you would hide or disguise the entry to food storage. Maybe it was an emergency shelter. He continued down the hallway.

The room next to the wine cellar was interesting. He tried the handle. Locked. He peered through the small window in the door, and in the shadows, he could make out microscopes, small racks of slides, medical centrifuges, and other equipment he didn't recognize. It was a laboratory. Was it to test the wine? Was it to type and match the donor and recipient blood or to filter whole blood to plasma? He took out his iPhone and snapped pictures. He continued.

The next room held six pairs of what looked like dentist chairs with a stainless steel table in between. On the side of each chair stood a pole with two arms stretching out, reminding him of the IV poles at a hospital. His heartbeat quickened. Gruesome images raced through his mind. Was this where the blood of kidnapped children was stolen to satiate the lust for eternity? He swallowed hard and took snapshots of this too. Sneaking on, he came to the last door and the hall's end. To his left, a corridor resumed and terminated at what looked like a loading dock. The concrete deck was closed to the outside by electric roll-down doors. Was this where the food and wine stores were delivered for the household? Or was it where abducted children became nothing more than a commodity?

Silently, he turned the handle to the last door on the right. It opened. He slipped inside. In the dim light from the hallway, he noticed two huge biomass incinerators. They could be used to convert household waste into electricity. But they were also the perfect size for disposing of bodies. Tim opened one of the incinerator's front door. One by one, the children's faces on Elias's cards scrolled through his mind. At the end of the reel, Tim was hyperventilating. Bending forward to catch his breath, he sank to the floor.

FIFTY-SIX

Beebe was nothing if not observant. Charlie Hayes whispered something in Shearer's ear, and the private security guards scampered throughout the ballroom, looking for someone. She wondered what was up and quickly found Miguel. Tipping her head, she asked him to step aside and talk to her. She hitched up her strapless gown and made her way to his side.

"What's going on?" she whispered, lifting her left eyebrow.

"Have you seen Tim?" Concern was etched all over Miguel's face.

Had she? Yes. She watched him slide mostly unseen up the stairs and enter the first door on the right. She assumed he was using the restroom.

"Um, not for a while," she lied. She had already made her plan. She would follow where she'd seen Tim last go. Get him alone. That thought made a sigh escape her lips. She tried to cover up with a smile.

"Yeah, okay. Let him know I'm looking for him if you see him. Gotta go," Miguel said his gaze dashing over the crowded ballroom. Something was going down. Something bad. Something involving Tim. Beebe watched until Miguel strolled out on to the deck through the French doors. She searched through the guests until she observed Dani chatting up President Trenton. Good. No. Great. At least the little wifey was occupied.

She wove her way through the gathering. At the bottom of the steps, she scanned the crowd. No one noticed her. She felt a half smile curl the right side of her mouth. She adjusted her red leather purse on her shoulder. Something was going down, and she was going to be a part of it. Beebe could barely keep herself from bounding up the stairs. But this was the first time since her skiing sprain without crutches, and she didn't want to go backward. Carefully, she removed her spike heels and carried them with her. Opportunity only knocks once, and this was her chance. In her imagination, she was already in his arms, and they were kissing, kissing like she'd seen him kiss Dani. It was unrealistic, but she had to try. Besides, Tim was always in the action. If nothing else, there would be a news story.

She reasoned Shearer's bodyguards were looking for Tim. They suspected him of doing something he shouldn't be. McAndrews? Naw. Never. No chance. But why would they be in such a secret frenzy? When she reached the top stair, she turned. When one of the guards looked up the stairs, she pressed herself against the left wall and into the shadow of the hallway, hoping he didn't see her. Oooh! This was fun. James Bond stuff. She felt the rush as her adrenaline surged.

Quickly, Beebe crossed the hall and slipped through the door to the room she'd watched Tim enter earlier. She softly pressed the door closed. Frozen for a second, Beebe let her sight adjust to the faintly lit room. She hunted for Tim as she slipped her heels back on. She frowned. She was all alone in this creepy room. The waning fire flickered shadows on the wall of bookcases. Damn it! He must've moved on when she wasn't paying attention. She started back for the door and stopped cold. The buzz of an electric motor stirred to life. The bookshelves began to move. She stumbled sideways and plopped down on the backrest of the sofa, watching. Tim emerged from the blackness, quickly turned, and fiddled with a book, causing the shelves to close.

"Well, well, well, Jackass. You found a secret passage," she said, mockery ringing in her voice. Tim wheeled around, surprise and concern scrawled all over his face.

"So, what's down there?" She grinned and stood, heading for the bookshelves. She adjusted her purse across her body.

"Don't. It's just wine." He shook his head. The look on his face was pained, serious.

"Just wine? Ahh, whatever it is has all the bodyguards in an uproar. They are all looking for you," she said, lifting both brows. "Did you steal a priceless bottle or what?"

Tim looked at the floor and back up into her eyes. Sorrow? Was that what she was reading? "Tell me, Tim."

He shook his head. "You don't want to know."

What was he thinking? Of course she wanted to know. She started to push her way past him. "Try me." When he didn't respond, she said, "Try and stop me."

He sidestepped and blocked her with his body. "Don't," he repeated, this time with more force. That made it irresistible. There was a story down there.

At that moment, she heard the doorknob rattle as it turned. Instinctively, she knew if they thought Tim had found the passageway, there was going to be trouble—big, capital T trouble.

"Kiss me, Tim. Kiss me like we're lovers." She threw herself in his arms and rolled up on to her tiptoes. Her lips found his as the light from the hallway spilled into the room. Every dream she'd had since the first day she'd seen Tim at the news conference a month ago, every flight of fancy, every imagining, every head-in-the-clouds musing came true in that kiss. His lips were deliciously soft, his aftershave heady, and she was dizzy with desire. She'd heard of women swooning in a man's arms. This had to be it. She surrendered to her emotions. She wanted to touch and explore every inch of him.

He backed away, his palms firmly on her shoulders, pushing her away and keeping her at his preferred distance. "Stop," he demanded.

Someone cleared their throat. "So, sorry. I didn't mean to intrude."

The look on Tim's face said it all. He didn't want her kiss. He never wanted her kiss.

Buddy Shearer stood in the doorway. Beebe couldn't even turn around and acknowledge him. Her eyes filled, and trickles started down her cheeks. She quickly wiped them away. She stared at Tim, begging him not to feel what she knew he felt.

"No. Excuse us. Miss Knoll was just leaving. Beebe?" Tim was clear. She needed to go. She could feel her cheeks flush hot. Quickly, she lowered her head and rushed from the room, not letting the senator see her tears.

FIFTY-SEVEN

Beautiful girl," Shearer commented after she'd gone. "Don't blame you one bit."

Tim didn't answer. Incredibly, Beebe had ignored him when he'd told her to leave him alone. He knew that her presence here in the library with him was enough to evoke suspicion of an affair. Her kiss was a problem—more than a problem. Shearer coveted Dani. Beebe had just handed him a cheater card to play.

"So, your bronze statue, is it Moloch?" Tim changed the subject, turning toward the bullheaded beast. He had to figure a way out of this.

"It is. Do you know about him? Charlie gave me the bronze as a gift when he came back from the Middle East," Shearer answered. He studied Tim as if trying to ascertain where he stood. "The artifacts' dealer said it was a valuable piece. The eyes are genuine rubies. Beautiful, isn't he?"

Tim ran his tongue along the front of his teeth. "The

Canaanites sacrificed their children to Moloch. Terrible might be a better description. My understanding is that they built a bonfire under him and burned their babies alive by placing them in his arms. They banged drums and played trumpets to keep the fathers from hearing their babies scream, changing their minds, and attempting a rescue. The Israelites were warned by God not to sacrifice their children to the fires of Moloch." Tim was squinting, forcing away the vile taste of evil.

Shocked, Shearer stared at Tim.

"I minored in history," Tim explained. "I've always been amazed at how superstitious man can be. And how wicked."

"Is that why you are in law enforcement? You see yourself as a hero, saving the day?" Shearer asked, a sneer coloring his voice. "Saving babies from the fires of Moloch?"

Tim couldn't determine if he was sarcastic because he was making fun of his goals, personally, or if he couldn't believe anyone would sacrifice a child to a false idol.

"Probably. I go after people who harm the most vulnerable in our society," Tim returned a challenge. He stood straight and looked Shearer in the eyes, not backing down. Shearer shifted his weight. For a moment, Tim thought he saw fear slide down his face like a cloud shadow passing over a meadow. It left him wondering where the man was coming from and what he knew. Tim wanted to confront him right here, right now. He could feel his nostrils flare, giving oxygen to the anger. But there wasn't enough evidence to link him to the missing children. Not yet.

"Is everything all right between you and Miss St. Clair?" Shearer said, reminding him he'd use Beebe's kiss against him.

Tim acknowledged his threat with a half smile. "Miss Knoll was thanking me. I just gave her the news story of the decade." Tim returned his dare. They stood—a face-off. *You fuck with me, I fuck with you* hung silently in the air.

Shearer's eyes opened wide and then focused in—an unspoken warning. "Then it's not romantic between you?"

"Miss Knoll is all yours if that's what you're asking," Tim replied with cold confidence. He'd make Beebe tell the truth if it came to it. But for now, all he could think about was saving the children.

"Shall we rejoin the party? You were a hit with some of the ladies; they've been asking about you." Shearer patted Tim's arm, but the menace circled like a supercell thunderstorm.

"Sure." Tim followed Shearer. Once at the doorway, Shearer turned around, blocking his route.

"Frisk him. Call Charlie if you find anything," he commanded his bodyguards. "Then we will decide what to do."

The guards slammed Tim up against the hall outside of the study. They kicked his legs apart. His arms were wrenched from his sides and roughly placed above his head. One of the guards shoved him against the wall, pinning him with his forearm against the back of his neck and forcing him to rest uncomfortably on his cheek.

"If we find anything, you're dead, motherfucker," Russ growled.

Tim was silent. He felt the larger man's hands slide down his right leg. He clenched his teeth in dread. He tried to work out how to reach for the pistol strapped to his left ankle before they could find it, but he couldn't move. The pat-down was intrusive. They turned out his pockets, and out of the corner of his eye, he watched Anita's business card flutter to the ground.

"I'll take it from here." Tim was relieved to hear Miguel's voice but understood he couldn't show it. The smaller of the two guards stepped back. The bigger man seemed not to want to let him go. Although surprised, he showed no emotion.

Tim was still pinned against the wall while Miguel finished the search. Intentionally, he took time to search Tim's legs. It was a show. Tim knew Miguel felt the gun still resting inside his boot.

"He's clean," Miguel reported.

The larger man released pressure. Tim slowly turned to face his captors. He watched as they went through his wallet. The smaller man pulled out his Department of Justice ID, stared at it, and handed it to the large man, who passed it on to Miguel. He slipped it into his pocket.

"Are you a cop?" the big guy asked.

"FBI Criminal Profiling Unit," Tim answered. "Former prosecutor." There was no reason to lie. The senator already knew he worked for Cain.

"Sorry for the rough treatment," Miguel said. "What were you doing in the senator's library?"

Tim knew he was giving him a chance to establish a logical alibi. "The bathroom downstairs was occupied. There was a line. Too much champagne. Didn't know it was out of bounds. Sorry."

Miguel guffawed. "This is your bad guy?" he said to the other bodyguards. He rolled his eyes. "The guy had to pee."

"That's a lie. What about the woman?" the smaller guard snapped, his expression tainted with distrust.

"Woman?" Miguel asked, his tone loaded with intrigue but dread flashing from his eyes. Tim understood his first alibi was in jeopardy.

Tim tamped down the sudden urge to wring Beebe's neck. He realized the two guards had seen her leave the study. He quickly made an excuse. "So, taking a leak was one reason. We don't have to tell my wife, do we?"

The guards mumbled and began to chuckle to themselves. For once, Tim hoped they thought he was a scoundrel.

"How about we go have a chat at the guard station?" Miguel suggested.

"I should get back to my wife," Tim said, getting a good laugh from the two guards.

Miguel joined the merriment. "That wasn't a question."

The two guards sobered immediately.

"I've answered your questions," Tim said, pretending a protest.

"I have a few more," Miguel said. He was playing his part to perfection. Tim started to worry. It was reasonable to believe they had surveillance tape. Miguel couldn't blow his cover. He would have to sacrifice Tim.

"Okay. Whatever you need. I'm a cooperative guy." Tim lifted both hands in surrender.

The two guards stepped forward to compel Tim to make his way to the station.

Miguel winked at them. "I've got this. Why don't you see if the senator needs anything else? Hands behind your back, McAndrews."

Tim complied, and Miguel tightened flex cuffs on his wrists. For a moment, Tim paused. What did he know about Miguel? Miguel encouraged him forward with a jolt. Tim had no choice now. He had to trust him.

FIFTY-EIGHT

Miguel shoved Tim forward into the room the guards called their station. He locked the door behind him. A rectangular table filled the room, and around it, staring at him, were two men. Tim wondered what was going to happen next. Was this rescue or the beginning of a grueling and maybe torturous interrogation? Miguel forced him to sit at the head of the table. The men shared a silent moment sizing up one another. Miguel finally flicked his fingers, and one of the agents tossed Miguel a pocketknife.

Still unsure of his fate, Tim waited for Miguel to speak. He didn't know what they knew. He didn't know whose side they were on.

"Oh, by the way, this is Special Agent Chad Montgomery and Special Agent Dave Ramírez from the Boise field office. I got them into this shindig under the guise of being the extra Blackhawk Security we needed for the party," Miguel said.

"Tim McAndrews, with the profiling unit. I've got to get you out of here, man." Miguel started pacing.

"Dani?"

"She's safe. I had her leave the party a half hour ago, and Elias picked her up with two agents. They're waiting at your house," he answered.

"Beebe?"

Miguel tipped his head slightly in question. "Beebe can take care of herself."

"She has something we need. I dropped it into her purse when she—never mind that. We need what's in her purse." Tim grimaced.

"What's in her purse?"

"Bones," Tim answered. "I recovered some charred bones from one of the incinerators in the basement. They may be ..." he could hardly say it; he didn't want to believe it. " ... Children's bones. A forensic anthropologist would be able to tell."

Miguel blinked, sighed, and looked at the left side of the table. "Little blonde, sparkly, red, minidress, pretty, red shoes," he said, drawing the-woman-has-curves sign with his hands. "Thanks, Chad, Dave." The two men rose and exited the room.

"Does the senator have me on tape?" Tim asked.

"He did. But somehow someone accidentally erased the hard drive on the surveillance cameras' computer. Lost the backup thumb drive too. Charlie was already down here looking for it." Miguel lifted his shoulders as if he couldn't imagine how that happened. After a few seconds, a big grin stretched across his lips.

Tim couldn't help but smile. "But I still can't just walk out of here, can I?"

"Probably could. Yep. I think you could slip out the back.

But we've been tasked with getting the president out of here. And pretty much now."

"But?" Tim encouraged Miguel to continue. He was obviously in conflict.

"Oh, you know, the usual, the I-can't-stand-to-let-a-criminal-walk thingie." Miguel swiped his hand down his face.

"The president?"

"And that's the million-dollar question, isn't it? There's no direct evidence he's involved in anything. There are a few pictures of him on Houseman's jet on the way to the Isla. Taken years ago. Guilt by association isn't enough. That and how do we get him out without tipping our hand? There's at least twenty security guards and Secret Service agents between us and our goal." Miguel started to pace down and back along the length of the table, fiddling with the knife.

"Can you get Secret Service on board?" Tim asked.

"When their job is to *protect* the pres? Right or wrong?" Miguel grimaced. Tim wouldn't want to be in Miguel's position right now.

"What does Elias say to do?" Tim asked.

"Get Trenton out."

Tim bent his head forward on his neck. He closed his eyes. He remembered how he felt when Goddard lectured him about winning some and losing others. The solid right and wrong, black and white ideals of youth clashed hard with squishy reality.

"On the good news front, we have been tailing Hayes for days. We followed him to a small house outside of Sandpoint. When you clued us as to the motive for the abductions during your little chat with Dr. Hope this evening, Elias called in a SWAT team to raid that house," Miguel said.

"Cut me loose. The kids are still alive and can be saved. Let's go now." Tim started to stand. Miguel pressed him back down into his chair. His expression changed to trepidation. "What's wrong with you? The twins found in Seattle were exsanguinated. Do you know what that means? They are killing the kids. They are draining all of their blood while they are alive!" Tim pleaded. "I get it; you're not sure. But trust me, it's true. Here is what we do: we bust this thing at the Sandpoint house." Tim's jaw was set with determination.

"The raid went down. The kids aren't there. There is a truckload of evidence that they had been there, just no more."

"Houseman's jet?"

"Sitting empty on a taxiway in Spokane," Miguel answered. "Houseman is here. My guess, the kids are here. Somewhere."

"I didn't find the kids." Tim sighed. "Raid this damned place. Search it top to bottom. Whoever stays for the treatments after the party gets arrested."

"Even if that whoever is the president?" Miguel asked quietly.

"No one is above the law. No one. Especially where the lives of young children are at risk," Tim argued.

Miguel stared as if making a judgment about whether Tim understood the impact of putting the president in this situation.

"Cut me loose, Miguel," Tim begged. "Let me try to find the kids."

Miguel moved behind him. He lifted his arms as if he would remove the cuffs but was suddenly distracted by three raps on the door. He pulled the door open.

FIFTY-NINE

You *pig*. You don't have to be so rough!" Beebe was furious. She was harshly shoved through the door to some small guard breakroom. Her interview with the president had been suddenly and unceremoniously canceled. And worse than all of this, McAndrews was sitting at the head of the table, here in this very room, probably laughing his ass off because she'd kissed him like a jerk and made a complete fool of herself. He told her to stop loving him. Why couldn't she?

"I said knock it off," she complained to the taller of the two guards, stumbling forward in her spike heels. The bodyguards let her go and slammed the door shut behind her. Miguel locked it.

"What do you want?" She glared at Tim, then at Miguel. She was in no mood to be manhandled.

"Your purse. Hand it over." Miguel was stern.

"You're robbing me? Are you kidding me?" she blustered. "Are you going to just sit on your hands while this brute robs

316 / SARAH VAIL

me?" She directed her question at Tim. He shook his head in answer.

Miguel grabbed her purse and set it closer to the end of the table. Beebe contemplated lunging for it and running, but knew she wouldn't get very far in her stupid but very pretty shoes.

Miguel sliced through the flex cuffs around Tim's wrists, and the plastic fell to the floor. He adjusted Beebe's purse to a spot in front of Tim. Tim first rubbed his wrists, restoring circulation. Then carefully, he took a folded white napkin out of her purse, set it on the table, and opened it, protecting the contents inside. She expected jewelry, rare coins, something of value—a thumb drive with top secret information perhaps. The contents were disturbing, and she blinked to make sure she was seeing what she thought she was seeing.

"Looks like a partial humerus and maybe a half of a femur," Tim said, looking up at Miguel, ignoring Beebe.

"Could be animal," Miguel replied.

"Could be anything, but with the lab, the medical chairs, the after-party, the incinerators, the weird statues of Moloch, I'm going with human, a child-sized human to be exact," Tim said as Miguel leaned forward to study the gruesome prize.

"What the hell is that? It's not mine. Why was that in my purse?" Beebe complained defensively. She began to feel she was in trouble. Big, capital T trouble. She looked over at Tim. His brow wrinkled with concern. "Why are you sitting there staring at me? Listen, that's not my stuff. I don't know how it got in my purse, honest." Panic cracked in her voice. She glanced at Miguel and did a double take. He was making a mental calculation. What did those bones have to do with anything? What were they talking about statues for? Who the hell was Moloch? Suddenly, she realized she was right there in the middle of a case. Something was going down, and her instincts about McAndrews had been right all along. He was always in the thick of the action. For a moment, she just stared at him. Awe, admiration, and love overwhelmed her. But as much as she felt for the man, she wasn't going to let that get in the way of a breaking news story. She swiped her hand down her jaw and leaned forward to get a better look. Her phone was in her purse, and if she could just grab some pictures. She reached for it.

Miguel slapped his hand on top of hers, keeping her from touching the purse.

"Ah, ah, ah," he warned her, wagging his index finger.

"We've got to get this to Elias," Tim said, all business, not even acknowledging her. "Can you sneak me out of here?"

"I can. We'll need to wait to see if it's all clear," Miguel said.

"I didn't find the kids," Tim said, sorrow in his eyes. Beebe followed their conversation like following volleys on a tennis court.

"They're here. They've got to be," Miguel countered.

"I'll get this to Elias and come back with a team. We can go over this house top to bottom," Tim said, folding the white napkin back over the bones. "This thing still on?" He pointed to the tiny video camera on his sweater.

"Yes."

"Elias, are you getting this?" Tim made sure he captured video of the bones on the table and then stuffed them back into the napkin and into the pocket of his slacks. "Okay how do I get out of here?"

"Hello?" Beebe said, trying to get their attention.

"There's a back door. But last time I looked, Russ and Rich were standing guard just outside," Miguel said. Tim scowled. This wasn't what he wanted to hear.

"Hello?" she said louder.

"We'll have to distract them unless you can think of another way out. You know the layout better than anyone," Tim said.

"I'm not the one who found the passage to the underground."

"That was an accident," Tim reported.

"Hello!" she screamed, finally getting them to look at her.

"What! What do you want, Beebe?" Tim asked, exasperated.

"If you're done patting each other on the back, I was just wondering what you were going to do about me?" She sat up tall in her chair. "I want out of here too."

The two men were silenced and stood to stare at her.

Finally, Miguel asked, "What *are* we going to do with her?"

Tim breathed out. "If we leave her, she knows too much, and if the kids are here, Hayes and the senator are in on it and will kill her. If I take her with me, she'll go straight to her editor, and she'll expose the raid before we can pull it off, and I'll need to kill her," he reasoned out loud, adding the last part sarcastically.

"Wait. What kids? I won't tell a soul, I promise. Take me with you," she pleaded. Tim shook his head no. Beebe could see Tim was adding up the pros and cons when the knocking on the door started.

"Miguel! You in there?" a familiar voice said, and the pounding began again.

They scrambled. They had to keep up the ruse for as long as they could.

"Don't blow this, Beebe. Keep your mouth shut," he warned her. Tim put his hands behind his back, signaling that Miguel should cuff him again. "If they ask questions, here's what you tell them."

SIXTY

Shearer strolled into the small guard station when Miguel opened the door, a satisfied grin curving his lips. "McAndrews, Miss Knoll," he said in a sarcastic greeting.

Charlie Hayes followed, with his ever-present security. The big man was called Russ, and the athletic one, Rich, trailed behind. Tim tried to get Beebe's attention to warn her again to play along. She was near panic, and he couldn't tell if he'd made the connection or not. She knew too much. Hopefully, fear would keep her quiet.

"So, Mr. McAndrews. Did you enjoy my library?" Shearer asked; the smug look on his face made Tim want to punch him. He gritted his teeth because he couldn't.

"Didn't get the chance," Tim retorted. His reward was a hard slap across the face from Rich. He should've expected the bad treatment when he suggested Miguel put the cuffs back on. Plans on the fly never worked. Never.

"Why did you hit him, asshole? He answered you straight," Beebe complained. She started to get up as if to see if Tim was okay. Immediately, she was cuffed, her wrists behind her back, a measure of duct tape pressed across her mouth, pushed down into her chair by Rich. Beebe's muffled protests became nothing more than background noise.

"Did you get any information from them at all, Miguel? What were they doing in my library?" Shearer asked.

"They said they're having an affair. They intended to use the study for a little amour," Miguel lied with a straight face, staring at Tim as if getting his consent. Beebe's eyes were bugging out, and she was trying to protest. "Isn't that right? Getting a little somethin'-somethin' behind the wife's back, eh, McAndrews?"

"Is that true, McAndrews? You'd cheat on your beautiful wife? Your very desirable and rich wife, I might add. This is how you treat her?" Shearer taunted him, then turned his gaze on Beebe and frowned at her antics. "Bring Mrs. McAndrews here to see this." Two guards were dispatched to find her.

Tim didn't answer but looked over at Miguel, trying to confirm that Dani was out of here and safe. Tim showed no emotion, but inside, his stomach roiled. He would never cheat on Dani. It pained him to have anyone think he would, even Buddy Shearer. Miguel held his gaze long enough to reassure him. Dani was long gone, safe with Cain.

Beebe, on the other hand, was bouncing and fighting her bonds and wildly shaking her head no as they accused her. Tim guessed if she was going to be blamed for it, she wanted to be doing it.

"What are we going to do about this? Because I don't believe you." Hayes grinned with pure evil in his eyes.

"Believe what you want," Tim said, narrowing his eyes in a threat. The second he got free, he was going to bring the hammer down on Hayes. Hayes stared back, but he understood it.

"We have surveillance video of you. The main computer failed, but you forgot that there would be backup because of the president's visit," Hayes sneered. "You certainly aren't as smart as you think you are. I don't even believe you're really married to Daniela St. Clair. You're not her type. Just a player in an FBI game, and not a very good one at that."

Every so slightly, Miguel flinched. It was clear to Tim he'd thought he got all the video. They knew he'd found the laboratory, the medical chairs, and the incinerators. Lying about it would neither buy him time nor freedom.

"Is that right? So, Charlie—I can call you Charlie, right? Tell me what you do with the incinerators. Do you sacrifice living children there? Is that what you do at the winter equinox?" Tim confronted Hayes. He noticed Shearer's eyes widen. Miguel, too, was shocked. Though he'd heard from Cain, he hadn't had the chance to get the whole story.

"Charlie?" Shearer asked, concern furrowing his brow.

"First, you take their blood and sell it as the elixir of eternal life to your pathetic, depraved followers. How much money are you getting for that, Charlie? Are the kids dead when you burn their bodies? Or are they still alive? What do you get, Charlie? Is it sex or just a sadistic thrill?" The second blow was unexpected and had Tim barely holding onto consciousness. His head bobbed forward to his chest in pain. But he'd had these kinds of hits in football and knew he'd quickly recover. Rich grabbed Tim by his hair, forcing his head back so he'd look at Hayes and reared back, preparing to strike him again, but Miguel intervened.

"Knock it off. He's FBI; he goes missing him, they'll come calling," Miguel said. "We need to think this through."

"It's a little late to worry about that. Besides, he'll just have a tragic accident. It's snowing, and the roads are icy. Happens all the time. Or he'll just disappear, never to be seen or heard from again," Charlie said, enjoying the thought of Tim's demise a little too much.

"Whatever you're doing needs to stay inside these walls," Miguel said emphatically, as if he were on their side. Rich let go, and Tim let his head loll forward again as if he were unconscious. He knew his recording device was still active, and he hoped Cain was organizing a raid.

"What do you suggest? We've already said too much. He knows too much," Charlie answered.

"What does he really know? The basement is for food and wine storage. The incinerators are for biomass power generation to supplement your electricity. Everything has an alternative explanation." Miguel offered up what Tim had earlier suggested. "Now, go on. Get out of here. Don't worry about it. I'll take care of him and the woman too. And I'll enjoy doing it," Miguel volunteered, allowing a sneer to cross his lips.

"Good." Charlie lifted an eyebrow and then narrowed his eyes. "Just so we're clear, McAndrews, what I get out of it is having power over little pieces of shit like you," Hayes growled.

"Charlie! Stop!" Shearer protested. "Charlie?" Once again, Shearer wanted answers. "Charlie, are you doing what he says?"

"What do you care what I do to keep you in office? Where do you think your money comes from?" Charlie glowered at his boss. Tim could see Shearer's expression morph to horror. "Just take what I give you, be grateful, and shut the fuck up," Charlie snarled. "I'm counting on you, Miguel."

Miguel stepped forward to a cabinet and took out a vial and a cotton cloth. Tim felt his stomach flop over. They were going to put him under with some knockout drops. He tried his best, but there was no way to get his gun. Beebe's eyes were as round as saucers, and she began to rock her chair as if knocking it over would help. Tim watched her fight with muffled screams until they covered her mouth and nose with the chloroform.

Charlie grabbed a handful of Tim's hair, forcing his head up. He bent forward to look in Tim's eyes. "Since you are so fascinated with the idea of burning humans alive in the incinerators, McAndrews, why don't you learn all about the experience firsthand."

"Fuck you, Hayes," he hissed just as Russ covered his mouth and nose with the saturated cloth.

SIXTY-ONE

In the dream, he was running, running through a mist-covered forest. His muscles were stiff and sore. Suddenly, he ascended from somewhere dark, and he was breaking the surface of consciousness, like water. It all came back to him. Tim remembered resisting the chloroform until he couldn't fight any longer and slipped into blackness. How he'd gotten here to this dark, cramped space, sitting on the cold floor, he wasn't sure. The weight slumped against his chest and positioned between his legs with her back to him was a woman. It was not Dani; he could tell by scent of her perfume and her size, but his mind couldn't wholly focus on who she was. He tried to rub his eyes but found his wrists were bound behind his back and behind a six-by-six post. He saw light—a small sliver, at the most an inch—between the door and the floor. No help. As his thoughts cleared, he realized he was in the pantry he'd noticed off the guard's station. He was still in Shearer's house with Beebe, and if he remembered correctly, just about ready to become biomass to save money on the senator's electric bill. He had to get out of here.

"Beebe, wake up," he whispered.

Beebe moaned sleepily and twisted her neck to try to look behind her but settled back against him, exhausted. She was still drugged.

"Beebe, do you hear me?" Tim asked. He struggled uncomfortably against his bonds. The dark pantry was too small for them both.

"What?" she whispered, dazed. They had given her the same tranquilizer. He remembered she fought furiously as they gave her the chloroform. Her anger had dissipated. She seemed to be lost.

"Your cuffs, there's play in them. About six inches between the wrist links," he said again for the third time. Miguel had intentionally made it easier for her to break free. But unfortunately, he'd only had time to loosen Beebe's cuffs. At least he'd pulled the tape from her mouth before shoving them in this closet.

He remembered some whispers. Chad and Dave from the Boise office had been tasked with getting the president out. Dani's house was being used to set up SWAT raids. But if this was only a drug dream, they had to escape. Charlie Hayes had proven himself insane. He'd admitted, though not directly, to the murder of children and pretty much confirmed they were taking their blood.

"Lean against me and try to bring your hands underneath you and around to the front," he said softly.

"You do it if it's so easy," she whined.

"I can't. My wrists are bound behind the post."

"They are?" she asked, leaning drunkenly against him and looking over around his side, nearly falling into a position she would have difficulty recovering from. He couldn't help her. "Oh, so they are."

She righted herself by ramming her elbow into his stomach. He grimaced with pain. She twisted again and gazed up into his eyes, and that lost expression returned. She rested her head on his chest. "I can hear your heartbeat," she slurred.

"Beebe, listen to me: this is our chance of getting out of here, getting free. Can you try?" He bounced her awake by moving his body forward as far as he could.

"What? Okay. I'll try." For the next few minutes, he could feel her struggle against him and hear her grunts, groans, and occasional giggles when she lost her balance.

"That's it, lean on me. That's it. Now try to wriggle over. Like that. Now the other leg, just like that," he coached her, pleased. She did it. Her hands were still cuffed but in front of her now. Panting, she collapsed against his shoulder.

"Beebe, listen to me. Can you stand?" After a few seconds of effort, Beebe was on her feet—unsteady at first but standing.

"See if there is a light switch on the wall." He waited while she felt for it.

"No. It must be on the outside." Her voice was clearer now, more awake.

"Check the post I'm tied to. Are there cross members, or can I slide up to my feet?"

Beebe leaned into him, her beaded dress scraping against his face. She pressed her left knee into his shoulder. "Cool, I think you can stand."

She helped him to his feet and then leaned against him again.

"Miguel left me my phone. In my slack's pocket, there is an iPhone. Get it."

"Right." She began, and he grimaced, eyes tight as she

searched him. He struggled against the post, digging the cuffs deeper into his skin.

"Here, I found it." Her arm shot up to show him, and she banged him in the nose with it. He flinched away.

"Thank God. Okay. Now tap it and hold it up to my face. When it opens to my apps, find the flashlight, and turn it on. Now, find something to cut these bonds. If nothing else, find a glass jar, break it, and use a piece of glass to cut the cuffs," he said.

She started to hunt and gave him a report. "There's no knife, no glass jars, only this stupid can opener." She held it up, flashing the phone light on it so he could see. It was one of those pathetic old-fashioned jobs that the world had abandoned years ago.

"That'll work. Open a can, take the lid, and slice it through the plastic cuffs," he instructed.

"That'll never work," she mumbled under her breath.

"Try it," he said softly, still irritated. "Must you fight me on everything?"

She sneered at him and went back to work. At last, she opened a can after some false starts. She pressed her body against his and reached around him, feeling for the cuffs. She began sawing the rough edges of the lid against the plastic. After a few minutes, he could feel the cuffs start to give way. He pulled as hard as he could each side against the other as she sawed. Finally, they broke apart with a snap. He wrenched his arms forward, rolling the pain out of his shoulders. He moved Beebe aside, leaned forward, and yanked the gun out of the holster in his left boot.

"You had a gun? All this time, you had— ..."

"I wasn't going to let you shoot the cuffs off. I wanted to keep my hands. Besides, the noise would've brought them running," he quipped. Beebe had no common sense. "Time to get out of here." Quickly, he unfastened her cuffs. He tried the pantry door. It was locked.

"Stand back. Give me as much room as you can." He barely gave her enough time to get ready. He stepped back, and as he did, he grabbed hold of the post he'd been cuffed to. He heard an electric motor whir to life. The shelves along the back pantry wall began to roll open. A bare bulb illuminated a concrete stairway spiraling downward.

"What is this?" Beebe asked, stumbling forward and into his back.

"Wait here. I'm going to go look," Tim commanded.

"Not on your life. I'm going with you. I'm not staying here alone."

"Yes. You are. Keep guard. Yell if they come back. I'm not playing around." Tim made sure she understood he was dead serious by his glare. She finally backed down.

"Damn it, I'm scared. All right? Hurry."

"I mean it, Beebe. Stay here." He could tell by her face that she would stay put for a little while, a very little while. He shook his head and started quietly down the stairway. When at the bottom, he observed the same type of walk-in freezer doors he'd seen when he investigated the basement from the library. They were to his right this time. In this hallway, there was only one other closed door to his left. He looked up and noticed the round, dark bubble of a video camera. He took in a deep breath. *It is what it is.* If they saw him and caught him, he'd have to deal with them. At least this time, he had his pistol. He hoped Miguel had disarmed the system.

As he studied the hallway, he started formulating a plan in case he found the kids. He'd organize it with stronger, older boys in the front to lead. Then younger and younger, with him following behind to help the weakest. He was sure Beebe would help once they started to pour through the pantry opening.

He approached the left side door. He carefully opened it. It appeared to be a small guard station. One empty chair sat in front of a thirty-two-inch flat-screen television. A *Game of Thrones* episode played quietly in the background. He didn't dare flip on the light, so he left the door to the outside hallway wide open. At the far side of the room, he saw another door. Stacked beside it and against the wall were black plastic garbage bags. He recognized the smell of death and almost gagged. He forced himself not to speculate about what they held. It might paralyze him with horror. He had to find the kids. Had to get them to safety.

"Do you see this, Elias?" he whispered into the small recording device still on his lapel.

Slowly, carefully, he opened the door. He stood in shock. On rows of cheap air mattress were at least fifty sleeping children. They were covered by sparse, filthy blankets. Not one child moved, and for a moment, he panicked, thinking they were dead. But finally, his eyes adjusted to the dim light, and he could see the rise and fall of their shallow breathing. Tim squatted down to make sure and touched the child closest to him. The boy's skin was warm; he was alive. The boy stirred and blinked up at Tim with big brown eyes. His pupils were dilatated. His mouth expressionless. It was all Tim needed to see. They were drugged. He felt his hope sink. The boy's eyes fluttered closed, and he slipped back into the drug-induced world.

Tim let out a breath in frustration. He wasn't going to be able to get all these drugged kids out. He couldn't—but Elias could.

"Elias, I found the kids. They're drugged. Send in a SWAT Team. Do it now, before Hayes and company can do anything else to them."

The children were kept like animals while the elite

partygoers ate and drank in warmth and comfort, waiting to take their blood. He forced down his anger.

There was no need for search warrants now. Tim had found the kidnapped children. He had no idea if Elias heard him. He wished for two-way communication, but wishing wouldn't make it so. He had to get out alive, get a SWAT team as help, and come back for them. He had to save them.

Cautiously, he left the room, closing the door silently behind him. He slipped through the anteroom and into the hallway. He stopped cold. From the end of the corridor, he heard voices. He rushed to the stairway and pressed his body flat against the corner wall. He positioned himself so he could see down the hallway, but no one could see him.

Charlie Hayes walked with Mo and Raphael Houseman toward the children's holding room. Mo. Tim's heart sank. His suspicions that some of the children were being trafficked internationally were confirmed. He had to stop this. He needed help.

"You can take your forty. But the FBI has been sniffing around, so you need to do it now. They sent in a guy posing as Daniela St. Clair's husband to the party. FBI thinks I'm stupid. I've sent my boys to take care of him and that crazy reporter. Months from now, they'll find them when the snow melts." Hayes laughed.

Tim felt his jaw tighten. He wanted to arrest them. But if Elias hadn't seen and heard his video recording, then he'd have no backup. He had to get out of here. Tim decided he would come back with a SWAT team and take Hayes down personally. With that thought of encouragement, he silently wound up the stairs. He closed the panel behind him.

"Thank God you're back." Beebe nestled close to him, setting her head on his shoulder.

"Not the time for this, Beebe." He tested the knob on the pantry door. There was no deadbolt.

"When is?" Beebe asked.

Tim ignored her. He had to get the kids out before Houseman could take them and escape in his jet.

"Elias, if you can hear me, there is a white van behind the house at a loading dock. They will be moving the children from there," he said into the pin.

"You're talking to Elias Cain? What's going on, Tim?" He pushed Beebe back away from the door. He armed his pistol's firing chamber, and with everything he had, he kicked the door. The jamb splintered, and the door fell open, barely hanging on its hinges. He took a shooter's stance as he eyeballed the room. It was clear. He knew he couldn't wait. Hayes had sent someone other than Miguel to finish them off. They were on borrowed time.

"Let's go." He reached for her hand and pulled her forward.

"What about Miguel?" Beebe asked.

He stopped. Miguel had blown his cover in front of her. "We get out, enlist the cavalry, and I come back for him. For now, he's safe. They think he's one of them."

"What's down there?"

"The less you know, the safer you are. Now, let's go." He was annoyed. Suddenly, he paused.

"Did you hear something?" she asked in a soft voice.

He shook his head. "It's minus eight degrees outside. You can't go out dressed like that."

"I can stand it."

"You'll have frostbite in five minutes."

Beebe looked down at herself. The red beaded dress was beautiful, but it was a strapless mini.

"You can't leave me. You can't," she begged. He stared at her for a moment, wanting to do just that.

"I will come back for you, just like Miguel." He started for the small coat closet. He knew there would be outerwear in there. The guards needed it for their outdoor shifts. He groaned when he realized Beebe had started to cry. This was his weakness, his Achilles' heel. He was raised in a family of rough and tumble boys. Weeping wasn't part of their makeup. And Dani, the most feminine woman he knew, had never used tears to manipulate him. He knew Beebe was scared. She should be.

"All right. But, Beebe, I'm warning you, if you hold me up, if you slow me down, I'll leave you where you fall. This is urgent." Tim shook his head. He ripped open the doors to a coat closet. He tossed out a large puff jacket and a huge pair of bibs. "Hurry. Put those on."

Sniffing back her tears, she complied. Tim pitched out a pair of snow boots to her. When he looked, she'd managed to put the outerwear over her dress. She was lifting the snow boots, studying them. They were many sizes too big. He tried to remember if any of the Secret Service agents were female but couldn't. He found a little bit smaller pair of boots for her and slipped into the bibs he scrounged for himself, but unlike Beebe's, his fit perfectly. He stepped into a pair of boots.

"The boots will have to do," he explained.

"I look like a damn clown," she whined.

"This isn't a fashion show. Hustle butt. We've got to go." He started for the door that led to the hallway, slipping his arms through the sleeves of the jacket he'd stolen. "If we get out of here alive, at least you won't freeze."

SIXTY-TWO

Tim waited on the outside of the six-inch-thick concrete wall for Beebe to climb down to his side. He promised her he'd catch her, knowing that even if he didn't, she'd fall in a soft drift that would be like falling into a mound of pillows. But she was slowing him down, and he needed her to hurry.

They'd made it out of Shearer's house. Before them, spreading out white and sparkling in the moonlight, stretched the two acres between where he stood and the wrought iron gate that separated Shearer's property from Dani's. While Tim waited for Beebe to gather the courage to drop the ten remaining feet, he studied what he could see of the upper deck. He knew Russ and Rich were there, armed with Heckler and Koch MP5K personal defense weapons. Its folding stock quickly turned the weapon into a highly efficient submachine gun. He had a five-round .380 pistol, with a short range, and one extra clip. Stealth was their only option. He studied the small wash between the houses, mapping out where they could stay in the most cover. Too bad all the winter outerwear he'd found for Beebe and himself was dark in color. Though that design was meant to absorb as much of the low winter sun as possible, it was no good when one was trying to disappear against a background of white, glistening in the light of a half-moon. He looked up just as Beebe dropped from the wall. He broke her fall by catching her just before her feet touched the ground. He turned and started to move, but she grabbed his arm.

He reversed, tipping his head with a question. This close to the house, it was imperative they stay as quiet as possible. He worried that even the swish of the waterproof fabric of the bibs, leg against leg, would alert a prepared and vigilant guard. He lifted a gloved finger to his lips and shook his head no to silence whatever she had to say. He'd warned her before they crossed the lower patio: no talking, no laughing, no coughing, not even a sneeze until they were out of earshot of the guards on the upper deck. He also assumed the guards had night vision and infrared. They couldn't hide their heat signature. Once they were on the move, there could be no stopping. His only hope was that Miguel had compromised some of the guards' gear.

Beebe pointed and directed Tim's attention to several SUVs. The president's entourage was driving at high speed for snow conditions away from the mansion. Elias must've gotten in touch with the director of the FBI, who in turn must've contacted the director of the Secret Service and had them hastily remove the president from danger, both physical and political. Tim felt a rush of urgency. He needed to get home and protect his girls. He motioned for Beebe to move out. He knew he would have to help her as she struggled in the deep snow. He decided that the president's leaving might draw the private security agents' attention away from their duties long enough for Beebe and him to cross to Dani's property.

"Stay in my tracks," he whispered to her. "I'll tamp down the snow, make it easier for you."

She nodded her agreement.

Tim started his trek. This was the easy part. The snow was only three or four inches deep on the concrete walkways maintained by the senator's gardener. He kept an eye on Beebe and an eye on the security guards. They had not noticed the two making their way quietly in the cover provided by the moon shadows moving across the ground with the sway of the ponderosas in the frigid breeze. Tim noticed that storm clouds were boiling up from the mountains to the west. He hoped it would soon start to snow. That would drive the security guards back indoors.

When he glanced back, Beebe had fallen. He turned back and helped her up.

"Damn it!" she said, too loud. "It's these stupid clown shoes."

Tim quickly put a finger to his lips to shush her. He rushed her to take cover. If the guards used their night vision or infrared, it was game over. Beebe sat on the far side of a tree in the snow. Tim plopped down beside her, rolled to his stomach. He wished he had binoculars. He looked up at the two men on the deck. The light from inside the senator's house illuminated them, and he could tell by their silhouettes that it was the two men that had earlier used him as a punching bag.

Tim hoped the trees would shield Beebe and him from view. The big one called Russ stubbed out his cigarette. He seemed to be peering out in their direction, but Tim could not see a scope. A gust of wind whipped through the top of the trees, and the shadows on the ground swayed across the snow. Within seconds, the moon disappeared behind a storm cloud, and darkness descended thick and heavy.

Tim motioned to Beebe it was time to go. He helped her

stand. He knew how deep the drifts were in the small draw halfway to Dani's property. There they would cross the creek in the trees. Most of the thick cover could be found there. He hoped that even if the guards saw them, they wouldn't be able to get off a clean shot. Tim took hold of both of Beebe's hands and placed them on his hips. If she held on to him, it would make it easier for her. He could feel her fingers curl into the fabric of his jacket as if her life depended on it. It did. He had wanted her in front of him to shield her if the bullets started to fly, but she wasn't tough enough to push through the deep snow. She had to rely on his strength to pull her through the drifts. As he started forward, he could see the top curl of the wrought iron gate in the distance. Dani's property was so close yet so far away.

As he plodded on, he occasionally studied the upper deck. In the dim light from the house, he could see one man's profile and the orange glow of the tip of a cigarette. His relaxed demeanor informed him they had not noticed the fleeing pair. He once again admonished Beebe to be quiet and began to slog forward. He was practically waist-deep in powder now. What he wouldn't give for a pair of snowshoes, skies, a sled— but dreaming about those tools only made the pull harder. He focused on the goal.

They reached a spot just about twenty feet from the iron gate, where Tim planned to rest for a few seconds. There was cover here. Tim heard a loud thud, like a large book slapping down on a table. A bullet splintered a branch above their heads. It was a suppressed gunshot. Tim whirled and shoved Beebe down into the snow. He covered her with his body. A second shot fractured the silence and whapped another branch in the distance. The owl that had startled him the other night screeched and took flight. Its giant wingspan momentarily blocked his view. He heard distant laughter. Beebe looked up into his face, panting with fear. She started to scream, so he covered her mouth with his hand. She struggled against him. When she settled down, he shook his head no. She needed to keep quiet. He waited until she acknowledged it. He removed his hand. He wasn't going to complain but thought she had no common sense.

Stillness returned to the forest. The owl resettled in its favorite branches. He listened for sound: the accidental cracking of frozen branches underfoot, the swish of waterproof fabric, anything that would tell him the guards were near and looking for them. Another cloud scurried along in the icy wind, obscured the moon, and engulfed them in inky blackness. He rolled off her and looked back at the deck. The guards were scanning the woods in their direction, but they still weren't using any scopes.

"Shoot back," Beebe whispered.

Tim shook his head no and again put his finger to his lips. Tim knew the muzzle flash would give them away if the guards were shooting at the owl for sport. He also knew that at this distance, the pistol's accuracy was greatly diminished. If he had to, he would lay down fire to distract when they needed to cross through the gate. If the guards were instead shooting at them and he and Beebe stayed still, they would think they were hit. When they came looking, the odds of survival would be even. Tim could use surprise to ambush them. He needed to tip the scales in their favor. He searched his surroundings to see if that was even possible.

Time came for them to move. Twenty yards to go. He looked back at the upper deck. A new figure emerged, backlit by the lights inside the house. It was Miguel standing at the edge of the wall, looking in their direction. He was using the high-powered night vision scope he'd used to keep Tim apprised when Graden tried to break in. They were sitting ducks.

For the third time tonight, Tim was in the position of having to trust Miguel. Could he?

Tim remembered the app on his phone he'd used to keep track of Graden's position. Luckily, he'd forgotten to delete it. Wondering if it was still working, he grabbed the iPhone out of his pocket. He unzipped his jacket to shield any light that might give their position away, took in a deep breath, and engaged it. After a few seconds, the screen became dark. Immediately his stomach sank like a stone. Both to his right and his left, the heat signatures of the bodyguards appeared glowing in a spectrum of colors; bright yellow hot where there was exposed skin, and darker orange, red, and purple painted the outline of their bodies. They were less than ten feet to each side of them and approaching fast. Tim pulled his pistol from its holster and maneuvered to a crouch, so he'd be able to spring up as a surprise. It was apparent they'd come looking for Beebe and him. In a split second, he weighed their fate. He knew he could take out one, but his unsuppressed gunfire would give the other man the advantage. He looked at Beebe's pretty face. He wished for Dani. He'd willingly take a bullet for Dani. Beebe parted her lips as if begging him for rescue—but more, begging him to love her. Those feelings were not there for him. All he could think of was getting home, getting back to Dani. He had to try. It was now or never. Tim picked his target. He stood and took aim.

Tim was startled when two silenced shots in rapid succession took the men on either side of him to the ground and left him standing. He looked up to see a full SWAT team pouring through the wrought iron gate. The arrest teams had arrived, and he and Beebe were standing directly in the crossfire.

SIXTY-THREE

Shearer tried his best to make casual chitchat with his equinox guests, but McAndrews's accusations of Charlie Hayes roiled in his stomach like rancid meat. He withdrew, went to his ground floor study, and sat heavily behind the huge mahogany desk. Almost in a daze, he rose, slowly walked to the west wall, and lifted the hinged painting that covered the compartment he had built into the wall. He pressed in the digital numbers that unlocked the safe. He was glad that MaryAnne was gone and that she would never know what he had become. He opened the safe's thick metal door. The small red thumb drive sat on the front edge of the compartment's floor, next to the neat stacks of emergency cash still in their bank wrappers, a passport, and several high-limit credit cards he'd set aside for a night like this one. Fingering the drive, contemplating making a run for it, he tried to decide if he should look at the damning pictures again or if once was enough. In a moment of weakness, drowning in loneliness and despair after MaryAnne died, he let Charlie convince him going to Houseman's island was a good idea. He'd allowed himself to be plied with drugs, alcohol, and the beautiful, young girls with their supple bodies and smooth skin. Houseman was black-mailing him.

He'd surrendered constituents and country and his own beliefs on two separate occasions. When he balked at self-serving legislation proposed by his fellow senators, he'd been threatened with exposure.

He brought the thumb drive with him, sat heavily in his leather swivel chair, and calmly slipped it into a USB port.

Shearer knew that the rumors of Charlie the pedophile, Charlie the Satanist, were true. Though he'd claimed it was only grist for the guilt-by-association mill and dismissed the gossip as rantings of political enemies in public, he knew it was true. Something had always been off about Charlie. Dread swept through him like an electric current. Shearer had willingly participated in the parabiosis treatments. He assumed it was a legal and legitimate medical procedure. He never suspected they'd murdered underage children. How did this get so out of control? He blamed himself for doing what was convenient despite any misgivings he had about Charlie. But now, in this heated atmosphere, if any of this came to light, his campaign was over. How on earth could he salvage it? They were already behind in the polls, behind in fundraising. And now they'd be accused of murder. He should've fired Charlie long ago, but they had been together for all these years, from the beginning of his political career.

He wondered if the early exit of the president had anything to do with the rumors. No one else knew about Charlie except Miguel, McAndrews, and Miss Knoll. There were the two guards that always seemed to be with Charlie, but they were disgustingly loyal. Could he keep the lid on this? Put the genie back in the bottle?

Never in his life had he condoned violence, especially against an unarmed man, handcuffed and without any way to defend himself or block the blows. He appreciated that Miguel had stepped in. Miguel was the voice of reason at a time of crisis. He thought about calling him for his advice now.

Charlie was on board with physically abusing an FBI agent. And now, there were no options but to allow Charlie to dispose of McAndrews and Miss Knoll. They knew too much. There was no way out.

This wasn't the first time he'd suspected Charlie of murder. There were suspicious accidents that the conspiracy theorists had dubiously linked to his campaign and staff. He felt nausea beginning again. If Charlie really had murdered children, no voter would support him if this came to light.

Then there was the matter of Trenton's endorsement. After he and McAndrews first discussed the artifact in the upstairs library, the support seemed to evaporate like steam from the top of a boiling pot. Trenton suddenly excused himself, claiming to be late for another engagement. But Shearer knew better. The Secret Service had studied his house, the ski lodge, the ski runs, and trails for days before even allowing Trenton to step foot off Air Force One. Trenton had changed his mind or had it changed for him. The latter was a frightening thought. Would that mean Shearer's arrest was imminent for crimes he didn't commit? Crimes that Charlie had? Ultimately, he was responsible. Wasn't he the one who craved power? Wasn't he the one who told Charlie, "Whatever it takes"?

Slowly, he opened the bottom righthand drawer of his desk and pulled out an unopened bottle of Jim Beam. It was a unique reserve blend he'd been given when he and a colleague visited their brewery last year. He unscrewed the top. Rather than use a glass, he took a long pull straight from the bottle. He reminded himself he hadn't done this since MaryAnne died. Nor had he felt so confused and desperate. He took another swig, feeling the fire all down his throat to his stomach, knowing the pain-dulling effect of the alcohol would soon follow. He gulped down another swallow.

He swiveled in his chair to look through the paned window to the crowd of press gathering outside in the cold by his ice-covered fountain.

Shearer assumed they were all speculating about the president's early departure. He could imagine them spewing their theories to their enthralled viewers. Had Trenton pulled his endorsement and why? What did that mean for the embattled senator? Was this the end of his career? He grabbed the whiskey bottle by the neck and gulped down another swallow. What if the press knew about Charlie? How could a man win the presidency if he was linked to a child murderer?

Charlie's familiar knock sounded on his study door. Shearer took another nip of whiskey before answering.

"Come in," he called out, dreading what he knew he had to do. "Lock it after you, okay?" Charlie turned on the light and hustled into the room, then closed and locked the door behind him.

"Why are you sitting in the dark? Are you ready? The press is waiting." Charlie pulled out a clean shirt and new complementary tie from the credenza along the east wall, as if expecting Shearer to dress for the occasion.

"We didn't get Trenton's endorsement," Shearer said, noticing the slur in his speech. He couldn't face them now anyway. They'd accuse him of being a drunk.

A small smile slipped across Charlie's lips. Shearer felt a rush of fear tingle at the back of his neck. He had to confront this.

"He had another engagement, that's all."

"Tell me, Charlie. Is any of what McAndrews accuses you of true? Any of it?"

"I've handled McAndrews. My men are on the way to take care of him and Miss Knoll as we speak."

"Your men? I thought you were going to let Miguel handle it. Are you going to kill them?"

"You don't need to know. Better if you don't," Charlie answered. The look on his face was clear. His jaw became rigid, his eyes black and narrowed, almost as if a mask of evil had replaced his face. Shearer sat back in his chair, amazed. How had he missed this?

Shearer continued. "Are you having children abducted and their blood taken for the parabiosis treatments? Are you sacrificing them? Here? In my house?" The alcohol started to hit him full force, and he blinked away the wooziness. He was far too intoxicated for the small amount he'd had to drink.

"We don't need Trenton's endorsement. He needs ours. Don't you see? We have all the power now. The presidency is ours. We just stay the course for one more year. It's right there at our fingertips." Charlie reached out for the air.

Shearer was shaken by disbelief. Charlie was insane. Drunk with power. Shearer felt everything slipping from his hands. His eyelids fluttered rapidly as he tried to hold onto consciousness.

"Charlie? Did you drug my whiskey?" The reality hit him when he saw Charlie's evil grin.

"It's just to help you sleep. You know that."

Fear squeezed at Shearers's heart, and it began to beat uncontrollably. He slumped forward across the desk, barely holding on. He had to fight. He had to. He propped himself up.

What he saw next solidified what he had to do. Through the panes in the French door, he watched as black FBI SUVs raced up the driveway and SWAT vans descended from all sides, police lights flashing color across the snow.

With every ounce of energy he had left, Buddy Shearer silently slid open the center desk drawer and fingered the cold metal of his Colt .45 revolver.

SIXTY-FOUR

Tim ducked and covered Beebe by putting his arm around her when two more shots rang out and shattered the silence, echoing off the surrounding mountains. These rounds were not suppressed, and they were not coming from the SWAT team. In seconds, it seemed every door to the mansion burst open, and party guests exploded out, screaming and scattering in every direction.

Tim scrambled, wrenching Beebe up to her feet. One of her snow boots fell off. Desperation flashed from her eyes. He took in a deep breath, bent forward, and slung her over his shoulder as if she were nothing more than a sack of potatoes. He clambered with every ounce of energy he had for the iron gate. When he was close, both he and Beebe were roughly pulled through. Tim fell to his knees and lost control. He reached for her but watched helplessly as Beebe fell flat on her back into the snow, exhaling as her breath was knocked out of her.

"Damn! I'm sorry!" He crawled forward to see if she was

hurt, but she was no longer there. He looked up to see Beebe being carried to Dani's house by a man in a black bulletproof vest, its back emblazoned with gold letters—FBI. Breathing a sigh of relief, he glanced up just as Mitch offered him his hand.

They made it. They were safe.

"The kids, we've got to go back and get the kids." Tim gripped Mitch's hand and pulled himself to his feet. Tim and Mitch jogged the rest of the way to the house on the walkways that had recently been cleared of snow.

Tim studied the group standing in the cold in front of the house. Dani had opened her home to the SWAT teams and the profiling unit, and agents were everywhere. They were staging here.

Tim searched for Dani in the throng. When he picked out her face, his whole body warmed with relief. Dani ran to him. Her embrace was wonderful. He held her against him, finding her mouth with his, losing himself in the joy of her kiss.

"You're safe. Oh, God, thank you. You're safe," she whispered.

He lifted her off the ground in his arms and held her tight. He couldn't even speak. When he set her down, she linked her arm in his. They walked toward the house, gazing into each other's eyes. When Tim glanced at the door, he noticed Elias standing there. The big man took in an exaggerated breath and tossed a bulletproof vest in Tim's direction. He disengaged with Dani and caught it before it hit the ground.

"Game's not over yet. You need to help us free the kids. SWAT is ready to enter the senator's house. Let's go," Elias said. It wasn't negotiable.

When Tim looked at Dani, she covered her mouth with her hand as if biting back her words. Her eyes were asking him to stay. She closed them briefly.

"Go. Go. I'll see you later." There was no anger.

He jogged after Elias, putting on the vest as they ran to his black Escalade SUV.

"Buy her flowers," Elias said as Tim closed the door to the front seat and fastened his seat belt.

"I'm going to owe her more than flowers," he said, laughing.

SIXTY-FIVE

The final part of the raid was poised and waiting when Elias and Tim arrived. This was another new experience for Tim. He undid his seat belt and slipped out of the front seat.

The SWAT commander, Jesse Radcliffe, made his way to Elias. Elias made the necessary introductions.

"We've ascertained that the gunfire you reported came from inside the house. That caused a panic. We've rounded up the fleeing party guests," he said, bringing the men up to speed. Radcliffe gave Tim a quick once-over, seeming to evaluate his suitability and readiness in that instant.

Tim looked around and saw many of the party guests in a line, hands on top of their heads, awaiting handcuffs. Elias decided to take them all to the sheriff's office. They would be evaluated and separated into two groups—first, innocent guests and second, trafficking gang and abusers.

Tim searched for Miguel, finally picking him out in a small

group of agents getting into vehicles to block all traffic attempting to leave the mansion. They made eye contact, and Miguel gave him a quick smile. Tim suspected when the chips were down, and Hayes's bodyguards were closing in on Beebe and him, Miguel called in the sniper strikes. Miguel had saved his life. Tim nodded his thanks.

Radcliffe approached Tim and handed him communication gear.

"We have the house plans. Show me where you believe the children are being held."

Tim followed him inside an electronics-laden van to a table with the house plans electronically imaged on its surface.

Tim oriented himself and began to map out the stairs from the pantry and the upstairs library to the dreary room where the children were being held.

"Tim, you and I will take a team through the pantry, confirm the location of the kids, and report. Sergeant Willows will lead the second team through the library," Radcliffe instructed. "Sadowski, Waters, Morgan, Bytters, you're with us." He called out names for his team, but by then, Tim was no longer listening. He was ready to save the children before anything else could happen to them.

"Remember, it's the third book on the third shelf down, left side, that opens the bookcases to the staircase. Pull it forward as if you were going to take it down and read it," Tim said to Willows as he started toward the house. He turned back to Radcliffe. "The kids are drugged. We need medics and transport. We should notify the local hospitals."

"Done." Radcliffe issued the order over his radio.

Radcliffe handed Tim a .40-caliber Sig Sauer semiautomatic pistol. Tim took it. The men made eye contact for a moment. Radcliffe waited for Tim's acknowledgment that he was ready. Grim reality sat heavily like a black raven on his shoulders. To save the children, he might have to take the life of another human being. Black and white, right and wrong, and good and evil squared off, face-to-face. He never expected to be here. Tim nodded he was ready. He was as ready as he could be. Two teams hurried to the house.

Once through the open door, Tim noticed the once elegantly appointed ballroom now held a group of adults on their knees, hands on their heads, waiting to be cuffed by the arresting SWAT team members.

He retraced his steps and led his team to the guard station, through the shattered pantry door, and down the spiral concrete stairs, to the secret underground. He stopped at the bottom stair landing. He held his hand up for everyone to stop. Down the shadowy hallway, he watched as Rafael Houseman, Mohammad Rashad, and two unknown men carried sleepy children down the corridor away from them. They walked briskly but seemed unaware of the full raid happening on the floors above them. Tim signaled to his team that he saw four suspects, waited for a few beats, then followed. He assumed they were taking the children to the white vans that remained at the cargo bay, as Miguel had earlier reported.

The team cautiously entered the hallway. There was no cover, and any gunplay would be deadly. The FBI team crept to the anteroom door, quickly opened it, and slipped inside. An empty chair sat in front of the TV, blaring an episode of *Game of Thrones* from its flat screen.

"Sadowski, Waters, lock this room down," Radcliffe commanded in a whisper. "Check on the children and report." He wanted to know that the kids were still there and safe. But he couldn't wait.

Tim felt an overwhelming need to make sure that Houseman didn't take a single child to his sex slave island. He pointed to the remaining agents on his team, and they continued quietly down the hallway.

At the end of the corridor, after a dogleg to the right, the team would encounter the cargo bay. Tim knew Elias was listening, watching through the tiny body cam Miguel had earlier given him, tracing their movements on the blueprints embedded in the electronic surveillance van's table. They'd planned for the second team to enter from the library side. Miguel and his men cut off the escape route from the house. When the traffickers realized they were boxed in, they would either fight or surrender peacefully. Tim hoped for the latter. He needed to take these men without gunfire.

Glancing back down toward the room where the children were held, he noticed a new team of at least a dozen agents slipping soundlessly into the anteroom. Children were being carried one by one to safety.

His team's mission had just been defined. They had to rescue the little ones that were already in the van parked at the loading dock.

Tim let out a deep breath. He motioned and moved his group forward. Suddenly, Tim realized he had no tactical experience. He was a suit-and-tie courtroom lawyer. What on God's green earth was he doing with an FBI SWAT team on a raid? He thought of Dani and her beautiful smile. He thought of Chloe. He thought of the children drugged in that filthy room. An angry calm filled him—first starting in his gray matter and seeping into every cell like floodwater. His courage returned and usurped all brain function, driving him forward with purpose. Saving the children became his only priority.

Tim refocused his attention on the dock spreading out a few feet in front of him. Houseman stood at the back end of the truck; both hands were visible. No weapon. At the dock's corner, up against the west wall, two Heckler and Koch MP5Ks were balanced on their shoulder rests. Unless they had handguns, the two men he'd seen earlier carrying children to this van were unarmed. Good news.

Tim crept across the hallway and flattened himself against the wall. Slowly he slid closer and closer to the opening. He stopped short. The team followed, and they lined up against the wall next to him. Then the two agents positioned themselves on the other side without prompting. Tim was grateful; at least someone knew what they were doing. Radcliffe quickly passed by Tim and silently snaked a tiny camera on a pole around the corner. He watched an image unfold on a device about the size of an iPhone.

"One on the deck, one driver," he whispered. "Wait. Two more—three on deck."

In his earbuds, Tim heard the report.

"Roadblock is in place. No one can get in or out. Team two is in the library side hallway."

They had cut off all avenues of escape. Tim knew he had to go now before the two guards realized they were surrounded and picked up their rifles.

"We are go," he heard Lieutenant Radcliffe say over his radio.

From both hallways, FBI SWAT team members surged into the cargo bay. Shouts of "FBI!" and commands to surrender came from every direction and reverberated off the walls. Within seconds, the seasoned agents quickly disarmed and lined up the suspects on their knees on the cold concrete floor. One at a time, each trafficker was handcuffed. There were five total in the cargo bay.

Tim felt as though his whole body was vibrating with adrenaline-fueled energy. Slowly, he walked down the line, studying each of the men in handcuffs. Houseman, Russ, Rich, the van's driver, and finally his gaze landed on Mo. For a moment, he just stared. This man had sworn to uphold the law, to protect the innocent. He felt his stomach wrench with disgust.

"Help me, Tim. You've got to help me," Mo pleaded, his voice quivering with fear.

Tim's jaw tightened. He ground his teeth together. His blood went cold as the images of the twins filled his mind. He couldn't find even a tiny smidgeon of mercy. Anger flared in its place. "I can't help you," Tim answered.

"Can't or won't?" Mo motioned with his head for Tim to move closer. Tim leaned forward to listen. "There's money, lots of money."

Tim rocked back, shocked. "Is that a bribe? Are you asking me to accept a bribe in exchange for your freedom?" Then a wry smile twisted his lips. "I won't help you."

Sergeant Ratcliffe moved forward and lifted Rashad to his feet. "Mohammad Rashad, you are under arrest for child trafficking—and attempted bribery of a federal agent. You have the right to remain silent. Anything you say can and will be used against you in a court of law. You have the right to talk to an attorney and have your attorney present during questioning …" He finished the Miranda warning. "Get him out of here."

Tim turned away as his team members escorted the traffickers to the waiting police transport. He took no pleasure in this, but Kathy's feelings about Mo had been vindicated.

Tim followed as several of his team members briskly walked into the van. Huddled in filthy blankets, eyes still dilated with a lingering drug fog, cheeks smudged with grime and smeared where tears had been wiped away, the remaining children stared up at him. Choked by emotion, Tim continued into the van.

"You're safe now. It's all over," Tim said softly, crouching down to help a little girl stand. Several of the older kids began to cry. Tim hoped they were tears of joy.

SIXTY-SIX

A team of CSI officers meticulously gathered every possible shred of evidence as Tim walked up the empty corridor toward the room where most of the children had been found. The large, cold cement basement was empty. The stale smell of longtime unwashed children lingered in the air. Tonight, they would be hospitalized, fed, washed, clothed, and given a warm, safe place to sleep.

Not one member of this law enforcement team intended to let these scumbags get away with this. One at a time, they acknowledged Tim with a nod. He continued through the anteroom and into the room where the captives had been held. The floor was covered with cheap air mattresses, and several badly soiled blankets were strewn about. Scattered here and there, small, dirty plastic toys lay haphazardly on the ground. The children were kept like animals while the elites waited in Shearer's mansion in warmth and comfort for their blood and for who knows what else. Tim had not found Hayes. He assumed he was arrested, along with the senator upstairs. Somehow, he needed to see this through court. In his mind, he began to formulate his opening statement for the prosecution.

He turned back and noticed one of the CSI agents had opened one of the plastic garbage bags and recoiled dramatically. Tim immediately needed to get out and into the fresh air but stopped. A sound. Soft, scared. A sound. He listened. In the darkness, he recognized a child's whimper. Rapidly, he made his way through the mess to a partially closed cabinet and opened the door all the way. He pulled out his iPhone and turned on the flashlight.

All Tim could see in the dim blue light was big brown eyes with thick dark lashes, a sweet face framed with brown ringlets tied up in a ratty pink bow. The little girl was dressed in a filthy pink dress. Her pink lace tights were tattered almost to shreds, and she shivered in the cold. Her tiny hands held a grimy white unicorn, a miniature of the one Tim had given to Chloe, tight to her chest. Tim's heart broke. Quickly, he peeled off his FBI vest and puff jacket. Once she was out, he'd wrap it around her shoulders.

"I'm here now. You're safe." He reached for her to help her out from her hiding place. She recoiled defensively and tightened into a ball, her eyes glazing over as if too frightened to even move. "I'm here," he said softly. Then he remembered what Chloe had asked him when he'd rescued her.

"I'm here, baby. You're safe. I've come to save you. I'm your angel."

SIXTY-SEVEN

Tim looked at his watch. Three in the morning. Another late night he needed to make up to Dani. She would understand, and he felt satisfied that they had dismantled the child trafficking ring. The kidnapped children would be returned to their families or assigned new foster ones. Hopefully better ones. He had no illusions that this was over. Break up one ring, and another springs up to take its place. He entered the code for the door and went inside, stripping away his winter outer clothing and hanging it on the rack. He pulled off his snow boots and placed them on the boot dryer. From the entryway, he could see into the decorated living room and remembered he and Dani had promised each other they would lavish Chloe with a memorable Christmas. Somehow, someway, he had to take time to make that happen. And now there was someone new on his gift list. Letisha Kay Watson. She'd been chosen for abduction for her AB negative blood type. She'd been taken in broad daylight while riding her bicycle, just as summer changed to fall four months ago. According to Kathy, the timing indicated they might have used Lettie once for a blood donation and were just about to do it again when Tim and the SWAT team intervened.

Tim walked across the living room in sock feet to the small bar. He took out a glass, filled it with ice, and splashed a couple of shots of Pendleton Stampede whiskey into it. He was still keyed up from the night's escape, arrests, and rescues; he needed to take the edge off. He took a sip.

He wondered, since Dani was willing to take on Chloe, would she be open to a second little girl? Hell, he would've taken home all fifty-five kids they rescued tonight. Little Lettie had been so vulnerable, so frightened, so needy; he'd been completely won over, just like he had been with Chloe. He felt bad leaving her with the others at the hospital, even though he knew she needed medical attention and that was the best. He would take Dani to meet her tomorrow.

He leaned back against the bar and took another sip of whiskey, looking out over the decorations, which were glittering and magical. Though he'd never expected to feel like this, he knew his family was going to be complete, and that made him smile.

He heard a creak on the stairway and turned and watched as Elias descended, dressed in blue striped pajamas covered by a white terrycloth bathrobe. Dani had invited the profilers to stay and rest up before they headed back to Quantico.

"Couldn't sleep," Elias explained, shrugging his shoulders.

"Want one?" Tim asked, holding up the glass.

"Yes. You can't sleep either?"

"Just got home from the hospital. Doing some thinking," he said, retrieving a clean glass. "Ice?"

"Sure."

"Whiskey? Or something else?"

"Whiskey," Elias answered.

When Tim handed him the glass, they clinked them together in a toast. "Good job tonight, Tim. The director is impressed. Very impressed." Elias took a swallow and grimaced as the alcohol went down.

"How many of your playing-card kids did we find?" Tim asked.

"Twenty-five," Elias answered. "Nearly half." There was no smile. Tim understood. Like Elias, he didn't want to think about the fate of the others. Facing that in the light of day tomorrow would be soon enough.

"I guess you heard that Shearer killed Charlie Hayes and then himself," Elias reported. "SWAT team found them locked in his study."

"Really?" Tim hadn't heard. "Saves me the trouble of kicking Charlie's ass." He wasn't shocked, and he hated to admit it, but he wasn't sorry either. He took another sip of whiskey. Elias chuckled.

"So, Tim, what are you down here thinking about? Joining us permanently, I hope."

"I'm down here thinking about the children. About adding Lettie to our family." Tim took another drink. "I'm down here hoping Dani will see it my way. And about joining you, for at least six months." He grinned.

Elias's eyebrows shot up, and he laughed. "Usually, the major concern for adding kids to your family is money. You don't have that concern." Elias was right, Tim thought. But Dani could keep him grounded if he was thinking with his heart instead of his head. They both had busy careers.

"In this household, time is in short supply, not money." Tim pulled out the bottle and offered Elias a refill.

"The fact that Lettie is black, that's not an issue for you?"

Tim was surprised and softly laughed. "I hadn't noticed. I

guess I'm color-blind." He knew Elias understood. "She was just a little girl in need of rescue. She's just a little girl in need of a family."

"And when the time comes for you and Dani to have children of your own? Have you thought of that?" Elias asked. Tim hadn't even told Scott and Kathy, his best friends, that Dani couldn't have children. Kathy would've tried to talk him out of marrying her. His mother would have a heart attack. This secret was best kept locked up.

"Clare and I adopted two girls after ours went off to college. I figure you need to be sure. Think of all the angles. Kids in situations like these can have problems. They were already in foster care for some unfortunate reason."

"Are you sorry? Disappointed? With your adopted kids, I mean," Tim asked and then took a gut-warming sip from his glass.

"No. They make life pretty sweet. Clare says they keep me young."

"That they were fosters makes a loving home even more necessary, doesn't it?" Tim reasoned. In his mind's eye, he could see two happy little girls babbling on about their new Christmas dolls together, half-lost in a sea of brightly colored wrapping paper.

"It does." Elias grinned his approval. "Now, how do you think this case goes together?"

"Me? Is my opinion important? I'm the junior guy." Tim studied Elias, surprised that his contribution was worth anything.

"I like to hear from all team members. But you especially since you saw the evidence firsthand. How would you present this case in court? Do you think Shearer thought up this whole scheme or—"

"Hayes. Hayes was involved in the parabiosis. Houseman

is just a pervert. They both found a way to make money by exploiting vulnerable children. No telling what else they were doing. That's my take anyway." Tim started to formulate a complete theory. "Someone resurrected parabiosis from the dustbin of crazy. Who in their right mind would pair two creatures' circulatory systems together? How could you even think up doing something so cruel, even to lab rats? Leaves me to wonder if they were scientists or sadists."

"Humans do weird stuff in the name of science. And sometimes there are breakthroughs," Elias offered.

Tim glared at him, clearly questioning his premise. "Anyway, our mastermind saw it as a way to make money, big money. But I don't believe the abducted children were used only for this. I think they were trafficked for anything and everything, for the right price. Internationally, here at home. They didn't care what happened to the kids. How many of our rescues were undocumented illegal kids shuttled across the southern border? Any guesses?"

"Half," Elias answered.

Tim shook his head; his heart ached in his chest. "Our parabiosis kids were carefully selected by blood type from the foster care system, the abductions staged, and the foster parents paid. We know that from the roundup day before yesterday.

"Our hapless kidnapper was once a big-time drug dealer. He had routes all over the US. He knew the roads, highways, and byways like the back of his hand. Mo from my office sprung him from a ten-year no-parole sentence," Tim explained, gulping back his distaste. "What did Mo get out of it? I think he was offered a position in a Shearer cabinet."

"There are gangs that drug and pass little girls from one man to the next." Elias took a sip of whiskey.

Tim stared. His words were lost. He could only breathe in and then out.

"Do you think Goddard is involved?" Elias's question hit Tim at his core. He felt the muscles in his jaw grow tight.

"I don't want to believe it. It was Mo. We busted him in the cargo bay." Tim felt a heaviness like a gym weight across his chest. Goddard was a friend. "I guess we're about to find out, right?"

"You were in the office with them. Did you notice anything? Anything at all?" Elias asked.

"Clueless. I was busy with my cases. I didn't have time to think about the others in my office unless they asked for help. I avoided social engagements. And then Dani came along, and I was—distracted." Tim felt a smile cross his lips for a second.

"The Seattle field office will interview Goddard tomorrow. Still you suspect Hayes, not Shearer."

"There's no longer an answer to that question." Tim chuckled. "Shearer thought he'd avoid all consequences by killing himself. Now, there will always be speculation and gossip about how he fit in. If he was trying to save his legacy, he trashed it instead. The word on the street about Hayes is now verifiable. All over the internet and social media, there were rumors about his pedophilia and Satanism. I thought it was fake news—conspiracy theories. There is so much of that these days. But the equinox celebration, the incinerators, the bones, the treatments—that's hard evidence. One of the partygoers, Anita Brustow, told me there were drugs at the party. Roofies maybe." Tim sighed. Suddenly, he felt tired.

"CSI is in the house now. If there are drugs, we'll find them. We'll know all this by morning." Elias drained his whiskey glass. "We found Chloe's foster parents."

"Where'd you find the living scum? They abandoned her."

"They intended to. We found them on their escape route. Some linemen with the electric company located the rental van in a ravine. They were murdered, shot with a forty-caliber. Their truck was shoved off the road and over a cliff."

Tim sucked in a gasp. "Forty-caliber? Just so happens Graden had a forty-caliber in his van."

"Yep. And a clip with three cartridges missing. That changes everything. His plea bargain? Gone." Elias snapped his fingers.

"Ah, couldn't have happened to a nicer guy." Tim shook his head. "Van Hatten was killed with a forty too. It looks like Graden was busy with more than kidnapping."

"I'll say. It will take us several weeks, maybe months, to wrap this up and arrest everyone involved." Elias handed Tim his empty glass. Tim set it in the bar sink. "You should go up now. Get some sleep. We'll need it. Tomorrow is going to be a long day."

"Just one question. What happens now? Do we see this all the way through?" Tim asked. Leaving this in the hands of others wasn't what he was used to doing. He'd already started forming his arguments for court.

"We leave all the evidence in the capable hands of the Department of Justice. You'll be called to testify. But this isn't our fight anymore. We will be moving on to others."

Tim stared for a moment. He dumped out his remaining whiskey in the small bar sink and set his glass next to Elias's.

"Oh, you wanted to know the significance of the rainbow duct tape. Remember? Why would someone use something so unique?" Elias paused, and then a wide grin spread out below the handlebar mustache. "It was on sale. Graden said it was a BOGO."

Tim shook his head and laughed. "Sleep well. I'm going to make sure the house is all locked up," Tim said and watched as his friend climbed the stairs.

Tim checked the doors and the alarm system, making sure

it was armed. Slowly and deep in thought, he strolled through the living room. He was ready for a hot shower and bed. As he walked down the hall, he stopped for a second and opened the door to Chloe's room. He could see her blonde waves against the pillow and TimTwo's pink nose peeking out from under the comforter. He closed the door quietly. Tomorrow he'd get another big unicorn for Lettie.

His thoughts turned to Dani. He soundlessly crept into their room. For a few minutes, he stood still watching her breathe as she slept in tranquility.

He slipped into the shower. For a long time, he stood under the cleansing warmth of the water. He finished by shaving and brushing his teeth. He realized he was still too on edge to sleep, but he needed to hold Dani. He gently climbed under the sheets next to her. She immediately snuggled up against his shoulder and kissed his throat.

"Are you awake?" he asked softly, stroking her hair.

"Yes. Waiting for you. You're home safe," she purred.

"I'm home." He closed his eyes, drifting in the perfection of her familiar touch. She knew exactly when and where to caress him. There was nothing on earth like it. Without realizing it, he was instantly asleep.

SIXTY-EIGHT

Beebe watched as Tim weighted his downhill ski until he turned a one-eighty and finished gliding backward so he could see his three girls swooshing down the beginner hill behind him. At least that's what she'd heard he called them—*his girls*. She made certain that her cameraman had a high-powered telephoto lens trained on the family for her new article "Tim McAndrews, the FBI's New Secret Weapon." He was going to hate it. She felt a smile of rebellion cross her lips. Plopping an advance copy on an SBC thumb drive on his desk was going to be one of the most satisfying things she'd ever done. She sighed with a massive measure of envy. Why were guys like him always taken?

"Beebe, you gotta see the footage. It's priceless." Hank Noble, her lanky, redhaired cameraman beamed. "Come on. I'll show you." He backed two steps and then turned in the ice-covered lodge parking lot toward the SBC news van. They would edit the film right on the spot, and she'd do her voiceover in front of the Selkirk Lodge. They'd run her story right along with the breaking news confirming that Buddy Shearer had murdered his campaign manager and then killed himself while Tim and the FBI were rescuing the children they used for experimental medical treatments. That Charlie Hayes was involved in some crazy Satanic cult and that children were ultimately being exsanguinated and what was left of them burned in huge biomass incinerators would be left out. No one would believe something so fanciful anyway. She decided that was her Alice Carroll story for the *National Globe*.

"Be there in a sec," she said. Tim's family was still unaware of the filming. They were having too much fun.

McAndrews. Where was she when this guy was out looking for a woman to share his life? It was the story of hers though—never at the right place at the right time. She watched Tim help one of the little girls on to the lift back up the mountain. Dani took charge of the other one. Though she couldn't see them, she imagined them waiting for each other and skiing down together as a group.

She was trying to formulate the rest of the copy for her voiceover as she watched the happy family come into view and ski down the slope again.

McAndrews. Devoted family man, madly in love with his wife, rescuer of helpless children, and ready to lose his life protecting yours, even if you were a stranger. Wasn't this what they were now calling "toxic masculinity"? She'd take some of that poison any day. She remembered how she felt when he caught her when she finally dared to jump down off that wall at Shearer's, how she felt when he covered her when the bullets began to fly, and how he carried her the final twenty feet to safety. But more than that, she remembered kissing him. Wow! She hoped Dani appreciated what she had.

Watching them skiing together as a happy family was one

of the hardest things she ever had to do. Replacing Dani as the woman in his life might've been hard but doable, in her opinion. But taking him away now, with the kids in the equation—another story altogether. Of course, that made him all the more desirable. She needed to move on. Why couldn't she? Slowly, she turned toward the news van as the family took the lift up for another go.

Deep in thought, she missed the tall black man moving in behind her until she turned at the last second. She was shocked when she saw Hank in the news feed chair, his eyes as big as saucers with fear. Standing behind him, looking vastly more handsome than usual, was Miguel. He was holding the pages of the voiceover script she'd written so far.

"Hey, what ...?" she asked as she was lifted into the van from behind and pushed forward. She heard the door squeak closed behind her and tried to make sense of it all.

"Take a seat, Miss Knoll." She recognized the voice as belonging to Elias Cain.

"What do *you* want?" She sank into the chair next to Hank.

Miguel finished reading and handed the pages over her head to Cain. Silent moments passed as he perused her work. She fidgeted nervously.

"I take it this is an editorial review?" she finally asked, her tone clipped and snippy.

"Nice work, Miss Knoll. You aren't just a pretty face and a newsreader after all." Cain handed the paper back to Miguel. He reached across Hank and pushed a few buttons, and the footage they'd recorded began to play on the editing computer. "This is very good too. Don't you think, Miguel?"

"Very good. Colors are crisp. The zoomed shots aren't blurry. Good quality, I'd say." There was a ring of laughter at the edge of his voice. He began to rip the paper into shreds and then deleted it from her laptop.

"Oh, come on. It took me all night to get that together," Beebe protested. Miguel studied the video camera.

"Here it is," he said. He pushed the left side of the computer mouse and the word *Delete?* with a small box around it came up across the computer screen. Miguel clicked the button to the simultaneous groans of Beebe and her cameraman.

"All that work," Hank complained. Miguel permanently deleted it all. Beebe was pretty sure she knew what was going on.

"Miss Knoll, shall we take a little walk?" Cain asked.

"Are you going to snuff me?" She was truly frightened. Cain looked at Miguel with surprise. Beebe wondered if it was because she figured it out or because it had never crossed their minds.

"Miss Knoll, we are usually considered the good guys," Cain reassured her. Though he didn't exactly answer her question, he opened the van doors and encouraged her to step out. She had an impulse to run, but then she remembered in the movies that character always took a kill shot in the back. Cain ducked through the opening after her, unfolding to his impressive height once out in the cold morning air. He took her hand and linked her arm through his. It was a soothing gesture, gentle, but still meant to intimidate. Miguel followed them out and closed off her left side.

"Miss Knoll, did you actually believe I would let you expose Special Agent McAndrews and his family to the world, with every sort of criminal looking on? What kind of boss would I be?" Cain asked, but Beebe knew it was rhetorical. No answer required.

"May I have your phone please?" Elias held out his right hand.

"That's my personal—you don't have the right ..." When she stared at Cain, she realized he wasn't negotiating on this point. Reluctantly, she took it out of her jacket pocket, handed it over, and watched helplessly as he permanently deleted her video files of McAndrews.

"You've been following McAndrews for some time, I see," Elias acknowledged. Miguel grinned and obviously got some sort of satisfaction out of her crush being exposed. She rolled her eyes and let her head loll back for a moment in despair.

"He's news," she defended, not sure her excuse would hold water.

"Ah, I guess so." Cain smiled. "If you have a problem with this, take it up with your boss or the director of the FBI." Cain twisted the ends of his handlebar. *Who wears handlebar mustaches these days, anyway?* Beebe thought. "We in the Behavior Science Unit work quietly, behind the scenes. We like keeping a low profile, if you get my drift." Elias gave an almost imperceptible nod to Miguel, and he quietly withdrew from their conversation. Beebe felt a rush of panic, but Cain wouldn't kill her right here in front of the ski lodge in broad daylight, would he?

"It isn't just that he's news now, is it, Miss Knoll?" he asked. Once again, no answer required.

"Why would you say that? Why would you even—did he put you up to this?" Beebe felt her stomach drop as if she were on a carnival ride. She hadn't been paying attention, but now as she looked up, they were at the base of the beginner run. Elias Cain was going to make her face the reality she'd been avoiding for all she was worth.

"Miss Knoll, does that look like a man available for a cheap affair to you?"

She had to look. Tim was helping a little girl ski. He held her hands on the poles, his skis outside of hers, guiding her into a series of slow turns. They were laughing together as he helped the child through her fear, just like Beebe's dad used to do. When they reached the bottom of the hill, he helped her remove her skis, and they joined Dani and the other little girl. They were holding hands, connected by love. They were a family. Beebe closed her eyes.

"I want it to be me. That's all." She looked at Cain, beseeching him as if he could make it happen.

"You need to let go. Let them live. It's going to happen to you. Just not with Tim." Elias started to turn her away from the scene, but she couldn't tear her gaze away. Tim was everything she wanted. Elias patted her gloved hand she'd slipped under his arm. Beebe's eyes filled, but she refused to let tears fall. This time, unlike the times before, the truth was there in the glaring light of day.

At the bottom of the beginner run, Tim looked up to see Elias and Beebe standing together talking. His gaze met Beebe's. She parted her lips, and her face filled with what he interpreted as longing. She had made her feelings known. He thought he'd made his clear, but he had failed, or she'd given them no weight. There was no one for him but Dani. He belonged with her and with the family they'd cobbled together from the castaway children they'd rescued from despair. This was the life he wanted. Beebe had no part in it. He looked away.

Dani slipped her arm under his, and he smiled at her. He leaned in for a kiss, but his attention was ripped away by the two little girls that grabbed hold of him in happy hugs. He felt warmth rush all through him. This was definitely the life he wanted.

AUTHOR'S NOTE

As I sat down to write this book, I learned that on June 8, 2018, the FBI and thirty-eight other law enforcement agencies conducted a sting, code-named Operation Safe Summer, that resulted in the rescue of at least 160 children, some still in diapers, from a child pornography and child sex trafficking ring.

The law enforcement officer in charge reported that grown men were involved in assaulting the children and filming it for others to watch. But sexual abuse isn't the only way children are exploited. Countless children from third world countries are trafficked across our southern border for who knows what. Children are a precious but vulnerable part of society, and their innocence and inexperience leave them open to every sort of evil conceived in the human heart.

To my dismay, as I finished this novel, Operation Safe Summer II was in the news. More than two hundred children were rescued during this raid.

I am heartbroken that anyone could be so evil as to steal childhood from another and submit them to a world of darkness, pain, and horror. Children should be joyfully running and playing under the watchful protection of a loving family.

Parabiosis clinics have sprouted. They use legally obtained blood plasma, and the donors are old enough to give consent. In my novel, I explore a hypothetical—the frightening but possible predation of children, in pursuit of eternal life, robust health, and a drugless high.

I thank God for the men and women of law enforcement who pursue evil twenty-four hours a day, even if we don't always see it. This book is dedicated to those who keep us safe.